ROSE O'BRIEN

Inside the Flame

First edition

ISBN: 978-1-7328730-1-8

This book was professionally typeset on Reedsy.
Find out more at reedsy.com

For Deidra

Thank you for reaching down into the pit and giving me a hand up.
You are the truest of friends.

Chapter 1

Jen Jiang felt the vibration of the blast more than she heard it.

Car bomb. Not close – half a mile, maybe a mile to the east.

The sound of a car bomb in Baghdad was a pretty common one these days. While the thrum of the concussion was like standing too close to a speaker at a rap concert, the bass shaking her ribs, there was a primal awareness of the danger. All the living things along the street, including Amal, the elderly woman Jen had been photographing, turned their heads toward the sound of the blast.

Jen looked up from the viewfinder of her old Nikon camera and began scanning the skyline for the inevitable plume of smoke. A small spike of adrenaline tingled in her blood, an old familiar friend.

"Do you mind if I come back to finish the interview and the photoshoot tomorrow?" Jen asked her subject in Arabic.

Amal was the subject of a profile she was writing on shifting attitudes on women's education. The retired architect and professor nodded, a little distracted as she looked down the street in the direction of the blast.

Jen looped her camera strap around her neck, settled her messenger bag across her chest and threw her leg over her scooter, starting the engine with a push of a button.

"Be careful," Amal called. "Sometimes there are secondary blasts."

Jen waved to her as she pulled out onto the dusty street. She'd lived in Baghdad on and off for five years now. She knew about secondary blasts and the damage they could do to rescue personnel and those who rushed to a blast site to help.

As she maneuvered her little scooter through traffic, she kept jerking her gaze to where smoke was rising over the squat buildings. She cursed as she realized the likely location of the blast. Not the market again.

This neighborhood had already been through so much. The walls she flew by were marked by discolored lines of new plaster patching the damage of past explosions, if the locals had managed to repair them at all. Many hadn't—the low, scarred houses often held multiple families trying to claw their way into middle class status. Every new bomb threw new debris into their path.

Leaning into a turn, she shot around a slow-moving taxi and gunned it down the street. The little scooter hit its top speed of thirty-five miles an hour, the wind whipping her long, black braid over her shoulder.

She hit another turn a bit fast, and her back tire skidded on the rough, crumbling street. With another curse, she righted the bike and almost rear-ended the pickup truck that slammed on its brakes in front of her.

"Come on!" she shouted in Arabic, gesturing with her right hand for the driver to hit the gas already.

The lonely cry of a siren went up to the east. First responders were on their way, at least. The pickup was moving again, and Jen twisted the throttle, giving the scooter as much gas as it could handle. The smell of smoke in the air said she was getting close.

As she rounded the corner, she came up on the edge of the marketplace.

The Al-Bayaa Market was a popular one on this side of the city. Built in an open square with an entrance off the main road, it was packed with stalls selling food, clothing, electronics and books.

Now, it was something out of Jen's nightmares. Voices filled the air, screams from the injured, shouts, and nervous chattering from bystanders who had rushed to the scene. Those were the easiest parts to tune out.

Not so easy was the smell. Explosives, burned wood and plastic, charred flesh, hot metal and brick.

Billowing clouds of black smoke rolled over the street and obscured anything farther than twenty feet away. She raised her camera's viewfinder to her eye and twisted the lens to bring things into focus. The shutter clicked in rapid succession as she snapped several wide shots of the devastation.

Jen abandoned the scooter on the sidewalk, but had the presence of mind to stick the keys in her pocket before she waded into what was left of the market.

She stayed low, crouched slightly to keep her lens in the middle space. As objects or people caught her attention, she'd bring them into focus, snap several pictures, and move on, trying to keep her footing on broken bricks and rubble.

A woman held a hand to her forehead, red blood leaking through her soot-stained fingers. A man carried a little girl on his hip as he ran toward the main road, black smoke offering contrast with his white tunic. She heard the ambulance arrive and turned to snap several shots of the rescuers jumping from the vehicle.

To many, her seemingly callous documentation of the scene might seem macabre. She'd been called a vulture and worse, but this was her job.

There was nothing she could do for victims since she had zero medical training. The one thing she could do was document this so the rest of the world knew what was happening here. She always gave herself a handful of minutes to shoot and then waded in to see how she could help.

She let the camera hang by its strap and pulled out her smartphone. Bringing up its camera, she took some wide shots of the scene, trying to ignore the ash and the scents that threatened to choke her, so much stronger here than on the street. The phone's camera couldn't touch the quality of her DSLR, but it was faster to upload pics this way.

In seconds, she had a tweet sent out with the photo attached.

"The scene at Al-Bayaa Market in Baghdad following an explosion. Multiple injuries. Updates to follow."

She sent the message out to her hundreds of thousands of followers and got down to work.

She approached a young man in his twenties who was standing off to the side watching the mess with a slightly dazed expression. His shirt was smudged with ash, and he was holding a gash on his arm.

Jen pulled off the long sleeved button down shirt she wore over her T-shirt and pressed it to the wound.

"What happened?" she asked him in Arabic. "Did you see?"

He shook his head and tapped his ear, a confused look on his face. Hearing loss, Jen assumed. Sure enough, there was fresh blood marking the dark skin of his neck below his ears on both sides.

She asked again, loudly and slowly, exaggerating the movements of her mouth so he could read her lips.

He looked away as he started speaking, just staring straight ahead. Shellshocked. She'd seen it before. Had to make sure the paramedics knew to get him a head CT when they got him to a hospital to check for traumatic brain injury.

"A truck pulled up at the edge of the market. I saw someone get out and walk down the street, like he was in a hurry to make an appointment. I had to leave my stall here at the front to get something from my uncle. He has a stand near the back of the market. I had just started back this way when I heard a noise and it felt like a big, angry fist knocked me to the ground."

His words were halting, as if his thoughts were jumbled. Jen peeked under her wadded shirt. Still bleeding. The bone was visible. She pressed it back against his skin.

"ISIS dogs," the man said. "Why can't they leave us alone?"

Jen pulled out the reporter's notebook she always kept in her back pocket and wrote down what he'd said. It was word for word.

She asked the man's name and got him to spell it for her. It took a couple of tries for him to get it out. Catching the eye of one of the paramedics, she waved him over. As the rescuer climbed over what had been a fruit stall to reach them, Jen curled the young man's fingers over her shirt, making sure he applied enough pressure to staunch the flow of blood.

As the paramedic knelt down, she stepped back, bringing her camera up. No one heard the clicking of the shutter as more screaming ambulances rolled up.

Speaking next to the paramedic's ear, she told him the man probably had a TBI. The medic looked at her and nodded before pulling a pressure bandage from a green duffle bag.

With that, Jen melted away from them, a part of the chaos, but apart from it.

How many of these had she covered over the last few years? God, she couldn't remember. There was almost a formula to it now.

Snap photos of the scene. Talk to survivors to see if anyone saw anything. Snap photos of the rescue operation. Talk to the cops when they arrived. Check with the hospital in a couple of hours to get the number of dead and wounded. Check with police headquarters in the morning to get the name of the group that claimed responsibility. Revise dead/wounded toll as necessary. Repeat.

Off to her left, she saw rescuers cover a prone form with a green plastic sheet. Shit.

"Blast has claimed at least one life. Rescuers working to clear wounded." She sent the tweet out.

"Help me!" A woman's voice screamed nearby.

Jen's head snapped up as she tried to locate where the voice was coming from.

"Why can't you hear me? I'm right here. Help me! Please!"

Uh oh. A prickling awareness danced across Jen's skin. Not this. Not now.

She turned and saw a young woman in a black abaya. She was standing beside a paramedic who was leaning over a man with a severely broken leg, the compound fracture leaving the bone showing stark white against soot-stained skin. The woman was practically shouting in the medic's ear, waving her hand in front of his face. No reaction.

Shit.

The shouting woman caught Jen looking and marched over to her.

"You can hear me, can't you? What is going on here? Why won't anyone help me?"

Ignoring them never worked. Once eye contact was made, there was some kind of connection, an awareness.

The dead just knew.

Jen turned slightly away and pretended to dig in her camera bag and tried to move her lips as little as possible as she spoke. No sense in spooking the locals. "Yeah, I can see you. And, no, you don't need to shout," she told the spirit.

"What's going on here?"

"There was a blast. Do you remember that?" Jen asked.

"A blast? What blast?" Confusion passed over the woman's face, and aggravation made her spectral form vibrate.

Jen sighed. It was like this with violent deaths sometimes. The spirit didn't know that it was separated from the body. Jen had been seeing the dead since she'd hit puberty. It had terrified her at first. Now it was just a part of her life. An annoying part.

She looked up and met the spirit's gaze. Deep within her, there was a tiny ping of something like empathy. It was more like a remembered sensation, a phantom pain from a part of her that wasn't there anymore.

"I'm really sorry to be the one to tell you this, but you didn't live through the blast. In fact, I'm pretty sure that's your body over there under that sheet," she said, trying to keep her voice soft and quiet.

She'd had to tell a few people over the years that they were dead, and it went about as well an L.A. traffic jam. This time was no different.

"What do you mean I'm dead?"

Jen put her hand out, palm up.

"Touch my hand."

The spirit reached out, the look on her face clearly saying that the she thought Jen was messing with her. Her expression turned to shock and then to fear in an instant when her spectral hand passed through the flesh of Jen's palm.

"Told you."

The woman's stricken face looked like she was crying, but the dead had no tears.

"What is my family going to do without me?"

Jen summoned up the words that she had developed over time for situations like these.

"Your family will miss you, but they will survive. They'll be sad at first, but someday, they will be happy again."

The specter shook her head. "No. There has to be something I can do, something I can do to fix this."

Jen put on her best I'm-trying-to-be-sympathetic-here face and just shook her head slightly, letting the specter see the truth in her eyes. There would be no going back this time.

The specter crossed her arms over her non-existent stomach and let out a frustrated half scream.

"Why me?"

Jen sighed, "Because death is a random bastard."

"This is a lot to take in."

"I know it's sudden. Just try to think calming thoughts."

The spirit seemed to gather herself as she looked around at the devastation.

"What's next? Where do I go?"

Resignation was written on the specter's features now, clouding her dark eyes.

"I don't know. I think it's different for everyone. Some people see a light. Others see family members. My advice? Calm your mind and think of the time you were happiest in this world. But whatever you do, don't stick around here. Anything is better than this place."

The specter nodded and looked back at the body under the green plastic sheet, her expression grim.

"Would you do something for me?"

Jen hesitated. She'd heard requests from the dead before. Most of them were of the "Tell my family I love them" variety. She hated those because if she fulfilled them, she wasn't telling them anything they didn't already know, and the family usually thought she was some whackjob psycho.

"I'll do what I can," was all Jen said.

"If it wasn't destroyed in the blast, there should be a bottle of pills in my—the pocket, over there," the specter said, gesturing toward the body. "It's medicine for my son. He'll die without it. It's a three-month supply, and we don't have enough money to replace it. I had just picked it up from the doctor and was buying bread for dinner when…" she trailed off, putting a hand that was fading to translucence to her mouth.

"What's your name?"

"Rukia."

"Where do you live?"

The spirit gave the address, or as close to one as any house in the slums had. Jen could find it. She had more experience navigating those neighborhoods than the well-off ones on the other side of the river.

"I can't believe I'm never going to see them again."

Jen stayed silent. A kinder person would have told the spirit that she would see her family again one day. But in reality, she had no idea what was on the other side. The spirits she saw might just be echoes of consciousness, the last electrical discharge of a dying brain. She wasn't sure if she believed in a soul or an afterlife.

She'd seen spirits fade out before and this one was headed in that direction. Jen had no idea where they went or if they went anywhere at all. Maybe they just became...nothing.

This spirit had little tying her to this plane of reality. She was ready to go and leave this hellish place behind. Her hands and feet had already disappeared.

Jen wasn't sure what possessed her to speak. Maybe it was the hopeful expression on the specter's face. Maybe it was the shitty, unfair way she'd been taken out.

"I'll take the medicine to your boy. Don't worry," she said, her voice soft. "Now, go with God, sister."

The specter closed her eyes and dissolved like a plume of smoke in a gentle breeze.

Why had she said that? Jen didn't even believe in God. She believed in exactly two things: the ability of humans to fuck over other humans and the inherent brutality of the universe.

Jen put her hands on her hips and looked up at the sky, blowing out a long breath. She was such an idiot sometimes. And a fucking bleeding heart to boot.

She looked around and found that the paramedics were moving the wounded toward the ambulances at an efficient rate. The police were just starting to arrive to cordon off the area. Anyone that could walk had left what remained of the market, probably fearing a secondary blast. Now was her chance.

No one was paying attention to the corpse. Typical. It wasn't like it was going anywhere. Not until the cops came, photographed the scene and hauled it off to the morgue.

Picking her way over the rubble, she knelt by the sheet and looked around again. Still in the clear. She put her camera bag down to block the view and darted her hand under the sheet.

She found the pocket of the woman's abaya and fished out the glass pill bottle.

Glancing at the label, she saw it was medication for hemophilia. Yeah, the kid probably would die without this. Shit.

She stowed the pill bottle in her camera bag, rummaged around in it like she was looking for something and stood. Looping the bag over her head, she headed for the blockades the police were putting up.

"Who's the scene commander?" she asked one of the cops. She recognized him from the neighborhood. Young guy, tall, with a trim beard. He nodded to her, clearly recognizing her as the local vulture reporter.

"Talk to the sergeant," he said, nodding in the direction of an older man with four bars on his uniform. "But they won't have much yet."

"Yeah, yeah. I know the drill," she said, waving him down.

* * *

Theron Blackwell's boots pounded against the pavement of the alley as he ran. He put a hand out and caught the rusty ladder bolted to the side of the building, using his momentum to leap onto the rungs, scrambling for the roof.

He'd heard the blast a few minutes ago and it froze his blood. Had the ones he'd been watching been responsible for this?

He reached the top of the four story building a block over from the blast site and crawled on his belly so as not to be seen by anyone below. Reaching the raised edge of the roof, he pulled out his binoculars and started scanning the crowd.

Wounded were being loaded up in ambulances. Police were

putting up barricades. All normal.

No sign of his targets. Good news there. He breathed a sigh of relief. Maybe they hadn't been behind this particular act of murder and mayhem.

Wait a second.

He zeroed in on the woman standing amidst the debris. She stuck out like a hipster at a biker rally. Her long black hair hung in a braid down her back and she wore no head covering. Her slender form was clad in khaki pants and a plain T-shirt. Not exactly the normal fashion for women in this part of the world. Either she was clueless or she gave zero fucks what anyone thought.

Most interestingly, though, she was talking to herself. He focused in on her face, but he couldn't make out the words.

He zoomed the binocs out and looked again.

Hold up.

She wasn't talking to herself. The body language was all wrong for that. She was focused on the space about three feet in front of her, and though she was trying hard to minimize the gestures, they were still there.

She was talking to someone no one else could see. He jerked the binocs away from his face as surprise speared through him.

Holy shit. Could it be?

He looked through the lenses again. She'd stopped talking and was heading over to where a body lay draped with a sheet. Her back was to him and her bag was blocking his view, but he was almost certain she'd retrieved something from the corpse. He'd bet dollars to doughnuts that was a seer down there.

As she rose to her feet, he focused the binocs on her face, maxed out the magnification and pushed a button on the side, activating the device's recording feature.

He'd never seen a seer before. None of his kind had for almost a hundred years. He'd been taught what to look for, though, just in case he ran across one in his wide travels.

She didn't look all that special. When you found the Holy Grail, you kind of expected it to sparkle.

As a ranger of the Mage Corps, it was his job to tag and flag unusual entities that could become assets of the Council. The woman was talking to people, writing things down in a notebook and snapping pictures. A reporter, then. Shouldn't be too difficult to track her.

The Council, the representatives of the five magical races in the Earthly Realms, would be extremely interested in a seer.

He was officially in Baghdad to find the group that had murdered half the team of mages in Damascus. He'd tracked his suspects here and now, he had a sneaking suspicion that they had something to do with this bombing. The brass had warned him that something was brewing in the region. The seer, while interesting, could be flagged for a later pick up. Once he'd eliminated his targets and uncovered whatever nefarious plot they were up to, maybe he could snag her on his way out of town and turn her over his superiors.

As Theron tracked her movement across the pavement, he zoomed the binocs out and froze, every muscle in his body setting like concrete.

One of the targets he'd been tracking for weeks was watching from the crowd that had started to gather at the barricades. His gaze was locked on that seer.

* * *

As Jen pulled her scooter up and parked it in the shadow of

one of the towering cement T-walls on the edge of the slum near the Amil neighborhood, she took a deep breath. She was nervous about going into the slum, but she was more nervous about speaking with Rukia's family. There was no telling how they would react when she told them the news of her death. It was very likely police hadn't identified her body yet, much less located her family. So, she would be the one to deliver the devastating news.

She planned to hand over the medicine and leave as quickly as possible and hoped no one asked too many questions.

The T-wall towered twenty feet over the squat little houses and shacks of the slum. The walls had cropped up all over the city to funnel traffic to the security checkpoints and to protect some of the larger development projects that were beginning to spring up around the city now that the war was over.

Jen knew—thanks to her reporting—that the T-walls were also used to separate slums from the areas that were targeted for revitalization. It outraged her, but the stories had been buried inside publications back in the US and hardly noticed.

People in the west had stopped caring about Iraq when the majority of the US troops had left a couple years ago. Her stories on the Iraqi government and the rebuilding effort sold, but they didn't make the front page anymore. There was more demand for her magazine profiles these days. Except for her reporting on ISIS and the offshoot groups that were rising to take its place. Those stories always made a splash.

Jen walked along the cracked pavement and stopped an elderly woman who was sweeping her doorstep. The shack was made of plywood and corrugated metal that reflected the brutal sun, causing Jen's skin to shrivel a bit.

"Can you tell me where to find Rukia's house?" she asked the woman.

The woman gave her some serious side-eye. Jen knew she didn't look or dress like most of the women in Baghdad. Her features, a gift from her Chinese-American parents, clearly marked her as a foreigner, though, and that usually earned her a pass.

"A woman with that name lives up the hill. Look for the white door."

The old woman turned her back on Jen, signaling that the conversation was over, and went back to sweeping.

As she moved deeper into the slum, the smell became stronger. The sewers were problematic in the best parts of the city. In the slums, they were nonexistent. Most people used communal latrines in this area, and garbage was piled periodically along what passed for a main drag in this neighborhood.

Men in long white tunics sat outside their doors, trying to escape the heat and catch the breeze that came dancing down the dusty street. Their eyes followed her. Most were wary, others curious, but a few were narrowed with hostility. Those gazes she met dead on.

Her spine was straight, her gait loose, and her expression set on resting bitch face. Everything about her said, "Don't fuck with me. I will straight up cut you."

She found the house with the white door and knocked. A bearded man in his thirties answered the door, a little boy with huge dark eyes hiding behind his father's hip and peeking at her.

"Are you Rukia's husband?"

The man nodded, a look of confusion crossing his face at her appearance and, likely, her mastery of Arabic.

"I'm sorry to be the one to tell you this," Jen started. "There was a car bomb at the market and your wife—she didn't make it."

A look of disbelief crossed his face, then white hot pain. He picked up the boy and put him on his hip, holding the skinny body against his chest.

"Before she died, she asked me to bring this to you," Jen lied. It was a white lie and one the man would never know about.

Jen turned on her heel and started walking down the dirt road toward her scooter.

"Wait!"

Her heart pounding, she froze, but did not turn around.

"Did she suffer?"

The pain in his voice caused her throat to tighten. Damn it.

"I don't—I don't think so," she said, her voice cracking a bit. "It was quick."

Her feet started moving again and she didn't dare look back.

"Thank you!" the man called to her. "Blessings upon you."

Jen practically ran to her scooter, overwhelmed with emotions she thought she had left behind a long time ago. The look on that man's face would haunt her. The sound of his voice was trapped in her ears.

HIs pain was like an echo of her own, blending with it in a kind of sickening harmony.

The streets of Baghdad flowed by in a stream of grey and brown as Jen navigated on autopilot to her little apartment near the Green Zone. Her thoughts were as blank as she could make them as she shut off the scooter and unlocked the front door of the building.

There was a bottle of Blue Label scotch upstairs with her name on it, and she was probably going to kill it before the night was over. She trudged the three flights to her floor feeling a thousand years old. Her clothes stank of smoke from the blast site, she had that guy's blood on her pants and that dead woman's words bouncing around in her head.

She pushed the thoughts away as best she could. She'd certainly had a lot of practice over the past few years.

Her little building was one of the nicer ones in the neighborhood. It had an open stairwell running through the middle of the structure. Each floor held two apartments, each door at the end of a long landing.

Twisting her key in the lock, she pushed her door open and pulled the strap of the camera bag off. A blow to the back of her head staggered her, sending her crashing into the little side table in the front hall where she usually tossed her mail and keys.

The switchblade she kept in her pocket was in her hand in a second, the quiet *snick* of the blade sliding free a welcome sound.

She kept the blade in an underhand grip, hidden against her body. Her back was to her attacker. Footsteps sounded behind her, and she tried to gauge the distance. Wait for it. Wait for it.

She'd drawn the drapes before she'd left that morning, and the apartment was cast in deep shadows. Her attacker must have slipped in behind her from the kitchen, which opened to the left off her front hall.

Now. She lashed out with the blade and felt it slide into the flank of her attacker, earning a surprised grunt. He was tall, well-muscled. She couldn't make out much more than that in the dark.

The blade slid free, and she stabbed again, once more. He screamed that time. She lashed out with a booted foot and knocked him back against her closed door. As she flipped the knife to an overhand grip and prepared to drive the blade into the juncture of his neck and shoulder, a hand clamped around her wrist and hauled her backwards.

An arm snaked around her middle, and the knife was wrenched from her hand. So there were two of them. At least.

Kicking out, a scream tore from her throat. It wasn't like anyone would ride to the rescue, but it made her feel better. Maybe it would make her attackers' ears ring while they killed her. She was dragged backwards and slammed face first on her bed. Bile and panic rose in her throat, a terrifying mix that threatened to choke her.

Her hands dug into the bedding and she tried to scramble away, but her attacker had her hips pinned against the foot of the bed.

Had her worst nightmare finally come to life? Was this how it was going to end? Were all the risks and all the mistakes she'd made catching up with her at last?

Hell if she was going down without a fight. They wanted her blood, they'd have to work for it.

Jen continued to struggle, trying every dirty trick in the book to get away. Her elbow strikes failed to land, she couldn't find a body part to dig her nails in. Her kicks struck only empty air.

Another scream, ripped from her throat, this one of frustration. Another blow landed against the back of her head, silencing her and causing little dancing lights to appear in her vision. Damn, the guy was strong.

A crashing sound echoed through the tiny apartment from the direction of the front door. Her attacker's weight shifted like he was trying to look out into the hall. He said something in a language that she didn't recognize. A tiny alarm went off in her brain. There weren't many languages she didn't know enough of to identify. She knew all the local ones. These guys weren't from around here, which spelled trouble. A new and terrifying kind of trouble. These weren't local gangbangers.

Another crashing sound was accompanied by the sound of the first attacker, the one she'd stabbed, screaming. Did she smell smoke?

Her attacker shifted again, like he was digging in his pocket, and she took advantage of his momentary distraction to shift her weight, bring her right knee to her chest and plant a solid backwards kick right in the guy's balls.

A strangled sound escaped his throat as he cupped himself. A capped syringe fell from his fingers and clattered on the concrete floor. Shit, whatever was in that syringe was for her. She prepared to kick the guy in the face, but a figure appeared in her bedroom door, and she froze.

It wasn't the first attacker she had been expecting. This guy had to be six and a half feet tall and built like a linebacker. Instead of the dark hair and dark skin she had glimpsed on her attackers, she could make out light hair and light skin in the dim light.

He was dressed head to foot in black clothes that looked vaguely like the tactical gear she'd seen on some of the soldiers.

And his hands were on fire.

Her brain slammed to a screeching halt at the sight. What the fuck?

Blue and yellow flames covered his clenched fists and licked up his forearms, but he didn't appear to be in any pain. The light cast by the flames lit his face from below, throwing his features into terrifying relief. His eyes were a deep indigo and almost seemed to glow in that light.

With a movement that was almost too fast to track, his right hand shot forward, and a fireball hit her attacker square in the chest just as he was scrambling to his feet. The guy flew backward into her nightstand, turning the wood into splinters.

Whoever this guy was, he'd just taken out her attackers. But that didn't make him an ally.

Jen suppressed another scream as the blonde stepped further into the room, but he ignored her. He pressed his attack, and Jen took that opportunity to slip past him and out the bedroom door.

She wasn't about to stick around and find out how that guy's portable flame thrower worked. As Jen scrambled into her front hall, she almost tripped on the body of her first attacker. There was a smoking hole where his throat used to be, and his sightless eyes were staring at the ceiling.

Bile rose in her throat again, but she pushed it down. Whoever the firestarter was, she wanted to be as far away from him as she could get. Now.

Jen had the presence of mind to scoop up her bag from the hallway floor where she'd dropped it and threw open her front door, heading for the stairs at a dead sprint.

"Wait!" she heard a male voice call behind her over the sound of her sawing breath.

Fat fucking chance.

Heart clawing its way out of her throat, she flew down the stairs, skipping treads and crashing into walls on the way down, her hands scrabbling against the chipped paint of the railings.

Jen was halfway down the street when she realized that she'd left her scooter behind. Fuck it. There was no way she was going back for it. Thighs burning, she slowed to a jog. Note to self, more cardio.

The next road over was a busy pedestrian thoroughfare. She hit the crowd and pulled a drab grey scarf from her bag. Twisting her long black braid on top of her head, she had the scarf tied like a hijab in seconds. An oversized pair of sunglasses helped further obscure her appearance.

Jen Jiang knew how to disappear.

Chapter 2

Three hours, two cab rides, and a bus ride later, Jen walked into the cool, dim lobby of the Palestine Hotel. She approached the registration desk, recognizing the clerk from when she'd stayed in the hotel before. When she'd first come to Baghdad five years before, she'd lived in the Palestine for several months. Since then, she'd bounced into the hotel a few times when she was between places or just passing through Baghdad.

The place had been the height of luxury in the 1980s, but it hadn't been updated much since then. The ruby carpet was threadbare, the wood paneling shabby, the furniture chipped and worn.

The hotel was a popular one with foreign journalists. When she'd first arrived during the height of the surge of American troops, it was common to see broadcasters doing live spots in the lobby and on the balconies of the eighteen-story hotel. It was quiet now.

"Got any rooms, Hassan?" she asked the clerk.

"Welcome back to the Palestine, madame. Just let me check and see what we have available."

Hassan flipped through a book behind the counter.

"I have a room on the twelfth floor. Is that acceptable?"

She nodded and passed him her credit card.

"Do you know how long you'll be staying with us?"

"Charge me for the week and we'll go from there," she told him.

"Very well, madame. What name would you like the room under?"

"Ida B. Wells."

She always used the name of the nineteenth century black journalist and anti-lynching activist when she was staying anywhere. Her editors and colleagues would be able to track her down if they needed to, although none of them were likely to get panicked and come looking for at least another three weeks, when she started missing deadlines.

The hallway on the twelfth floor was dark and dingy and the room was slightly shabby. It felt a little bit like home.

Jen put her bag on the bed. She fell, exhausted, next to the bag. Her face pressed into the threadbare bedspread. It smelled like cigarette smoke. Images from her apartment, the man on fire, flashed behind her eyelids.

She'd managed to focus on moving around the city, doubling back on her trail and losing any possible pursuit for the last few hours, keeping all those thoughts at bay. That asshole must have hit her harder than she'd thought. There was no way she could have seen what she'd thought she'd seen.

That guy hadn't been on fire. She'd just had her bell rung and was seeing things, that's all.

Her stomach clenched as she thought of her two attackers. She hadn't imagined that syringe. Someone wanted her. Alive.

She'd known for years that her work could get her killed. Plenty of journalists had died over the past fifteen years covering conflicts in Iraq, Afghanistan, Pakistan, and Syria. A few had been captured and beheaded or shot on camera. It was a risk anyone reporting in this part of the world assumed when they took the job.

Jen took a lot of steps to avoid that fate. She wrote under several pen names and never used her real name on anything. She had layers of identities online and in the real world. Only her editors knew who she really was, and they were all stateside.

She had no idea who those guys had been or how they'd found her or what they wanted. It wasn't like it really mattered, she supposed. Ditching her life was something she'd gotten good at over the last few years through plenty of practice. She had everything she needed: her camera, her laptop, her phone, and her wallet.

She had credentials and documents stashed in a safety deposit box at a bank in the Green Zone. There was nothing she needed in her apartment. She could walk away from that place and never look back, having learned a long time ago not to get attached to any material things.

She pushed the attack out of her mind. There was nothing she could do about that. She wasn't going to worry about it. What she needed to worry about was checking in with her editors on the car bombing story.

While she'd been riding around town, she'd managed to file a preliminary story with the international desk at a major newspaper in New York using her smartphone. Thank goodness for technology.

Hauling herself from the bed, she fired up her laptop. There were several urgent emails from her editor. He wanted updates and the high-resolution photos.

She sent the photos and captions first so the art department could start processing those. They were using the pics she'd tweeted earlier as placeholders online and were eager to upgrade.

Next, she called her usual sources in the Baghdad police and emergency services department to update her info. Death toll was officially three, and no one had claimed responsibility for the bombing.

Jen glanced at her watch. It had been hours since the bombing. No one had claimed responsibility? Weird. Usually there was video from some psycho fundamentalist group posted by now.

The official line was that the investigation was ongoing.

She hammered out the updated story in about ten minutes and sent it off. Ten minutes after that, her editor had sent her a list of questions. She answered them, and the story was posted five minutes after that.

She updated her Twitter account with the latest info and a link to the story, then closed her laptop and headed downstairs.

Calling one of the young runners over, she handed him the equivalent of fifty dollars US. The kid was about fourteen, one of the many errand boys that hung out in the hotel to run messages or pick things up for the journalists and tourists that stayed here.

In Arabic she told him, "I need you to run out to a clothing store. Buy some pants like this." She pointed to her khakis. "And some shirts like this," she pointed to her T-shirt. She gave him the size. She gave a list of toiletries she'd need, too, and added socks and underwear to the list.

"I'll get you a hairbrush, too," he added.

She touched her frazzled braid and realized that she probably looked frightful. Yeah, not a bad idea. Nodding, she sent him on his way.

She thought about sending another errand boy for her scooter and decided against it. It could lead whoever was after her right here.

Back in her room, she hit the shower, eager to wash the fear sweat off her body. The water pressure left a lot to be desired, but that wasn't unusual for this time of day. She was just lucky the water was on in this part of town right now. There were a lot of days when it wasn't.

What she wouldn't give for a hot, pounding shower. But she'd settle for a lukewarm trickle because that's what was available. The story of her life.

As she washed, her fingers brushed the gold phoenix necklace she wore. It had been a gift from her mother, and she was relieved it was still with her after everything that had happened. The Chinese phoenix had been an important symbol to her mother. Jen took comfort in it. Even when the worst happened, it was possible to rise from the ashes.

Her mind raced with a list of things she needed to do, thoughts careening from one place to the next. Her apartment was a loss. She'd have to lease a new one.

Crap! There was probably at least one dead body in there, if her recollections were correct. The Baghdad police had their hands full and then some, but even that overworked department was going to notice a corpse.

She'd have to burn that identity.

What if the cops talked to her neighbors or the landlord? There weren't exactly a lot of single Chinese-American women running around Baghdad. They might be able to track her down, and she really didn't want to answer any questions.

Maybe it was time to leave town for a while. She'd been meaning to take a trip to Turkey to report on the continuing Syrian refugee crisis for a while. Now was as good a time as any. Hell, she was already packed.

Still in her towel, she hopped on her laptop and had a flight to Gaziantep out of Baghdad booked for two days later. She marveled at the ease with which she could just book a flight and go. Five years ago, that had not been the case. She'd been so broke when she'd first come to Baghdad, but she'd found surprising success as a freelance reporter and photographer.

If someone had told her five years ago that she would claw her way from dead broke to making more money than she ever had at her cushy reporting job at the L.A. Times, she would have laughed.

Anger rose like acid in her throat at the thought of her old life and the way it had all ended. That Jen was long gone. She pushed the thoughts away and emailed one of the editors she worked with in New York.

"Heading to Turkey to report on refugee crisis. Should arrive Thursday. I'm giving you first dibs on my stories," she wrote.

The editor for the New York Times responded within two minutes.

"We're relying on wire copy right now. I'll buy anything you write and shoot. Usual rates. Can you give us an exclusive?"

She responded that she was happy to give the exclusive and that she would be in touch when she landed.

What a difference five years made. When she'd first come to Baghdad, she'd had a hard time selling her photos and stories to low-level outlets. Now, she had a direct line to one of the most desirable papers in the world.

But she would never let herself get comfortable again. She'd learned her lesson the hard way. She wasn't on anyone's staff, and she kept a stable of newspapers, magazines and broadcast outlets hungry for her work. She could never become dependent on anyone for a paycheck again.

Her runner arrived with two shopping bags and she handed him a few extra bills through the crack in the door so he didn't see her in the towel. Slipping the bags through, she shut the door and flipped the lock. She popped tags off a tank top and ripped open a package of cotton briefs before slipping on a pair.

A knock sounded at the door. Had the runner forgotten something?

Later on, she would realize that she didn't check the peephole. Stupid move. She'd assumed she knew who it was and that it was safe here in the hotel. What was that old saying about assumptions?

As she opened the door, she found herself looking at a very broad chest. As her eyes traveled upwards, she registered the indigo gaze, the blonde hair.

The firestarter.

Her eyes snapped wide in panic and she opened her mouth to scream, but his hand shot out and clamped like an iron band over the lower half of her face. In a split second, she was shoved backward through the door and up against the wall of her room.

The door slammed shut behind them.

Those eyes were inches from hers. The breath was frozen in her lungs.

His voice was low and dark.

"We need to talk."

* * *

Theron looked into the seer's dark eyes and realized that he had probably made a terrible mistake.

While she had shown the appropriate amount of fear for a moment, those eyes were narrowed and focused like lasers on him now. A frightening intelligence was working in those shadowy depths, likely planning his death. Or castration.

But he lived his life on a philosophy of "damn the torpedoes, full speed ahead," and he wasn't dead yet, so he was sticking with it.

"I'm going to say three things, and then I'll take my hand off your face. I'm begging you not to scream," he told her in a low voice. "One, I swear on my mother's life I'm not here to hurt you. Two, I saved you from getting kidnapped by some really scary dudes, so I'm hoping that buys me just a little consideration. And three, we have a severely limited amount of time to get you out of here and to a safe location before more bad guys show up."

He gave her a steady look and he slowly took his hand away from her mouth. Her jaw looked like it was clenched hard enough to crack teeth, and her eyes flashed with anger. She was breathing hard. That's when he noticed she was only wearing a tank top and underwear, and her legs were bare.

Theron's brain ground to a halt for a second at that sight. That was all the opening she needed.

Her little bare foot lashed out in a well-placed kick to the side of his knee that could have shattered the joint. Luckily, he was able to shift his weight and take the blow on his calf. He grunted at the impact and scrambled to grab her as she tried to dodge around him to the door.

There was no way she was getting past him, though. His shoulders had only a few inches of clearance on either side of the mini hallway and his back was almost to the door. His hands clamped around her biceps, but her skin was still wet from the shower and she had used some sort of girlie lotion crap, causing his fingers to slip. It was like trying to catch a greased pig.

"Just listen to me! I'm here to help you!"

She ignored him and tried to kick him in the balls. He was able to take that blow on the thigh. He didn't realize he'd picked a fight with a martial arts expert and he was going to walk away from this encounter with some serious bruises.

Thankfully, she hadn't started screaming yet. He hadn't been kidding about having limited time before another round of bad guys showed up. He'd been able to track her. There was nothing stopping the men he'd been after from doing the same. They could be here, even now.

He hated to do this, but he was running out of choices.

Reaching in his pocket, he cracked a plastic capsule in his fist, filling it with Svarturan knockout dust. He took a deep breath and blew across his palm, filling her face with the stuff. She fell to the carpet in a sprawl that somehow managed to be graceful

He felt like the world's biggest asshole. This woman had been attacked in her home and had a stranger barge into her hotel room while she was partly undressed. She must have been terrified and he couldn't blame her for the ass kicking she'd tried to give him. And he'd just drugged her into unconsciousness. He was so going to hell for this. Just add this to his long list of sins and screwups. One more thing for his guilt to feed on.

He just hoped it was worth it.

Careful not to breathe in the knockout powder, he knelt beside her. Glossy black hair, damp from a shower, pooled around her head and contrasted against tanned skin. A dusting a barely-there freckles highlighted high cheekbones. Her body was slender, almost willowy. If she hadn't just tried to beat the life out of him, he might have said she looked fragile lying there. She fought like a much larger person.

A spark of awareness flared inside him and he pushed it away.

Objectively, she was a beautiful woman and he was a sucker for a gal who knew how to throw a punch. But this was the absolute worst timing. Trouble was hot on their heels and they'd both be lucky to survive the next few hours. He sighed and only blushed a little as he started looking around for her pants.

* * *

The first thing that Jen became aware of was a pounding headache. The second thing she noticed was that she was moving.

Her eyes snapped open, and she immediately wished they hadn't. Even in the dim light, the headache ratcheted up several notches, causing her to moan and grip her skull.

"Mornin' sleepyhead," a low voice drawled with a barely perceptible twang. "Drink this."

A plastic water bottle hit her left palm. She eyed it through narrowed lids but decided it was probably a safe bet since it was still sealed. With a shaking hand, she reached to twist off the cap. And came up short.

Frowning, she looked down and saw that her right wrist was handcuffed to a door handle. And she was in the front passenger seat of some kind of SUV or truck. It was moving. Where were they going?

It was dark outside the windows. How long had she been out? There were lights from buildings and homes and streetlights overhead. They were still in the city, then.

Fuzzy brain rattling with questions, she paused for a second before she figured out that she needed to move the bottle closer to her right hand so she could open it.

The water was the best thing she'd ever tasted.

"Sorry about that," he said. "Svarturan knockout powder can leave you with one hell of a hangover. But the water will clear it up pretty quick."

Jen continued to chug, letting the water slide down her throat in big gulps. As she drank, she looked sidelong at the man in the driver's seat. Blond hair, dark blue eyes, black clothes. Yup. Same room-crashing asshole as before.

As she finished the bottle of water, she calmly put the little plastic cap back on it. And proceeded to hit him in the head with it over and over.

"Ow! Hey, quit it! I'm trying to drive here!"

"Fuck you!" Jen shouted, slamming her booted foot against the floorboard. "Fuck your handcuffs! And fuck your god damned driving skills!"

Unfortunately, the bottle was one of the thin plastic ones, so it crumpled on impact and didn't do any damage.

The guy actually had the nerve to laugh.

"That's some mouth there, princess."

She threw the water bottle at him and went after him with her nails. Her kidnapper was in the process of taking her someplace. She wasn't going to let him. Better to make him kill her on the street than to get wherever it was they were going. They'd find her body on the side of the road, but that was better than getting murdered on camera.

"Shit, lady! What the hell?"

The blond jerked the wheel and pulled to a stop.

"You're going to have to kill me here," she growled as his hands clamped around her wrist, holding her slashing nails at bay.

She met those stunning indigo eyes for the first time since he'd pushed inside her hotel room and that gaze locked her in place for a moment. Was this what the mouse felt like when it looked into the mesmerizing eyes of the cobra?

"I don't want to kill you," he said slowly. "For the last time, I'm here to help you."

He released her and held his hands up. She rubbed her wrist, not taking her eyes off him.

"Kidnapping and help are kind of mutually exclusive terms, dick cheese."

"I'm not kidnapping you...exactly," he said, taking a deep breath. "Look, we had to get moving. The guys who are after you are seriously dangerous. They're the ones that want to kidnap you. I'm just trying to get you to someplace safe. Let's call this what it is: protective custody."

"And who are you, exactly?" Her tone was sharp as a razor.

He extended his hand. "Theron Blackwell."

She ignored that hand and continued with her questions, going into full reporter mode.

"Who do you work for? Everything about you screams military, but you're not. Are you CIA? NSA? A merc?"

"You've never heard of the organization I work for, but we're the good guys. We keep people safe and do everything we can to prevent conflict and bloodshed," he told her.

"Ha! First off, there are no such thing as good guys in this world, just people seeking to protect their own self interests. And second, you caused plenty of bloodshed back at my apartment."

"I was trying to protect you!" he said, frustration tightening his shoulders.

"Who were those guys who attacked me?"

"Operatives of a fanatical cult. They are well armed and well organized and I'm almost certain they set off the bomb in the market today."

That brought Jen up short.

"Really?"

"I've been tracking them for a few days. We think they took out agents in Damascus and Baghdad, and now they've set up shop here," he said.

She paused, thinking hard on that bit of info. Operatives and fanatical cults. Her smarter brain cells said this was not something she wanted any part of. The piece of her that liked adrenaline too much was suddenly very curious.

"Why did they attack me? I hadn't even filed my story on that bombing yet."

He looked away from her, gazing out at the dusty street and the traffic passing by them. After a moment he turned back and stared at her again.

"Because you can see and speak with the dead."

Jen felt her eyes widen and she let out a tiny gasp at his words.

"How did you know that?" she blurted.

He turned and gripped the steering wheel, shifting his weight and making the huge slabs of muscle in his chest and arms ripple. It suddenly hit Jen that Theron was massive and ripped out with enough muscle to bench press three or four of her. And she'd just slapped him around like she was the one with a tactical advantage. If this guy wanted to, he could snap her in half. She needed to keep that in mind.

"I saw you at the market after the bombing," he said, finally. "I got there a few minutes after the blast. I had been tracking some of those operatives, but I got on the trail of the wrong ones. I had no idea they were planning that bombing. I was a couple miles away when I heard the blast. I rolled up and saw you, talking to someone only you could see."

Shit. He knew what she was. And for some reason this had

made her a target? Of all the things she'd thought would get her killed, her stupid ability hadn't been on the list.

"Talking to the dead? Are you serious? That's ridiculous," she said, trying to play it off. "I just talk to myself sometimes."

"Too late, princess. I already know you're a seer. Might as well cop to it."

In her head, she let out a string of curses. She didn't usually give stuff like that away, but she was a little new at being kidnapped and the situation was kind of stressful.

"A seer?"

The question slipped out, her reporter mode still engaged and, apparently, on autopilot.

"Yeah, that's what we call people like you," he said. His eyebrows were raised, and he was giving her a look that said, *duh.*

"I never knew there was a name for it," she said, absently looking out the window.

She'd hated this ability since it had shown up. She'd turned twelve, gotten her first period, and seen her first spirit all within a week. Welcome to freaking womanhood.

His eyes narrowed on her and he frowned slightly in confusion. He regarded her for a long moment, his hard gaze making her skin itch.

"You don't know what you are," he said softly, disbelief coloring his voice.

"What I am is a freak," Jen said. "You're the only person who's ever known about my little problem."

He blinked a few times, clearly finding it hard to believe, before he shook his head.

"You're not a freak," he said, meeting her eyes again. The streetlight caught in his hair, revealing bronze sparks in the depths. "You're incredibly special. Quite possibly one of the most valuable humans alive. We haven't seen one of you for over a hundred years. And my people really need your help."

Jen's mouth fell open at his words. Could he be serious? What kind of game was this? "And that's why I need you to come with me to Damascus."

* * *

Theron waited to see how the seer would react to his words.

He was taking a gamble here. There was a chance that the woman was just crazy and thought she saw dead people, but that's not what his gut was telling him. All of his internal alarm bells were screaming that she was the real deal.

First off, fakers and crazies were only too willing to talk about their conversations with the dead. But a real seer, without any support or training from the people in her world, would do her best to hide the ability so as not to be labeled an outcast.

From what he'd read, that kind of power could be a terrifying thing. Like a mage's powers, it usually showed up right around puberty. Being able to see and communicate with entities that existed in a different phase of reality was pretty scary stuff for a kid.

No one knew exactly where a seer's ability came from. While it could run in families, it also showed up randomly in the sapien gene pool. The Council's last seer had died more than a hundred years ago.

There was a slim chance that she wasn't actually a seer, but he was willing to take the risk. It meant abandoning his hunt for the group that had taken out half the team in Damascus, but he was sure his superiors would understand and forgive him.

Especially if he came home with a brand new seer.

Besides, the group he'd been tracking probably knew he was in town after that encounter at Jen's apartment. Both of her attackers were dead, but it was a good bet his cover was blown. It was time to get back to headquarters and report in.

His new priority was to get Jen to the Citadel, the Council's underground headquarters deep beneath the heart of the Rocky Mountains. To do that, he needed to get to a hub.

Hubs were weak places in the fabric of reality that made portal travel a snap. Portals were a tricky business, and the nearest permanent one to the Citadel was in Damascus.

"Whoa, whoa, whoa," Jen said. "I'm not going to Damascus. I'm going to Turkey. I have a flight day after tomorrow."

"The airport is the last place you want to go. These guys are going to be watching like hawks and they'll grab you before you can make so much as a squeak."

She winced and pinched the bridge of her nose.

"Well, how were you planning to get to Damascus if I can't go through the airport?"

"I was hoping to call in for an emergency extraction," he said.

He'd been trying to get through to his contact in Damascus for the past several hours without any luck. Jerimiah was new to the job of team leader. He'd been promoted after the former leader had woken up with his throat slit in his own bed. That and the execution-style murder of the team's medic was what had brought Theron to this part of the world in the first place.

Jerimiah was an earth mage and a solid operator. They'd been at the Academy together, but not in the same class. If he wasn't responding to messages, there was a damn good reason. Theron was quietly getting worried, but Jen didn't need to know that.

If he couldn't get anyone on the horn in Damascus, he could

call HQ for help. The brass was notoriously unhelpful, most of the time, but stranger things had happened and they might come through for him.

One way or another, he needed to get her to Damascus.

"We just need to sit tight for about twenty-four hours," he said. "Then, we'll be headed stateside."

"I'm not going anywhere with you."

He took a deep breath, clenched his teeth and tried to let the frustration drain away. This was not how he pictured his day going.

"Lady, you have a fanatical group of murderous bastards on your tail. They've already taken out two extremely skilled fighters, so they won't even break a sweat taking you down," Theron said, leaning into her and speaking in a low voice. "And they don't want to kill you. That should scare you most of all.

"On the other hand, you have me. So far, I've saved you once, and I'm keeping them from locating you as we speak. I have given you no indication that I want to hurt you. I didn't even fight back when you tried to insert that water bottle into my skull," he said, a slight smile tugging at his mouth.

He caught her gaze and held it again.

"I'm your best bet, and we're getting out of here."

* * *

Jen met Theron's steady glare with one of her own.

"We're not going anywhere until you tell me everything that's going on and exactly who you're working for," she said, crossing her arms over her chest. She put every ounce of steel she had into her voice. "Until then, I will fight you every step of the way and make your life a living nightmare. You think I left bruises

38

before. Ha! Just wait until—"

"Fine! Geez! Apparently, saving someone's life doesn't buy you any kind of leeway anymore."

She just gave him a look that said she wasn't budging an inch until he downloaded his info.

"All right, where to start?" he mused.

"Who do you work for?"

"What is this, an interview?" he asked.

Jen had found over the years that holding her silence after asking a question was a surefire way to get an answer. Human beings were socially programed to fill the silence. Eventually, everyone said something, if you waited long enough. After a few moments of Theron staring at the roof of the SUV, squinching his eyes shut and nervously rubbing the back of his neck, he started speaking.

"I work for the Council of Magickal Creatures. They have five elected members, one each for the vampires, the shape shifters, the elves, the fey, and the mages," he said.

Jen tried to keep her face blank, but she couldn't help it. She felt one eyebrow arch toward her hairline.

"Oh, come on," she said. "Seriously? You can do better than that. Space alien is far more believable. Or how about you tell me that you're from the underwater city of Atlantis? Look, if you're some sort of foreign operative, I'm not gonna bust you. Just drop me off on the outskirts of town or something..."

He was the one staying silent this time. His gaze was steady, his features impassive as he studied her. Oh, god. Was he being serious? No way. Her eyes narrowed on him.

"Fine. Which one are you?"

"Mage."

What's that?"

"Magick user."

"Like a wizard, or something?" she asked, incredulity still coloring her voice. She'd humor him for now and see how far he took this. Although she was starting to get a little nervous. He sounded like he believed this stuff.

"That's one word we've been called over the centuries," he said.

"Uh, huh. Sure." Sarcasm dripped from her tone.

He snapped his fingers, and suddenly his right arm was covered in blue flame. It wasn't a roaring kind of fire, and it didn't even singe the SUV's headliner. It was like the delicate, barely there flames that danced over cherries jubilee.

It had to be some kind of optical illusion. Putting her hand out, she could feel the heat.

She jerked back, slamming up against the car door. Her fingers scrambled for the door handle, but it wouldn't open. Holy shit, she had to get out of here. Right. Now.

Fear gripped her lower belly, and her breath started coming fast. Her shaking left hand clawed at the seat belt release, but couldn't seem to find the button. A scream was building in her throat.

He snapped his fingers again. The flames disappeared.

Jen slammed her eyes shut and gulped big breaths of air as her nails dug into her knees. It was real. What she had seen at her apartment was real. She'd tried to rationalize it, pass it off as some sort of trick, some sort of hallucination, but it was real. He was real.

Opening her eyes, she saw concern marking his features. Those indigo eyes were calm, and he was leaning toward her, one hand on the steering wheel. The other gently touched her shoulder. She tried not to jump or shudder under that touch.

His hand was warm through the cotton of her T-shirt.

Not taking her eyes from his, she reached a hand out, like she would with a growling dog. She wasn't exactly sure what she was doing. Her brain must still be fuzzy from whatever he'd knocked her out with. Or maybe this was shock.

Her fingertips touched his cheek, just beside his lips. There was the tiniest rasp of stubble. It was the barest hint of contact, but it was enough. This was no spirit or illusion. This was a man. A mage.

"So, you're a fire starter?" she heard herself ask.

"Basically, yeah. Although, I prefer the term fire mage. I didn't go to school for ten years to be called a starter." His tone was light, a smile touching those lips and he was obviously trying to break up the tension.

"Are there others like you?" she asked absently, her mind still spinning like a carnival ride, all flashing colors and screeching noise.

"Yeah. A few thousand in the world, maybe. Others can control the other elements. My brother is a water mage. My two sisters, they're an air and an earth mage."

He had siblings. This strange creature had siblings.

Suddenly, her whirling mind jerked to a stop on something he had said earlier. "You said vampires and shape shifters. Those are real, too?"

"Yeah. Most of them are pretty regular people when you get to know them."

"I fucking knew it," she almost shouted.

The sound of his laughter filled the SUV. It was a rich sound and she felt her mouth tug up at the corner.

"I'm from LA, and I always knew there were probably vampires and werewolves and all that. There's just too many freaking weirdos."

She felt herself relaxing just a little and could see the tension was bleeding out of Theron, as well.

"What are you doing in Baghdad?" Jen asked.

"Two of our strike team members turned up dead in Damascus," he said. At her questioning look, he quickly continued. "The strike teams are like the police for the non-sapiens. They keep our existence on the down low and make sure all the magickal folk don't eat each other."

"Sapiens?"

"Normies," he replied. "Technically, mages, vampires, and shape shifters are human, just a different subspecies."

"Okayyyyyyy," she said drawing the word out and settling back into her seat.

"Anyway, we've had several team members turn up dead in a bad way. Something or someone has been picking them off. They called me in to neutralize the threat. I'm a ranger. That's my job."

He filled her in about tracking the suspects to Baghdad and spotting one at the bombing site.

"I saw them following you and tracked all of you back to your apartment. Sorry I didn't make it there in time to stop them from ambushing you." He sounded genuinely contrite. "I tried to stop you when you ran out of there, but you're really fast. Like, seriously, props."

"Thanks," she said, struck by how surreal the conversation was. "I ran track in college."

"It shows. You were out of the building and gone before I was done taking care of that second guy."

"Wait. Then, how did you find me at the hotel?"

"Simple locator spell. I found your hairbrush in your bathroom. DNA was enough to get me right to the door of your hotel room," he said, holding up a small crystal that was glowing bright blue. "This glows brighter the nearer it gets to you."

Jen's eyes widened as she stared at the thing. It quickly disappeared into the pocket of his combat fatigues. A plan was already forming in Jen's mind.

She needed to get away from Theron.

He'd said they had about twenty-four hours before he could arrange for an extraction to Damascus. Unfortunately, he had that magickal locating crystal, which she didn't quite believe was real, but better safe than sorry. She'd work on the assumption that it was real and steal it before she took off.

At some point, he'd have to take these handcuffs off her, and she could make a break for it. He was just one guy. Eventually, he would slip up. And then she was gone.

Until then, she would talk with him, build a rapport, build trust. She'd read a lot of first-hand accounts of journalists and others who had been kidnapped and held prisoner. Building trust was her best chance at getting away from this guy.

A terrifying thought occurred to her.

"What's to stop those guys from making another little glowing tracker crystal?" she asked, stifling the note of panic that wanted to creep into her voice.

"Don't worry. I torched anything in your place that might have had usable DNA. But they have plenty of tricks they can use. We're a long way from safety."

Theron reached down and put the big SUV into gear again and pulled into traffic.

If she could get free from Theron and steal that crystal, she could activate one of her other identities, disguise herself and make that flight to Turkey.

Feeling better now that the seed of a plan was taking root in her mind, Jen began to catalog her resources. She'd lost her switchblade at her apartment. Her boots were on her feet, and she was dressed in khakis and a tank top.

She glanced behind her and saw that her camera and laptop bags were on the backseat, along with the bag of clothes and toiletries.

Her thoughts ground to a halt.

When he'd busted in, who knew how long ago, she'd just gotten out of the shower. She'd been in her underwear.

"You son of a bitch!" she screamed at him, punching his shoulder hard.

Unfortunately, her left hand was the one that was free, and it was her weak hand. In the confines of the car, there wasn't much room for a windup, so it was more of a solid jab, but it was enough to get his attention.

Theron raised startled eyes to hers and jerked away while trying to keep the vehicle on the road.

"What did I do this time?"

"I was in my underwear! And unconscious!" she hollered. "And now I'm not. You want to explain how that happened?"

"I couldn't carry you down the stairs like that, now could I? It was suspicious enough carrying you to the truck, but thankfully it was easy to convince the staff members I ran into that a reporter got drunk and needed some help home."

She gasped.

"Don't act surprised, princess. Your profession has a reputation. There's a reason the Palestine doesn't stock mini bars."

That earned a low growl from her.

"And don't worry," he added. "I'm a professional. I got pants and boots on you without anything inappropriate happening."

She stayed silent to see what he would say next. There was the barest hint of color in his cheeks. Holy shit, could he be, no way, blushing?

"Believe it or not, you're not my type," he stammered slightly. "And I would never do anything to an unconscious woman. That's just gross."

His nervous chatter trailed off and Jen just held his gaze.

Theron changed lanes and made a right turn. This street was darker than the main thoroughfare. His face was suddenly lost in shadow.

From the darkness, she heard him say, "If I touch a woman like that, she's awake and begging for it."

Chapter 3

Theron breathed a sigh of relief as the metal rolling door slid shut behind the big SUV and plunged the old brick warehouse into darkness.

The building had been the HQ for the local Mage Corps strike team up until a couple years ago. It was empty now.

He clicked his flashlight on and hopped out of the vehicle. To Jen he said, "Sit tight. I'm going to get some lights on in here."

"Not like I have much of a choice," she snapped, rattling the handcuffs against the door handle.

Turning away, he moved over the concrete floor and noted the thick layer of dust. No one had touched this place in a while.

After a little searching, he was able to locate the breaker box and started flipping switches. He was rewarded with a handful of lights popping on. Clicking off the flashlight, he noted he was standing in what had probably been the office once.

There were seven metal desks scattered around the room. Laptops were still open, papers still scattered. All were covered in dust. A weapons locker across the room stood open, rifles, handguns, and an assortment of blades and blunt weapons visible, untouched.

There was a conference/interrogation room off the office. A plexiglass window looked out to the main area where he'd parked the SUV.

Moving back out to the huge main floor, he noted training mats that were torn and frayed on the edges. Rats had gotten to them.

As he moved through the room and past the SUV, he took a deep breath and focused, sending his senses out into the building around him. The wards were still in place, thank the gods. The physical security on the place was minimal.

He'd been given a copy of the keys before he left on this mission. When he'd landed in Baghdad more than two weeks ago, he'd swung by and grabbed the SUV, but had decided not to bunk here. It was just too creepy. Aside from the dust, everything felt like the Baghdad team had just left it and would be back any minute.

But the place he'd been renting wasn't set up for guests. At least, not guests in handcuffs. This place had holding cells, wards, a security system (if he could find the controls), and had plenty of privacy. He opened a door off the main floor and found a hallway with dormitory-style crash rooms opening off it. A small kitchen and bathroom were at the end of the hall. The beds were still made, and there was non-perishable stuff in the kitchen. Small bits of luck.

Across the warehouse, he found three windowless cells with heavy duty doors, concrete walls, floors and ceiling. Each had a cot and a toilet.

Heading back to the SUV, he hit the switch for the overhead lights. Jen came into view inside the SUV, and he stopped in his tracks for a second.

Her long black hair was loose around her face and a little mussed. She was looking out the window, not at him. Her dark eyes were full of questions. And, no doubt, sarcasm.

But, for the first time since he'd seen her in that bombed out market, she looked almost vulnerable. Something in his chest twisted as realization dawned on him. She was beautiful.

He'd been focused on other things up until this moment, but here in relative safety, his brain could stop spinning long enough to take in the sight of her.

She wore no makeup, but her skin was flawless. She was just a little too thin, and while he normally didn't go for that look, she managed to look strong, not sick. It made her collar bones and cheekbones stand out. The dark circles under her eyes were like bruises.

And those eyes. They were so dark they appeared black and were filled with a dangerous intelligence.

Everything, coupled with that feisty attitude, had certainly grabbed his attention. He hadn't been lying when he said she wasn't his type, but damned if there wasn't something deeply appealing about her unique blend of looks and personality.

He shoved that thought away and tried to stuff it into a mental footlocker. Okay, so she was hot. Big deal. Acknowledging any kind of attraction to her was profoundly creepy on his part. He was acutely aware that he held all the power in this situation and she was strictly off limits. He'd only have to be around her for a few days, then he could turn her over to the Corps brass and be on his way.

He pulled the driver's side door open and leaned over to unlock the cuffs from the door handle.

"What is this place?" she asked.

"Local headquarters for the Mage Corps strike team."

"Where is everyone?"

"They're all dead."

At her alarmed expression, he added, "The war was hard on the Baghdad team. We lost some good people. There were bombings, the insurgency. Then there's just the natural attrition of the job. Our work is dangerous. We go up against some pretty scary stuff, and not everyone comes back. A couple of years ago, the team was down to three members. One of them got killed, and the brass transferred the last two people out. We couldn't afford to keep throwing personnel at this site."

"Why not?"

He should have known better than to get her talking. He should have just stayed silent. Answering one question always seemed to lead to more with this woman.

"There's not that many mages left. We've been policing the magickal world for over a thousand years. Our numbers are running a little thin."

"Why is it the mages' job to police the other groups?"

"We can most easily pass in the sapien world. Elves and fey have to throw glamour—that's a type of illusion spell—so the normies don't see them for what they are. Vampires can go out in the daylight, but they don't like to. They have to feed more and use a lot of sunscreen to keep from blistering. And the shifters have never expressed much of an interest. They're pretty tribal and keep to themselves.

"But there are a few representatives of the other groups in the Mage Corps. Come to think of it, we really should get around to changing the name someday," he said.

She just raised an eyebrow and looked at him.

He leaned in and watched her eyes widen a fraction. Her breath was coming just a little faster. Did he make her nervous? Guilt pinged within him, but he didn't know how to put her at ease.

"In case you hadn't noticed, I tend to talk a lot when you get quiet," he said. "I don't know what that's about, but maybe you could save me from myself and tell me a little about you."

"Like what?" she asked.

"Well, we could start with your name."

She laughed. It was a quick explosion of sound and it almost startled him. He hadn't been expecting that. The sound was like breaking glass.

"All this and you don't even know my name?" she asked, that eyebrow cocked again. "It's Jen. Jen Jiang."

Grasping her right hand, which was now cuffed to his left wrist, he said, "Nice to make your acquaintance, finally."

He helped her climb over the gear shift and lifted her down from the SUV. Their bodies came into contact for one brief moment before he stepped back. She looked like she was all angles, but he'd felt a hint of softness under that tank top. "So, you're a reporter," he said. "Where can I read your stuff?"

"I don't write under my real name," she said, distracted, looking around the warehouse floor and peeking into the office.

"What name do you write under?"

"Sean Jameson," she answered.

With a start, he realized that he recognized the name.

"Holy crap, I've read your stuff. I did a bunch of reading on the plane down here. You're like one of the undisputed experts on Iraq politics and ISIS."

"Thanks," was all she said.

"But why that name?"

"I needed a pen name that would throw off anyone trying to track me down and murder me because of my work. Writing about ISIS is very dangerous. So, I picked the most white-boy name I could think of, hoping no one would ever figure out it was actually a Chinese-American chick at the keyboard."

She continued, "I do write under Jen Chang, which was my

mother's maiden name. That's mostly stuff on the rebuilding. My editors know all my names and, surprisingly, they can keep track."

"How's that headache?" he asked her.

"Better. Could use some food, though. You kidnapped me before I could order room service." Her tone held just a little bite to it.

It was his turn to laugh.

"First of all, it's protective custody. Come on. I think I saw some MREs in the kitchen. If we're lucky, there might even be some Spam."

"Eww," she said.

He'd seen the inside of the cabinets in her apartment when he'd been looking for anything with DNA on it to run his locator spell, and she was turning her nose up?

"Sorry. I know it's not an entire cabinet full of ramen noodles, but it'll have to do," he teased.

At her shocked expression, he flashed her a knowing smile.

"Come on," he said, clasping the hand that was cuffed to his own and guiding her down the hallway.

* * *

"Well, that wasn't...terrible," Theron said, pushing away the remains of his MRE. "How was yours?"

"Caloric," she responded.

They had somehow managed to eat with her right hand cuffed to his left, but they'd made it work. The meal had passed largely in awkward silence, both of them intent on getting through it as quickly as possible.

Jen was a little afraid to ask what was next. She'd noticed the crash rooms down the hall. Her brain began to spin with escape routes. If she could convince him to cuff her to one of the metal cots and if he went and slept in one of the other rooms, maybe she could get free and...she kept picking up and discarding ideas with lightning speed.

"I think it's probably time we both got some sleep. It's been a hell of a day," he said, rising from the small table that dominated the kitchen. "Hopefully, by morning we'll have heard back from HQ with instructions for the extraction."

"Why are you so keen to get me back to your headquarters?" she asked, unable to hide the slight nervousness in her voice as she rose to follow him. "Are we running late for my dissection or something?"

"What? No! Geez," he said, a little flustered. He ran a hand through that blonde hair and met her gaze. "Look, you're a seer. We haven't seen one of you in a hundred years. And the Mage Corps needs all the help it can get right now. Your gifts may save lives. You're so important that I'm abandoning a mission I've been working for weeks so I can get you to safety."

As they continued walking, she asked, "What happens when we get where we're going?"

"Certainly not your dissection," he said, clearly still marveling at her earlier conclusion. "Most likely, the Corps brass and maybe even the Council members themselves will fall at your feet and beg you to work for us."

"Really? All I do is talk to spirits. I'm pretty sure there are some fortune tellers in New Orleans who can do that, too."

"Those are charlatans. You're the real thing. I'm pretty sure you could ask the brass for whatever you wanted. And we're magick, remember, so feel free to get creative."

His smile was a like a beam of sunlight in the dim and dingy hallway. Something twisted in her stomach at the sight of it. She chalked it up to the MRE settling.

Gorgeous, smiling, charming six-and-a-half-foot strangers aside, she wasn't going anywhere with him. She didn't trust people in general and especially not people who were something out of a fairy tale. Or a horror movie.

Maybe it had to do with her job. She'd had it drilled into her from her first days of journalism school not to take anyone at their word or anything at face value.

An editor had once told her, "If your mother tells you she loves you, verify that with two other sources."

She practically had that tattooed on her. It wasn't only how she conducted her professional life, it spread to her personal life as well. She wasn't sure if she was in a professional or personal situation right now, but it didn't matter.

With a start, Jen realized they had left the hallway with the little crash rooms and had crossed the main warehouse floor. There was a concrete room with no windows and a heavy steel door. Inside was a cot and a toilet. It was a cell.

She spun on her heel and ran smack into Theron's huge chest. Jesus, it was like walking into an oak tree.

She stumbled backward and would have gone down hard, taking him with her, had he not caught her around the waist. His free arm came around her and brought her up against his hard body.

"I'm not going in there," she said, trying hard to keep the panic from her voice.

His arm was a hot band of iron across the small of her back. She'd thought the nylon tac vest he was wearing was armored before, but she'd been wrong. No, that was just him. The guy felt like he'd been carved from granite.

Ugh. She hated muscle heads.

"You'll be more comfortable," he argued. "I can take the cuffs off. You'll have privacy."

"No way!" She said, anxiety bleeding into her words. "I don't do small spaces. You lock me in there, I'll be screaming inside thirty seconds and a gibbering crazy person by morning."

He'd had his mouth open to argue, but shut it, giving her a thoughtful look. He looked at the cell, then back at her once more.

"Okay," was all he said.

She followed as he moved back toward the crash rooms. It was that or be dragged. On the way there, he stopped at the SUV and grabbed the bags with her extra clothes and toiletries.

Opening one room, he grabbed the metal frame of the Army-style cot and dragged it to the room across the hall, positioning the twin beds so they were about a foot apart.

"Will this work?" he asked.

"It's not perfect, but it's better than the cell, I guess."

Sighing with resignation, she kicked off her boots, pulled back the slightly dusty blanket and shook out the sad little pillow one handed while Theron stood over her. She climbed between the sheets, still fully clothed.

The pathetically thin mattress barely kept her from feeling the cot's springs.

As they lay down, their cuffed wrists hung between the bed frames.

Theron was asleep in minutes, but she didn't fool herself into thinking that it was a sound sleep. She knew his type. He'd be on his feet in two seconds flat if there was a sound much above a whisper.

She lay awake for a long time, listening to the quiet sounds of his breathing and feeling his gentle movements where their hands were linked.

There was no hope of escape like this. The guy was too smart, too cautious. He knew she'd run the first chance she got.

She wasn't sure how much later it was, but she felt her eyelids growing heavy. She rolled on her side toward him, her arm still extended and watched the gentle rise and fall of his chest in the shadows.

A part of her wanted to acknowledge that Theron's heart was in the right place in this situation. He genuinely just wanted to protect her, it seemed, and keep her from ending up in the hands of dangerous people. There was no malice in him. He was just a guy trying to do the best he could. In other circumstances, she would have liked him.

It was just that she didn't trust anyone to look out for her interests but her. No one made her choices for her and she would never be at the mercy of other people's decisions ever again. That way lay disaster.

She shifted just a little, and the fingers of her right hand came to rest against his. They were warm. Something in her said she should move, but she didn't want to.

Jen felt him stir, just a little in his sleep, and his fingers curled around hers.

Chapter 4

As Theron came to consciousness, he was instantly aware of Jen. By the sound of her breathing, she was just coming awake. He rolled toward her and saw her stretch and yawn, her eyes squeezed shut and a slight smile touching her lips.

As her beautiful dark eyes opened, they came to rest on the handcuffs that bound them together and then his face. It was like a storm cloud passed over her features. Those eyes became chips of flint and her mouth narrowed to a hard line.

She turned her head toward the door and jerked like she'd been slapped. A sound like a strangled scream was caught in the back of her throat.

Jen turned to look at him and then back at the door. She sighed. "You can't see him, can you?"

"See who?"

"The dark-haired creep standing in the corner," she answered. "Yeah, I'm talking to you, dead guy. You know, it's not nice to scare the crap out of people like that."

"There's a spirit here?" Theron asked.

"If you can't see him, it's a good bet that's what he is."

"What does he look like?"

"About six-foot-two, black hair, muscular build. He's dressed in black. Hard to see his eyes, they're really shadowy and sunken.

They might be blue," she said. "Someone you know?"

At her description, a hard knot had formed in Theron's stomach. It sounded like Rafi, the water mage and team medic that had been assigned here. He and Theron had been at the Academy together and in the same year. They hadn't been friends or anything, but Rafi had been a good guy.

"Yeah, I think I do," Theron said past a throat that had gone as dry and rough as sandpaper. Jen sat up and faced the corner, her right arm stretched behind her from the cuffs.

"Did your friend have a birthmark, right here?" she turned back to him and indicated her throat.

Theron's stomach felt like it was in his socks. There was no way that Jen could be making this up. Rafi had, indeed, had a small, dark splotch of a birthmark on the right side of his neck.

"His name is Rafi. He was a mage. I knew him," Theron ground out.

Jen nodded and rose slowly from the bed and he went with her, eyeing the corner she seemed to be focused on. He didn't see a damned thing, not a shimmer, not a shadow. It didn't even feel cold in here.

"Hey, Rafi. I'm Jen," she started. "Yeah, I can see you."

She paused like she was listening.

"Yeah, I've been told that's rare. Hence my new silver bracelet, here," she said indicating the handcuffs. "Your friend, Theron, thinks I'm some kind of unicorn and he's hauling me back to your secret base. Or something like that."

She paused again and then a slight smile touched her mouth.

"Rafi laughed and said you always did do things the hard way."

"Ask him what he's still doing here," Theron told her.

Jen glared at him.

"He can hear you, dude. And he says he's not sure why he's

stuck here. He didn't even die in the building."

The concept of spirits was a little new to him. He'd always thought you died and that was it. No white light, no pearly gates, just oblivion.

But here was hard evidence that they were real. And that Jen was the real deal. A small part of him had held out the possibility that Jen thought she saw the dead, but was really just mentally disturbed.

But she was talking to Rafi, who'd been dead for years.

"Can you do anything for him?" he asked Jen. "Direct him to the light, or something?"

"It doesn't really work that way," she said. "Especially for the ones that have been stuck here for a while. He's in pretty good shape mentally, I'll say that. Usually the ones that have been without a body for a while start to get...weird. He must have had a strong mind in life."

"The strongest," Theron replied. He spoke to the area Jen had indicated that Rafi was occupying. "What happened to you, man? I read the report, but it sounded like no one was really clear about how it all went down."

After a pause, Jen spoke, "They were raiding a compound outside of the city. Suspected rogue mages. It all went to hell from the moment of entry. Intelligence was wrong. More badies than they expected. All of a sudden, it was lights out for him. The next thing Rafi knew he was here and no one could see or hear him."

Jen fell silent and listened intently. It was the weirdest thing, watching her face react with little expressions as she made soft sounds to indicate she was listening, but there was no one there. That he could see, anyway. Theron could see her taking mental notes.

"It was Bridget, the air mage, and Anslem, the earth mage, left. They were upset. Sometime after he died—he's not sure how long, but it didn't seem like more than a week or two—they packed up and left. The next person to come through here was you, Theron."

Burning stars, there was nothing they could do for Rafi now. The guilt made him sick to his stomach.

Running a frustrated hand through his hair, he said, "That's good, man. Real good. Info is everything in this business and that's valuable intel."

It didn't tell him much more than he already knew, but he thought it might make the guy feel better. If someone had told him just a few days ago that he would be telling white lies to a dead guy, he would have laughed.

Jen narrowed her eyes at him, but didn't say anything.

Theron again trained his gaze on the spot where he thought Rafi was.

"I'm sorry about how it went down, man. It's a raw deal. Seriously, is there anything I can do? Anything that will help you...move on?"

Jen turned and slid her eyes from Theron back to the corner.

"Can you find out what happened to Rebecca Jurowska?" Jen asked. "She's a water mage stationed somewhere in South America, last he heard. She was special to him, he says. He'd just like to know how she is."

"Done and done," Theron said. "I've got to put in a call to HQ for our extraction anyway. Jen, see if you can talk to Rafi and find out what might help him move on from this place."

"I'm not really the best person for that," she said in a low voice. "I'm not a ghost shrink, you know."

"Do you see anyone else around here who can speak with the

dead?"

Theron was desperate to escape the room and the sick feeling in his guts. Digging in his pocket, he came up with the handcuff key. In less than 10 seconds, he had Jen handcuffed to one of the cots. It wasn't ideal, because the thing wasn't bolted down, but it wasn't like she could go walking around Baghdad with twenty pounds of metal Army cot shackled to her wrist.

Theron hit the office and breathed a sigh of relief. He flipped on the equipment he would need to make a secure call to the Citadel, the underground fortress and headquarters deep in the Rocky Mountains that housed the Mage Corps and the Council.

He dialed in, was met with a series of staff members that answered the line as a hotel, a beauty salon and a grocery store. He identified himself each time and said the necessary passphrases before the call was handed to the next level of security.

Eventually, his handler picked up the line.

"Theron, good to hear from you," came Desic's gravelly voice.

"We've got a situation here in Baghdad."

"So I've heard."

"I've secured the seer, but she's not exactly enthusiastic about coming with me. We've got likely bogies on our tail and we could use a portal out of here."

"No can do, buddy," Desic said. "Baghdad is strictly a no portal zone. Fabric of reality is too weak from all the violence."

Theron nodded. He'd suspected that was going to be the answer, but it didn't hurt to ask. Baghdad had seen a lot of concentrated violence in the last few years. That kind of death, pain and prolonged suffering could damage a place on a fundamental level. The fabric of reality, the barriers between dimensions, could start to warp and even fail completely.

There were things, creatures, drawn to suffering and pain and death that would take advantage of those weakened barriers. Heck, they probably already were. An elf- or fairy-made portal from the Citadel had the potential to weaken the fabric even more. Might even leave a permanent scar or rift those creatures could take advantage of, one that could be ripped back open, revealing a portal right into the heart of the Council's fortress.

"How about a flight out of here?" Theron countered.

"Sorry, man. Zone's too hot. Can't even get a chopper there. Your only option is to get to Damascus and use the secured portal there."

"The airports are being watched, no doubt about that. How exactly do you suggest I get there, genius?"

"By any means necessary. Brass wants that seer so bad they are practically salivating. She could be invaluable in dealing with our new problem."

Theron had heard the rumors over the last few months. Strange things had been occurring all over the world. Members of the supernatural community were going off the rails at an alarming rate. There were reports of murders, disappearances and abductions. Just a few weeks ago, his sister had to deal with a former Corps team member, a vampire named Dominic who had been one of her closest friends once, flipping out and trying to demolish Austin with an army of horrific revenants.

There was some indication that Dominic had been hearing voices that told him to do horrible things. It was possible that the young vamp had just lost his mind, but Alayna and the Corps brass were convinced it was demonic influence.

A spear of guilt ripped through his chest at the thought of what his little sister had done to stop Dominic's maniacal plan and the part Theron had played in the whole disaster.

The Mage Corps, along with the rest of the supernatural community, had been scrambling ever since to find out as much about demons as they could. Long thought to be nothing more than the imaginings of fevered sapien brains, it now appeared they might be real. The working theory, for now, was that they were likely extra-dimensional beings. It appeared they were non-corporeal in this realm, but had a way to communicate with some people. Demons might be just out of phase with this reality, like spirits, but unseen by humans, elves, or the fey.

Being able to communicate with spirits, given the possible incursion of demons in this dimension, could be invaluable, and the brass was justified in their desire to secure the seer. Hell, it was even possible she might be able to see demons as well as she saw spirits.

"How do you suggest we get to Damascus?"

"At last report, the Baghdad office had an armored vehicle," Desic said.

"Are you suggesting that we drive to Damascus?" Theron hoped his disbelief at the absurd suggestion was coming through the connection.

"I didn't say it would be easy, but if anyone can do it…" Desic's voice trailed off, and Theron felt a growl of frustration claw up his throat. This is what he got for being good at his job.

"You're talking about an eight hundred kilometer sprint, most of it across the open desert. We'd have to pass through Ramadi and Fallujah, which I don't have to tell you aren't exactly Disney World these days. In the desert, we've got bandits and militants. Then we've got the Syrian border to contend with. Between there and Damascus, we've got several hundred miles of battlefield controlled alternately by militant terrorists, rebels, and the army of a vicious dictator. And we get to make this sprint with unknown magickal hostiles on our tail. Have I got the shape of that?"

"Yeah, but it's still your best option," Desic said. "I'll do everything I can from this end to make it a smooth trip."

Theron snorted.

"Fine. I've got the sat phone. I'll report in as much as I can," he said. "One more thing. I need you to check on the status of Rebecca Jurowska, water mage, last known location was South America."

"That's random. What do you need to know for?"

"I'm asking for a friend," was all Theron said.

He heard keys clicking over the line as Desic ran a search.

"Looks like she's stationed with a team out of Buenos Aires. Reported in two days ago. All quiet."

"Thanks, man. Could you email me her file photo?"

"You're weird," Desic muttered. "It's coming to you."

"Thanks. I'll try to check in at my usual time."

Theron signed off and pulled up his email on one of the dusty laptops. Thing still worked just fine. Rebecca Jurowska was a beautiful woman. Startling blue eyes were set in a slender face framed by auburn hair.

He printed the photo out and carried it back with him to the crash room where he'd left Jen and Rafi.

As he entered the room, Jen was focused on the spot he assumed Rafi was occupying. Her mouth was turned up at one corner, like she found something funny. It was just the barest hint of a smile, but it transformed her face. Just like last night, he was struck for a moment by how beautiful she was. What would she look like with a full smile on her lips, mirth turning up the corners of her eyes?

He shook that thought off and stepped into the room. He set

the picture down on the cot beside Jen.

"Rebecca's alive. She's working in Buenos Aires right now and she's doing fine," he told the area he thought Rafi might be in. "Sorry I couldn't get more info, but I thought you might want this."

Jen was silent for a moment as she stared at the empty space. She ducked her head and looked away before she said, "He really appreciates it. You don't know what it means to him, to be able to see her face, even if it's just a photo."

"Yeah, man, no problem."

Theron met Jen's obsidian gaze and she said, "Rafi and I have been talking. He's not sure how to move on to what's next, but he thinks he can leave this building. Now that he knows where Rebecca is, he might try to find her, watch over her."

"Whatever you gotta do, Rafi," he said. "In a way, that's kind of romantic."

"It's more of a purpose than he's had in a very long time. Before he goes, he wants to know if there's anything he can do to help us here."

Theron thought for a moment.

"You got any contacts between here and Damascus? Any safehouses, supply caches, anything?"

Jen listened intently before turning back to Theron.

"He says there are some files on his laptop that could help us."

She rattled off a password and the location of Rafi's laptop in the office.

Theron spoke to where he thought Rafi was. "We'll give you some privacy, man. Jen, let's talk in the office."

* * *

As Jen reached the office a step behind Theron, she was still squashing her disappointment that he'd remembered to lock the handcuffs back around his own wrist before taking her. He would slip up eventually, and when he did, she was out of here.

"Here's the situation," Theron began.

As he told her of his plan to take that monstrous SUV and drive to Damascus, her jaw dropped. And then dropped even further. Then, she laughed, the derisive sound exploding out of her throat. This was not a joyous or mirthful sound, but grating and dripping with derision.

"You're talking about a flat out run down Highway 1," she said. "They call that the Highway to Hell, and for good reason. I've interviewed some of the long haul truckers that run supplies back and forth to Damascus. That road is like a Mad Max movie without all the warm fuzzies. Bandits roll flaming cars in front of drivers so that they can rob and murder them. There are checkpoints, and you don't know who's controlling them, the Iraqi Army, ISIS, or a random warlord until you're staring down the barrels of their guns."

She paused only briefly for breath and noted Theron's stoic expression. His square jaw with its dusting of red-gold stubble was set hard. His arms were crossed over that huge chest and those dangerous dark blue eyes that didn't miss a damn thing regarded her levelly.

"You're talking about going through Ramadi and Fallujah. Those two cities fall under ISIS attack on the daily. ISIS forces could take either one of those cities at any time, and even if they are not under ISIS control, you still have to deal with their IEDs and snipers."

She looked away and ran her free hand through her frizzy hair, which was messily coming loose from its braid.

"And that's just the shit on this side of the border. Once we hit Syria, we're in an even hotter situation, if you can believe that."

She met his gaze again as she ran out of steam. He was quiet a beat, clearly wanting to make sure her little rant was over.

"I'm fully aware of the situation," he said evenly. "But it's our only option to get where we need to go. And it's still safer than trying to stay here. Eventually, the guys on your tail are going to track us down, and they'll come in numbers I won't be able to stop this time."

A shiver of fear crawled through her belly. For just a moment, the memory of being pinned to the bed in her apartment came roaring back.

"Who exactly were those guys?" she asked him.

"I've been tracking them for a few weeks. They're an elven death cult and I'm pretty sure they're responsible for murdering some mages in this region."

Jen snorted. "Elves? What, like, Lord of the Rings?"

It was Theron's turn to laugh. Jen caught herself before she smiled at the sound. It was a warm sound that made her toes tingle.

"Tolkien got the descriptions of their physical appearance right, which always lead me to believe that he actually knew one or two in real life," Theron said. "But the similarities end there. Elves are scary intelligent, calculating, and ruthless. They're actually aliens from another dimension called the Fey Realms. And they are not to be trusted. Ever. They will cut your throat as soon as look at you if it's politically expedient and they have the strength, speed, and magickal abilities to do it before you can blink."

That indigo gaze locked with hers and her stomach did a little flip.

"And you managed to take one out with a pocket knife."

She cocked an eyebrow at him. She was sorry she'd lost that knife and would give up a lot of things to have it back in her pocket right now.

"That switchblade was hardly a pocket knife. And it sounds like they were overconfident and I got lucky."

Lucky Theron had come along when he had. The reality of her situation was really beginning to sink in. She was going to have to get the hell out of Baghdad. Theron was probably the best way to make that happen, but once they were beyond the city, she'd ditch him and take her chances running on her own.

She'd been surviving in warzones for five years now. Between her false identities and her contacts across the world, she could disappear if she had to. And she wouldn't have to deal with whatever Theron and his Council wanted her and her abilities for.

"All right," she said, stepping into him and grasping the hand that was cuffed to hers. It was big and rough, with calluses on his fingers. "I'll come with you. No resistance."

Her chest nearly touched his, and the heat of his body wrapped around her, pulling her toward him. He smelled like leather, with a hint of gun oil and sun-warmed cedars.

His lips thinned in a cynical smile, but he didn't break the contact. "Sure thing."

Chapter 5

Theron settled into the driver's seat of the monster armored SUV. The thing might have started life as an armored State Department vehicle and retained a shape vaguely like that of a Chevy Suburban, but the modifications were numerous and extensive.

The engine was scary powerful, the glass was bulletproof, and the armor plating had been upgraded to withstand everything but a direct hit from a shoulder mounted rocket. It was painted a matte sand color from its wheel wells to the equipment rack on the roof. All the emblems had been pulled off, and the thing sported an LCD screen instead of a license plate. He could control which letters and numbers appeared on the screen from the dashboard panel.

He wasn't sure who had created the beast, but he was certainly thankful for all their work.

Theron had spent the last couple of hours outfitting the truck for their mad dash. He'd left the back bench seat on the concrete floor of the garage. The two bucket seats up front were all they were going to need.

The cargo area was packed with guns, ammunition, explosives, food, water, spare parts for the SUV, along with his personal equipment. He'd transferred Jen's meager possessions, the clothes and toiletries the errand boy had bought, into a spare duffel he'd found. It sat next to her laptop bag behind the passenger seat.

"I just want to reiterate that this is an absolutely terrible idea," Jen said. The handcuff around her wrist rattled where it was attached to the door handle as she gestured at him, herself, and the SUV.

"You have my permission to tell me I told you so when we're both dead," he said, his tone light and a smile pulling at the corner of his mouth.

He leaned over the dash and clipped his smartphone into a cradle and plugged in a cable that connected it to the SUV's computer system. With a push of a button, screaming guitar riffs poured from the speakers.

He put the massive SUV in gear and hit the gas as the building's doors began to roll up.

Jen had a pained look on her face.

"Our adventure's soundtrack will be provided by Ozzy, Avenged Sevenfold, and Five Finger Death Punch," he said over the music.

"Ugh, metal. The only music genre that can be confused with the sound of pennies in a blender," she said, turning to look behind her. "I'm going to need some ibuprofen to put up with this." "Oh, and what do you listen to, the break music between segments on NPR?"

Her mouth fell open and she turned sharp eyes on him.

"Knew it," he said.

Her jaw snapped shut and she glared at him before turning to stare out the window. For a split second, though, he'd seen a spark of humor in those eyes. Was it possible she was warming up to him?

This trip was going to take three or four days by his estimation and it would certainly be easier if they didn't have to pass it in stony silence. Maybe he could use the time constructively, to soften her up to the Council's cause and prepare her for what she would encounter on the other side of the portal in Damascus.

The Citadel was an overwhelming experience for creatures who had grown up among the shadow races. It was going to be a hell of a shock for this poor sapien. But maybe he could answer her questions and build a little bit of trust before she was thrown in the deep end and expected to swim.

He tried to concentrate on the road as he maneuvered through the morning traffic, but he found his gaze drifting to Jen. Her long black braid hung over her shoulder. It was still glistening from the shower she had taken while he waited outside the locker room door. Her face was caught in profile as she looked out the window. Her jaw was as delicate as fairy glass, ending in a pointed little chin. Her cheekbones were high and sharp enough to cut himself on. They framed a small nose that was downright adorable. If there hadn't been a perpetual frown making little creases between her dark brows, she would have been magazine cover pretty.

But the snapping intelligence in those dark eyes coupled with her hard expression transformed her into something else. There was a fearsome quality about her beauty. It was like coming face to face with a tiger. The beauty was awe-inspiring, but you knew that you could be eaten alive any second.

Her voice snapped his thoughts back to the road.

"Why are you going this way? If you want to hit Highway 1, we need to take Rabie Street to the Abu Ghraib Expressway."

"I was going to take the hospital road," he countered.

"Trust me, you want to take the expressway. There are more

checkpoints on the hospital road, and we'll be all day."

"Are you in a hurry to get where we're going?"

"If these guys on my tail are as bad as you say, then I'd like to get the hell out of Dodge."

He switched lanes and prepared to do as she instructed. They passed a Taco Bell on the right, and he was struck for a moment by how often this city surprised him. The last time he'd swung through Baghdad, the Americans had been here in force, and Sadr City had been erupting in violence.

This area of the west side had been bombed out the last time he'd seen it. Now, there was a line of Toyotas and Hondas waiting in the drive-thru line to get their tostadas and quesadillas.

He checked the rearview and his stomach clenched. They'd picked up a tail. The little black two-door was hanging back three or four cars, but it had been with them too long and there was something in the motions of the driver that was setting off his spidey sense.

"We've got company," he told Jen.

Surprisingly, she didn't snap her head around to look, which might have given them away. Instead, she casually checked the side mirror.

"Black car, three cars back?" she asked.

This one was way too sharp.

"They've been with us awhile."

"Could be nothing," she said.

"Better safe than sorry."

He slid into another lane without signaling and at the next intersection jerked the vehicle into a sharp right turn. The engine roared as he accelerated and hung a left, almost clipping a Dumpster.

His heart rate kicked up several notches, and his senses sharpened, routes and strategies pouring through his brain.

The black car was with them, accelerating hard to keep up, sparks flashing under the belly as it bottomed out on the uneven road.

Theron continued to manhandle the SUV through a series of turns that had Jen gripping the oh shit handle above her seat with her free hand.

Her dark eyes were narrowed and trained on the mirrors, watching to see if their tail stayed with them, with the occasional glare directed his way when she was thrown against the door.

Theron's adrenaline surged as he maneuvered around a guy on a motorcycle and sprinted for the intersection ahead. The light was red. He ignored it and gunned it, shooting in front of a group of cars just starting into the intersection.

Horns blared, but they were already well past. Jen shouted to take a right at the next intersection, a four-way stop that he completely ignored. He scooted around the corner with only a slight squeal of tires.

"No sign of the tail," Jen said.

"Best news I've heard all day. The bad news is that I have no idea where in the hell we are."

"I do," she said.

She rattled off a series of directions. He'd slowed down now and was following the pace of traffic, constantly checking the mirrors to see if their tail had caught up.

"I think we should head south of the city, circle around the airport and pick up Highway 1 way west of town," she said, still checking the mirrors.

This was clearly not the first time the woman had been forced to lose a tail. Theron wondered what kind of things she must have seen in her life to have stayed as cool as she had during that little chase.

"My exit route's been blown to hell," he said. "Lead the way, princess."

Her glare landed on him at his use of the nickname.

"Why do you keep calling me that? I'm about as far from a princess as I can get. I haven't worn a dress or a pair of heels in five years. I've forgotten how to put on makeup. Tact and grace got left behind a long time ago. And I say fuck way too much to be considered a princess."

He shot her a quick look as he followed the series of turns she'd given him.

"I don't know," he said, a little puzzled. "Princess just seems to fit somehow. I think it's the air of unshakable confidence and command."

"Whatever you say," she snapped. "Captain America."

"Wrong comic book. I'm a little more Human Torch."

"Same hair. Same apple pie attitude. Same aw shucks smile. Same ridiculous shoulder to hip ratio. It fits."

"Ah, come on! If you knew me, you'd know that I have more of an edge than that." He felt a smile tugging at the corner of his mouth again. "I take back the princess comments."

She looked out the window, deliberately avoiding his eyes.

"Sorry. It's too late now," she said. "Cap."

"Damn it."

"Language," she said, sliding a sidelong look his way, a small smile tugging at the corner of her mouth.

* * *

T hough they had lost the tail, Theron was still driving like a bat out of hell and was clearly enjoying it. The big muscles in his arms bunched as he twisted the SUV's wheel, maneuvering in and out of traffic like an oversized shark through a school of minnows. A cocky little grin pulled at the corner of his mouth.

God save her from adrenaline junkies.

She had the handle over the door in a death grip, but she was starting to relax, despite the song on the sound system featuring a guy screaming about bodies hitting the floor. Theron had lost that tail like an expert. The guy was clearly well trained. If she had any hope of ditching him, she'd have to get very creative.

Jen mentally catalogued her resources and didn't like what she was coming up with. Her laptop, phone and camera were in her bag behind her seat. Without a WiFi signal, the laptop wouldn't be of much help in getting free. Her phone might be a better bet for getting a message out, if she could find an area with a signal and find a way to use it away from Theron's ever watchful eyes.

Who could she contact? Jen had no family left. The old familiar sting of pain bloomed in her chest at the thought of her mother. She hadn't spoken to her so-called friends in five years. The only people she communicated with were her editors, her contacts and her sources.

Even if she could get a message out to one of them, what would she tell them?

Been kidnapped by pyrokinetic claiming to work for magical shadow government. Running from elven death cult that supposedly wants to use my ability to see and communicate with dead people for some unknown nefarious purpose. Driving somewhere west of Baghdad. Send help?

Yeah, that wasn't going to work.

The handcuff rattled against the door handle and she wanted

to scream at the annoying sound. Theron had been far too careful to always keep her locked to him or something equally immovable. Fury at her situation burned like acid in her gut.

The man clearly did not trust her, despite her assurances that she recognized the danger of her situation and wouldn't resist his efforts to get her to safety. She'd been lying through her teeth. Was it possible he had sensed that, or was he just being cautious?

Jen had no hope of overpowering Theron. She knew how to fight dirty, but the guy was gigantic. He was somewhere around six and a half feet tall and two hundred fifty pounds, if she had to guess. His muscles were ridiculous, he was clearly a trained fighter, and, oh yeah, he could throw fire around with his brain.

No, the only shot she'd have at getting away was to convince him to lower his guard.

Once she got free, she wasn't sure what she was going to do. Theron had loaded water and food in the back of the SUV. It might be possible for her to sneak some into her bag, should she get the opportunity to make a break for it. She didn't like her chances hiking across the desert, but it was a gamble she was willing to take.

But how to get him to trust her enough so that she could slip away?

Her thoughts were interrupted as the SUV slowed to a stop. There was a double line of vehicles ahead, their brake lights glowing in the wan morning sunlight. Checkpoint.

Theron reached behind her and pulled her ID and press credentials from her bag. Shifting slightly, he pulled his own ID from a back pocket. With the push of a button, he released a catch at his waist and his black leather gun belt slid free.

He stashed one of the twin .45s in a hidden compartment just below the steering wheel and stowed the belt under the driver's seat.

"Good thing I was wearing my day guns," Theron commented as they rolled toward the group of Iraqi soldiers checking IDs and looking under vehicles with mirrors. "My evening rig is so much flashier and harder to hide."

Jen had to purse her lips to keep from laughing. He should be worried that the sniffers were going to pick up on the plastic explosives and ammunition he'd stashed in a compartment in back. Instead, he appeared casual as he slapped their papers against the steering wheel.

A thought occurred to her. Maybe she could alert the soldiers at the checkpoint that she was being held against her will. Maybe Theron would let her go rather than take them all on. There must have been at least a dozen manning the checkpoint. All were armed with automatic weapons.

Theron lowered the window and turned off the music as they rolled up to the soldier checking IDs. He handed over the papers without a word. Jen tried to catch the eye of the soldier and bring his attention to the handcuff on her wrist. She did her best to look uncomfortable, agitated and nervous, all behaviors the soldiers were trained to look for. At least that's what officials had told her when she was writing an article about checkpoint guards last year.

She was afraid to draw Theron's attention to her plan. She needed the soldier to notice what she was doing, alert his comrades and surround the vehicle. On a gut level, she understood that if she wanted Theron to let her go without a fight, the odds against him would have to be overwhelming.

"You're with the press?" The soldier asked, only a slight accent coloring his English.

"She is," Theron responded. "I'm just her private security."

The soldier glanced at her for a split second then back down at the ID. She realized too late that the drug dealer tint on the SUV's windows made the interior pretty dark. It was likely the guy couldn't even see the handcuffs from where he stood, barely able to see into the window of the jacked up vehicle.

Mentally, she cursed the tendency of Arab men to ignore women.

"Open the back," the soldier said.

Theron hit the release on the back gate and another soldier looked over the case of protein bars, the jugs of water and miscellaneous equipment.

The guns and explosives were in a hidden compartment in the floor. Jen had seen Theron lift a section of carpet to reveal a keypad. He'd entered the code too fast for her to follow from where she'd sat in the front seat.

The explosives had been in airtight cases, as had his ammunition. The soldier in back pulled a handheld scanner from his belt and ran it over the carpet and around the sides of the cargo area. A knot formed in the pit of Jen's stomach as the man stared intently at the device.

If they found the explosives, they'd haul her and Theron out of the SUV and place them under arrest. She'd have a hell of a time explaining her way out of that situation, but it was better than the mess she was in now. Wasn't it?

She started to open her mouth to say something, though she wasn't sure what. Her gaze landed on Theron's indigo stare and something in his look froze her. There was a pleading in his level gaze.

Trust me. I'll protect you. She almost heard the words in her head. For several seconds she was transfixed, lost in his eyes.

The scanner beeped once and a green light glowed. The back gate was shut before she could blink.

The soldier at the window nodded and handed the paperwork back to Theron. Theron touched his forehead with a two-finger salute and put the behemoth in gear. "Whew," Theron said as they moved back into traffic. "I was a little worried the seals on the back compartment wouldn't be enough."

Jen stayed silent, internally cursing her inaction. It always came down to bad timing, the story of her life.

Theron hadn't turned the music back on, so she heard him clearly when he said in a quiet voice, "They can't protect you."

She turned narrowed eyes on him. Had he noticed? What was he going to do?

"Your poker face is good, princess, but I'm better," he said, keeping his eyes on the road. "Let me be clear: just one of the people after you could cut down an entire squad of those soldiers without breaking a sweat. You want their deaths on your conscience?"

Jen clenched her jaw as rage surged through her, but she stayed silent.

"I'm your only ticket to safety," he said evenly. "Have I given you any reason not to trust me?"

Afraid her voice would come out hoarse from rage, Jen silently raised her cuffed wrist and rattled metal against the door handle.

"That's for your safety and mine," he said. "I know how sharp your knees and elbows are."

Jen kept her mouth shut, crossed her free arm across her chest and stared sullenly out the window, watching as the buildings became more sparse as they neared the city's edge.

Several minutes passed in silence while Jen beat herself up

over the missed opportunity, the impossibility of her current situation and the infuriating man in the driver's seat. Her mind spun, trying to analyze her way out of here.

Theron's voice broke the silence. "I know you didn't sleep well last night. Why don't you try to catch some shut eye? I'll keep the music off. We should be in Fallujah in a few hours."

Without saying a word, she closed her eyes. Sleep was an impossibility, but this way, she could more clearly picture all the ways she'd love to kill the guy sitting next to her.

Chapter 6

J en woke with a start when she felt the SUV slow down. She was disoriented for a second until her gaze came to rest on Theron. Her eyes narrowed.

"How long was I out?"

"About an hour," he said, not taking his eyes off the road. "We'll be there soon. When we get there, please, for the love of all that's holy, keep your mouth shut and let me do the talking."

"Expecting trouble?" She couldn't help the hopeful note that crept into her voice.

"Hopefully not." He shot her a look from beneath his brows that reminded her of their conversation earlier. *They can't protect you.*

"I'm not exactly sure what our reception is going to be," he continued, his eyes returning to the road. "I'm flying by the seat of my pants since you blew my mission plans to hell. This situation might be a little delicate, so just stick with me and follow my lead."

"Sure thing, Cap," she drawled, letting her voice drip with a sarcastic sweetness.

He growled in annoyance. She smiled to herself.

Looking out the window, Jen could see that they were on the outskirts of the city, the squat buildings visible in the distance. They were headed slightly away from town, a compound wall rising in front of them. Stucco buildings peeked over the top of the wall and a lake or reservoir glittered nearby.

Jen turned a confused look on Theron as she realized where they were headed. Dreamland. The nickname had been given to the opulent Ba'ath Party headquarters after it had been built by Saddam Hussein. The place was part resort and part fortress. Infamous tales circulated of the depravities committed within its walls by Saddam's two sons.

After the invasion in 2003, the compound had been occupied by several different U.S. military units and had been renamed Camp Baharia by the Marines. Since the drawdown, the place was home to several units of the Iraqi Army and the private lake that had been a playground for a dictator was being used as the main source of drinking water for Fallujah.

Eyeing her kidnapper, she wondered if he'd lost his mind. He'd done everything he could to avoid the notice of the authorities in Baghdad. Now, he was walking into one of their fortresses? What was he playing at?

Theron slowed the SUV as he pulled up to the gate, greeting the guard in halting Arabic.

"I'm here to see the base commander," he told the guard.

The guard sported a dark beard, an automatic rifle and a skeptical expression.

"The brigadier general?" he asked.

Theron nodded and looked a little impatient.

"Do you have an appointment?"

"Not exactly—"

The guard cut him off.

"Without an appointment, I cannot allow you to enter the facility."

"Get the brigadier general on the phone and tell him that

Theron Blackwell is at the gate. Tell him that I'm cashing in for that night in Athens."

The guard's expression remained blank as he repeated that he couldn't let them in without an appointment.

"Trust me when I say that the brigadier will be very upset if he finds out I was turned away. I suggest you place the call."

The guard stepped back and paused, caught in a moment of indecision. As he turned away to the guard booth and picked up a landline receiver, Theron turned to her, closed his eyes and mouthed, "Phew."

After a tense couple of minutes, the guard came back.

"Sorry for the delay, sir. He'll see you immediately."

He handed Theron a piece of paper and told him to put it on the dashboard, then he gave them directions where to park.

A young looking first lieutenant was waiting for them when they got there. Theron leaned across her body with a quickness that had her jerking back against her seat. He froze and held his hands up, wiggling the handcuff key in his right hand.

Her lips thinned and she nodded. His elbow brushed her breast as he worked to get the handcuffs off and she jerked again. "Sorry," he said, shooting her a sheepish look and trying to hurry. The metal cuff snapped free and Jen tried to track where that key went, but it disappeared into his clothing faster than she could track it.

Theron bailed out of the driver's side door like his ass was on fire and shook the hand of the young lieutenant.

Jen grabbed her messenger bag. No way was she leaving it behind. If the opportunity presented itself, she was going to make a break for it. With the cuffs off, this might be her best chance. As they walked past a line of military vehicles, Jen's brain was churning with possibilities.

She might be able to get free and hide in the compound until she could sneak out. Maybe she could let one of the officers know that she'd been kidnapped somehow and they could detain Theron long enough for her to get away. There were easily a hundred soldiers in the compound and they were well equipped. It certainly didn't solve the problem of the bad guys on her tail, but if an entire company of Iraqi soldiers couldn't keep these guys at bay, what could?

As they entered a side door of one of the larger buildings in the compound, Jen was immediately struck by the ostentatious decor. The floor was white marble veined with gold. The walls were covered in glittering glazed tiles in blues and greens. The ceiling was done in an intricate mosaic of geometric patterns.

As they moved down a hallway toward a central foyer, Jen could see evidence of military occupation among the opulence. An olive drab filing cabinet was stuck in a hallway, a stray office chair had been left abandoned, supply crates were stacked against the wall.

Ahead, a marble fountain burbled in the foyer. The lieutenant ducked down another hallway and pushed through a set of double doors with gold filigree handles.

An imposing man rose from behind a large desk and came around to greet them. He was in the dark green uniform of the Iraqi Army and his shoulder featured three stars and a Republican Eagle, marking him as the brigadier general.

The man stood in front of Theron and glared at him. Jen looked between them trying to figure out how they knew each other.

After a tense moment, the general laughed and pulled Theron, who was several inches taller, into a hug. She saw Theron's eyes widen slightly as the general pounded him on the back.

"Blackwell! What a surprise! What brings you to this part of the world?" the general said in English.

The man's voice was loud and rich, a British accent rounding out the syllables.

"Work," Theron said, straightening and giving the general a level look.

Jen could tell the two knew each other, and clearly they were friendly. So the general was unlikely to help her in her bid for freedom.

"I hope it's nothing too serious," the general said, returning to his seat behind the desk.

"I'm afraid it is," Theron said, lowering himself into one of the two chairs facing him.

Jen remained standing, looking between the two of them. Theron shot her a look and then pointedly glanced to the chair beside him. No thanks, she'd stand.

Theron continued. "Are you telling me that you haven't gotten a call already?"

The general looked momentarily surprised at Theron's words. Then he started laughing.

Pointing at Theron and looking at Jen, he said, "Can't get anything by this one."

Theron wasn't smiling.

"All right. Yes. I got word this morning. There's a substantial bounty on the head of a blonde fire mage traveling in the company of an Asian woman. I had no idea it was you until you walked in."

Theron tensed, his features becoming grave. Jen saw his right hand inch toward the .45 on his hip.

"Are you about to get rich, old friend?" His voice was even, but his eyes had a predatory alertness.

The general laughed again, a booming sound. "Oh, do unclench, old boy. I honor my debts. You know that. You have my word, on my blood, that you are safe here."

Theron relaxed and sat back, taking a deep breath and letting it out slowly. Eyeing the other man's insignia, he said "Brigadier, huh? Couldn't make yourself a full general? Field marshal?"

"I'm working my way up. Fewer questions this way," the general said. "It's not like I don't have the time. I'm immortal, after all."

"I didn't quite believe it when I heard you were hiding out in the ranks of the Iraqi Army, but here you are," Theron said. "Quite a step down from king, isn't it?"

Jen's brows lowered in confusion at that remark. King?

"Quite the step up from where I was when we met in Athens," he countered.

"Fair enough," Theron replied. "And you can drop the glamour. She's cool."

He nodded in Jen's direction. She was still reviewing the conversation, trying to figure out what they were talking about.

The general chuckled. "Very well."

Before her eyes, the air around the general shimmered. His darkly tanned skin shifted to a color somewhere between lavender and blue. His brown eyes became solid silver, without even a pupil. A swirling, shifting pattern moved in those eyes, and the breath caught in Jen's throat.

The general's close-cropped military haircut was replaced with a mostly bald head that was adorned by an elaborate topknot of black silken strands.

The bottom fell out of her stomach, and she almost screamed. She felt herself begin to fall, when suddenly strong, muscled arms clamped around her middle. Theron's massive chest pressed into her back, supporting her weight as her knees buckled.

From behind her, she heard his voice and felt his warm breath on her neck.

"Jen Jiang, meet Djinn ben Jaan, King of the Genies."

* * *

Theron supported Jen's weight easily in his arms. Her head whipped back and forth, her gaze flipping between his face and Jaan's.

She hadn't taken the reveal quite as well as he'd hoped. Apparently, being able to see spirits didn't quite prepare one to see one of the legendary djinn in the flesh.

He put one of her arms around his shoulders and worked an arm around her slender waist. He was struck again by how little she weighed. When they got her back to the Citadel, he was going to have to make sure the woman got something more to eat than protein bars and MREs.

He maneuvered her into the second chair and knelt in front of her, taking one of her hands and rubbing the back of it. Her eyes were a little wide, and panic was creeping in around the edges, her breath coming a little fast.

"Hey, eyes on me," he told her, catching her gaze and holding it. Her eyes were dark pools, nearly black, and he had to fight the urge to get lost in them.

"Jaan is my friend. He's not going to hurt you." Over his shoulder, he called, "Isn't that right Jaan?"

That cultured voice answered, "Of course, old boy. She's safe as houses here."

The snapping intelligence behind those dark eyes was already processing what she'd seen. Her breath was slowing, and she was back in control, which impressed the hell out of him. There weren't many sapiens that could witness that kind of reveal and keep from screaming or passing out.

Finally, her eyes drifted from his and it felt just like when the sun went behind a cloud. She focused on the being behind him.

"You're a genie?"

"We prefer the term djinn, but yes."

"And you're a king?"

"For a very long time I was," Jann answered, a wistful note dancing through his words. "I suppose I still am, but it's in name only. My people are scattered and have no interest in taking orders from anyone, least of all me."

As Jen continued her questions, Theron rose and settled himself back in his chair. Jaan didn't know what he was in for. Jen had entered reporter mode. When the woman asked a question, there was something in her eyes and her voice and her body language that made you want to answer. It made you want to tell her your life story.

"So you're in exile?"

Her hands twitched as if they missed the weight of a pad and pen. Fortunately for him and every other member of the shadow races, this was one story she'd never get a chance to write.

"In a manner of speaking," Jaan replied, leaning back in his chair and putting a boot on the desk. "I'm just trying to survive, like everyone else."

Wasn't that the truth? All Theron wanted was to get himself and Jen back to the Citadel and safety. Jaan was a professional survivor. Theron's eyes narrowed on the djinn. If the monarch was helping them, Jaan stood to gain something. It had little or nothing to do with the debt for that night in Athens and Jaan's honor. Djinn only honored one thing: the wishes of the ones who held their soul homes. And even then you'd better be damn careful what you wished for.

Djinn had phenomenal power, but they couldn't use it for themselves. Their powers were only activated when another being took possession of the object their soul was bound to, their soul home.

A wish made by someone in possession of a djinn's soul home was instantly fulfilled, but the djinn had some discretion in how it was fulfilled. They resented being the servants of other beings and they took particular delight in fucking over anyone stupid enough to make a wish with the most literal or unexpected interpretation of their words.

Theron had no idea what Jaan's soul home was or where to find it. Even if he did, he wasn't crazy enough to take possession and make a wish, no matter how dire their situation. No one in their right mind wanted to tango with an immortal being of near limitless power with thousands of years of experience and knowledge.

"Your girl is utterly charming, Blackwell," Jaan said, drawing him back to the conversation. "Why would anyone want to put a bounty on her beautiful head?"

Theron leaned forward and flashed a smile. "Maybe the bounty is on me and she's along for the ride."

"They were very specific. They want her alive and you dead."

"Who's they?"

"Word came through a third party. No one knows who's offering the payout," Jaan told them. "But you can bet that word has spread far and wide among those who walk in the shadows. You'll need to watch your back, old boy."

Theron knew who was behind the bounty, but the question was, did Jaan?

"So, what is so special about one sapien woman?" Jaan said, raising his eyes to the ceiling, like he was posing the question to the heavens.

Theron debated telling him. He could keep the fact that Jen was a seer a secret. Jaan wouldn't appreciate it. HIs friend was insatiably curious, a hallmark of his race. They needed him in a good mood.

On the other hand, a seer was a valuable asset for anyone, especially a power hungry former regent with advancement on his mind. If Jaan had a mind to, he could take Jen from him without breaking a sweat.

"I'm a seer," Jen told him.

Theron winced. That decided that.

He glared at her, but she was fixated on Jaan. Sapiens could be really susceptible to persuasion from a djinn. Suggestion and illusion were the only powers the djinn could call at will. They could draw sapiens in like a cobra could hypnotize its prey.

Jaan released her gaze, and she shook her head a little, as if to clear it. The old king looked a little troubled, a crease appearing between his dark brows as he frowned. Silence descended around them and the djinn appeared lost in thought.

"Damn it," Jaan said after a moment.

Theron remained silent, waiting for Jaan to fill him in.

"Is it a death cult or some demon possessed fiends on your tail?" Jaan asked him in a low voice.

"Both, probably," Theron said matter-of-factly.

"So the rumors I've been hearing of demons making their return to this side of the rift is true?"

"We've had some reliable reports that they may be exerting

some influence," Theron said cautiously. Didn't want to give too much away. "But what do you mean a return?"

Jaan steepled his fingers and placed his chin on his thumbs, mulling something over. After a few tense and silent moments, he said, "This isn't the first time the denizens of Hell have invaded our dimension. In the earliest days of humans, demons wandered the Earthly realms. They are formless here, just thought and energy, but they can whisper to the weak-minded, twisting their thoughts and actions."

This was certainly news to Theron. Jaan wasn't even looking at him as he spoke, his eyes fixed on some distant point. Or was it a distant time?

"How do you know that?" Theron asked.

"Because I was there," Jaan said. "No one knows this anymore, but the djinn were created by the demons."

Theron's jaw almost fell open.

"We were their servants, imbued with their power, under the control of the humans they possessed. The soul home was the built-in control switch for us."

"Why did they leave?"

"They didn't. At least, not voluntarily. My soul home fell into the hands of a young man that was strong enough to resist demonic influence. I convinced him to wish for the demons to be banished."

Theron whistled. "Heck of a move there."

"You have no idea," Jaan said. "A rift between the earthly realms and Hell was formed and the demons were tossed out of this dimension. My people were free, and I lost my crown."

"But the demons are back..."

"It seems the rift is not as wide as it once was. In places of death and misery, battlefields, war zones, massacre sites, it leaves scars on a place. You know this. It's why the elves are so careful with opening a portal when traveling between two points. Once a door is open, it can never be completely closed."

"So the demons are breaking through these scars," Theron said.

"They've had millennia to slowly work on those scars. A few scouts managed to slip through."

Theron decided to give as good as he was getting. Jaan had suddenly become the best source of information on the new enemy.

"There was an incident a few weeks ago in Austin. We think the demons were trying to open a portal by destroying a city."

"Well, that certainly might do the trick," Jaan said. His gaze was still a bit distant, as if he was processing his shock.

"What do they want?" Theron asked.

Jaan looked at him and his head rocked back on his neck slightly. "You don't know? Demons feed on the emotions of other beings. Negative ones, like sorrow, anger, hatred, fear. They latch onto people, whispering to their minds, influencing them, on very rare occasions possessing them. But they are really after spirits of the dead. They can drag spirits back to Hell and feed on them for eternity."

"Fuck me," Theron said, stunned. "So, Hell is real?"

"It's more than real. Word has it that thought has form on that side of the rift. Spirit becomes flesh. Energy takes a solid shape."

Jaan's eyes fixed on Jen.

"You have to keep her safe, Theron. If they get their hands on a seer, it could be the advantage they need for a successful invasion."

Theron realized that Jaan had a hell of a dog in this fight.

The djinn would be slaves again if the demons returned to this dimension.

"That's what I've been trying to do. My resources and choices have been somewhat limited so far."

Jaan got up from his desk and came around.

"You'll stay the night here and you'll be off in the morning. I'll put the facility on alert. If the death cult comes sniffing around, I'll throw them off the trail."

"We need to get to Damascus and the portal to the Citadel. I don't suppose you could lend us a chopper or an armed escort?" Theron asked, a hopeful note in his voice.

Jaan laughed big and loud.

"Helicopters are more precious than gold these days. And besides, I don't trust any of my sapien personnel to go with you. Demons are undetectable, even to a seer's eyes. If I send an escort with you, they could be possessed and turn on you. No, old boy, the safest way is for the two of you to fly under the radar. A military escort would stand out like a gunshot in the silence."

Theron paused for a moment, a sickening thought occurring to him.

"What's to stop them from possessing me?"

Jaan laughed again. The sound was beginning to grate on Theron's nerves.

"Mages are immune. Only the weak-minded are susceptible. All that training and discipline to control the elements leaves you as malleable as brick walls."

Good to know. At least he wasn't a threat to Jen.

Jaan ushered them to his office door.

"Here I am rambling on when you must be tired. I'll set you up in one of the guest suites. And then I'll strongly suggest that the few personnel that have seen you should forget all about that."

Theron nodded and thanked his friend.

"We're square for Athens. More than square."

"Thank you, my friend, but my greatest interest right now is seeing you safe for the night and on your way. The sooner she is behind the walls of your mage fortress, the better."

Theron couldn't agree more.

Before he knew it, a junior officer had swept them down an ornate hallway and shut them in a suite that wouldn't look out of place at Caesar's Palace. It was all white marble, gold fixtures and colorful silks.

There was a sofa along one wall done in gold brocade. A large mahogany wardrobe loomed in the corner. Another corner featured what Theron assumed was a wet bar. And against the far wall was a raised platform that sported a gigantic canopy bed. The canopy was missing, and the sheets were a functional cotton. Apparently, all of the luxury items hadn't made it through the war.

The problem was there was just the one bed.

He eyed the gaudy gold couch and sighed.

"You take the bed. I'll take the sofa," he told Jen.

He did a quick survey of the room and the attached bathroom, noting that the door to the hall was the only entrance and exit. The room had a balcony that overlooked a sunken courtyard that had probably once featured a beautiful garden and fruit trees. The trees were leafless and the beds were full of blackened stalks. The drop was too far to make it a likely escape route. No need to put the cuffs on the seer.

It was late in the winter day, and the sunlight was fading fast. He had maybe an hour left and hoped it would be enough.

Turning his back on Jen, who was standing near the locked entrance, he strode out on the balcony and stripped his shirt off. Next was the gun belt. As he turned to place it strategically beside him, he cast a glance over his bare shoulder. She was watching him.

Probably contemplating where to stick the knife.

Straightening, he turned his back to her again and undid his pants with a deliberate slowness. If she wanted to watch, he'd give her a show.

The material slid down his legs, and he stepped out, leaving him standing in a pair of black jockey shorts. HIs pulse was coming just a little faster. He smiled to himself. He'd been in some pretty nasty firefights over the years and that cardiac muscle had been steady as a metronome. But this wasn't about fear and adrenaline.

He was dying to know if Jen was still watching him with those gorgeous dark eyes of hers, but he didn't want to break the crystalline tension of the moment. One word, one look could shatter it.

If he listened carefully, he could hear the sound of her breathing behind him, soft and even, not moving around the room.

He stretched his body out on the cold tiles of the balcony, his right side toward the balcony railing, his left side toward the open door to their room. He was banking on a threat coming from outside the room and not from within. The guns lay within easy reach. He closed his eyes as the sun's rays fell across his skin. The stores of energy, his internal fire, surged.

Thirty heartbeats passed before he heard her ask, "What are you doing?"

The woman's curiosity never failed to get the better of her.

She was still pissed as hell at him for taking her into protective custody and would probably love nothing more than to never speak a word to him on this trip, but she couldn't resist asking him questions.

"Recharging," he said, not opening his eyes.

His voice sounded even and detached. Yay him.

"Like a battery?"

"Yeah. All mages have to do it. Air mages just go stand out in the wind. Water mages go for a swim. Earth mages go walk on the ground. Fire mages lie in the sun. We got the shaft if you ask me. Our recharge is time sensitive."

His eyes were still closed and she was silent for a moment.

"What happens if you don't recharge? ' Should he tell her? It was one of his few fundamental weaknesses. And it wasn't just his weakness. All mages needed to recharge. That wasn't known outside the shadow races.

But if she was going to stop fighting him, she had to start trusting him. And he had to earn that trust by offering it to her first.

"I'll die," he said. "A mage's powers are fueled by the energy in our bodies. I have a lot, but if it gets drained completely, my heart will stop."

Turning his head slightly, he opened his eyes and met her gaze. She'd been staring at him.

Her eyes widened and her cheeks flushed because he'd caught her looking. Fighting a smile, he looked deep into those dark depths, holding her there for one breath, two. Like a cable snapping, she turned away and grabbed her bag. Practically running for the adjoining bathroom, she tossed words over her shoulder. "I'm going to take a bath!"

At the sound of the slamming door, Theron settled himself

again, closed his eyes and let that smile spread over his face.

* * *

Jen leaned back against the closed bathroom door and pressed her palms to her heated cheeks.

She mentally cursed and kicked herself for her reaction to getting caught looking at Theron.

She'd blushed like a virgin, stammered and stumbled her way into the bathroom. That was so not her. She hadn't reacted that way to guy since—her mental brakes slammed into place for a moment—oh, god, since Trevor.

Nope. No way. She did not like him. Sure, he was a traditionally attractive man. He had big shoulders, narrow hips, a tight ass, and more muscles than anyone really needed. He moved with the grace of a well-trained fighter and had an easy going confidence and sense of humor that urged her to relax around him. Add in that hair, with its shifting red, gold, and platinum strands that kept falling artfully over his brow, the devastating indigo eyes framed by those long bronze lashes, and you had a package that was designed to push female buttons.

Her body had reacted to the sight of him taking his clothes off, not her brain. She'd been horrified by the warmth that had spread through her lower body and the clenching she'd felt between her legs.

He was practically a walking cliché. And he was so not her type. At all.

She preferred dark-haired men, not too tall, with slender builds that looked good in designer suits. Trevor invaded her thoughts again. That had been him to a T. He'd checked all of her boxes. The perfect boyfriend that had fit into her perfect life.

Jen shoved thoughts of her ex in the corner of her brain where she kept everything she hated. He was shelved right next to her former bosses, LA traffic, and little yippy purse dogs. When she realized that she was scowling, she relaxed and looked around the bathroom.

It was more of the white marble that seemed to pervade the former pleasure resort. The walls were done in hand-painted tiles. A double vanity marble sink was along one wall. The toilet was tucked into a little closet. And a giant sunken pool, complete with jets, dominated half the room.

A tiny levered window was set about eight feet off the floor. No way to reach it, and even if she could, she'd never fit through it. Disappointment had her frowning for a moment, but she shook it off. She'd find some other way, a better way to get out of this mess.

Not seeing a shower anywhere, she resigned herself to a bath. Under the sink, she found soaps, shampoos, oils and bath salts. She grabbed a bottle of shampoo and bar of soap that smelled like jasmine. The old her, five-years-ago Jen, would have loaded up on the salts and oils. Taking long baths had once been like a hobby for her. She realized that she hadn't taken an actual bath since she left the States. There were months since she'd left when she'd been lucky to find a shower.

Jen pulled off her boots and socks and lowered her feet into the tub, watching as the hot water slowly rose to cover them. The khakis she folded up on the edge of the tub, her shirt and underwear joining them.

Slipping into the tub, she waited until the water was up to her neck before she shut it off. She sat in the still and humid silence, turning over escape plans in her mind, running contingencies and rejecting them all.

Theron seemed like a good enough guy. She believed him that he wouldn't hurt her and that he genuinely wanted to get her to safety. It was the people he worked for that were the unknown quantity. He was clearly some kind of soldier or operative, following orders. When they got to this Citadel he mentioned, she was afraid she would lose all control over her future. They could lock her up under the guise of protective custody because she was somehow of strategic importance thanks to her powers.

If this Mage Corps was full of people with powers like his, she didn't stand a chance of resisting. And apparently they were just one segment of a shadow government full of vampires, shapeshifters, elves, and fairies. She couldn't quite wrap her head around that one, but she knew she didn't want anything to do with it.

Her life was her work and her work was her life. There were stories on the refugee crisis that needed reporting. Nothing and no one was going to keep her from that.

Leaning over the edge of the tub, she dug in her messenger bag and pulled out her steel flask. She took a long pull of Johnny Walker Blue Label she always kept in the thing and sighed at the sting and the spreading warmth.

So, how to ditch Theron before she ended up in the hands of fairy tale monsters for the rest of her life?

The guy was careful and those eyes didn't miss a thing. He was too strong for her to overpower, even with the fighting techniques she'd picked up over the past five years of living in warzones. The memory of her near-collapse in Jaan's office came back to her. He'd moved so fast, faster than anyone she'd ever seen. And he'd supported her like she'd weighed nothing. The chest that had pressed against her back had felt like a brick wall.

If violence was not the answer and he was too vigilant for her to slip away, that left one option: subterfuge.

She had to lie to him, get him to lower his guard. When he was vulnerable, she could incapacitate him. As for the people after her, she might not be able to fight them, but she could run and she was damn good at hiding.

The best, most sure-fire way she knew to get a man to lower his guard was to fuck him senseless.

It wouldn't exactly be a chore. The guy was hot. And it had been awhile for her. She took another long swallow from the flask and turned the idea over in her head. Turned out, it was an appealing one.

Under different circumstances, she would have really liked Theron. He was funny and a little charming.

As she laid her plan out in her head, her pulse began to pick up. Despite the cooling water, her skin felt warm. Was she actually turned on at the idea of seducing him?

But a seductress she was not. That much she knew about herself.

She'd taken a handful of men to bed over the years. Most she had known very well before she got physically involved with them. A couple had been virtual strangers. But she'd never made a move on a guy. They'd always come to her. She wasn't exactly sure how to go about this.

She took another long swallow from the flask and felt her thoughts go a little fuzzy around the edges.

Guys responded to physical stuff. They were also visual creatures. Naked things appealed to them. Boobs were pretty high up on their lists, generally. She could work with that.

Stepping from the now cool water, she saw through the tiny

window that the sun had set. It was now or never.

Blotting her wet hair with one of the Egyptian cotton towels that were neatly folded on the edge of the bath, she left the strands a little wet, their long black lengths falling over her shoulders.

She wrapped the towel around her, covering her breasts and tucking the end between them to secure it. Checking herself in the mirror, she looked as good as she was going to get. For a moment, she missed the makeup she used to wear, the pretty dresses, the spike heels, the push-up bras. Those things had been her armor. But they were long gone now, lost remnants of her old life.

Her clean clothes had been left in the SUV, so it was totally legit for her to be walking around the room in a towel, she told herself. Taking one more long pull from her flask before tucking it back in her bag, she realized she'd almost drained it. Hopefully, the liquid courage would do its thing.

Opening the bathroom door, she peeked out, steam escaping around her. Theron was leaning over the railing of the balcony, his back to her. He'd put his pants back on, but his shirt was off. A black leather cord hung around his neck, a large black claw, like a panther's, hung suspended from it, resting in the valley between his pectoral muscles. The last rays of the setting sun touched his golden tan skin, the muscles in his back highlighted by shadow.

Taking a deep breath, Jen felt her pulse spike. *You can do this.*

On bare feet, she padded toward him. A Cosmo article she'd read as a teen popped into her head and she licked her lips and pinched her cheeks. It was supposed to make you more kissable. She felt like an idiot, but she needed all the help she could get at the moment.

She moved to stand beside him, her left arm brushing his right bicep. The thing was like granite.

He looked at her and his brows lowered in momentary confusion at her.

"Hey," he said cautiously, his tone wary. He was giving her serious side-eye. "I can get your clothes from the SUV." The words "you weirdo, what are you doing?" were left unspoken, but she could still hear them.

Crap. This was not going how she had expected. He was on edge, and that was the opposite of what she wanted.

She turned and let her cotton-covered breast brush his arm. Eyes widening a bit, he froze.

"I don't need them right this second," she said, keeping her voice low and trying to make it sound husky.

She stepped into him, sliding her hand along his waistband, her fingers dancing over his muscles until she flattened her palm against his lower back. Pressing her full length against him, she touched that square jaw with her other hand. He stiffened slightly. Afraid to meet his eyes, she rose on tiptoe, closed her eyes and pressed her lips to his.

His mouth was soft and warm and he smelled ever so slightly of sun-warmed cedars. His lips remained motionless, unresponsive to her kiss. Panicking, she slid her hand from his jaw to the nape of his neck, her fingers running through the short hair there. Still nothing.

She felt him pull away and opened her eyes to find him scowling at her, his face as dark as a storm cloud. He reached up and gently pulled her hand off his neck, his other hand pressing against her shoulder as he stepped back, disengaging from her.

"What are you doing?" He asked, his voice hard and suspicion narrowing his eyes.

"Ummmm…" was all she could get past the knot of panic in her throat.

He'd seen right through her clumsy attempt at seduction. And now he was pissed. Oh, shit. She'd messed up big time.

"Sorry," she mumbled as she turned away and covered her mouth, embarrassment heating her cheeks. Jeez, that was a stupid move. What had made her think she could possibly lure him into bed?

There was a rustling noise behind her and she turned to see Theron had put his shirt back on and was pulling his boots on.

"I'm going to get some things out of the SUV. I'll get your clothes." His words were coming fast and clipped. Was he angry? Annoyed?

Before she could move, the handcuffs were closed around her wrist and the balcony railing. Rage surged through her. How did he always move so fast?

"Don't go anywhere," he snapped.

"No problem," she threw back, sarcasm and anger dripping from her words as she rattled the handcuffs against the railing. The click of a lock engaging sounded just after the door closed behind him. He wasn't taking any chances.

What seemed like a small eternity later, but was probably only a few minutes, Theron came back in the room with a duffle over his shoulder and her bag of clothes. He tossed the bag at her feet and unlocked the cuffs, careful not to meet her eyes.

His posture was tense and he still sported a scowl. His silence was unnerving her.

Picking up her clothes, she walked slowly to the bathroom even though everything in her was urging her to scurry. She did not scurry. Ever.

Just as she turned to slam the bathroom door, she met his

dark blue gaze from across the room and it was hard and sharp as flint.

* * *

Theron heard Jen come out of the bathroom about half an hour later, having taken her sweet time.

He was lying on the couch, his eyes closed, trying to calm his thoughts. Her bare feet made almost no noise as she moved past him to the bed. The only light in the room came from a lamp he'd left on beside the bed for her.

Anger and confusion roiled through his brain battling for supremacy and making his chest tight. Why had she done that?

She was trying to seduce you to get past your defenses and escape, a part of his brain chimed in. Talk about stating the obvious. Her attempt had been beyond clumsy. No one went from indignant and resentful to amorous that fast. Sure, she'd seen him in nothing but his skivvies, but even he didn't have that kind of power over people.

It was the pure cynicism of her actions that left him so angry. He was risking his life to protect her and throwing out weeks of work and his original mission in order to get her to safety. And she'd thought she could use sex, use him that way, use her own body that way? Ugh, gross.

When she'd pressed her lips and her body against him, it had taken every ounce of his will and resolve not to kiss her back. His arms had ached to wrap themselves around her and pull her close. Her hands had felt so damn good against his bare skin, sending little electric shivers through him. The lingering hint of scotch on her lips was simultaneously intoxicating and a warning. It had snapped him back to reality. She'd had to drink to work up the courage to touch him.

He was proud of himself for not outwardly reacting to her. And he was shocked at his internal reaction. And angry at her for trying to use him like that. Mostly, he just felt dirty.

The sheets rustled as Jen climbed into bed. The lamp clicked off and the glow he could see through his lids disappeared. There was more rustling as she settled in. When it was silent, he spoke.

"Jen, don't ever touch me like that again."

He heard her breath catch, but she didn't answer.

Chapter 7

As Jen woke the next morning, she pushed the tangled black mess of hair out of her eyes and was momentarily disoriented.

As she looked over all the white marble and gold accents, her gaze landed on Theron's sleeping form. And it all came rushing back.

Don't ever touch me like that again.

The anger in his voice had been tangible. She'd crossed a line.

Oh, god. She flushed and pulled the covers over her head. What in the fucking hell had she been thinking last night? If she was being honest with herself, she hadn't been. At least, she hadn't been thinking straight. It was never a good idea to formulate plans on too little sleep and most of the way through eight ounces of premium whisky.

Slowly lowering the covers from her face, she looked up to find Theron's blue eyes staring at her and she almost jerked in surprise.

"Morning, sunshine," he said sharply. That scowl was back.

"Morning," she said levelly.

Swinging his legs off the couch, he rose to his feet.

"Get yourself ready. I want to make Ramadi by nightfall."

Jen once again walked slowly to the bathroom under his withering glare.

She'd worn a pair of cotton panties and a T-shirt that barely covered her ass to bed last night. This had been her only option. She'd have never been able to sleep if she'd worn the khakis.

Holding her head high, she wrapped her pride around herself and walked to the bathroom, feeling Theron's icy eyes on her the whole way. She kept herself from running across the huge room by pretending her T-shirt and panties were a ball gown and that it was Theron who was standing in his underwear. It sort of worked.

Shutting herself in the bathroom, she broke land speed records getting dressed, brushing her teeth and running a comb through her hair.

When she came out, her clothes were in the duffle and she scooped up her messenger bag. Theron motioned for the door.

At her look of confusion, he said. "I took care of things while you were getting your beauty sleep, princess."

At her glare, he said, "Let's get on the road."

"Aye aye, Cap."

His sigh of annoyance was a beautiful sound.

* * *

Hours later, they were back on Highway 1 and crawling along at thirty-five miles per hour. Theron kept to the snail's pace out of fear of hitting a roadside bomb. The explosives still littered the roads around Iraq, and he didn't want to risk hitting one.

As a fire mage, he might be able to control and redirect a blast, but he didn't want to bank on his reflexes being fast enough. He was good, but why take the risk?

His eyes were constantly scanning the roadside, looking for telltale triggers and markers of the homemade devices, and

106

it left his lids tired and itchy. The music was cranked in an effort to discourage conversation and Metallica's Unforgiven was blaring through the speakers.

Jen was staring out the passenger window, watching the empty, flat landscape roll by. They hadn't said a word since they'd said goodbye to Jaan this morning.

The old king of the djinn had restocked some of their supplies. He'd provided them with paperwork that would get them past any Iraqi Army checkpoint. He couldn't do anything about the ISIS blockades or the bandits, though, and told them to be careful. Most importantly, he'd given them some official looking documents that would help them get past the border guards and into Syria.

As he'd shaken Jaan's hand in farewell, the djinn had leaned in and whispered, "Take care of her, Theron. Everything may depend on it."

He'd met the eyes of the ancient being and nodded. Jaan's words were still echoing in his head.

Jen's voice invaded his thoughts and he jerked in surprise, not catching her words. He turned the music down.

"What?" he asked her, shooting her a look.

"I said I'm sorry."

"Why did you pull that shit last night?"

"I—"

"You know what," he interrupted. "I know exactly why you did it. And it was a cynical, ugly thing to do. What I honestly don't understand is why you are so hell bent on escaping and getting yourself captured by some of the scariest bastards in this or any other dimension."

She was silent for a long time and when he glanced over, her hands were folded in her lap, her head down, her eyes closed.

Finally, she spoke. "My life was ripped away from me once." Her voice was a little sad, but mostly it was flat.

"It was a life I'd worked so hard to create for myself. Everything was perfect. And then, because of other people's actions that were out of my control, that life disappeared. I tried so hard to get it back, and I was left with nothing and no one. So I started bouncing around war zones, and I told myself I was deliberately not building a life. I could pack up and leave it all behind at a moment's notice."

After a pause and a deep breath, she continued. "And then those guys came along, and you came along, and I'm realizing that I had built a life. It wasn't much of one, but I want it back. I have stories to write and deadlines. But once again, I'm not in control of my own life, and it's all being ripped away. I swore that would never happen again."

Jeez, he felt lower than dog shit. He'd understood that she wasn't happy about coming with him, but he didn't realize that he was hurting her like this. She was trying hard to hide it, but there was pain and fear in her voice.

He hit the brakes and pulled to the side of the road. Grabbing her hand, palm to palm, he couldn't bring himself to look her in the eye.

"I'm sorry," he said. "I didn't mean to hurt you."

"You didn't."

"Not physically," he said. "I was focused on the mission, and I didn't think about things from your point of view."

What had he taken her away from? Was there a boyfriend back in Baghdad that was worried sick about her? Parents that couldn't reach her? Siblings that were calling every twenty minutes trying to get her to pick up? Suddenly, he realized how much he didn't know about her.

"Is there someone missing you right now?"

He stared at her small hand, with its slender pale fingers.

"Nope. I have no family left. I haven't spoken to my friends in more than five years, which I'm pretty sure means they're not my friends anymore."

"No one?"

She thought for a moment.

"There are going to be some editors back in the States wondering where my articles are in about two weeks," she said finally.

He breathed a sigh of relief, tension uncoiling in his stomach.

"I'm sorry I ruined your life, Jen."

"I'm sorry I came on to you in order to catch you off guard long enough to knock you out. We're even."

He looked up and she flashed him a little smile. It was close-mouthed, just one corner turning up ever so slightly, but it transformed her expression from harsh into almost playful. Something in his chest started to flutter at the sight and he rubbed absently at the skin above the spot.

Easing off the brake, he pulled them back onto the road.

Silence stretched between them for several minutes, and Theron began to wonder. What had happened to her? How had her life been ripped away? What had turned her into the hard, cynical creature with armor a mile thick? He was rarely curious about people, but with her, he was dying to find out more.

"Control is an illusion," he said. "You know that, right?"

"I had a therapist tell me that once. I think it's bullshit," she said. "I make the decisions that affect my life. I don't always know the outcome, but they're still my decisions. It was my decision to go to the bomb site. It was my decision to talk to that spirit. It was my decision to go home. I may not be entirely in control of what happens next, but I can affect the outcome."

He just hoped that the outcome was her safe in the Citadel.

"It's in the quest for control that you lose it because the quest starts to control you," he told her softly, his father's words spoken in Theron's voice.

Her eyes narrowed and her brows lowered for a moment. She opened her mouth to say something and then closed it, sitting in silence for a long time.

"Damn, Cap, that's deep," she said finally.

"Just call me Yoda," he replied.

She snorted. She actually snorted. And he smiled.

* * *

Hours later, Ozzy was singing about Iron Man, and Jen was asking questions. A lot of questions.

"What are vampires like? Do they really burst into flames in sunlight?"

If she was going to join the world of the shadow races, as Theron called them, she was going to need to know as much as possible.

"Of course not. You'd hear about a lot more cases of spontaneous human combustion if that was true," he told her. "They evolved as nocturnal predators, though, and they tend to avoid the sun. Their skin can get seriously burned pretty quickly in direct sunlight and it hurts their eyes. But some of them just cover up and wear sunscreen and sunglasses."

He glanced her way and continued, a small smile touching his mouth, "You've probably met several and never even knew it."

"They can pass for human?"

"They are human. Just a different subspecies. Same with shape shifters and mages."

She took a minute to process that. Theron had explained that there were more branches of human evolution than sapiens—that's what the shadow races called all the other humans—knew about.

"Do vampires drink blood?"

"Yeah," he said, quickly adding, "but it's always from willing donors. We've had laws about that for hundreds of years. There's elements in sapien blood they can't live without. But they eat regular food, too. These days, most of them get their blood delivered in bags."

Jen couldn't help it, she made a disgusted face at the thought of drinking blood.

"Can they turn huma—I mean sapiens—into vampires?"

"Yeah, they can turn humans, but they have to get permission, and that almost never happens. They also have live births. Contrary to your folklore, they're not undead. And they're not immortal, they just live a really long time, like hundreds of years."

"Do mages live a really long time?" she asked.

A bitter laugh escaped from him.

"Normally, we live about as long as sapiens, a little longer." His voice was harsh with a touch of sarcasm. At her confused look, he continued. "Most mages have a short shelf life. We're the cops and soldiers of the shadow world. We're lucky if we make it to forty before we meet a violent end. Some mages are healers, librarians, teachers. They live longer."

Jen frowned. To her, he seemed like some kind of superhero. He was faster and stronger than anything she'd seen. And then there was that whole controlling fire thing. It hadn't occurred to her that he probably bled like everyone else.

HIs iPhone picked that minute to switch songs to Rob Zombie's More Human than Human. Fucking apropos.

"That doesn't seem fair," she said.

"Fair doesn't come into it," he responded. "A thousand plus years ago, the shadow races formed the Council. Someone decided that the mages, because we could most easily pass for sapien, would serve as the buffer, enforce the laws and punish those who broke them. So ever since then, mage children are taken from their parents at age seven and sent to the Academy. Attendance is mandatory. Obedience is absolute. Mages serve or die. All rogues are hunted down and eliminated."

"That sounds barbaric," she said, anger at the thought of a little seven-year-old blonde boy being taken from his parents.

"It's what's required to keep everyone safe," he said.

The world she was being dragged into was a dangerous and harsh one, and she wasn't sure if she wanted to keep going.

"Why hide from the sapiens? If everyone lived together, it wouldn't fall on the mages alone to protect everyone."

He shot her a "really?" look.

"Because sapiens have such a great track record of treating those who are different with unconditional love and kindness? You people kill each other by the millions over differences of opinion. What do you think they'd do to us? The shadow races are just one percent of the population. We're vastly outnumbered. Does the phrase 'torches and pitchforks' mean anything to you?"

Jen shrank back in her seat. The man had a point, and she felt like an idiot. It was so easy to see oneself and one's people as the good guys. After all the war zones she'd been in over the last five years, she knew that better than most. And yet, she'd fallen into that trap.

She kept her mouth shut, afraid to say something else that would make her sound like more of an idiot.

"Sorry, that was harsh," he said, his voice quiet. "But I've lost friends and family in the fight to protect sapiens from rogue shadows and protect the shadows from being discovered by the sapiens."

As usual, she'd pushed too far with her questions. It wasn't uncommon, a side effect of her job. When you asked questions for a living, it was hard to turn that off. Sometimes she walked into conversational back alleys and caught a knife in the ribs.

She nodded at him, briefly meeting his eyes, but kept her mouth shut. Turning, she watched the desolate desert landscape slide slowly by outside her window.

Theron's deep voice broke the silence.

"So, on chicken farms," he said. "Do you think the chickens that get fed an all vegan diet act all superior to the chickens that don't?"

The question caught her so much by surprise that a laugh bubbled out of her throat. Her eyes widening, she clamped a hand over her mouth, but it was already out, like a bird slipping from an open cage door.

It hit her suddenly that she was laughing a lot around this man. Not a sarcastic or a derisive laugh, but one of genuine amusement. Her surprised gaze met Theron's and she saw his mouth turn up at the corner. Another laugh slipped past her fingers, feeling like an alien thing in her throat and causing her mouth to stretch into a smile against her hand.

Taking her hand away from her face, she said, "Speaking as someone from LA, I can predict that vegan smugness is universal, even across species."

His smile widened as he turned his eyes back to the road. "Thought so," he said. "These are just the questions that pop into my head when it's too quiet."

"I better start talking then," she said, the smile refusing to leave her face. "Wouldn't want you to strain yourself."

* * *

An hour later, Theron could see Ramadi in the distance, silhouetted by the setting sun to the west.

He'd gotten Jen talking about her time in the Middle East. She'd landed in Baghdad a little over five years ago after "shit blew up stateside."

She deftly steered the conversation away from her life before then, but was willing to talk about the places she'd been and the stories she'd covered since. She'd arrived in Iraq at the height of the US military occupation. As a freelancer she'd been unable to afford a translator, so she'd started out by embedding with a unit of Marines.

They'd treated her like a little sister. She'd picked up enough Arabic from the veterans of multiple tours to get a conversational grasp on the language. As someone who'd had to learn that language, Theron knew how hard it could be to pick it up.

That had also been where she'd picked up the vicious fighting skills she'd used on him back at her hotel. There had been a lot of downtime during her weeks with the Marines, and they'd taken it upon themselves to make sure Jen could keep herself safe.

They'd taught her their dirtiest, bone-breaking moves, and she'd taken to it like a fish to water. She'd let slip that she never would have considered something like that in her former life back in LA. That left Theron wondering what she'd been like before she'd landed in this hellhole.

The woman sitting beside him was a hard, jaded survivor with a mountainous intellect and no compunctions about eliminating all obstacles in her path. Somewhere along the way, she'd left behind the ability to look on the bright side and had forgotten how to laugh.

But she knew how to tell one heck of a story.

"So, there I am in the middle of this huge protest, hundreds of thousands of people crowding the streets. Word starts making its way through the crowd that the president, who was a total dictator, has stepped down, and the crowd erupts."

The only time Theron had seen her open up was when she was telling a story about some place she'd been or some interview she'd done or some article she'd written. He'd take it. For now.

"People are dancing, there's music, screaming, cheering, crying. I'm trying to take pictures, and all of a sudden this guy grabs me. The crowd was so crazy that no one realized the guy was trying to drag me off to god knows where."

She must have been terrified, but she didn't show that in the retelling.

"I fight back, kicking and punching. I swing my backpack at the guy and catch him across the face. I tried to run, but the next thing I know I can't breathe, and my side is on fire. I look down, and there's a knife sticking out of my shirt, just below my ribs. I scream, stumble back and get swept up in the crowd."

Jesus. He'd never have guessed at some of the stuff she'd been through.

"These three women saw the blood and the knife. Luckily, one of them was a nurse and she was able to keep me from bleeding out until we could get to a hospital."

Jen lifted her shirt and pointed to a thin white scar about two inches long just below her right short rib.

"Only took a handful of stitches to close it up," she said. "And I got to keep the switchblade."

He reached into the pocket of his fatigues.

"It wouldn't happen to be this switchblade, would it?"

The knife was cheap stainless steel, with a maroon plastic grip. The release for the blade was a black metal catch near the top of the grip. He'd found the thing, covered in blood, on one of the elves in Jen's apartment.

Her face lit up. "That's it! That's my lucky knife."

She started to reach for the blade, and he pulled his hand back. Could he trust her not to stick it in his carotid the second his back was turned? They'd made some progress today. She seemed less hostile, but maybe that was all an act. Just last night, she'd tried to seduce him so she could knock him out.

On the other hand, it was her knife. Did he have the right to deprive her of the chance to defend herself if their pursuers caught up with them?

As he pulled the knife away, her face fell a little. Something twisted in his chest at the sight, and he frowned.

"I need your word," he began. "I want you to be able to protect yourself, but I also don't want to find this sticking out of my back."

He leveled his best attempt at a stern look at her.

"I'm putting my trust in you," he continued. "I'm asking you to do the same with me. Promise you'll stop trying to escape and that you'll work with me to get you to safety?"

She looked back and forth between his face and where he was holding the knife. Her lips thinned and her eyes narrowed in thought. That pause, more than anything, convinced him that if she gave her promise, she would honor it. If she'd given the promise immediately, without thinking about it, he wouldn't have trusted her completely.

"Okay," she said, finally. "I'll stop trying to get away from you. And I'll work with you to get us to Damascus."

He sighed in relief and slapped the handle of the knife into her open palm.

* * *

As they neared the outskirts of Ramadi, Jen felt her nervousness mounting. Until just a few weeks before, Ramadi had been under ISIS control. Republican forces had recently retaken the city, but the area was still reeling from the assault, and who knew how many ISIS operatives were still in the area. It wasn't like the guys wore uniforms.

Jen had bounced around a lot of dangerous places over the last few years. She'd interviewed warlords, rebel leaders, insurgents. No one scared her like ISIS. Through all the incarnations of terrorist groups in this part of the world, she'd always encountered people who thought on some level that they were fighting the good fight. ISIS was a different animal. The craziest, most vicious, ruthless, sadistic killers had formed a well-organized machine. It was like the leaders had put up recruiting posters for the most evil motherfuckers they could find. And they'd found them.

She'd filled Theron in on the situation in Ramadi as they'd neared the city. There was a small hotel on the north side of town that was friendly to journalists and foreigners, and they'd agreed to stay there for the night. Jen just hoped the place was still there.

"Be sure to have those military papers ready," she told Theron. "The checkpoint guards are going to be extra jumpy."

Digging in her messenger bag, she found her press credentials and her passport, complete with a journalist's visa tucked inside. She handed them over to him.

"I suggest we stick as close to the truth as possible. Tell them I'm a journalist covering the conflict for an American publication, and you're my private security. Are your IDs and visas in order?"

"They'll stand up to any inspection," he told her.

Her eyebrows popped in surprise.

"We've got mages inside the State Department that can get us perfect documents," he told her.

"That's not creepy at all," she said sarcastically.

"We're just there to help. There are members of the shadow races at every level of every government. They protect the interests of the Council, sure, but they're also tasked with nudging players toward peace."

"Where were they in 2003?" she said, referring to the US-led invasion of Iraq that had destabilized the entire region, perhaps irrevocably.

"We can't stop every war," he said. "But we've stopped a few. Dark forces thrive in the chaos of war, and it makes it difficult for our people to operate. So we try to keep the bloodshed to a minimum when possible."

A thought occurred to her and the question fell out of her mouth before she could stop it.

"ISIS—they're not any of yours, are they?"

He shot a look that was very similar to the one she'd gotten earlier.

"We talked about this," he said, a touch of anger creeping into his tone. "Sapiens are capable of far more depravity and on a much larger scale than the shadow races."

He was quiet for a moment.

"But I wouldn't be surprised to find a few shadows lurking in the ISIS ranks. There are bad apples in any bunch and we're no different. And there are certain elements that have been chafing under all the rules lately. They don't understand why we have to hide from the sapiens."

He opened his mouth to say something, seemed to think better of it, and shut it again.

Just as she was about to ask him what he was holding back, they reached the edge of town. Traffic was backed up waiting to get through the first checkpoint.

It took them well over two hours to clear both checkpoints into the city, inching along in the lines of cars. Fortunately, the papers that Djinn ban Jaan had provided them with proved to be invaluable. One look and the checkpoint guards were waving them through.

The delay meant that it was well after dark as they rolled into what passed for a downtown in Ramadi, these days. The last time she'd been through here, she'd been writing about the American troop withdrawal. The place was a little the worse for wear, having come through a recent ISIS occupation and subsequent Republican assault with major damage to the infrastructure.

Large sections of the city were without power, the street lights were a distant memory, and the traffic lights—when they were working—were treated like suggestions. Traffic was a mess, and as Jen tried to help Theron navigate the behemoth SUV, they kept running into closed streets with bombed out craters and shattered pavement.

Night held the city firmly in its embrace, making navigation even more difficult.

Theron slammed on the brakes and narrowly avoided hitting a car that ran a red light. A large truck behind them laid on its horn and flashed its brights.

"Fine, fine. I'm moving," he mumbled under his breath to no one in particular.

Rather than trying to cross the intersection, he turned right, easing into the flow of traffic.

"Head west," Jen suggested. "We can skirt around some of the residential sections.

Theron frowned, "That truck is still with us. And he's tailgating."

Looking over her shoulder, Jen confirmed he was right.

"Maybe he's just in a hurry to make a delivery," Jen said, trying to fight down a rising moment of panic.

"Could be," he said. "Let's find out."

Jerking the wheel to the left, he cut across several lanes of traffic, leaving horns blaring in their wake as he darted down a side street. Jen gripped the handle above the door and closed her eyes, flashing back to the wild driving he'd done in Baghdad. The Powerbar she'd eaten for lunch suddenly wasn't sitting so well.

Theron gunned the engine and made several quick turns before easing off the gas. The truck hadn't made the turn off the main drag.

"Guess he was just in a hurry," Theron said, not the slightest bit apologetic for the automotive acrobatics.

There was a loud crunch ahead of them and Theron slammed on the brakes again, throwing Jen into the seat belt. Cursing, she looked up to see two cars blocking the intersection, smashed plastic and broken glass littering the pavement.

It looked like just a fender bender, but Jen reached and undid her seat belt.

"We should help them," she told him, reaching for her door handle.

"Stay where you are," he growled, a deep scowl making his handsome face appear harsh in the glowing lights of the dashboard.

He threw the SUV in reverse and slammed his foot on the accelerator, tires screaming as he reversed down the street at a high rate of speed. Another car was coming up fast behind them, the headlights a glaring warning in the darkness, but Theron was able to switch gears and turn down a side street.

Jen bounced in the passenger seat as they rocketed over potholes and cracked pavement. Coming down hard on her tailbone, she swore and braced one of her hiking boots against the dash.

They continued heading west for a few minutes, and eventually Theron began to slow, wary of attracting the attention of military units.

"Don't you think you're being a little paranoid?" Jen said. "Do you really think that accident was staged?"

"I think it didn't feel right," he said, his eyes never leaving the road ahead of them. "I trust my gut. It's saved me more than a few times."

Jen stayed silent, watching him. The muscles in his massive shoulders and arms flexed where he gripped the wheel. His right hand dropped to his waist to touch the .45 holstered there. He was nervous, she could see, and trying to reassure himself.

Theron's frown deepened, if that was possible, and he slowed the SUV. About fifty yards ahead, a large group of people were moving across the road. It was just five or six at first, then ten or twelve. By the time they got within twenty feet or so, the crowd looked closer to forty or fifty.

The people were all dressed in white robes, their heads covered and moving slowly. Beyond them, Jen could see the gates of the city's cemetery looming like sentinels in the night. The necropolis was a large one, with the above ground mausoleums, large and small, crowded close together and glowing white in the moonlight.

"It's a funeral procession," Jen said, realization dawning on her.

Jen turned and looked behind them. The nearest intersection was about half a mile back. The street was narrow, crowded with homes and a few shops. With a sinking feeling, she noted that there was not a single light on in any of them, and the majority of the windows were boarded up.

They'd probably be here for a while as the mourners made their way to the cemetery. Night burials were not uncommon given the level of violence in the area and the strict rule that Muslim dead must be buried within one day of death.

As the crowd filled the street and sidewalks, heads slowly began to turn toward the two of them. Most of the faces were obscured by various head coverings, but Jen caught a glimpse of one of the figures that made her want to scream.

Grey skin hung in strips and bone shone through at the cheeks and forehead. Empty eye sockets were like black pits. She blinked hard and almost didn't trust what she'd seen. Then she caught a glimpse of a hand peeking beneath the edge of another figure's robe. It was skeletally thin and bone white.

"Turn around," she urged Theron.

"Don't gotta tell me twice."

He was already manhandling the steering wheel into a K-turn. Unfortunately, the street was narrow, and the SUV was big.

Suddenly, Jen was thrown against the door as a tremendous impact rocked the SUV, and the sounds of twisting metal and a roaring engine filled her ears. She looked up and saw the grill of the truck that had been tailgating them earlier through the shattered glass of the driver's window.

The fucking thing had just T-boned them in the middle of the road! Her ears were ringing and her head was spinning. She put her hand to the side of her head where it had hit the window. She caught the sight of blood through blurry vision.

Theron was half conscious beside her, shaking his head and clutching his shoulder. A groan escaped his lips.

"Hit the gas, Cap, we gotta get out of here!" she shouted.

Theron struggled to sit up and reach for the gear shift. A loud thunk brought her eyes around, and she found herself staring into the rotting face of a corpse. The thing was crouched on the hood of the SUV and drawing its bony fist back. There were already spiderweb cracks in the glass of the windshield. Another hit and the thing would shatter.

More corpses were gathering around the SUV, skeletal hands reaching out. The panic-inducing scent of gasoline reached her and sent her heart pounding. The crash must have ruptured a fuel line.

As she opened her mouth to scream for Theron, she was suddenly showered with broken glass, but not from the windshield. The window beside her head exploded inward. For a split second, she met Theron's wide indigo eyes before a dozen nightmare hands dragged her backward through the window.

She had just long enough to wish that she'd put her seat belt back on earlier before a blow to the back of her head had her seeing stars.

* * *

"Jen!" Theron screamed as he watched her boots disappear out the busted window, unable to move fast enough to stop it.

His vision was blurry, his ears ringing. It was almost like he'd been hit by a—oh, yeah. He had, in fact, been hit by a truck. The same truck that was backing up and no doubt getting ready to hit him again.

He tried to lift his left hand to the door handle, but pain screamed from his shoulder, sending shocks dancing across his already scrambled nervous system. Probably dislocated then. Possibly broken.

It took more effort than it should have, but he managed to get his right hand on the handle and yanked. Nothing. The door was wedged shut from the crash.

Levering himself around in the seat, he pulled his knees under his chin and smashed both his combat boots into the door, funneling a sliver of his magickal energy into the effort. With the sound of twisting metal, the door popped open, swinging with enough force to send several of the walking corpses flying back.

Tucking his injured left arm against his body, he brought his right hand up, letting his inner fire coalesce above his palm. He mentally formed the energy into a white hot ball of flame about the size of a basketball.

Theron thrust his arm out, palm forward, and sent the fireball through the windshield of the truck. It passed through the glass like it was no more than tissue paper, leaving glowing orange edges. There was a scream from the driver, a low boom and the cab was filled with flames, the heat causing the windows to explode outward.

Scratch one threat from the board. Only forty or fifty more to go.

The flying tackle came from his left and slammed into his injured shoulder. His breath left him on a scream as fresh pain ricocheted up and down his arm, skittering across his chest and causing his vision to go black around the edges.

Anger, pain, and fear surged through him, and his fire came without being called. Orange flames leapt to life in his hands, pouring up his arms like a trail of gasoline igniting.

It was dangerous to let his emotions fuel his power. If he lost control, his power could consume him, draining every bit of his energy and stopping his heart. At the moment, though, he was a little more concerned about the ravening dead closing in around him.

The one that had tackled him, was wrapping skeletal fingers around his neck, rotting flesh slipping against the skin of his throat. Fuck, that was gross! His punch caught the creature in the jaw, shattering the skull and setting its ragged robes on fire. As the creature fell back, twisting and twitching in the flames, Theron hoisted himself to his feet, head spinning at the sudden shift.

"Jen!" he called, casting a glance in the direction she'd been dragged. "Talk to me!"

No answer came from the other side of the SUV, and he couldn't see her through the shattered windows. Fear for her gripped his gut. He had to get to her.

Bringing his eyes back to front, he saw that the walking corpses had arrayed themselves in a semicircle around him, corralling him against the side of the SUV. It was times like these, he wished he was an air or earth mage like his sisters. Alayna could call a hurricane gale to knock these fuckers back, and Kayla could have opened the earth and swallowed them all.

The problem with fire was that it didn't carry force on its own. It was just energy. He could call the flames and set every one of the hideous creatures on fire. But then, he just had a dozen or so rotting corpses that also happened to be on fire.

As the creatures advanced, he formed another fireball above his right hand. This wouldn't be enough to take them all out, but it might give him an opening. He launched the fireball at the ground just behind the corpse in the center of the group. It burned right through the creature, setting it on fire as it went. As it hit the sandy ground, the fireball's concentrated heat exploded outward, igniting the oxygen in the air and sending burning hot earth to sizzle against the surrounding corpses. They didn't flinch.

Oh, great, they didn't feel pain. This situation just kept getting better and better.

The force of the explosion knocked two of the creatures to the ground and Theron darted through the opening, skidding around the front grill of the SUV in time to see Jen's unconscious form being carried away by about a dozen of the corpses.

He couldn't risk throwing fire; he might burn Jen. His hand went to the .45 at his hip. He was a crack shot, even at this distance, but he didn't want to risk hitting her.

His right fist clenched. He'd just have to do this with his bare hands. He looked down at his useless left arm cradled against his chest. Make that bare hand.

Pain erupted at the base of his skull from a blow he never saw coming. As darkness swept up to claim him, his last thought was that he had failed again. And yet another friend would pay with their life.

* * *

Jen was barely conscious and dimly aware of the hands gripping her clothes, hooked under her arms and behind her knees. She was being carried, she realized, becoming aware of the jostling movement.

Cracking her eyelids, adrenaline shot through her at the sight of rotting flesh and protruding bones that greeted her and her limbs jerked, her body trying to run even as her mind reeled. Zombies were real.

If she'd known the cast of the Walking Dead was one of the things that might potentially come after her, she would not have signed up for this little trip.

Her brain began observing, recording, cataloging, as it always did. These creatures weren't behaving like zombies in the movies, she noted. They moved slowly, but they packed a wallop. Anything that could punch through bulletproof glass, even as a group, was not to be messed with.

Jen had hated zombie movies growing up. Her mom had never liked her watching scary or violent movies, anyway, but zombies in particular had terrified her. There was something so sad and desperate about those films, the humans trying to survive against the relentless onslaught of the dead.

And someone always got bit. And their friends or family always had to make the terrible choice to end them before they turned into a zombie. That terrifying and inescapable inevitability of a death that was minutes away had hit her younger self in some soft place.

After the series of events that had torn her life apart and left her completely alone in the world, she took a kind of sick delight in watching every zombie movie she could find on Netflix. She'd felt a kind of kinship with the characters trying to survive in a world gone to hell, everything they'd ever known ripped away, isolated and huddling against the darkness.

These things weren't trying to bite her like the zombies in the movies. It appeared the group was carrying her to the cemetery. A flicker of panic lit up in her gut at that realization, but she squashed it. Clear heads were needed right now.

So, they weren't biters. And they weren't fast *28 Days Later* zombies. More like slow, listless Romero zombies.

All the creatures were looking ahead and shuffling in lockstep. An image popped into her head of a line of ants carrying a leaf that she'd seen in some nature documentary.

There was no intelligence in their eyes, no awareness. Heck, some of them didn't even have eyes. How did that even work?

They were under orders, a part of some hive mind maybe. If these were the worker ants, where was their queen?

Jen had a sneaking suspicion she was about to find out.

A small explosion sounded behind her, in the direction of where she thought the SUV might be, and it sounded like a grenade going off. Theron!

Panic made her limbs twitch again, but the zombies didn't seem to notice. Worry for him tightened her chest and she was shocked for a moment. Hadn't she been doing her damndest to get away from him? But that big, stubborn ox might be the only one that could take on this army of the undead. She needed him alive.

Fighting the urge to twist around and look for him, scream for him to help her, she forced her limbs to relax and her eyes to close, appearing as close to unconsciousness as she could.

Her ears straining, all she could hear was the shuffling of feet over dusty ground and the rustling of tattered robes against rotting flesh. No shouts, no grunts, no booms, no sounds of fighting at all.

Jen fought to keep the panic from making her hyperventilate. He couldn't be dead. Maybe he'd run away. Maybe he was hiding and preparing to ride to her rescue when the moment was right?

Oh, sure, like that ever happens.

More likely, she was on her own. Well, wasn't that just the god damned story of her life?

Cracking one eyelid for a second, she caught a glimpse of the stone arch over the cemetery entrance. They were inside the necropolis now, moving among the white stone above-ground graves.

After what seemed like a small eternity but was probably only a minute in reality, she heard the grating sound of stone on stone and felt a blast of chillier air that smelled of earth. The sound of bony feet on stone stairs reached her ears.

They were going down.

She let her head loll back on her spine and risked cracking an eyelid again. The entrance to the crypt was distinguishable by the grey light of the outside against the blackness they were descending into. As she watched, a stone door began to slide back into place behind them, replacing the grey with black and emitting that grinding noise again.

The darkness closed in around her and she shut her eyes again because there was suddenly no difference between keeping them open or closed.

With only the sound of the shuffling feet and her own breathing in her ears, her thoughts turned to Theron again.

How would he find her? They'd taken her into some kind of cave under one of the mausoleums. Was he even alive? And if he was, how could he possibly fight all of these things? There had been at least forty of them around the SUV. Theron had powers she didn't really understand. If he found her, could he just turn all the zombies into the prom scene from *Carrie*? Jen almost smiled at the thought.

After a time, she became aware of a glow against her eyelids. Cracking one eye, she saw firelight flickering along the walls of what looked like a tunnel. The surface of the walls was white and uneven. Opening her other eyelid a sliver, her stomach gave a sickening roll. The walls were lined with skulls. Human skulls. Hundreds of them. No, thousands.

They were bleached white and stacked row on row up the curving wall, the empty dark sockets staring out at her. Some had lower jaws, some didn't.

Jen gave up any pretense at being unconscious and opened her eyes fully, pain lancing through her optic nerves as the light began to increase. The zombies were carrying her into a cavern of some sort, the ceiling opening up suddenly, soaring up into the darkness where the light of the torches along the walls couldn't reach.

The stone walls of the cavern were lined with skulls and long bones, human femurs and tibias, ulnas and humerus bones forming intricate patterns. It would have been beautiful if she didn't know what it was all made of.

Lifting her head, Jen saw a raised ledge cut out of the stone of the floor. A throne, again made of bones, sat on it. She was beginning to sense a theme.

A voice that sounded vaguely feminine echoed through the chamber. "Release her."

The bony hands were suddenly gone, and Jen landed hard on the dusty floor, her breath leaving her in a rush. Aside from coughing and trying to regain her breath, Jen stayed down and as still as possible, eyes searching for the source of that voice.

The queen of this little hive had presented herself.

From the darkness behind the bone throne, she emerged. Her skin was as pale as moonlight and glowed in the shadows like a ghostly specter. As she came around the throne and the firelight touched her, it gleamed in flowing ebony hair. Black robes flowed from her milky shoulders, looking like they'd been made from an oil slick. Obsidian horns—or was that a headdress of some kind?—rose from her skull in a U shape that curled out at the ends. That shape called some memory to mind, but Jen's thoughts were racing, and she couldn't pin it down.

Raven black wings spilled down the female's back, and a smile touched inky dark lips. She was a study in contrasts. Black and white, light and darkness. And a knot of terror formed in Jen's throat at the sight of her.

"At last, the seer," the woman said lazily, almost bored.

Jen remained silent, not trusting her voice. Something in the vicinity of her diaphragm was trembling and she didn't want to give away how scared she was right now.

Whatever she was, this being was not human. She was one of the dangerous residents of Theron's world. Jen had no idea what this creature wanted her for, but it was a good bet she didn't want to go get mani-pedis together.

The woman's midnight gaze suddenly lifted in the direction of the tunnel and narrowed. Jen heard more shuffling footsteps and risked a look over her shoulder.

Jen felt her eyes widen as another group of zombies dragged a half-conscious Theron into the cavern, his combat boots scraping in the dust. His body hung limply as they held him by the arms, but his eyes were half open, his head moving. His left shoulder was at an odd angle, and bright blood had trickled down his face from a cut near his hairline.

Poor guy was looking rough. He wasn't going to be rescuing anybody.

The corpses released Theron, who landed on his knees before that heavily-muscled torso tipped forward and slumped to the dusty floor. He tried to catch himself on the way down, but his left arm buckled painfully under him, and he moaned loudly, coming to rest on his right side.

Jen eyed the five or so zombies clustered around her and the eight or so surrounding Theron. She had her switch blade in the pocket of her khakis, but considering these things didn't look like they had vital organs, that might not be of much use. The woman with the wings didn't look like anything that would be afraid of her knife.

A word danced on the edges of her thoughts and it scared the hell out of Jen. Goddess.

It hit her where she had seen horns like the ones the female sported. They were like the ones in paintings and statues of ancient Egyptian, Babylonian, Sumerian, and Mesopotamian deities she'd seen in museums.

The thing with the wings spoke again, disdain clear in her voice. "The fire weaver is not necessary. Kill it."

As the zombies moved to obey, a voice screamed, "No!"

A dozen sets of eyes, including Theron's indigo ones, landed on her. With a start, she realized that had come from her.

The woman smiled, but there was something twisted and alien about the expression that put Jen even further on edge. In the shocked silence, the being moved forward, seeming to glide, her footsteps making no noise.

"I am Ereshkigal, Queen of the Dead. Do you dare to give me orders, human?"

As the woman drew closer, Jen rose to her knees. Preparing for what, she didn't know. One of the zombies grabbed her braid and yanked her head back on her spine. Jen gritted her teeth, her lips pulling back with a hiss and her eyes glaring at the woman.

"Silence is wise in the presence of a goddess," she said, bending down and trailing a finger down the side of Jen's face. "But you will answer me. Are you willing to bargain for the mage's life?"

Fear squeezed Jen's lungs and made it hard to breathe. Jen's gaze shot to where Theron was pushing himself up with his uninjured right arm. His eyes were on her, that dark blue stare pleading with her. He shook his head and mouthed, "No."

"Depends on what you want," Jen said.

"You have gall."

"You're not the first one to tell me that," Jen replied. The longer she could keep the woman talking, the longer she and Theron might be able to come up with a plan.

Jen's eyes roved the walls, the floor, the ceiling, looking for a way out, a weapon, anything they could use to get out of this situation.

The goddess seemed to be considering something.

"Put yourself under my control, under my command, and I will let the mage live."

The .45s on Theron's gun belt were gone, probably taken by the zombies or lost in the fight. She had no idea if he could use his powers, especially given his injuries. Then, she remembered that she'd seen him strap a backup .38 into an ankle holster that morning before they'd left Dreamland. Theron might not be as helpless as he looked.

"Not good enough," Jen told the woman. "He walks out of here unharmed."

A look of anger twisted Ereshkigal's face for a split second before her pale features settled into serene stillness once again.

Jen's mind whirled, turning over scenarios, possibilities, contingencies, searching for any way out of this. It wasn't looking good.

Then it hit her. Damn it! Why hadn't she noticed before?

With this many dead and rotting things filling the cavern, crowding around her, touching her, she should be choking on the odors of putrefaction. It should stink to high heaven in here. But the zombies didn't smell like death. They smelled like clay. The smell reminded her of the pottery class she'd taken in college.

She wasn't sure how she knew it, but these things were fake. And she was willing to bet her life that this creature in front of her was anything but a goddess of the dead.

Jen brought one foot under her, leaving her down on one knee before the creature.

"Impossible," the thing claiming to be Ereshkigal said. "The mage is mine."

"Then no deal, bitch," Jen said, throwing all of her weight back against the zombie holding her hair. She planted her boot right in the woman's gut and shoved her backwards, sending her reeling.

As she did so, she shouted to Theron, "The zombies are fake! They don't stink!"

* * *

Jen's voice still ringing in his ears, Theron's thoughts spun for a second.

She was right. The things surrounding him smelled like fresh clay, not rotting flesh. Something had been niggling at the back of his brain ever since the attack began.

Zombies—the walking dead, the undead, whatever you wanted to call them—were not supposed to be possible. Legends of necromancers who could raise the dead had existed for millennia, but there was no credible evidence to suggest the legends held any truth.

That was, until his sister had faced a horde of revenants just a few weeks ago. The undead result of a human who died during transition to vampire, revenants were supposed to be a legend too.

It seemed Blackwells were running into legendary things left and right.

Theron had been a little too busy trying to survive to wonder why things that were supposed to be a myth were trying to kill him. He'd almost bought the goddess ploy. His experience with goddesses was somewhat limited, but he was pretty sure some of them could raise the dead if they wanted.

But this was no goddess.

Now that he knew what to look for, he could see through the illusion. The zombies were just constructs, animated clay forms wrapped in illusory magick. A few things made sense now. The creatures were strong, but fragile, and they felt no pain. They obeyed commands but appeared to have no thoughts of their own.

That "goddess" was just an elven sorceress with delusions of grandeur. Still a threat, but not invincible.

Theron watched as Jen planted her boot in the woman's gut

and sent her sprawling ass over tea kettle. He wanted to cheer and kiss that stubborn spitfire at the same time.

"Destroy the heads!" he shouted to Jen.

Pushing his pain aside, he pushed to his feet, drawing strength from his internal fire. As he rose, he let the flames loose to leap up his left arm and drew his six-shot .38 from his ankle holster with his right.

He extended his left arm toward the group of zombies that had been guarding him, sending an arching gout of flames across them all. Their tattered, dry robes caught almost instantly.

Reaching forward, he wrapped his big hand around a skull, his palm scraping against the raw bone of the forehead. He concentrated. It took a couple of seconds to heat up the space inside the skull until it exploded outward, popping like an overinflated balloon.

A frustrated screech sounded to his right, and he spared a glance just in time to see the sorceress claw her way to her feet. Her wings had disappeared, the illusion dissolving without the concentration necessary to sustain it.

The horned headdress had been knocked askew, and she was clawing that ebony hair out of her eyes. He leveled the .38 and squeezed off a shot. Theron caught her surprised look as she threw up a shimmering field to catch the bullet before it could reach her.

Damn, it was worth a try. At least she was focused on him and not Jen.

The seer currently had a zombie in a headlock and was stabbing it in the skull with her switchblade. It was starting to crumble as she brought the blade down over and over again, acting more like brittle clay than actual bone. As he watched, the form shattered, disintegrating to dust in her hands as she released whatever essence had animated the thing.

Jen didn't see the sorceress rising behind her, a crackling ball of silver energy sparking in her hand. Theron shouted a warning and threw his own fireball. The dark haired elf dodged it, but she lost her concentration momentarily. It was enough.

Pulling the trigger on the .38, he saw her twitch as the bullet caught her in the shoulder. A thunderous expression crossed her face and she advanced toward him, Jen forgotten.

His plan was working.

At least it was until the full weight of eight flaming zombies crashed into his back, bearing him to the dusty floor.

The flames didn't bother him. He couldn't be burned, especially by his own fire. But the seeking, skeletal hands clawing at his throat were a big problem.

Through the dogpile, he could see the wounded sorceress coming closer, murder in her eyes. Jen growled in frustration has the zombies began to drag her down, too.

This was it. They were outnumbered, outgunned, and outmaneuvered.

But he was not without an ace in the hole. It was a nuclear option, to be sure, and it would most likely bite him in the ass, but he didn't have much of a choice.

His fingers landed on the black claw suspended on the leather cord around his neck. He managed to shift his weight enough to snap the cord free. Taking this claw in his fingers, he broke the thing in half and braced himself.

* * *

Jen screeched as another zombie latched onto her right arm, dragging her closer to the floor. There must be at least five of the things on her. Bony fingers clawed at her hair, arms and torso, raking her skin and drawing blood.

But if she went down, she knew she wasn't getting back up. She tried to lash out with the switchblade, but there was too much weight on her arm. Her legs began to tremble under the strain.

Suddenly, there was a bright flash of white light, and Jen was momentarily dazzled. Blinking against afterimages dancing across her retinas, she looked up to see a woman standing in the middle of the chaos.

She was at least six feet tall, with dark skin and long black hair that spilled down her back. A black leather catsuit hugged the curving body of a 1940s pinup. Four-inch spike-heeled knee-high boots dug into the dust of the cavern floor.

"Well, hello, lo—" the woman began.

The new arrival turned eyes that were yellow as a cat's and thickly lined in kohl on Jen. A puzzled look crossed her face. The bombshell turned to where Theron was buried under a writhing pile of zombies.

"I like orgies as much as the next girl, Theron, but I have to say, this is a bit weird, even for me," the woman said.

She spoke with a British accent and sounded just a little bit bored.

"They're trying to kill us, Bast. Help!" Theron's strangled voice emerged from the pile of zombies.

Those yellow eyes narrowed into a predator's stare and black daggers appeared in her perfectly manicured hands, delicately painted gold nails wrapping around the hilts of wavy blades that looked to be made of black glass or obsidian.

"The human is with me, Bast. Protect her, kill everyone else."

The woman sprang toward Jen, her daggers moving faster

than Jen could track. Before Jen could process what was happening, the crumbling remains of the zombies were falling around her. Jen stumbled as the weight pulling her down suddenly fell away.

The Serena Williams lookalike smiled at her, revealing canines that were long and sharp, those eerie yellow eyes flashing.

She was having fun, Jen realized.

The woman Theron had called Bast turned and caught the zombie queen as she moved toward Theron, cradling the shoulder he had put a bullet in. Bast glared and raised her hand. The zombie queen went sailing back, crashing into the bone throne with a scream, her body landing in a heap.

"I'll deal with you later," Bast said quietly.

While the newcomer stalked over to where Theron was struggling to rise under the flaming pile of zombies, Jen ran to him.

She tried to grab a body part that wasn't on fire to start pulling the creatures off him, but the flames licked out and left a blinding trail of pain across her wrist. She snatched her arm back with a hiss.

A hand landed on Jen's shoulder and yanked her backwards. As she stumbled back, a roar sounded from within the pile. An explosion sent the rotting bodies flying, flames leaping toward the unseen ceiling of the cavern.

Most of the zombies crumbled to dust in midair as Theron rose to his feet, smoke curling off his chest, shoulders and back.

His eyes were narrowed, and his jaw was set as he stood. Soot clung to the hollows of his cheeks and the creases around the muscles in his arms, making everything stand in sharp relief. He looked dangerous and terrifying, a warrior bent on destruction. A shiver chased through her at the sight of him, but it wasn't fear.

"We have incoming," Bast said, bringing their attention to a group of at least two dozen zombies moving into the cavern from the tunnel.

They didn't move quickly, but their advance was inexorable.

Theron launched a fireball into the middle of the group, and the explosion sent several flying. He waded in, fists flying as flames surged up his arms.

Bast took a running leap and launched herself into the horde, daggers flying, whirling at impossible speeds. She was a dark blur that left crumbling clay dust in her wake.

Several of the shambling forms broke away and headed for Jen. Switchblade in her right hand, she widened her stance and braced herself.

* * *

Theron palmed the skull of another zombie, poured his fire into the center of it, and felt it explode, the bones crumbling like brittle pottery in his hand.

To his left, Bast had become a whirling dervish of death and destruction, those obsidian daggers of hers flashing in the light of his flames.

It was a gamble calling the goddess here. She had a legendary temper and was notoriously quick to anger. She'd given him that claw as a way to contact her, but for a very different reason than saving his ass from a horde of fake zombies.

Still, Bast was a predator at heart and loved to kill, especially if she could play with her prey first. She might not be too mad at him for summoning her into the middle of a fight.

He turned in time to see a zombie rake its sharp, bony fingers across the back of Bast's dagger hand, drawing shimmering gold blood that stood in stark relief against her dark skin. Her scream of rage shifted an octave and morphed into something more feline.

Before his eyes, she released her other form, a gigantic black panther suddenly moving among the zombies.

Her obsidian claws flashed in her huge paws as she swatted three zombies to the ground at once. Long gleaming white fangs descended to crush the skulls of the three in quick succession.

Before he could blink, she was moving, her long black tail whipping back and forth as she impatiently searched for her next target.

But there were none. At least not in front of them.

A shout brought his attention around and he smiled. Jen had leapt onto the back of a zombie, her legs wrapped around its chest, one arm hooked under its chin. Her switchblade was stabbing over and over into the skull. As the creature disintegrated, she fell back, landing squarely on her ass.

She rose slowly and stiffly to her feet, her face grimacing in pain. Her right hand clutched her ribs, and he could see blood soaking through the cotton of her T-shirt from three long gashes. One of the zombies had gotten a good swipe in before she'd destroyed it.

He was by her side before he could even think about moving. He pulled her hand back from the wound, and she hissed. The gashes looked painful, but they hadn't hit anything vital.

"You'll live," he told her, feeling a little awkward as he released her hand.

He'd felt actual terror at the sight of her blood. What was wrong with him? Flaming zombies were annoying, but Jen bleeding was what got his heart pounding? He decided now was not the time to start analyzing himself. He'd made it twenty-eight years without doing much of that, no reason to start now.

A scream rose up from the direction of the throne. Bast was standing over the elven sorceress. The black fur was gone and she was back in human form, daggers gleaming in her hands.

The sorceress's face sported a long bloody slice that hadn't been there before, and she was trying to crawl away as Bast loomed over her.

"I am Ereshkig—" the sorceress stammered.

"Bitch, I know Ereshkigal. I saw her two weeks ago in Ibiza. You're an imposter, and I don't appreciate fucking imposters."

Her dagger flashed overhead.

"B," Theron's voice held a note of warning and her hand stilled in midair. "I need to talk to her. Please."

Those yellow eyes met his, and a look of mild annoyance crossed her face, but she stepped back. Whew. That could have gone badly. Bast didn't like being denied a kill.

He left Jen clutching her ribs and stepped onto the raised stone platform where the throne and the crumpled form of the sorceress lay.

"Who are you, really?" he asked.

"I am Ersh—" she began.

Cutting her off, he said, "Whatever. Doesn't matter."

Clearly the chick was off her rocker.

"Who do you work for?" he continued.

"I am death. I serve no one."

"Great. I knew it. You're the one stirring up all these death cult fuckers, aren't you?"

"My dark children go forth to do my bidding."

He was really starting to lose patience. This woman was deep in character. She really believed this shit, and so did the cultists following her. Now that he was up close to her, he realized that she had serious crazy eyes going on. They were just a little too wide, a little too bright.

"How did you track us?"

"I have eyes everywhere. It was easy enough to draw you here."

"It was the stupid traffic accidents wasn't it? We got herded."

His frustration was bleeding through into his voice. He could see now how the trap had been sprung, and even though he'd seen it closing around them, he hadn't acted fast enough to avoid it. His gaze landed on Jen's bloody wounds and guilt clawed at him.

The sorceress nodded, casting a nervous glance at Bast.

"What do you want with the seer?" he asked.

"It is another who seeks her, offering great rewards for her capture."

"Who?" His voice came out as more of a growl. He could feel his inner fire leaping to get at the one who had hurt Jen.

"It was one called Eurus. It promises that when the demons invade this realm, those who help them will be raised up."

The name of the unlucky east wind? That didn't tell him much.

"Where is this Eurus?"

"This I cannot answer. I do not know."

Fear was edging into the sorceress's voice now. She'd realized her usefulness had just come to an end.

"She's all yours, Bast. We'll see you upstairs."

He turned and took Jen's hand in his, leading her to the tunnel.

"Don't look back," he whispered to her.

Chapter 8

As he and Jen limped out of the cavern entrance concealed in the mausoleum, Theron scanned the graveyard. The white stone of the necropolis glowed in the bright moonlight, the above-ground graves stretching for acres around them.

Theron spotted a stone ledge nearby and steered Jen in that direction. His heart was still pounding. It didn't normally take him this long to come down from a fight, but seeing Jen's wounds had left him more worked up than usual.

He tried to lift her up so she could sit on the ledge, but pain screamed up his shoulder, nearly bringing him to his knees. That shoulder wasn't right, but he'd deal with that later, when they got someplace safe.

Theron used his good arm to hoist Jen up on the ledge, putting her eyes level with his. Her sigh of relief as she sat was music to him.

His hands rested on the stone on either side of her knees as he breathed through the pain in that shoulder. She leaned forward and touched the bare skin of his arm, just below the injury. He hissed in pain, but didn't jerk back.

"Dislocated," she said.

Glancing at the shoulder, which was quickly swelling and showing the promise of wicked bruises to come, he said, "You think?"

"It's not moving right and the angle's off. We'll have to pop it back into joint when we get somewhere safe," she said, looking around the graveyard, as if such a place might appear. "It's going to hurt like a bitch. Hope you've got some pain meds and some anti-inflammatories."

His eyes narrowed on her.

"I thought you were a reporter, not a doctor."

"I was engaged to one once, a long time ago. You pick up a few things," she told him, meeting his eyes.

Those dark eyes of hers were black as night, but there was something a little more open about them. The hostility had faded and had been replaced with something else, something that felt like connection.

His pain faded to the background for a moment as he got lost in those eyes. For once, they weren't narrowed at him in anger, snapping with sarcasm or searching for the nearest exit. Lines of exhaustion marked her face. Maybe she was just too tired to be pissed at him right now.

He froze as she reached out, gently touching his face.

"You're cut," she said. "We're going to have to stitch that up."

Her fingers were cold against the inflamed skin above his eyebrow where it had split. His eyes slid closed. Instead of being painful, her touch was like a balm as she wiped some of his blood away with her thumb.

Theron thought about telling her that stitches wouldn't be necessary. Mages healed too fast for that. But if it meant she would keep touching him and getting this close, she could do what she liked with him.

Opening his eyes, he realized that her face was very close to his as she inspected the gash. Her mouth was so close, her lips slightly parted as she concentrated. For a split second he had a crazy thought. What if he leaned forward and pressed his mouth to hers? What would she taste like? Would she kiss him back?

He mentally slammed the brakes on and squeezed his eyes shut to keep from looking at those soft, pink lips of hers. Not cool, man.

He was acutely aware of the insane situation he'd put her in. He'd basically kidnapped the woman, pulling her away from her life, her work, and had thrust her into his incredibly dangerous world entirely against her will.

Coming on to her would be unbelievably creepy, not to mention absurdly stupid. Can you say Stockholm syndrome?

Having put the kibosh on any thoughts about kissing her, he opened his eyes again, only to find he was staring down her shirt at a gorgeous pair of breasts. Jesus. He closed his eyes again and left them that way until he felt her move back.

Quiet footsteps whispered across the sandy ground behind him. Jen probably hadn't heard them, but mage senses were just a little sharper.

"Hey, B," he said quietly, knowing Bast would hear him.

"Hello, lover," she purred right beside his ear.

He opened his eyes just in time to see Jen's eyebrows shoot up at the endearment as she tried to look anywhere but at him and Bast.

Bast's fingers gently drifted up the bare skin of his uninjured arm.

"I hope that fight was just foreplay," she said, her voice dark and husky.

He turned and saw her wiping elf blood from her lips, the spaces around her canines showing dark in the moonlight where the blood had collected.

She was just as beautiful as he remembered. Dark skin, midnight eyes and hair as black as her obsidian daggers. Her curves were dangerous, betraying her true feline form, and her body was intensely athletic, that catsuit showing every muscle.

She was also just as terrifying.

"This isn't a booty call, B."

She pouted and tossed her silky black hair over her shoulder. "Are you sure?" she asked. "I was hoping we could recreate that weekend in Cairo."

He laughed softly and caressed her shoulder.

"I almost didn't survive that weekend in Cairo, if you'll remember," he said, trying to keep his voice light. "As busted up as I am, I wouldn't last a minute with you."

Bast gave him an up and down look that said she doubted that. She glanced behind him at Jen.

"If you're worried about her, your friend is welcome to join us," Bast said in that low sultry tone, her fingers continuing to drift up and down his arm.

Theron almost choked.

"Uh, it's not like that," he said quickly, trying to clear his throat.

Bast eyed Jen again and Theron glanced back to see her face was red and she was desperately trying not to look at them.

"If you're not into it," Bast said, "maybe she is."

Bast's eyes gleamed with sexual hunger. Jen's cheeks got a shade darker.

"Um, very flattered," Jen stammered, her gaze locked on the ground, "but, um, I don't really swing that way."

Bast sighed dramatically. "Humans."

Eyeing Theron, the goddess continued, "Well, if that's all you need me for, I'll be on my way."

"Don't suppose you could patch up our wounds?" he asked.

Bast laughed, the sound coming out like a low growl. She cocked a hip out, one hand resting on it. "I'm the assassin of the gods, the goddess of war, do I look like a nurse? You want healing, talk to Isis."

"I can't afford her," Theron said.

"Damn straight. Sister's got expensive taste."

"My ride's busted, and we could use a safe place to stay for the night," Theron said, not at all hopeful that the goddess would help.

"Those two things I can help with," Bast responded. "Lead the way."

He wasn't sure why the goddess was willing to help them, but he'd take whatever he could get. Anything Bast expected in return, he'd deal with that later, even if it meant being her cat toy for a weekend. But only after Jen was safe in the Citadel.

Theron helped Jen down from the ledge and they followed Bast in the direction of the wrecked SUV outside the cemetery gates. He had no idea how she could move so quietly across the rocky path in those spike-heeled boots. The goddess was all feline grace as she walked, moving with a boneless sensuality that made her hips sway.

As they made it to the SUV, Theron got a good look at the damage for the first time. The driver's side door was demolished where the truck had hit it. He was lucky to have only walked away with a dislocated shoulder.

The windshield was a mass of spiderweb cracks where the zombies had tried to smash through it, the passenger side window was a mess of jagged broken glass and all four of the tires were shredded.

Bast waved her hand and the bent metal began to mold itself

into its original shape, the cracks reversing themselves and the tires re-inflated themselves. It was like watching all the damage happen in reverse. In a few moments, the SUV looked just as it had before the attack.

"Your battle chariot is repaired, my warrior," the goddess said, waving at her handiwork and striking a pose, elbow bent, palm upraised. The pose was disconcertingly similar to paintings on the walls of ancient tombs. It also showed her considerable assets to their best advantage.

Theron's eyes were on Jen. Her mouth had fallen open, and her eyes had gone wide as she watched the transformation.

It was still odd to watch someone who could speak with ghosts get her mind boggled by his fire slinging or some light divine influence. It was all relative, he supposed.

Without a word, Bast stalked over to the SUV and slid into the backseat, before shutting the door.

"I think that's our cue," Theron told Jen. She shook her head, blinked and straightened her shoulders.

"Is she really an Egyptian goddess?" Jen whispered as they walked over.

"Yes," he whispered back, fully aware that Bast could hear them. "And I know this is going to be hard for you, but try your best not to piss her off."

As Jen reached for the door handle, she said, "Despite your limited opinion of me, I can make friends. I have people skills." A small smile tugged at the corner of her mouth and his stomach fluttered a little at the sight.

He frowned. It would be great if his body would stop reacting to her. Maybe he was just hungry? He hadn't eaten in—gods, he couldn't remember. That was it. It was the calorie deficit that was making him feel funny, not a certain elusive smile.

Climbing in the truck and starting the engine, he looked back at Bast, who was carefully cleaning dried blood from her fingernails with one of her daggers.

"Where to, your magnificence?"

Bast leaned forward and spoke in Jen's ear. "This is why I like him. He knows how to address a lady."

Jen almost smiled again. Theron kept his eyes ahead.

Bast directed them west and before long, they found themselves on the outskirts of the city, driving on a road that might have been paved at one time. They'd been driving for about fifteen minutes when Bast signaled for them to pull over. There was a little cinderblock house set back from the road and several hundred yards from any of its neighbors. The facade was spartan, and there were no lights on the exterior or shining through the windows.

"This is the place," Bast purred.

As Theron slid out of the SUV, his shoulder gave another staggering scream of pain that ricocheted around his chest. Holding back his grunt of pain, he was grateful Jen and Bast were on the other side of the vehicle and couldn't see his wince.

Jen was right. Something would have to be done about that shoulder.

"No offense, Bast, but this place doesn't seem like your style," he called.

In the darkness, Bast was nearly invisible, her hair, skin and black leather blending into the night.

"That's the point, darling."

With a wave of her hand, the metal door swung open.

"I have little crash pads all over the place. They're just places to sleep off a hangover or bring a hookup. No sense in making them conspicuous."

With a clang, the metal door shut behind them, sealing them in darkness. A sizzle of fear lit off at the base of his skull, but he ignored it. Fire mages had a fundamental distrust of the dark. It was anathema to their nature.

Bast snapped her fingers and candles flared to life around them. They were standing in a little entry hall. To the right, there was a traditional looking kitchen with a wood oven and basin. It was clean, but it clearly hadn't been used in decades.

"Bathroom's down the hall," Bast said, indicating a closed door ahead of them. "Never bothered to get the place wired for electric, but there's running water."

To the right was a large room. A double mattress with a carved wooden headboard sat against one wall. It had black satin sheets and was heaped with furs and pillows.

At his raised eyebrow, Bast said, "I make some concessions to comfort. I may be a war goddess, but that doesn't mean I have to sleep on an army cot."

He just smiled at her.

"Try not to get your mage blood on my sheets," she said.

He spotted a fireplace in the corner. It was a fat-bellied ceramic and stone number, with a metal chimney that led up to the ceiling. Wood had already been laid. It was a chilly night already, with the promise of lower temperatures in the air. The wood lit easily with only a second's concentration, but even that tiny effort left Theron feeling drained. He needed food, meds and rest, in that order.

Bast stepped in front of him, pressing her body in close and running those shimmering gold nails against the fairy leather covering his chest.

"It's yours for the night, gorgeous," she purred by his ear. "I'll ward the place when I leave. Nothing, and I mean nothing, will come anywhere near you."

She pulled back and he met those glowing yellow eyes. His head swam for a moment and he wasn't sure if it was from all the exertion or from the heavy energy Bast was throwing off.

She held up a black claw like the one she'd given him after their weekend in Cairo. She slid it into the pocket of his fatigues.

"Call me sometime," she said.

And with that, she was gone.

A noise behind snapped his head around. Jen was by the door, the bag with her camera and clothes was at her feet. In her hand was the first aid kit from the SUV. The thing was the size of a small suitcase.

"Let's get to it," he said, gesturing with his good hand to his busted shoulder.

Moving to the bed, Jen set the first aid kit down and started rummaging through it, pulling out some squares of canvas and some gauze. There was the rattle of a pill bottle and she turned, pressing six white pills in his hand.

"That's twelve hundred milligrams of ibuprofen. It ought to bring the inflammation down."

He swallowed them and stayed quiet. Jen's movements were nervous, her breathing a little uneven. He didn't want to spook her, but he didn't want to move away. She touched the items she'd pulled out of the case, one by one, like she was running through a checklist.

She turned and almost bumped into his injured arm before she jerked back.

"Sorry!" she said quickly and a little too loudly.

Reaching out with his good arm, he caught her hand in his and met her eyes.

"What's got you so jumpy, princess?"

She looked away, not meeting his eyes.

"I know how to fix your shoulder, but it's been awhile," she said. "If I do it wrong, I could really hurt you."

She was worried about hurting him? That surprised him. What had changed, and when did it happen?

He squeezed her hand and she met his eyes again.

"I'm already hurt. I doubt you can make it worse."

Her mouth was tight and lines of worry showed around her eyes, but she nodded.

"Okay." Her voice was strong and sounded confident. "Lay on your back on the floor."

He fought a groan as his shoulder blade came in contact with the floor, his left arm cradled against his body, and watched as she pulled her boots and socks off. She padded over to him on bare feet.

They were adorable feet. Nothing else about Jen Jiang was adorable, but her feet were. They were small and slender, with long toes and trimmed, plain nails. He hadn't expected her to be the type to paint her nails, but for just a second, he thought that paint belonged on those nails.

For all her fast-talking toughness and the absence of anything soft and feminine about her, he still had the niggling sense that it was a front. It was like a new coat of paint that didn't quite hide what was underneath it.

"I'm going to straighten your arm," she said, sitting beside him. Her fingers wrapped around his wrist and her other hand was under his elbow, gently lifting until his arm was at a forty-five degree angle from his body.

The movements caused a grinding pain in his shoulder and he winced.

Her movements were slow and steady and he concentrated

on breathing evenly, trying not to groan through his clenched teeth.

She put her left palm against his and wrapped her fingers around his thumb as he did the same. Her right hand gripped his forearm below his elbow. Her dainty feet were placed against his ribs, just below his armpit.

Leaning her weight back and using her legs for leverage, she started pulling, slowly and steadily. The pain began to build and his breath quickened until it was leaving him in short sharp puffs. He could feel the muscles and tendons in his arm stretching in directions they were never meant to go.

Jen was growling with exertion, pulling with everything she had. He was grateful she'd taken her shoes off. His ribs were sore from the collision with the truck and the fight. Her bare feet felt like branding irons. Her boots would have been even worse.

There was a sudden shift in his shoulder and with a loud pop, the bone slid back into the socket. Jen released his hand and leaned back. The pain had decreased by about ninety percent, he realized.

"You're amazing!" he said, starting to move his shoulder around to test it.

"Don't move it." That was an order if he'd ever heard one.

"Yes, ma'am," he responded, staying where he was on the concrete floor.

She knelt by him again, the canvas and gauze in her hands. With quick movements, she folded the canvas into a triangle and gingerly worked it under his arm, wrapping it around and tying it behind his neck in a sling.

While she worked, he watched her. A little crease had appeared between her thin, dark brows as she concentrated.

Her bottom lip was caught between her teeth. She was dusty, bruised, bloody, and exhausted. And she was gorgeous.

Jen began pulling long strips of gauze from the roll. As she leaned over him to work them under his back, he caught her scent. Her hair smelled like orange blossoms. And beneath the dust and sweat, her skin smelled like honey.

She leaned back and began tying knots in the gauze, binding his arm to his torso. Sitting back, she nodded.

"You can sit up now."

He rose slowly, trying not to move the shoulder.

"It feels good. Thanks," he told her, feeling a little awkward.

As she moved back to the first aid kit, he saw the blood on her shirt.

"Shit!" At her startled look, he continued, "Your ribs. I forgot about them. I'm sorry. We should have done you first."

She glanced down at the blood stain and the ragged skin showing through the tears in her shirt.

"I kind of forgot about them too, actually," she said.

She lifted the hem and touched the wounds with a hiss.

"Not deep, but they hurt like a bitch. The bleeding's mostly stopped. They could use some sutures, but I can't do it on myself, and you're one-handed."

Levering himself up off the floor, he went over to the first aid kit and pushed some things around until he found what he was looking for.

"Surgical glue and butterfly bandages. Works just about as well as stitches, and they're a lot easier to apply."

Between their three hands, they made quick work of cleaning the wounds. Jen hissed when the isopropyl hit the raw gashes, but otherwise didn't flinch. So, she could handle pain.

He applied the surgical glue since he had a better view of

the wounds. While she held the hem of her shirt up, he filled the three gashes with adhesive. Her skin was warm where his fingers brushed.

With his help, she was able to pinch the skin together and apply the little butterfly strips to hold it all together. Theron held a gauze pad over the wounds and she handed him strips of tape to hold it in place.

When he was satisfied that the wound was treated as well as it could be, he held up his right fist for her to bump.

"Now that's fuckin' teamwork," he said.

One side of her mouth twisted upward, and she rolled her eyes.

* * *

Jen made quick work of brushing her teeth. A shower was out of the question. The surgical glue would need a few hours to fully set, so she used about fifty baby wipes from a package she'd found in the first aid kit to clean all the blood and dirt off her skin.

Slipping on a fresh shirt and khakis, she unbraided her hair and started running a brush through it until it fell in dark, kinky waves around her shoulders.

When had it gotten so long? It was past the middle of her back now. That's what happened when you didn't go to a salon for five years, she supposed, but there weren't many of those in war zones.

Her bare feet made almost no noise as she padded back down the hall to the main room of Bast's little cottage. The place was clean, but clearly it was used very rarely. And judging from the satin sheets on the bed, it was used for one purpose only.

As she came into the room, she saw Theron standing by the little fireplace. The flames dancing inside were the room's only illumination and heavy shadows filled the corners of the room. It didn't get cold in Iraq very often, but it was currently the middle of winter. It was chilly and there was the threat of a freeze in the air.

The room was warming quickly and Jen was thankful. If it was one thing she hated, it was being cold. Having grown up in Los Angeles, cold was not in her vocabulary.

Putting her back against the wall, she let herself slide down to a sitting position. She pulled her knees to her chest, folded her arms across the top of her knees and let her head fall forward. As her eyes fell closed, she tried not to think about how much the gashes on her ribs hurt.

"You're not sleeping there." Theron's voice sounded loud and harsh in the near darkness. She looked up at him, eyeing the sling and the gauze that bound his arm to his chest.

"You're too busted up to sleep on the floor," she said. "Since you won't take the morphine, you're going to need to be as comfortable as possible to get any rest."

The big stubborn brute had refused to let her inject him with the painkillers she'd found in the first aid kit.

"It doesn't feel right," he said, turning his eyes to the gigantic bed that dominated the room. It wasn't so much a piece of furniture as it was a playground.

"I've slept like this more than a few nights." She put her head down again. "Don't worry about me.

She'd slept in this exact position in more airports than she could count, in armored personnel carriers when she was embedded with military units, and in other random places over the years.

"I can't help worrying about you."

His voice had softened and her eyes found him again in the darkness. The firelight caught in his hair and brought out red lowlights beneath the blonde. In the harsh shadows, his dark blue eyes looked black as they landed on hers.

"That's your damage, not mine," she told him, resolutely shutting her eyes and putting her head down again.

Footsteps moved over to the bed and she heard the rustle of cloth. She peeked and saw him sitting on that ridiculous black satin covered bed in his T-shirt and boxers. His fatigue pants were laid across the foot of the bed and he was settling that gun belt of his on the headboard, no doubt so he could draw his guns in a heartbeat if he needed them.

Despite his injuries and his weariness, his body was all coiled, deadly potential. He was a living weapon, always sharp and ready to cut. She'd do well to remember that, no matter how beautiful he looked in the firelight.

He settled awkwardly beneath the sheet and blankets, trying not to jostle his busted shoulder. As he stilled, he blew out an exasperated breath. She shifted slightly, trying to find a comfortable position and the sound of her feet against the floor sounded loud in the silence of the room.

They stayed like that for several minutes, each shifting uncomfortably, trying not to make any noise. When Theron's voice came out of the darkness, she almost jumped, the tension having wound her tight.

"Jen, I—" he began. Silence stretched. He started again, "I'm too keyed up to sleep, adrenaline is hitting me hard. How about you?"

"Same."

"So," he said quietly into the firelit darkness. "Tell me things."

"What kind of things?" she said, fighting a smile. The guy was relentlessly positive and it was a little infectious.

"Hmmm," he said, thinking. "When did you get into comic books?"

She almost asked him how he knew she liked comics, but remembered the nickname she'd given him.

"Not long after I got to Baghdad. I create and stare at long blocks of text all day for work, so I find reading for fun difficult sometimes. I discovered an online comics subscription and got sucked in. I was in a pretty dark place and those stories always felt really hopeful, good overcoming evil and all that. I like the movies, too."

She couldn't believe the number of words that were pouring out of her, but here in the dark, it felt good to talk. No other human knew about her comic book addiction or how much she loved superhero movies.

Theron shifted in the firelight, turning to look at her.

"I used to love them as a kid," he said. "But sneaking them into the Academy was damn near impossible. And these days I don't have a lot of time to read anything aside from dossiers and situation reports."

He moved slightly and groaned, his face contorting in pain in the firelight. Before she knew it, she was on her feet and striding to his side. Sitting on the edge of the bed, she checked the sling. Her fingers brushed his shirt and she could feel the heat of him in the fabric.

"Try to be still," she said, her voice soft.

"Just trying to keep eyes on the door. It makes me nervous having you all the way over there. If anything busts in here, you're in a bad spot."

Her eyes fell on the empty space beside him in the bed. The

satin sheets looked so much more comfortable than her place on the floor. It would make him relax and get some rest if she curled up next to him. A rested protector was more effective than a tired one. And it put him and his guns between her and the door.

Practically speaking, this was smarter. The logical part of her brain nodded in agreement.

And he'd be more comfortable. Wait. She cared about his comfort now? Considering he'd saved her life tonight, yeah, she did. But it was more than that.

She liked him. There had even been a moment back in the cemetery when she'd been leaning into him when she'd had the oddest urge to kiss him.

Another part of her brain sounded an alarm bell. How smart was it to sleep next to him?

The logical part chimed in again. He was badly injured. She was hurt. And he'd given her no indication that he thought of her that way. He'd angrily rebuffed her clumsy attempt at seduction the night before, after all. "What if I laid down here?" she asked, indicating the empty spot. "I could keep watch while you rest and wake you up if anything happens, but you're between me and the door. Would that help you relax and rest?"

He met her eyes and something fluttered in her belly.

"That could work," he said, his voice low. She eyed the space between the wall and his uninjured shoulder. That bed had looked a lot bigger a second ago. The space suddenly seemed about as big as a postage stamp.

Crawling across the foot of the bed, she managed not to jostle him and slid into the small unoccupied spot and laid on her left side on top of the blankets, facing him.

He was gigantic, his massive shoulders and chest taking up

entirely too much space. With a shift of his weight, he settled the blanket over her and brought his right arm around her so that she was cradled against him. Her hand came to rest on his chest.

Instantly, she felt a rush of heat and realized it was him. He was several degrees too warm.

"You're hot," she exclaimed.

"You're not so bad yourself, sweetheart." His teeth flashed in the darkness as he smiled. "I meant temperature. You're feverish."

"That happens," he said. "Mages heal faster than sapiens. A lot faster. The high body temp is a side effect. I just need rest. A good five or six hours of sleep, and that shoulder will be good as new."

She settled against him again and liked the feel of his chest beneath her cheek and hand. He was solid and so very warm. The pain in her muscles started to ease off. He was like sleeping with a heating pad.

"Would you do me a favor?" he asked.

"Depends on the favor."

"The pain's got me all wound up. I need a distraction," he said. "Tell me a story."

"What kind of story?"

"One about you."

"I'm boring," she said.

"Totally not true. Why don't you tell me how you learned to set a dislocated shoulder?"

Where should she start? How much should she share?

"A few years ago, I went on a hike with my boyfriend, Trevor, and some friends of ours," she began.

The six of them had all decided on a whim to hike up to

Sandstone Peak outside of LA one Saturday. Trevor had always loved hiking and outdoor stuff. She'd never really enjoyed it, preferring to stay home, but she went because he wanted to go. Her friend Monica had reminded her that it was important for couples to do things together.

It had been one of the rare Saturdays when she'd been off. Her reporting job at the LA Times tended to eat up evenings and weekends. Breaking news pulling her away at odd hours. Trevor had always gotten angry when she had to bail on plans because of a murder or some breaking scandal, even though as a medical intern at UCLA Medical Center he'd had to cancel more than a few dates because of work emergencies.

The hike was dusty, but uneventful. Near the top, the guy Monica had brought along had tripped and fallen off an outcropping.

"I think his name was Chad," Jen said. "Anyway, when we got down to him, he was screaming. His shoulder was way out of joint. We were at least two hours from the car. I watched Trevor do exactly what I did to you."

Trevor had always been a star student and during medical school and his hospital internship, he'd been no different. He'd moved quickly, positioning Chad on his back. He'd explained everything as he'd done it, taking the chance to show off his knowledge and skills to their friends.

"At the time, he seemed like such a hero. Now that I look back on it, he seems like a showoff and a pedantic little shit," she told Theron.

Theron laughed soft and low, creating a pleasant rumbling beneath her ear.

"I'm guessing Trevor's not in the picture anymore," he said.

"Definitely not." She could hear the venom in her voice and

she didn't care.

"Sounds like there's a story there."

She stayed silent on that one, not interested in sharing that bitter tragedy with anyone.

"Why doesn't your fire burn you?" she asked Theron.

"Changing the subject, huh?"

"Come on. I told you a story."

"You're good at telling stories. Really good," he said.

His right hand absently stroked her arm, his fingers trailing up and down her elbow. He probably didn't even realize he was doing that. It felt nice, so she didn't say anything.

"Telling stories is my job," she said. "But I'm also really good at asking questions. Now, tell me why your fire doesn't burn you."

"It's not just my fire. It's all fire," he said. "It's just that way for fire mages. It's probably some biological self-preservation mechanism. I've never thought too hard about it."

"And you were born like this?"

"I was born a mage, but I didn't come into my powers until I was twelve."

Mages got their powers around puberty, he explained. By that time, they were already several years into their Academy training. Theron described being sent to the Academy at age seven, as was mandatory for mages, and the intense training he underwent for the next eleven years.

"That sounds harsh," Jen told him. "Your parents were okay being separated from you that young?"

"I'm the third of four," he said. "Dad was a ranger, like me, and he was gone a lot. Mom is the chief healer of the Citadel and an adviser to the Council. They loved us, but in a way, I think it was easier when we all left for the Academy."

He'd spoken of his father in the past tense. Jen was afraid to ask what that meant, but the words slipped from her, quiet as a whisper.

"What happened to your dad?"

"He died when I was ten. Killed in combat. Like most mages." His words trailed off.

The darkness and the closeness of their bodies were weaving an odd kind of spell. She couldn't believe she was asking him these things, telling him these things. It felt like something was forming between them. It was tenuous, but it felt almost like a connection.

Theron had gone silent and the muscles of his chest tensed beneath her hand.

She moved her hand back and forth a scant inch or two, impossibly slow, and the tension left him.

"You have siblings?" she asked him. "Two sisters and a brother."

"You're lucky. I'm an only. I've always thought it would be nice to have a sibling."

"We're not that close," he said. "Well, my little sister Alayna and I were kind of close. Once. But I did something, and now I'm pretty sure she's never going to speak to me again."

"What could you have possibly done?"

He was silent for a moment before he said, "The Council made me deliver the orders for her suicide mission."

Jen stayed silent. Yeah, that was bad.

"She actually died, but her—this guy—managed to resuscitate her. Pissed the brass off. Word is, Citadel's in an uproar about it. And I couldn't be prouder of her."

Jen knew when to press a subject and when to come back to it. She'd have to dig a little deeper on this subject later.

She took a breath, about to ask another question, when Theron cut her off.

"My turn," he said. "I want another story."

Sighing, she thought back through the years, picking up and discarding experiences. Something funny? She didn't have many of those. Too many of her stories were sad, and she didn't want his pity. The rest were just scary.

"Where did you learn to fight like you do?" he said, bringing her thoughts to a grinding halt.

That was a pretty safe topic.

"When I first landed in Iraq, I didn't know my ass from a hole in the ground," she said, borrowing a phrase the Marines she'd been embedded with had taught her.

When she'd left LA, she'd been the quintessential SoCal girl. Her hair had always been perfectly styled and cut in the latest fashion. Her heels had been four inches minimum, and her hem lines had been knee-length maximum. Fashion had been her religion and Vogue her bible.

Having grown up Asian and middle class in Southern California and the daughter of an intermittent Tiger Mother, her after school activities had consisted of homework, tennis, and violin lessons, not martial arts. After graduation, her physical activity consisted of yoga and shopping.

"Those Marines were shocked at my lack of hand-to-hand skills. Here I was, a twenty-five-year-old woman who'd never so much as thrown a punch, sitting in the middle of a war zone. In retrospect, my career move to war correspondent wasn't the brightest idea, but I wasn't exactly in a clear frame of mind when I picked it."

Theron chuckled softly, the barest breath of a laugh, at her assessment of herself.

"There was a lot of downtime between runs with the Marines and they started teaching me how to fight. I think they considered it a humanitarian project."

They'd taught her how to handle a knife, a gun and every dirty hand-to-hand move in the book.

"They were good teachers. Didn't hold back just because I was a woman."

"No offense to your teachers, but your technique is a little more refined than you usually see from Jarheads."

"Well, I did have an on-again-off-again friends-with-benefits thing with an Israeli Mossad agent for a while," she said, well aware of the slightly wistful smile in her voice. "He showed me more than a few things."

Theron tensed and made a slight choking noise, which he tried to cover by clearing his throat.

Jen sat up, taking in his shocked expression.

"Don't worry," she told him. "I haven't talked to him in months. It's not like he's going to come riding to my rescue or anything."

Why had she just said that? Stupid move, Jen. She should have said just the opposite to make Theron think twice about this run to Damascus. With a start, she realized she wasn't even thinking about escape anymore.

Somewhere, somehow, she'd gotten on board with the plan, joined the team, signed on the dotted line.

When all this started, she'd fought so hard to hold on to the meager life she'd built for herself, but this kidnapping had succeeded in showing her that it wasn't much of a life. No one was going to miss her. Literally, no one. Her family was dead. When she stopped answering her emails, her editors, sources and contacts would just assume she'd disappeared, like so many others in the war zones of the Middle East.

Theron said that his people needed her. Her powers made her rare and special to them, and she wasn't going to lie to herself—that made her feel special. He made her feel special, like something to be protected.

Jen was good at looking at things objectively. It was what made her good at her job. A big part of the reason she was going along with this plan had a lot to do with the funny, infuriating, gorgeous, deliciously solid man lying beside her.

She tilted her head back where it lay against his chest and looked up at him through her lashes. He'd been staring at her and her gaze locked with his. They stayed like that for a moment, neither one moving. A tingling heat bloomed across Jen's chest and crept up her neck.

She swallowed hard and looked away. *Can you say, Stockholm Syndrome, Jen?*

Realizing that she'd been quiet for a while, she blurted the first thing that popped into her head.

"Do you have a girlfriend?"

Ugh. Smooth move, Jiang.

He just laughed. Hard. He groaned when the movement jostled his shoulder and Jen lifted her head rather than getting bounced around by his chest as he laughed. When he fell into a light chuckle, he said, "No. God, no. I'm never in one place long enough."

"Sorry, that question was out of bounds," Jen said, feeling supremely awkward. The darkness and the closeness had woven its spell too well and she'd started saying things and asking things she shouldn't have.

"I'll forgive you if you tell me what happened to Trevor," he said.

Chapter 9

Jen froze. Shit. No way was she going there. She was literally the only person on the planet that knew all the details about that tragedy. Trevor was one piece of the bomb that had gone off in the middle of her old life and left the bitter shell that used to be Jen Jiang willingly living in one of the worst hell holes on Earth.

That story was a pot of hot mess stew and the lid should be left on forever.

His hand pressed against her back and urged her to lay back down. She melted against him and felt his warmth flow into her. Every muscle within her relaxed and her anxiety bled away.

Maybe she could just give the short version.

"We were engaged. He left."

"How long were you together?" His voice was soft, barely above a whisper. It was like he was afraid he was going to spook her. She should have known that he wouldn't let her off that easy.

For some reason she didn't really understand, she told him. "I met him freshman year of college, so, six years."

"Why would he leave?"

Frowning, she thought, that was an odd way to phrase that question.

"I got pregnant."

She felt him tense beneath her, but she didn't dare look at him. The pain in her chest was a distant echo of what it had been five years ago when it all went down, but it still threatened to bring tears to her eyes.

A tense silence stretched between them and she felt compelled to fill it. She started talking.

"It all started a little over five years ago…"

Jen had been on top of the world then. She was one of the youngest metro reporters for the Los Angeles Times, the newspaper she'd dreamed of working at since she was a little girl. She'd worked her ass off and clawed her way up through unpaid internships, and shitty jobs at shitty regional papers until she'd finally caught the attention of the senior editors.

She'd sacrificed having a life beyond her work, but she'd broken some amazing stories. She'd exposed corrupt officials, given a voice to the voiceless, done everything that she had set out to do as a young idealistic reporter. Saving the world had been her goal, and in some small ways, she'd been doing that.

The awards had come early and often, but she hadn't cared about that. It was all about the work.

And Trevor had gone through all of that with an easy-going smile on his handsome face. She'd supported them both while he'd gone through medical school. He didn't mind the long hours she worked, because he also worked long hours. It wasn't unusual for them to go an entire week without spending any real time together. They would pass each other in their little condo, occasionally exchanging an exhausted kiss and asking how the other's day had gone. There had been a lot of days when he'd fall into bed just as she was getting up for the day.

She'd been in her second year at the Times and he'd been at the end of his internship at UCLA when everything fell apart.

Jen's mother had been diagnosed with late stage breast cancer, and it had fallen like a hammer blow. Jen had never known her father since he had taken off when she'd been a baby. It had always been her and mom. Her mother had demanded a lot from her, but they'd been close. It had been the two of them against the world for as long as Jen could remember.

"Up until then, everything in my life had gone exactly according to plan. I'd made straight As in school. Was the editor of my college paper. Landed the perfect job. Had the perfect doctor boyfriend. Had the perfect LA condo. Had the perfect LA wardrobe," Jen said, her voice surprisingly clear despite the pain throbbing behind her breastbone. "The diagnosis changed everything."

They'd tried chemo and radiation, but they both knew they were just buying time. Jen had taken vacation days for the first time in her career, desperate to spend every spare moment she could with her mother before it was too late.

Editors at the paper had started to notice, but Jen hadn't known that at the time. It was the unspoken rule in the do-more-with-less atmosphere of the Times that vacation days were given but were never to be taken.

For the first time, Jen had begun to resent the long overtime hours she was asked to work but was never paid for. The paper was struggling financially. *Just take one for the team*, she'd been told.

"Somewhere along the way, with the stress and everything, I must have forgotten to take some of my birth control pills," she said.

She'd had a moment of pure panic when that second pink line had shown up on the home pregnancy test, but a feeling of overwhelming joy that she hadn't expected was close on its heels.

It had never been a question in her mind that she would keep the pregnancy. With all the sadness surrounding her mother's terminal diagnosis, this pregnancy was a gift that she was gladly going to accept.

"Trevor hit the ceiling when he found out," she said.

A baby was not in his five-year plan. He was staring down the barrel of a three-year medical residency and at least a two-year fellowship after that. There was no way they could handle a baby, he said.

Jen had been adamant. This was a surprise, but they were keeping it.

Trevor had screamed at her that she had ruined his life. He'd stormed out of the condo and had never come back.

"That was the last time I ever saw him."

She'd gotten an email a few days later. He'd accepted a residency in Seattle instead of the one he'd had lined up in LA. Movers would come and collect his things. She could file for child support after the kid was born. He wasn't interested in visitation and would be happy if he never saw their child.

Theron tensed beneath her and she lifted her head to look at him. His jaw was clenched and his lips had thinned to an angry line. With a start, she realized that he was trembling slightly, his fists clenched.

She frowned, touching his arm. "What is it?"

He was silent for a moment before he answered.

"I just don't understand how he—how anyone—could do that." He looked down at the floor. "Ugh. If the woman I loved told me she was carrying my child, I'd get down on my damn knees and thank my lucky stars, the universe, and all the gods."

His words shocked her for a moment. Genuine anger was

written all over his body and face.

"That's the problem. I don't think he ever really loved me," she said, putting her head back down on his shoulder. "I was just convenient. I checked the girlfriend box on his five-year plan. I kept the condo clean. I picked up his dry cleaning. I was an assistant he got to sleep with."

The fist resting on his thigh clenched again.

Theron looked at her and seemed to be about to say something, but then he looked away and stayed silent.

"I decided to carry on without him. But it was really hard to make rent on the condo on a reporter's salary and without Trevor paying half. Mom was in the hospital around that time, so I moved in a ratty motel near the hospital."

Her mother had been thrilled about the pregnancy, and, in characteristic fashion, had told her that she never liked Trevor and that she could do much better.

"When I was about two months along, I told my bosses I was pregnant. I wanted to give them as much time as possible to arrange for coverage while I was going to be on maternity leave," she said. "About two weeks later, I got called into my editor's office. They were very suddenly unhappy with my performance and were putting me on an 'improvement plan.' The next three months, I worked like a crazy person, barely slept, convinced that if I put in a hundred twenty percent, I could save my job."

That three months destroyed her confidence and had jacked her into dangerous levels of depression and anxiety, all while trying to deal with horrible morning sickness, hellish fatigue and insomnia from the pregnancy.

"I didn't realize then that it wasn't about my performance at all. They were just dotting their i's and crossing their t's so they could fire me without a lawsuit. I was five months along when they fired me."

Jen couldn't believe that she was letting all of this spill out. No one alive knew this story, but at this point, she couldn't stop. The words just kept coming.

After she'd been fired, Jen had been incandescently angry and suicidal for a hot minute before resolving that, fine, it was her and kid against the world. The economy had been in shambles at the time. Jobs had been scarce. Reporter jobs had been nonexistent. She considered looking for reporter jobs in other cities, but she wasn't about to leave her mother during the final weeks of her life and her mom couldn't be moved by that point.

Her mother had been unable to help her financially as the medical bills had eaten everything she'd had and then some. Unemployment checks had barely paid for the motel room.

The few friends she had eased away from her after she lost her job. The three-hour brunches and the yoga classes were no longer in her budget. Her emotions hadn't been something they could handle. They just stopped returning her texts and calls. Those friends had never been what she'd call close, mostly because her job ate up all her free time, but it hurt to look around and find no one had her back.

The day after she'd been fired, she started applying for writing jobs, public relations jobs, social media jobs, anything she might be remotely qualified for. At that point, her baby bump had already been showing. All the potential employers who had been so excited during the phone interviews turned cold during the in-person interviews. Jen could see them mentally crossing her off their lists the second they saw her swollen belly.

She'd quickly started applying for any job, convenience store clerk, stocker at Target, and janitorial crews, despite the fact that she wasn't supposed to be around strong chemicals while pregnant.

A magna cum laude graduate from UCLA, she couldn't get a job scrubbing toilets. She'd sold her expensive shoes and clothes on Craigslist to pay the bills. When that money was gone, she'd had to go to the food pantry.

Stupidly, she'd thought that was the low point. She'd lost the job that had been her identity and her whole life and no one else wanted her. She'd felt worthless. If she hadn't been pregnant, she would have seriously considered losing herself in a bottle for a while.

After she'd held a pity party for a couple of days, she'd resolved to hold out until her mother passed, then she would have the kid and land a reporting job in another city. Her great comeback, her moment of redemption was still ahead.

Her mother had passed away the day she'd hit the seven-month mark on her pregnancy. The funeral went by in a blur. A handful of her mother's friends had shown, but it had been a pitifully empty service.

"I remember lying in my fleabag motel room afterwards, just thinking that it was going to be the same way when I died. My kid would be there to mourn me and no one else. In a way, it was oddly comforting," Jen said, her voice surprisingly steady and her eyes miraculously dry. "I started bleeding that night."

The bright red blood that trickled from her had been like a scream amid dead silence. It hadn't been much at first, and she stupidly waited a couple of hours. She'd had no medical insurance at that point and her Medicaid paperwork hadn't gone through. An unnecessary hospital bill at this point would put her on the street.

But the contractions had hit like a wrecking ball around midnight on a cold and rainy night. The doctors at the hospital had done everything they could, pumping her full of drugs to try to stop the pre-term labor, but it had been too late.

"I still remember the look on the doctor's face when he knew. It's frozen in my mind. His eyes were so kind and he had this sympathetic, thin-lipped frown. He held my hand and told me the baby didn't have a heartbeat anymore," Jen said, her voice dropping in volume the further she went. "My heart might as well have stopped, too."

She'd still had to deliver the fetus. The labor had been the most horrible experience of her life. The only thing that made any labor bearable was the knowledge that you got to hold your beautiful new baby at the end.

For so many months, the baby had been her light at the end of the tunnel. Jen had poured all her hope for the future into the tiny thing growing inside her. The baby was supposed to make everything worth it, her redemption in human form. But it wasn't meant to be.

"It was a girl. I named her Madison. And she's still the most beautiful thing I've ever seen."

With the kind of dawning realization that slams into you like a speeding car, Jen realized that she hadn't really thought about that time in her life in the past five years. The thoughts and feelings and images had cropped up like weeds every now and then and she'd yanked them out by the roots, using the stressful world around her to always keep her mind on something else. When that didn't work, there was always the bottle of Blue Label she kept around.

After all this time, it was the faces that stuck in her mind, frozen like photographs. There was her mother on the day she'd told Jen about the cancer, her face drawn in lines of despair and resignation. There was Trevor on the day she'd told him about the pregnancy, his face distorted with anger and hatred for her. There was the doctor who told her the baby was gone, concern and sympathy filling his eyes. There was her daughter, all her potential written in the curve of her little cheek, the tiny fingers that would never grasp hers, and the life they should have had together wrapped up with that perfect, lifeless body.

Theron's good arm tightened around Jen and he pressed his cheek against the top of her head. Her voice was steady as she continued.

"I was still in the hospital when I started making arrangements to come to Iraq. An old editor of mine was running the Baghdad bureau for a wire service and had emailed me right after I got fired and offered me a job. I'd had to turn it down because of the pregnancy.

"After I lost the baby, I felt like I had died, but somehow my body was still walking around. I wasn't about to kill myself or anything, but I suddenly didn't care if I died either. I knew the Baghdad assignment would be dangerous, but it meant I could be a reporter again, do some important work, and maybe the warzone would take out my walking corpse," she said. "I scattered my daughter's ashes at Redondo Beach and got on a plane to Baghdad two hours later."

* * *

Theron knew he was staring at Jen, but he didn't really care and he didn't want to stop.

As a storyteller, she was riveting and had him hanging on her every word. Her voice was clear and steady, but he still heard the little pauses, the subtle catches and the emotions that bled in around the edge of her story. She still carried a lot of anger over the way her former bosses had treated her. There was a well of grief about her mother and her child that she had locked away behind some pretty thick walls. It was clear she'd never really dealt with it.

The surprising part was the near indifference about her fiancé leaving her when she had needed him most. Anger surged within him again at the thought of what the man had thrown away. Theron didn't even know the sapien, but he hated him.

Her story had explained so much. He finally understood what had created the fierce creature that lay next to him.

"Dear gods," he said, the words slipping from him as understanding hit him.

All of that pain, all of that struggle had been the immense pressure that turned an ordinary piece of carbon into a diamond.

"Aren't you sorry you ever asked me?" There was a note of wry bitterness in her voice. She was trying to pull away, to diminish the weight of what she'd told him.

"No." He kept is voice soft, trying to stem her retreat.

She looked up at him then, her black eyes locking on his. The flickering firelight played over the planes of her beautiful face, the reds and yellows catching in the glossy black hair she'd left loose around her shoulders.

"I shouldn't have told you all that," she said. He had the feeling she was talking more to herself than she was to him. "If I catch even the barest hint of pity from you…"

She trailed off, not finishing the threat.

"Pity? Not likely," he said. "I'm actually feeling pretty intimidated over here."

One skeptical eyebrow shot up. "Intimidated?"

"You must be a warrior goddess to still be on your feet after all that."

She almost laughed at that, but stopped. Could she hear the respect in his voice? It was there. It took strength most people didn't have to come back from something like that.

"Not hardly. It wasn't strength that kept me going," she told him. "I think I went more than a little crazy after it all went down. It was some combination of insanity, self-destruction, and sheer stubbornness that got me here. By the time I came to my senses and really thought about what I was doing, I'd already been in Iraq for several weeks. To my messed up brain, living in a warzone was better than going back stateside because that world reminded me too much of what I'd lost."

It occurred to him that she'd probably never told anyone about what happened. They'd known each other three days and she'd bared that scar for him. The silence stretched between them, his chest rising and falling beneath her hand, but he wasn't sure what to fill it with, what to do with what she'd shared. Her voice broke the silence first.

"The blues," she said.

"Huh?" Theron wasn't following the abrupt change in subject.

"Yesterday, you made fun of my musical tastes. My iPod is not actually full of the 'break music between NPR segments.' I like the blues. The older the better. I really like the female artists from the thirties," she said. "No one understands pain like a black woman living in 1930s America."

Theron laughed, making the muscles in his chest bunch beneath her hand. She smiled at him.

"I also really like classic country. Willie Nelson. Johnny Cash. No one writes or sings sad songs like they do."

"I never pegged you for a country fan, Jiang."

"Yeah, not many Asian former-fashionistas from LA in the

Willie Nelson fan club, so it's an honest mistake."

She had managed to bleed the tension out of them both and he was glad for it.

"Tell me a story," she said softly.

"What kind of story?"

"Well, since I brought us down with my story, tell me a happy one."

He took a deep breath and let it out slowly, the motion shifting her closer to him.

"Don't have too many of those," he said.

"Come on, you must have one."

She glanced up at him. He wracked his memory, trying to fish something funny out of the muck of his life.

"You're a heck of an interviewer, princess."

"That's why they pay me the mediocre bucks. Now, spill."

"So this one time…" he began.

* * *

They'd been about twelve, little mages with shiny new powers. The instructors had wisely taken them to one of the training grounds far from the Academy. While the school was built deep within the Rocky Mountains and constructed to withstand the budding abilities of a bunch of teens who could move water and earth with their minds, it was standard operating procedure to take the kids out to the training grounds in the foothills until they had a basic handle on their abilities.

The training ground had once been a cattle ranch, it's former pastures in the rolling hills west of the mountains still marked with barbed wire fences. The old ranch house was the only structure on the property and the sole domain of the instructors.

Cadets slept in tents. It was safer.

"There was this one kid, Bren. He was an earth mage and cocky as hell. He was one of the first kids in the class to get his powers and one of the first to get a real handle on them. He used to levitate small stones and hit me in the back of the head with them."

"Sounds like a dick," Jen said.

"He kind of was back then," Theron said, memories that he hadn't dared to take out and examine in a long time flooding back to him now. "He thought he was hot shit and took every opportunity to pick on my best friend Jas and me."

The torture had gone on for weeks. Neither Theron or Jas were a match for Bren in the sparring ring. Jas, an air mage, had been able to muster stiff breezes and Theron had just about mastered lighting a candle with his mind and only occasionally set his tent on fire while trying. Bren, on the other hand, had been able to levitate rocks the size of his fist and shift patches of ground about two feet across just enough to send his opponents stumbling.

"We couldn't beat him head to head, so we plotted our revenge," Theron said.

The ranch house had always been a spooky place for them, and not just because that's where their intimidating, hard-ass instructors roosted for the night. The place must have been about a hundred years old by that point, it's weathered old boards looking like the scales on a diamondback rattlesnake. The place had never been wired for electricity and had no running water. At night, when the instructors put out their kerosene lanterns, the old house squatted among the trees like a goblin, watching, waiting.

Beside the house was an old wooden grave marker with a

single name carved into its cracked surface. Wallace. Every class of cadets that graduated from the training grounds made up scary stories to tell the incoming class about that grave. The most common one was that Old Man Wallace (no one knew his first name) had been a rancher a hundred years before and had lived in that house. Cattle rustlers (or bandits or bank robbers depending on the story) broke into the house one night and murdered Wallace. Someone, and the stories were never clear on exactly who, buried him beside his house, but his spirit was still around, restless.

"The older kids told us that if anyone disturbed him, Old Man Wallace would rise up out of that grave and get us."

"And you believed them?"

"We were twelve," Theron said defensively. "And remember, some of our teachers were elves and fairies, so ghosts and zombies were not outside the realm of possibility to our imaginations."

"No self-respecting ghost would haunt its grave. That's boring. Maybe the house. Spirits are drawn to people or to places they have an emotional connection with." She could have been describing the weather, her voice matter-of-fact.

Chance of rain, partly sunny, ghosts don't hang out at graves. He almost laughed at the absurdity of the conversation.

"Anyway, we were all convinced if anyone messed with that grave, the old man would crawl out of it, believed it deep down in our bones. So we dared Bren, being the cocky ass that he was, to piss on it."

A laugh burst out of Jen, startling them both. If sunlight had a sound, it would be that sound, Theron thought. It was only the second time he had heard her genuinely laugh with something other than sarcasm or derision in her voice.

He looked down at her to see her covering her mouth with her hand, her dark eyes wide. A slow smile spread across his face at the sight. She was magnificent. He realized he would do anything to hear that laugh again.

Pushing that dangerous thought away, he continued the story.

"One afternoon, Jas and I managed to sneak away from lessons. We dug a shallow hole next to the grave. We were very careful, mind you, not to disturb that grave."

They'd managed to put a plastic tarp over the hole and covered it with dirt and dead leaves. Jas had hidden beneath the tarp for hours in preparation for their ultimate revenge. Theron issued the dare around the dinner fire that night and Bren had no choice but to accept or risk looking weak in front of the other kids.

"I caught just a flash of fear in his eyes, but he was able to hide it from everyone else."

As a group, the twenty or so cadets had followed, laughing, joking, and jeering all the way to the grave to make sure that Bren completed the dare.

"So, there he is, midstream, and Jas reaches out from under that tarp and grabs his ankle. Bren jumped about six feet straight up in the air and hit the ground running when he came back down," he said, unable to hold back his own laughter. "There was a barbed wire fence a few feet from the grave and Bren didn't stop running until he was about a quarter mile away. We never did figure out how he didn't cut himself to ribbons on that fence. He either jumped it or dove through it somehow because he didn't have a scratch on him when someone finally caught up to him and told him to stop running."

Jen was vibrating with laughter, clutching her sides. And he loved it.

"What happened?" She asked. "Did he try to kill you guys when he got back?"

"He didn't speak to us for a week, but after that we were good friends, him and Jas and me."

In his mind's eye, he could see Bren's smiling, young face. They'd been so stupid back then, with no idea what was coming at them.

"We were inseparable," he continued, the words flowing out before he could stop them. "They called us Earth, Wind, and Fire. We were a great team, the best. Nothing could stop us."

Until something had.

He felt his smile dissolve and the laughter in his chest died as the happy image of Bren was replaced with his last glimpse of his friend. The flames hadn't left much. Theron had found Bren and Jas, their bodies lying together, as close in death as they had been in life. He hadn't been able to save them. And the flames had been unable to touch him.

Bottom line, they were dead and it was his fault.

"Hey," Jen's voice cut through the blackened memories. "Where'd you go?"

Concern filled her dark eyes.

"Nowhere good," he said quietly.

They were silent for a while when she asked, "How did they die?"

His gaze snapped to her face and he glared.

"I didn't say they were dead."

"You spoke about them in the past tense, and you look like you've been stabbed in the gut. They're dead and not too long ago, either. I know what fresh emotional wounds look like. I used to interview the families of murder victims. They looked just like you do right now."

"A year ago," he said. "They died a year ago."

The silence stretched between them while a clawing pain filled his chest. Bren and Jas had been closer to him than his own brother and sisters. They ate together, fought together, got drunk together, and on more than a few nights, they had slept within arm's reach of each other, secure in the knowledge that each one had the others' backs.

They had been a perfect trinity, perfectly complemented to each other. Where one was weak, the others were strong. They had shared every aspect of their lives and were never apart for more than a few days.

Now he was the only one left.

"It was my fault," he whispered.

"I'm sure that's not true," Jen said. "What makes you think that?"

As memories of that night threatened to overwhelm him, he slammed the mental brakes on, forcing the memories back into the dark lockbox in his mind where he kept them.

"I can't talk about it," he said softly.

"I understand," was all she said.

He looked at her, surprised. He'd expected her to press him on this. She'd bared her soul and he was refusing to even meet her halfway.

"A good reporter knows when to press and when not to," she said, her voice gentle as she lay her head back down on his chest. "But, in my experience, the story always comes out eventually."

His voice was a little rough when he said, "Tell me another story."

"Want to hear about the time I threw up during a violin recital in front of five hundred people?"

Chapter 10

Jen came awake slowly. The room she was in was dark, the only light coming from a flickering fire in a grate on the other side of the room.

The air was chilly against her skin, but she was warm. So warm. Whatever surface she was sleeping on was hard as stone, but as warm as a summer beach. Raising her head, she saw Theron's sleeping face and the night before came rushing back to her.

Oh, god. The things she'd told him. What had she been thinking?

And she'd slept in his arms. Well, arm. His left arm was still bound in the sling and gauze rig she'd improvised. But his right arm was around her middle, holding her gently against his side, even as he was relaxed in sleep.

His T-shirt was wrinkled where she'd slept with her head on the spot between his shoulder and chest. Her hand still rested on his ribs. Her first instinct was to snatch her hand back like she'd been burned, but she was strangely reluctant to move it.

He felt good. He was big and solid and so very warm. There was strength and power in him, so much it scared her a little. It was a thrilling kind of fear, like watching a horror movie alone with the lights off, just enough to get the blood pumping and the adrenaline flowing.

There was also humor in him and, although he tried to hide it, kindness, too.

Turning her head, she studied his sleeping face. He was actually kind of gorgeous. Long, coppery lashes that stopped just short of being feminine rested against his cheek. His cheekbones were high, his jaw was square and his lips were just full enough to keep his face from being harsh.

Jen caught herself staring at his mouth and she didn't care. The truth was that in the two and a half days she'd known him, she'd never really studied him. They'd been running or fighting or she was angry and couldn't stand to look at him. She'd also been afraid he'd catch her staring, but now, she could look her fill.

The firelight caught in his hair and it was spectacular. Right now, it was mussed and falling over his brow. There were so many different colors, a deep gold mixed with platinum highlights and red lowlights. Before she realized it, her hand was lifting off his chest like it had a mind of its own and reaching for that hair.

Would it be as soft as it looked?

Her fingers gently brushed his hair back from his brow. The strands slid through her fingers, feeling like silk. His eyes opened slowly and his gaze found hers. She stayed frozen for a heartbeat, caught in an embarrassing spot.

His brows drew together ever so slightly, and his arm tightened around her just a fraction, drawing her closer to him. Something searing flashed in the indigo depths of his eyes, and a shock of electricity jolted through her, sending delicious sensations skittering along her nerves.

They stayed locked like that for one breath, two. Jen was the first to snap out of it, pulling her hand back and turning her face away, hoping she wasn't blushing. Pushing off the mattress, she unfortunately had to use his chest to lever herself up. He pulled his arm away as she scooted to the foot of the bed, studiously avoiding his eyes.

She could feel his gaze, though, as she crawled awkwardly over the carved ebony footboard. It beat crawling over his legs.

When her feet hit the stone floor, she grabbed her toothbrush and a fresh set of clothes and headed for the bathroom, managing not to look at him.

The bathroom door slammed behind her and the lock was turned.

Shit. What was going on here? She was touching him, embarrassed around him, feeling little electric shocks when he looked at her.

Attraction. She was attracted to him.

Hold up there, sister. That guy kidnapped you. Thou shalt not be attracted to thy kidnapper. She was pretty sure that was an important rule written by someone smarter than she was being right now.

But had he really?

It may have started off as a kidnapping, but if she had the chance to run right now, she wouldn't. Somewhere along the way they'd become a team. She was on board with the plan now. The thought of going with him didn't scare her anymore. The thought of leaving her life in Baghdad, not that it had been much of a life, seemed, hell, appealing now.

What would this Citadel look like? What kind of people would she meet? What kind of creatures would she meet? Curiosity had her excited by the prospect. The idea of something so completely new had a feeling that felt a lot like hope blooming within her.

She wasn't scared anymore because Theron would be with her. He wouldn't let anything bad happen to her, he'd proven that last night.

Their conversation floated back to her. She'd talked with men like that before. It was the way two people talked when they'd been dating for a little while, when they were getting to know each other. That thought scared her a little and she pushed it away, dismissing it.

Lying beside him in the dark, his arm around her, their voices weaving a spell of comfort around them both. It felt like connection. It felt like...intimacy. But was it real? Or was it a product of stress, adrenaline, proximity and physical attraction, at least on her part?

Jen stripped out of her clothes and showered quickly, brushed her teeth and threw on a fresh shirt and khakis. She wasn't in a hurry to be in the same room as Theron this soon after her little realization, but she was also aware that the sun would be up very soon and they should get on the road if they wanted to make Rutba by nightfall.

* * *

Two hours later, Theron was nervously drumming his fingers against the steering wheel. Highway 1 stretched out before them, disappearing into the horizon. Empty desert stretched out on either side. Rise Against was pumping through the speakers singing about help being on the way.

Jen rode shotgun, staring out the window at the shifting sands. She'd been quiet since he'd come awake to find her fingers in his hair, her body pressed against his side. He'd been incredibly grateful for the silk duvet that had covered them both. It had hidden his massive erection from her view.

He normally woke up semi-hard, but the feel of her touch and the look in her eyes had left him instantly like steel. After she'd bolted for the bathroom, he'd had to focus on remembering how to draw protection wards for several minutes to get his dumb-stick to calm down. Wards had always been the toughest area of magick for him. So many symbols and loops and knots to remember. The trick worked, and he was able to stand up before Jen had finished the fastest shower in the history of females.

He tried to push thoughts about last night out of his head, but they kept creeping back in. The feel of her tucked against his right side, her head on his chest, it was one of the best things he'd ever felt in his life. The skin over his ribs tingled at the memory, and his right arm ached to be around her again.

He'd never just slept next to a woman. They'd talked until she'd fallen asleep during one of his stories about Academy life. He'd just watched her for a few minutes until he'd drifted off too. He'd never told a woman the things he'd told her last night.

There had only been two types of women in his life. The female mages knew his story. Most of them had grown up around him. They weren't interested in relationships. They'd all wanted his body. A few had wanted him to father their children, but he wasn't going there. All the female mages knew he was a bad bet for the long-term. He practically had "killed in action" stamped on his ass, but his genes were top notch.

Female mages, particularly the combat mages, were a practical bunch. They knew emotional attachments were not a good idea, but they also understood the need to carry on the subspecies. Mages were the line between the sapiens and the other races, after all.

The other women he'd been with were sapiens, and he'd never gotten close to any of them. They'd been one-night only affairs when he'd had an itch to scratch and it had been the same for those women. He hadn't even learned most of their names, and they hadn't gotten his.

That was the rule mages lived by. One night with a sapien was all that was allowed. Anything more was strictly forbidden. For both the safety of the sapien and the secrecy of the shadow races.

That thing last night with Jen was totally new. He'd only ever talked like that with Jas and Bren, trading stories and laughing until all hours. Mixed with the physical closeness, the warmth of her against him, the scent of her surrounding him, it was intoxicating.

He was hungry for more. It was so bad, he wanted to pull off the road and haul her into his arms. He thought he'd put a lid on his urges where she was concerned, but the way she'd looked at him this morning, the way she'd touched him, it had torn the lid off, blown up the lid and scattered the ashes of the lid to the four winds.

He just had to hold it together until they got to the Citadel. Then he could get some distance and figure out what this was.

The asphalt rolled beneath the tires at a much slower rate than he would have liked, but he had to be sure they weren't going to hit any roadside bombs. This stretch of Highway 1 between Ramadi and Rutba was supposedly a hotbed for bandits and ISIS operatives.

The big eighteen-wheeler trucks that made the runs between Baghdad, Syria and Jordan had this one highway through the desert. Those rigs looked a bit like something out of Mad Max, with huge spiked grills, run flat tires and a few even had gun turrets.

He'd give his left nut for a gun turret on the SUV, but if wishes were horses, beggars would ride.

That left them slow rolling so that he could visually inspect the roadway. It also limited them to traveling during the day, which made them targets for bandits. If it had just been him, he might have chanced it and run full out at night without the headlights. He had even odds of surviving a bomb blast, given his immunity to fire. The concussion and force of such a blast was still a danger.

His passenger changed all of that, though. She was precious cargo.

Theron's eyes scanned the horizon alert to the slightest glint of sunlight on metal or glass, the barest hint of movement from people or vehicles, the smallest inkling that danger was ahead.

Tension had already tightened his shoulders to the point of pain when a vehicle crested the slight rise behind them, popping up in the rearview. A couple of trucks had passed them since they'd left Ramadi around dawn. He hoped to hell this was another one of those.

As they crested another small hill, Theron saw figures ahead on the road and his stomach hit the floor. There were four vehicles parked, two on either side of the road and makeshift barricades had been set up.

Slowing the SUV, he pulled the binocs out of the console between the seats, very aware that the vehicle behind them was closing fast.

"Shit," he said, his voice sounding loud in the silence of the SUV. "They've got tire spikes."

Passing the binoculars to Jen, his mind raced with tactical possibilities.

The vehicle he'd spotted in the rearview earlier, which turned out to be a rusted out 4Runner, was idling about fifty feet back. There were two figures in the front seat, no telling how many were in the back.

With the number of vehicles ahead, there were at least four potential hostiles, likely armed.

They had a few options. Gun it and go off road. They ran the risk of getting stuck in the shifting sand, given how heavy the SUV was. They'd be sitting ducks then. There was also the risk that the bandits, and that's almost certainly what they were, had set up IEDs and landmines in the empty stretches of sand beside the road.

He could gun it and run down the barricades, but they would almost certainly take some fire, and as good as his run flats were, he wasn't sure they could stand up to those tire spikes.

They could turn around, but there were likely magickal baddies waiting for them in Ramadi. They had taken out that sorceress, but it was a good bet the rest of the death cult would be gunning for them, and now they had revenge on their mind. The only way out of this was to get to Damascus and this was the only road there.

Turning, Theron eyed the explosives, the grenades and the automatic weapons in the cargo area. If he could get close enough, he could light some shit up, mechanically, chemically and magickally.

His 1911s went in his holsters. He pulled an automatic M-16 across his lap and handed Jen a Belgian P-90. The rifle could churn out the lead and didn't have much of a kick. It could be fired easily without looking through the sights and he was sure she could handle it.

"It's set to semi-auto, three round bursts," he told her, speaking quickly.

She tucked the gun barrel down beside her right knee so that she could easily bring it to bear. The woman must have taken careful notes when she was embedded with those Marines.

Two frag grenades were placed in her lap.

"Grip and pull the pin," he said, indicating the bit of metal with a ring on it. "Count to three and throw it or roll it. The kill zone is about fifteen feet. Casualty zone is about forty-five."

Her eyes went wide and shot to his face.

"Shit is about to get real in a very bad way," he told her, wishing to the gods he'd thought to put a tac vest on her. "Keep your head down and do what you have to in order to get out of here."

"What about you?" Her voice was steady but higher than usual.

He flashed her a smile as he let his fire out to play, letting tiny flames lick up his hands.

"I got this," he told her. It took every ounce of strength within him not to lean in and steal a good luck kiss as he prepared to hit the gas and charge the barricades.

He'd just released his foot from the brake when she said, "Wait."

His foot hit the brakes again. The binocs were up to her eyes, and she lowered them just enough to look at him. She glanced back at the vehicle behind them, which was rolling slowly forward.

"I think I can get us out of this," she said, her voice quiet.

"How?"

"I'm going to talk to them."

"The hell you are!"

"I'm serious. They're not organized enough, and their equipment isn't good enough to be ISIS. They're bandits. I've heard these guys can be bought off. It's basically a toll booth."

She eyed the guns, ammunition and explosives behind them.

"Not a chance. I'm not going to give them any more weapons than they already have."

"They might take something else," she said, turning and fishing something from her bag. "If we try it and it doesn't work, we're no worse off than we are right now, having to fight our way through."

A long strip of black cloth emerged and she wound it around her head and face with the ease of long practice. She grabbed his sunglasses out of his pocket and put them on. Her face, eyes and hair were completely covered.

"Let me go with you," he said.

"Not a chance, Cap. You're too white. With my Arabic and in a niqab I can pass. This is going to work," she said, lunging for her door handle.

"Jen, wait!" he shouted.

She was too quick and he cursed his decision not to handcuff her. He opened his door just a crack and positioned the M-16 where he could draw it quickly. His fire was coiled just beneath the surface of his left hand.

Jen walked slowly toward the barricades, her hands above her head. He let the SUV roll slowly about ten feet behind her.

Glancing to the passenger seat, he saw she'd pocketed one of the grenades somehow. The woman had deft hands, that was for sure.

Theron's heart was in his throat as he watched Jen approach the barricades. He hung back about twenty feet, his finger on the trigger of the M-16 and a killer fireball brewing in his palm.

Two men appeared from one of the vehicles and approached, wariness written in their body language. There was no telling what they were going to think of a woman in pants and a niqab asking them to let her pass.

He flipped the weapons compartment shut and hoped like hell they didn't want to search the SUV.

Jen was talking with the men, and the tension in Theron's body as he watched them was painful. She pulled something from her shirt pocket and flashed it.

One wrong move and he'd burn the fuckers to ashes. But he'd have to worry about hitting Jen, too. Gods damn it!

What seemed like hours passed, but was in reality only seconds.

Jen turned and walked slowly back toward the SUV, her hands in the air again. When she reached the vehicle, she opened the back passenger-side door and pulled her bag toward her.

She pulled her laptop out, opened it up and clicked a few times, her eyes roaming quickly over the screen. Shutting the computer, she pulled a memory card out and stowed it in her bag. Next came her fancy cell phone. She pushed a few buttons, then killed the screen and added it to the pile along with the device's charger. Next was her digital camera, which she had always handled like it was something precious. She popped a memory card out and stowed that in her bag before adding the camera to the pile of electronics.

"What are you doing?" he asked her.

"Paying our toll."

Before he could stop her, she turned on her heel and marched back toward the bandits with the electronics in her arms. A sick feeling invaded his gut as he watched her hand the items over to the bandits.

Those three items were her prized possessions. She didn't have much in the way of material goods. He'd seen that when he'd been in her apartment searching for some way to track her down.

Her laptop allowed her to write. Her camera allowed her to record the way she saw the world. And her cell phone was her connection to the outside world.

And she'd just given them all up. To save them both. The enormity of what she'd done hit like a punch to the chest and he was left momentarily in awe.

In that moment, as he watched her walk bravely into a dangerous situation to hand over the last pieces of her old life and her only tools for escape, he felt something move through him. It wasn't a feeling he had a name for. It scared the hell out of him.

Focusing on what was happening ahead, he watched as the electronics disappeared into one of the vehicles. Jen motioned with her hand for him to drive forward. As he rolled up, the two men moved the barricades and the tire spikes.

Theron's left hand was on the steering wheel, his right was on his 1911, ready to bring the smaller weapon up and empty the clip before moving on to the M-16 if necessary.

As he got closer, he could see that each of the vehicles had at least four men, all likely armed. He was really glad they hadn't tried to charge through. They probably wouldn't have made it. Jen had likely just saved both their lives.

As he rolled up, Jen climbed in, her expression unreadable beneath the fabric of the niqab.

The SUV accelerated to about forty as he watched the rear view, ready for the bandits to change their minds.

* * *

Jen sat in the passenger seat, her face numb and her hands and feet tingling. She knew what it felt like to come off a sudden adrenaline burst, and it always left her a little spacy.

Theron held their speed steady and slow, the silence tense and yawning between them. She glanced at him. His knuckles were white on the steering wheel, his eyes nervously darting between the road and the rear view mirror.

After about ten miles, he pulled the SUV to the side of the road and threw the thing in park. He leaned forward until his forehead rested against the steering wheel between his hands. After a deep inhale through his nose, he let the breath out just as slowly from between his teeth.

Reaching out a hand, she asked, "Are you o—"

In a swift movement, his hand went to the back of her neck and he brought her mouth to his.

Surprise flared within her for a split second, before it was replaced with raw heat. His mouth was hard against her lips, his hand an unyielding pressure on her neck. Neither of them had buckled their seat belts, so as his other arm locked around her waist, she was hauled against his chest.

His mouth moved against hers, possessive, owning. She could feel his fear, the helplessness and anger he must have felt during that handoff burn off him in the heat of the kiss.

His arms relaxed ever so slightly and the kiss shifted. His mouth softened against hers and his hot tongue slid against her lower lip, sending a delicious electricity zinging between her thighs.

She realized with a start that she was frozen with her hands by her sides. She skimmed her hands over his stomach and up his chest until she was gripping his shoulders. At her touch, he groaned against her mouth and deepened the kiss.

Jen had lost count a long time ago of the number of men she'd kissed in her thirty years on the planet. In all that time, she'd never been kissed like this. She'd never felt this kind of raw need, this naked power, this unapologetic taking that was simultaneously incredibly giving.

Without warning, Theron broke the kiss and released her, leaving her at once chilled and feverish back in the passenger seat. She suddenly missed the feel of him.

"I know what you did back there," he said quietly, not looking at her. "I know what it meant to give up those things."

Thoughts raced through her head, but she didn't know what to say to him. She hadn't given it a second thought. Those electronics were valuable and easily sold for a hefty sum in this part of the world, where those items were hard to come by. They had been important to her, but they were just things. Their value was nothing when compared to her life...or his.

He was silent for a moment, before he met her eyes and said, "Thank you."

His voice was low and soft and she thought he might be thanking her for more than just giving up her gear.

"It's not a big deal," she said. "I wiped the memory on the phone and I was able to save my files and photos on those memory cards before I wiped the hard drive."

He was quiet for a long time, his eyes searching her face. "I'm sorry I kissed you without asking. I was so scared during that handoff and the adrenaline had me wound up and I wasn't thinking, but that's no excuse."

He looked away, turning his gaze out the driver's window.

She smiled and reached out, cupping his jaw in her palm and turned his face gently toward her. Meeting his gaze for a moment, she closed her eyes and leaned in, placing a featherlight kiss beside his mouth. She felt the vibrating tension leave his body on a sigh.

"Don't be sorry," she whispered. "I liked it. More than I should."

She pulled back.

"But we need to keep driving."

"Yes, ma'am," he said, putting the SUV in gear and hitting the gas. ===

* * *

Jen stared into the flickering flames in front of her and studiously avoided looking at the man across the campfire from her. That kiss kept replaying through her head and the thought of it kept sending blood rushing to her cheeks. And other places.

She and Theron hadn't said much to each other since it happened. They'd rode in silence, Theron concentrating on the road and Jen pretending great interest in the lyrics of the heavy metal songs pumping through the speakers, until they hit the tiny village of Rutba around sunset.

It was worse than she'd expected.

Rutba had been hit hard, first by an ISIS occupation, then by airstrikes from the Syrians. It was virtually abandoned now. The town used to boast seven thousand residents and was the last stop before hundreds of miles of empty desert between here and the border. Some of the buildings were intact, but not many. Most were broken, spilling rubble from partially standing walls. The open doors and shattered windows looked like the empty eye sockets and gaping mouths of shattered skulls. The broken walls appeared as skeletal fingers reaching from the sandy earth.

The streets of Rutba were a haunted place. Spirits of the

dead wandered aimlessly, taking no notice of the newcomers in the rumbling vehicle. The living peeked out of heavily fortified doors set in the few intact buildings. Stray dogs drifted between the houses, picking at scattered garbage.

Every shop was shuttered and even the lone gas station was out of commission.

She and Theron had found a mostly intact cinderblock house that had lost one corner in the bombing. Jen had looked it over and declared it spirit free, and Theron had pulled the front end of the SUV into the gap in the walls.

They'd made camp for the night, Theron collecting a pile of broken furniture in the middle of what had probably been the living room at one time. He'd set it on fire with a thought.

Jen had arranged a couple of carpets she'd found in another room so they had something to sit on instead of the dusty tile floor. The thing had cracks running through it that were wider than her hand.

Theron's voice broke through her thoughts.

"What did you say to those guys back at the checkpoint?"

"Huh?" she asked, not following his words.

"Back at that 'tollbooth,' how did you talk your way out of that one?"

"Oh. I, uh, I just kind of told them the truth. I said I was a journalist and I was trying to get to the Syrian border and that you were my bodyguard."

"And that worked? We're lucky they didn't take you hostage right there," he said.

"I just flashed them this," she said, pulling a laminated badge from her shirt pocket. It was black with white letters that said "VICE" and "HBO" and "PRESS."

Theron looked at it, his brows drawing together.

"You're kidding," he said.

"I know one of the producers and I did some reporting for them a few months ago. I discovered that this baby will get you past just about anyone. It's like the trump card of press badges."

VICE was doing some of the best journalism about the Middle East these days, and with the backing of a network like HBO, they had the budget to make it happen. This little laminated badge had got her interviews with warlords, insurgents and rebel commanders.

"Turns out," she said, "those bandits back there are big 'Game of Thrones' fans."

He looked at her for a beat with wide eyes and then burst out laughing.

Breathing hard and clutching his side, he said, "Jen, you never cease to amaze."

There was something in his eyes as he looked across the fire at her. Jen realized it was respect, deep respect.

"I'm just glad you decided to work with me instead of against me," he said. "When I took you out of Baghdad, I did it because I thought I needed to protect you. Have I apologized for that, by the way?"

"No, I don't think you did," she said, her mouth stretching in a smile despite her best efforts.

"Well, good. I wish I'd handled all that better, not gonna lie, but I'm not sorry you ended up here with me."

Jen felt her skin heat and it had nothing to do with the fire. Embarrassed at her reaction, she turned away and rummaged in her pack. There wasn't anything in particular that she was after, she just didn't want him to see her blush.

Because the truth was, if she was really honest with herself, she wasn't sorry she'd ended up here either.

She'd been living a tiny fraction of a life in a grim and brutal place that had her existing in a constant mode of survival.

She was still in survival mode, more so than she had been in a long time, but something had woken up in her. She was laughing again, smiling again, cracking jokes again. She'd been funny once, and she'd almost forgotten that.

For the past five years, she'd been living in a bubble of pain, anger, and sadness, but mostly boredom. As disruptive as Theron's appearance in her life had been, she was glad for it because it made her realize how little she'd been living.

Her hand landed on a protein bar, make that two, and she pulled them free of her bag, tossing one to Theron.

"Dinner's on me," she joked.

He caught it in midair and tore the crinkly wrapper open.

"I get to choose the restaurant next time," he said around a mouthful of protein bar. "The food here is terrible."

She smiled. "Yeah, and the service is atrocious."

A smile flashed across his handsome face, the firelight catching in the golden stubble that was starting to come in around his jaw.

"The atmosphere leaves a lot to be desired," he added.

"I give it one star," she said. "We should have checked the Yelp reviews before we showed up. Oh, well, live and learn."

They both dissolved into laughter, laughing so long and hard that Jen's side hurt.

* * *

Theron watched Jen throw her head back and laugh, and it was one of the most beautiful things he'd ever seen.

They were in a mountain of trouble, running from a death cult that was not only hell bent on getting their hands on Jen, but was now gunning for revenge for the death of their priestess/leader. They were in ISIS-controlled territory, running low on food and fuel. Desic's latest text said the temperature was expected to drop near freezing tonight.

Cold never bothered him, but Jen was a different story. He'd managed to snag two sleeping bags from the supplies back at the Baghdad HQ, but they were not designed for cold weather. To top it off, they didn't even have jackets. Jen was currently huddled close to the fire, hugging the long-sleeve cotton button up shirt around her and rubbing her biceps.

The sun had set, and the temperature was dropping fast.

As he eyed the sleeping bags sitting rolled up next to the fire, his thoughts turned to the night before. He'd never felt anything like what he'd felt holding Jen in his arms. Well, arm. They'd talked for hours in the dark, her head on his shoulder, the warmth of their bodies wrapping around each other, their breath mingling.

He hadn't slept that soundly in, well, he couldn't remember. There was a kind of peace and comfort in her arms that let him relax and let his guard down.

A voice in the back of his head said that wasn't necessarily a good thing. They were in an extremely dangerous position and they both needed to keep their guards up. If he was smart, he'd keep her on the other side of the fire tonight and sleep with one eye open.

But ever since he'd woken up to find her scrambling off the bed, there had been a small ache in the center of his chest. His arms felt her absence. He was hungry to feel her pressed against him again. He wanted that connection, that closeness, needed it.

The tactical part of his brain, that thing that had kept him alive through hundreds of sticky situations, told him he should stay away from her. They should set a watch, sleep in shifts.

But she'd be cold. And if she was beside him, he could protect her more easily. He'd just keep his guns close and not sleep at all. That would work. Sure.

A part of him that was about as far from the tactical part of his brain as it was possible to be, reminded Theron that there were other things they could do in that sleeping bag besides hold each other.

That ill-advised kiss popped into his head and had his blood heating. He still didn't know what had possessed him to put his mouth on her. It had to be the combination of adrenaline, stress, anxiety and, if he was totally honest, raw desire.

Iron control and force of will were as much a part of him as the skin he wore. A fire mage couldn't survive without them. He refused to let himself lose control. Not again. It had cost him too much last time. But he'd also never felt anything like this connection with Jen before.

That kiss hadn't been a conscious decision. It had just happened, almost before he'd known it. It scared him a little. Her mouth against his, her breasts pressing into his chest, the heat of her, it was one of the best things he'd ever felt. One kiss from Jen was better than the sex he'd had with anyone else.

And she'd kissed him back.

A part of him was screaming at him to kiss her again, pull her against him, strip her naked and make love to her. But he couldn't afford the distraction, couldn't afford to lose control like that.

He watched Jen chewing through her protein bar and was struck again with how lean she was. Last night, he'd seen how pronounced her ribs were and the way her hip bones stuck out. She was too thin. When he'd been in her apartment, he'd seen the distinct lack of food and she'd barely eaten since they left Baghdad.

That was going to change. From here to Damascus, he'd make sure she ate. And when they got to the Citadel, he'd make sure she didn't miss a meal. For a military installation, the Citadel had some of the best chefs this side of the Fey Realms.

He was really going to enjoy spoiling her. For a moment, a mental image of the two of them invaded his skull, them hanging out on a couch in one of the standard living quarters in the Citadel, surrounded by popcorn, pizza, and other junk food while Netflix played in the background.

He slammed the mental lid on that thought. In his experience, it didn't pay to fantasize about things like that. They never came true. For him, at least.

One minute, one hour, one day at a time, that's how they had to play this. Survival first, movie night later.

Across the fire, Jen shivered hard and put her palms toward the flames. He added a little of his own energy to the fire, pumping it up beyond what their meager fuel of broken furniture could provide. He was exhausted and even that small effort cost him, but it was worth it to see her relax a little as the extra warmth wrapped itself around her.

"Cold?" he asked her.

"Temperature's dropping," she said. "And someone didn't give me a chance to pack for the weather."

Her tone was playful, a smirk pulling at the corner of her mouth and the light of the fire dancing in her eyes.

"I'll make it up to you," he said, meeting her eyes, his voice low and soft. She looked at the sleeping bags and then anywhere but his face. It might be his imagination or a trick of the firelight, but her cheeks looked ever so slightly pink.

Rising to his feet, he moved to the sleeping bags. Didn't take more than a moment to unroll the black nylon bedding. They wouldn't offer much padding against the hard floor, or much insulation against the cold, but he could make it work.

Working the zippers and the elastic straps that held the bags when they were rolled up, he was able to maneuver the two bags into a configuration that would fit them both comfortably and keep them warm.

Jen eyed the setup, not saying anything, but her little pink tongue licked her bottom lip, and he almost groaned. Her gaze caught his for a split second before she slid her eyes away and started rummaging in her pack again. Coming up with her toothbrush, a water bottle, and toothpaste, she rose.

"I'm going to brush my teeth," she said, her words coming a little faster than usual. She stood by the rough gap in the exterior wall where the SUV was parked, little swishing noises reaching his ears over the crackle of the fire.

When she came back, she stowed her things in her pack and looked at the sleeping bags again, giving the setup serious side-eye.

"Kick your boots off and climb in," he said.

She hesitated, but then started pulling at the laces of her boots. While he finished with his own hygiene routine, he watched her climb in and scoot to one side of the pallet he'd made. Fully clothed. Her eyes kept watching him and darting away and she thought he didn't notice.

Sitting beside the fire, he pulled off his own boots and shucked his fatigue pants. In his T-shirt and boxers, he moved slowly, but as casually as possible to the nest of sleeping bags, laying his pistols carefully within reach.

He continued to move slowly as he slid in, facing her, careful not to spook her. Her shoulders were curled down and her knees were curled up between their bodies.

"Those khakis are going to get uncomfortable on this hard floor," he told her.

"I don't think it's a good idea to take them off," she said, not meeting his eyes.

He gave her a hard look.

"Are you nervous?" he asked, unable to keep the surprise out of his voice.

"No," she responded too quickly, her tone defensive.

"Look, if you're worried about shenanigans, I promise to keep my hands to myself," he said, bringing his hands up between them and showing her his palms. "Honestly, this is about warmth and safety. I'm worried you'll get too cold by yourself, and it's easier to protect you if you're right next to me if something sneaks up on us."

She stayed silent for a moment, staring at his chest, before she shifted around and he heard the rustle of fabric. The khakis hit the floor by their feet.

Her bare leg brushed against his, and the breath froze in his lungs. It was going to be a long, hard night. So very, very hard.

* * *

Big, he was just so god damned big. As Theron settled next to her in the nest of sleeping bags, she watched with fascination as the muscles in his arms and chest bunched. His movements were slow and deliberate and that was about her, she knew, about making her comfortable. Somewhere along the way, and she wasn't sure exactly when it had happened, her comfort had become important to him.

And his to her.

"I forgot to ask," she said softly. "How's the shoulder?"

He was lying on his right side on his uninjured shoulder. He moved the left in a circle, first backward then forward.

"Hundred percent as far as I can tell," he said.

"Most people would need to have it in a sling for a few weeks," she told him.

His face was mostly in shadow, his back to the fire, but she caught the flash of his white teeth as he smiled.

"I'm not most people," he said, his voice low. "Mages heal lightning quick, and fire mages have a metabolism like a furnace. Put the two together, and you can almost watch our skin knit back together when it's cut."

Her eyes went to the cut he'd had on his forehead from where it made contact with the window when that truck had plowed into them. It was just a pink line now. Those cuts on her ribs had barely scabbed over in the same amount of time.

"I wish I healed like that," she said, her hand going to the bandage over her ribs.

"Oh, hey, we never checked that," he said. As he sat up, his own hands went to her bandage, his fingers brushing hers aside.

"Let me look," he said, pushing aside her T-shirt and peeling the surgical tape away from her skin at one corner. She had no time to protest and his hands were gentle, so she really had nothing to complain about.

Shifting so the firelight hit her skin, he looked down at her side. That blonde hair of his fell over his forehead and the firelight danced against the skin of his throat. He was a strikingly handsome man, she thought.

Her gaze fell on his mouth, and the memory of that kiss invaded her thoughts again. Her breath came faster and her heart rate kicked up a notch. What would happen if she sat up, put her palm against that square jaw and put her mouth to his?

Theron's voice snapped her back to reality.

"Does that hurt?" He asked, his fingers lightly pressing the skin around her gashes.

"No," she said quickly, hoping that her thoughts didn't show in her voice.

"No bleeding, no sign of infection," he said. "I don't think we need to redress it tonight, but let's leave the bandage on for now. I don't want you knocking off those butterfly strips."

She nodded as he tugged her T-shirt back into place. As he laid back down, folding his left arm behind his head, his pecs strained at the material of his T-shirt. He stared at the cracked ceiling of their bombed out little shelter, his face and body silhouetted against the fire. The urge to touch him made her fingers tremble and her thighs squeeze together.

He turned his head to look at her and his low voice reached out to her.

"I'm going to stay up tonight, but can I ask you something?"

She nodded, not trusting her voice to sound anything other than breathy, not even thinking about his request. She'd give him just about anything in this moment.

He was silent for several seconds and anxiety began to build in the space around her lungs.

"Would you...would you sleep on my shoulder, like you did last night?"

Biting her lip, she closed her eyes. She hadn't wanted to ask him for that, but she'd been thinking about it ever since they'd made camp.

Sleeping in his arms the night before had felt good. Really good. Like maybe the best thing she'd felt in, oh god, she didn't remember when.

For a moment, she examined her reaction to his request. Somewhere between here and Baghdad, she had ceased to be his captive and had become his partner. Her physical attraction to him had an obvious source. But this connection, each craving the touch and comfort of the other, the way he longed to see her smile and laugh, that was something else.

Stockholm syndrome? No, they'd left the risk of that behind a long time ago. They liked each other. She genuinely wanted him. And underneath that was a feeling she wasn't nearly ready to examine yet. Maybe when they were safe behind the walls of his fortress, they could figure out what this spark was.

She nodded and inched toward him, ducking under his right arm, her breasts pressing into the solid wall of his chest. Her right hand rested just over his heart, its strong and steady rhythm reassuring under her fingers. Her head was pillowed on his shoulder, her black braid snaking over its bulk.

"Try to get some sleep, okay? The toughest part of this trip is ahead of us tomorrow," he told her.

She was far too keyed up to sleep, and judging by the tension in his big body, so was he.

Jen closed her eyes, but locked in the darkness of her own skull, all she could think about was the way he felt against her. Her bare leg brushed his again and the fine hairs tickled her skin. She was keenly aware of how soft the fabric of his T-shirt was beneath her fingertips, his incredible warmth radiating through her skin and sinking into her tired muscles.

She was also very aware that her button down shirt, which was open over her T-shirt, was bunching uncomfortably under her.

Awareness continued to ratchet up as she squirmed and tried to get comfortable, her every movement brushing against him some way. Finally, when she couldn't stand it anymore, her eyes snapped open.

And found him staring at her.

Those indigo eyes were almost glowing, like the blue flame of a blow torch. Her lips parted on a gasp, but her breath caught in her throat.

Jen was caught. Trapped. Ensnared by those eyes. Her heart pounding, her hand snaked up between them and touched his face, as she had longed to do.

The shimmering stubble on his jaw rasped against her palm, a delicious friction on her hyper-sensitive skin. He turned into her touch, pressing against her palm like he craved the contact.

His eyes closed and he let out a long breath, his lips parting gently.

He was beautiful. And she wanted him, more than she'd wanted anything in a long time.

She stroked her thumb just under his cheekbone.

"Oh, gods, Jen," he groaned softly. A slight, almost imperceptible tremor moved through his enormous body.

As he rolled onto his side, his other arm came around her and brought her fully against him. His erection pressed into her hip, and a shock zinged through her body, ricocheting along her nerves until it settled between her legs.

For a beat, she waited for him to kiss her, as he had in the SUV. She was hungry for the feel of his mouth on her again. When he made no move toward her, she leaned in and brought her mouth to his.

His lips were warm, and as she licked his bottom lip, the

rumble of his groan reverberated through her. As his lips parted, she seized the opportunity and slid her tongue into him. He tasted like toothpaste and male.

He groaned again, louder this time, and his arms tightened around her. That erection of his strained against the thin soft cotton of his boxers. In a bold move, she brought her knee up to his hip and positioned that erection right against her cleft. She could feel the heat of him through the cotton of her panties.

He groaned against her mouth and it was loud enough this time to shake the rubble around them. The big muscles in his chest and arms were jumping against her and she realized that he was holding himself back, keeping the full power of his body leashed.

Without warning, he broke their kiss and pressed his forehead to hers, his hands on either side of her face.

"You're killing me," he growled.

She didn't answer him. They were good at talking, but the time for words was over. She lived in a world of words, too many words. This was all about feeling something.

Instead, she leaned in and kissed him again, and he let her, his hands still cradling her face. His touch grew just a little harder, a little more urgent.

She ran her hands along the muscles of his chest, marveling at the solidness of him, the power in that big body. Jen had never been with anyone like Theron before and she was suddenly desperate to know what he'd feel like moving against her, inside of her.

He broke the kiss and his mouth found her throat. When his teeth scraped against the delicate skin beneath her ear, it was her turn to moan, her body arching against him.

He stilled, his breath tickling her wet skin and causing

goosebumps all over her.

"Is this really happening?" he asked, his voice incredibly soft.

She nodded vigorously and leaned into him, suddenly desperate to taste the skin of his throat. A wild surge of energy moved through her, a desperation and a hunger she'd never felt with a partner. His hands on her shoulders stopped her.

His eyes were locked on hers.

"I need to hear you say it," he said, his voice a husky rumble. "I need to hear you say you want this."

Her heart squeezed at the look in his eyes. How did this man, who held so much destructive energy within him, exude sweet concern at every turn? It had been so long since anyone had put her first, and when he did it, it unwound every defense she had.

Breathing hard, heart pounding, she looked into his eyes and said, "I need your cock inside me like I need my next breath."

* * *

The air in Theron's lungs froze as Jen's words hit him.

She wanted him.

That knowledge was like gasoline to his inner fire. Heat flushed his body and danced along his veins. In a swift movement, he pulled his shirt over his head and tossed it. He stripped the button down shirt from her shoulders with the same efficiency.

She wanted him.

The thought pounded through him again and he had to clench his hands into fists to keep them from ripping her T-shirt to shreds. Her slender hands caressed his bare chest and her touch cranked his inner fire up another notch. If he wasn't careful, he'd scorch them both.

She rolled her hips against his erection, and he wasn't able to hold back the groan that escaped his lips.

"Keep that up, sweetheart, and the party's going to be over before it gets started," he said against her throat.

She laughed, and it was deep and husky and throaty and quite possibly the best sound he'd ever heard.

As her laughter died, she seemed to sober for a moment. Pulling back a little, she met his eyes.

"I don't suppose you have any condoms handy?" she whispered.

"I don't, but I can't get you pregnant and we can't get each other sick."

"How is that possible?" She arched an incredulous eyebrow as she stroked his shoulder.

"Different subspecies, remember?"

"Good to know," she said, a devious looking smile spreading across her lips.

As he ran his hands slowly up her waist, pushing the T-shirt toward her shoulders, it hit him. It had never been like this before. Sex with anonymous sapien women had been nice, and he'd certainly enjoyed it, and the women had too, but it had been more a means to an end. Sex had always been a series of steps to get to a destination, which was at least a couple orgasms for the woman and one for him.

This pounding, demanding need coursing through him was new. It turned every touch, every kiss into something full of more sensation than he'd ever felt.

It's because you care about her, an accusatory voice echoed in his head. The realization was like a sledgehammer to the chest and it snapped his eyes open wide.

Any coherent thoughts he had fled his skull at that point. Jen's shirt was pushed up over her chest. She had on an adorable white cotton bra that gently cupped her small, tight breasts. Her small, dusky nipples were straining at the cotton.

He couldn't help it, his fingers trailed over the swells above the thin cotton, and his mouth sucked her nipple through the fabric. She arched against him, her moan of pleasure echoing in his ears, and he smiled while he tongued her sensitive flesh.

Snapping the front clasp of her bra open, he freed her breasts and blew across her damp nipple, smiling again as she shivered hard in his arms.

He moved his hand slowly down her stomach, watching her face. Her eyes were closed, lips parted, breath panting. It was important to him that she wanted everything he was doing. Sure she'd initiated, but there was a tiny portion of his brain that was still getting blood flow, and it was aware of the odd situation they were in.

He never wanted her to feel pressured to do something. He was her protector, and he'd defend her to the death, but that had nothing to do with what they were doing. He would protect her even if she were biting and clawing him the whole way to Damascus.

Right now, they only biting she was doing was nibbling his earlobe, and the only clawing she was doing was raking her nails down his bare back, causing a delicious frisson of pain that helped him focus again.

His hand reached her panties and dipped under the elastic. She was wet, his fingers slipping over her slick, hot pussy. She was so ready for him.

When his fingers found her clit and he started to circle her sensitive flesh, she arched against him and moaned. Her fingers dove into his hair and her nails raked his scalp. He let out a moan of his own.

Her hips began a subtle rhythm as he worked her, and he could feel the tension coiling within her. It wasn't long before she came apart in his arms, coming hard against his hand.

She was panting hard, her cheeks flushed red in the firelight, her dark eyes sparking as they met his, her braid coming undone around her face. Not unlike the woman herself. In this moment, Jen was raw and undone and quite possibly the most beautiful thing Theron had ever seen.

He brought his mouth to hers again, kissing down her throat as she came down. As he began to move his fingers again, she pushed at his shoulders.

"No, please, I need you," she said, her voice breathy and a little desperate. He chuckled softly.

"Yes, princess," he said against her throat.

She was reaching for him, pulling his boxers down, and her panties disappeared. He had only a moment to enjoy the feel of her hand wrapped around him before his body took over. He mounted her, the desperation to be inside her taking control of him.

He knew he should hold back, take it slow, but after a lifetime of rigid control, he just didn't have anything left. Not when it came to Jen. He knew he should stay sharp, that their enemies could find them at any moment.

Jen was a sapien, and he knew the law. They got one night. And he was about to spend that one night with her in a bombed out hovel in the middle of nowhere, huddled together in sleeping bags.

But this magnificent, fierce creature wanted him, and he was powerless to deny her. When the time came, he would give her up if ordered and deal with the pain and heartbreak. They were old friends of his.

He knew all of the reasons why he shouldn't give into his feelings for her, but he just didn't care anymore.

As he slowly slid into her, feeling her slick heat and the muscles of her pussy grip his cock, the chain that held his control snapped.

* * *

Jen gasped as Theron penetrated her. She'd known that erection was big, but the feel of it as it entered her left her feeling stretched. But he moved slowly, and her body was able to accommodate him.

He kept most of his weight on his elbows, but the knowledge of his body above her had her lost in the feel of him. She'd always loved the weight of a man on her, but Theron was hands down the biggest she'd ever been with, his body completely blocking her view.

For a moment she felt overwhelmed by the sensations, by the size of him, by some feeling she couldn't name that was bouncing around in her chest and head.

Then, suddenly, he began to move.

He had been holding back before, she realized, as the full power of his body was unleashed. The buildup had been like the long, clattering chain pulling her to the top of a roller coaster. Well, they'd just dropped into the first exhilarating freefall.

As his arms tightened around her, his hand clamped just below the base of her neck and pressed her to his exquisite chest. She parted her lips and scraped her teeth over the skin where his shoulder met his chest.

His groan of pleasure spurred her own arousal higher. Her nails dug hard into the steel cables of his back, and the ride got wilder.

The friction of his cock as he moved inside her was kindling a fire within. As the heat started to spread, a delicious tension began to build. Her internal flames ignited with a rush, and she was suddenly coming apart. The orgasm could only be described as explosive, and she arched hard against him, her head snapping back.

She caught sight of his face, and he was gorgeous, his blonde hair slightly damp with his sweat, falling over his brow. His eyes were open and on her. She fell into those blue depths as her orgasm continued to grip her, spinning her out of control. Sensation danced along her nerves like the tiny embers that rose from a fire, shooting up and floating back down again.

Suddenly, his eyes squeezed shut and he held her fiercely, his erection jerking inside her. A rush of liquid warmth filled her as his body continued to pound into her.

His movements gradually slowed, until he was mostly still. His muscles still spasmed and trembled around her. Reaching up, she brushed his hair back and looked into his eyes. They were intense and hot.

They stayed like that for a long time, just breathing, just feeling. She stroked his hair back from his brow and let her caress linger on his stubbled jaw. It had been so long since she'd shown tenderness to anyone or anything. She knew she shouldn't, but she held his gaze. If he saw the tiny sprouting feelings that she didn't have a name for, then so be it.

Within the blink of an eye, his expression changed, becoming concerned.

"Oh, gods, did I hurt you?"

She laughed.

"You're adorable," she said, patting his shoulder.

"I must be crushing you," he said, moving like he was going to get off her. She held his shoulders.

"I like the feel of you," she said as she pressed her palms against his back and watched the firelight dance over the perfect angles of his face "More than the feel of you."

She met his gaze, let him see her desire.

"I like you," she whispered, a little smile tugging on one corner of her lips. "All of you."

Something dark, like a slamming gate, moved in his eyes. He looked away and withdrew from her body, withdrew his heat. He moved so quickly, like he was desperate to get away from something disgusting. She suddenly felt very cold.

Theron stood and moved slowly around the fire, his naked flesh glowing in the firelight, his muscles thrown in sharp relief by the shadows. There was a rustling as he dug in her pack. Something landed in her lap. He'd tossed her a package of wet wipes.

"So you can clean up," he said, not even looking at her. His eyes were on the floor. She just stared at the plastic package.

What. The. Actual. Fuck?

Theron bent and retrieved his boxers from where they'd landed on the floor in their mad scramble. He pulled them up and covered himself. His T-shirt was next, falling into place at his waist. He bent again and scooped up his pistols, one in each hand, before moving to sit by the fire.

Without looking at her, he said, "I'm going to stay up. You should get some rest."

Jen stared at him in stunned silence for a moment, ice creeping along her veins, freezing her and leaving her hands and feet tingling and numb. Part of her wanted to question him, talk to him. Why was he shoving her away? But the words wouldn't come. In silence, she lay down in the sleeping bags, which seemed so frigid now, and curled on her side with her back to the fire.

Chapter 11

Stupid. Stupid. Stupid.

Theron stared into the flames, silently cursing himself. How could he have been so stupid?

He'd been prepared to deal with the fallout of escalating their relationship, he'd even been prepared to deal with his own feelings, but he wasn't ready for what Jen showed him. This wasn't purely physical for her. Jen cared about him. The shy vulnerability mixed with want he'd seen in her eyes had called to something in him, something that was desperate to answer.

He'd screwed up bad.

She didn't know their law. She didn't know that this was all they'd be allowed. She was a seer, but she was still a sapien. He was a mage. They'd be separated one way or another. Either the brass would pull them apart or his name would end up on the Wall of the Fallen, like most of the other mages. And Jen was going to get hurt. She'd already been through so much, a lot of which he'd put her through, and he was going to add to her pain.

Guilt poured through him, hot and nauseating.

He'd failed again, in so many ways. After he'd lost Jas and Bren, he'd sworn that he would never fail like that again. But he'd just put Jen in needless danger. Anything could have snuck up on them while he'd been distracted. Why was he so dangerous to the people he cared about?

He couldn't save his best friends. He hadn't been the one to save his sister. He should stay as far away from Jen as possible if he wanted her to survive.

There had been shock and anger in Jen's eyes as she'd turned her back to the fire and curled up in the sleeping bags. He was already hurting her. But maybe a little pain now was better than the pain she'd experience if they kept going down this path. It didn't matter that the feel of Jen in his arms, his erection buried in her pussy was the best thing he'd ever felt in his life.

He should have told her there could never be anything real between them. Given the way they'd started out and everything that had happened, he hadn't let himself hope for anything. Her desire had been a surprise, a beautiful surprise, but not one he'd prepared either one of them for.

Guilt squeezed his gut again and he shut his eyes to shut out the sight of Jen laying there, curled up in the sleeping bags, the messy remains of her black braid snaking down over the golden skin of that elegant neck.

Theron's grip tightened on the pistol in his right hand, but he was careful to keep his finger off the trigger. He was going to make it up to Jen by keeping watch over her tonight. And he was going to keep his hands to himself for the rest of this gods forsaken trip, damn it.

He focused his eyes on the gap in the wall and opened his other senses, alert to the smallest indication that something was approaching.

* * *

Jen awoke to the most heavenly smell. Thinking it was the

remnants of a particularly lovely dream, she opened her eyes slowly, only to find that it was real. A steaming plastic mug sat on the ground beside her and it was filled with what could only be—

"Coffee!" she shouted. Snatching up the mug, she sat up and brought the mug to her nose, inhaling deeply.

The sleeping bag slipped down to her waist and she remembered that she was naked as the cold morning air hit her breasts. She yanked it back to her shoulder and took a tentative sip. It was hot and wonderful.

"Theron, you made coffee, you're the—"

She'd been about to say, "You're the best," but then the events of last night came rushing back to her and she fell silent. As her cheeks flushed red with humiliation, she remembered that she was angry at him.

"Sorry, it's just instant," he said. "I found some packets hiding in one of the bags."

He raised his own mug and took a sip. He'd dressed in a T-shirt and fatigue pants, his gun belt firmly in place and another pistol holstered under his arm. The term "Loaded for Bear" came to mind.

He'd also shaved at some point, she noticed. And he had the unmitigated audacity to look really good. You couldn't even tell he hadn't slept. Fucker.

"I should probably get dressed," she mumbled. Without even asking, he rose and handed over her bag. Damn him.

"I'll give you a minute," he said, heading over to the SUV where he started loading a few things in the back.

Using the sleeping bag as a shield she scooped up the package of wet wipes Theron had tossed her last night. Pulling one of the hated things out, she swiped under her arms, repeating the process in other areas with fresh wipes. When she was done, she threw the wipes into the fire and watched them burn with a tiny bit of glee.

Digging out her last fresh set of clothes from her bag, she was dressed in record time. She shook out the tangled mess of her braid and ran her travel brush through it before she twisted it back into a new braid. A couple minutes with her toothbrush and she was ready to rock.

After she rolled up the sleeping bags, trying hard the whole time not to think about what they'd done in them last night, she threw them and her messenger bag in the back seat and climbed in the passenger seat without saying a word.

She was going to keep her fucking mouth shut today. Conversation was reserved for people who hadn't humiliated her down to her core. God, how could she have been so stupid? Why had she come on to him? He was gorgeous, yes, and touching him felt really, really good, and the sex, well...but that move had been beyond dumb. And he'd certainly shown her the error of her ways with his quick exit last night.

What had she done wrong? Was she that bad at sex? Was she that out of practice? Maybe he didn't appreciate the come on? Why had she told him she liked him? He seemed like a total alpha, maybe he needed to be the one to make that move? Had it been when she'd dropped her guard, just a little, and let him see her feelings in her eyes?

Stop it! She ground the mental wheels of her thoughts to a halt and threw it in reverse. Anger flowed through her and wrapped itself around her like a familiar, well-worn blanket. She would not think that way. He would not make her think that way.

If he didn't like the way she got down, if he couldn't deal with feelings, well, fuck him.

Crossing her arms over her chest, she settled back in the passenger seat and prepared herself for a long, quiet ride to Damascus.

* * *

Great, she was furious with him.

As Theron climbed into the SUV, Jen was already buckled in, arms crossed, jaw set, eyes straight ahead.

Honestly, he didn't really blame her. He was still pretty angry at himself over last night and the danger he'd put them both in because of his lack of judgment and control. Not to mention the fact that he had violated, like, the second most important rule for mages.

Rule number one: don't turn evil.

Rule number two: don't form romantic attachments to sapiens. Seer or not, she wasn't a mage.

Before he shut the vehicle's door, he concentrated on the fire, which was still burning low in the makeshift fire pit. He called the energy of the fire back into him, spooling it up and feeling the warmth of it take up residence in the vicinity of his diaphragm. When there was nothing left but blackened wood, he closed the door and fired up the SUV.

Jen wasn't talking to him, and that was fine. He'd need his concentration for the road today. They were heading into extremely dangerous territory. Several hundred miles of empty desert separated them from their destination.

It was this part of Highway 1 between Rutba and Damascus that had earned this stretch the nickname Highway to Hell. They might run into bandits, ISIS operatives, Syrian rebels, and who knew what else between here and the border and Theron wasn't so sure Jen could talk their way past them again, especially without anything left to bribe them with because he wasn't about to hand over any of the guns, ammo or explosives in the back.

Her press badge might get them past the border guards. They both had their visas in order, thank the gods. Even though his was fake, he wasn't worried about a Corps forgery standing up to scrutiny.

It was probably the stretch of highway between the border and Damascus that he was most worried about. Reports had ISIS and rebel forces clustered to the north around Homs and Aleppo, but that was no guarantee. A Syrian fighter plane had been shot down by shoulder mounted rocket just a couple of weeks before near the Ad Dumayr air base, which their route took them right by. Reports were unclear if it had been rebel or ISIS forces that had taken the shot.

Rebels they could deal with. Jen had told him during the drive from Fallujah to Ramadi, that she had spent a few days with rebel forces some months ago in the northern part of Syria while she'd been reporting a story. She could drop some names if she had to, even had a couple of cell phone numbers for top commanders if they needed them.

Theron wasn't sure how much time had passed, but when he looked over at Jen, she'd fallen asleep, her obsidian lashes resting against her cheeks. He was suddenly worried that she hadn't gotten enough sleep. Hell, she probably hadn't gotten any real sleep for several nights. Totally his fault. Add it to the ever-increasing tally of things he had to feel guilty about.

He suspected, though, that Jen hadn't gotten a healthy amount of sleep for a long time before he'd shown up. Those dark circles had been there when he'd met her.

That would change when they got where they were going. Once they were safe behind the underground walls of the Citadel, he'd make sure she got enough rest. Without warning, an image popped into his head. It was Jen, and she was lying in a bed. His bed. The one back at his ranch in Texas.

Her black hair was loose, spilling over the white cotton of his sheets and pillows. The sheets clung to her in all the right places, because in this vision she wasn't wearing anything but the soft smile that curled her lips as she slept. She looked like she was having a nice dream.

The enormous bed was made of polished cedar posts and was big enough to sleep a family of five normal sized people, or just him, with enough room for one other person. Maybe. If they were small.

Jen is small, his brain pointed out unhelpfully.

Shut up brain, where were you eight hours ago when I needed you? he thought.

Being overridden by his other, smaller, more southern brain, that's where.

Theron sighed and looked at Jen again, pushing away his little fantasy. It was really dangerous to start thinking like that. Forbidden, in fact.

He understood why relationships between sapiens and mages were forbidden. Secrecy was the only way the shadow races would ever survive. Mages, shifters, and especially vampires just weren't prolific subspecies. Nature liked balance, and the low birth rates were the trade off for the physical advantages.

As for the elves and the fey races, immigration was tightly controlled from the Fey Realms for the same reason, to maintain balance.

If the sapiens ever found out about the existence of the shadow races in their midst, the sapiens would vastly outnumber them. And judging by sapien history, every member of the shadow races would be rounded up and, best case scenario, locked up. He didn't even want to think about the worst case scenarios, but he'd seen documentaries about the Holocaust, and that was what sapiens did to their own people.

And because the mages were not a prolific subspecies, it had been stressed to them all from day one that it was their duty to keep the bloodlines pure and produce more little mages to keep the balance and provide future protectors for the shadow races.

Jen would never see his ranch and she'd certainly never sleep in his bed. He wouldn't be the one to worry about how much sleep she got or if she was eating enough.

When they got to the Citadel she would become a well-guarded, highly-paid instrument. The Council would insure that she was never unprotected.

Theron knew that it wasn't safe for her out in the world on her own anymore, but he worried about how her new life was going to sit with her. Jen was strong, fiercely independent and valued her freedom. She'd never go anywhere without an armed escort again, and she was going to hate that.

She'd probably have to give up reporting. He really had ruined her life.

Better this than dead, he told himself, keeping his eyes locked on the faraway desert horizon. He was almost convinced.

Chapter 12

"For the fifth time, I'm her private security contractor," Theron told the border guard, tapping his passport and visa paperwork.

Jen translated his words to Arabic, but used more diplomatic language and hoped the guard couldn't pick up on the snark in Theron's tone.

She and Theron were standing outside the SUV in an open parking lot, the squat building that housed the border guards, the checkpoint and a few offices set back several yards. Six guards were searching the SUV and Jen had to fight the urge to keep glancing nervously at the vehicle. Theron assured her that the compartments hiding the guns, ammo and explosives were undetectable. She hoped he was right. If those guards found the small arsenal they were carrying, they'd be arrested and charged with gun running. In the current political climate in Syria, they'd be lucky to see the inside of a jail cell. More likely, they'd be shot on the spot.

"If you are a journalist, where is your equipment? Your laptop? Your cameras?" One of the guards asked.

"We ran into some trouble on the road outside of Rutba," she said, opting for the truth because it was easier. It might even gain them some sympathy. "I had to give the bandits my equipment in exchange for passage."

"That's what you get for traveling through Iraq. That place is a shit hole full of thieves and rapists," the guard spat.

Syria wasn't exactly Disney World these days either, but Jen wisely kept her mouth shut, just nodding respectfully at the guard. God, how many checkpoint guards had she talked her way around in the past five years? More than she could count and enough to have it down to a science by now.

She'd covered her hair with her scarf, put on a very small, closed-mouth smile, kept her eyes downcast, her voice small and polite. It galled her, but she made herself small and totally non-threatening, calling the guards *sir*, keeping her hands in plain sight, and doing her very best to appear less than she was.

No Pulitzer finalists here, no sir. Little ol' me ain't no threat to your horrible, corrupt, gas-your-own-people regime. Nothing to see here. Move along.

One of the men searching the SUV signaled to the guard, moving his index finger in a circle in the universal "all clear" sign.

The guard nodded, stamped something on a clipboard, and handed Theron a handful of papers.

Jen mentally sighed in relief, but didn't let her body language change. This was the first piece of good luck they'd had this whole trip. Thank god for small miracles.

"The road from here to Damascus was clear of insurgent activity as of yesterday," the guard told Theron, even though, as far as he knew, Theron didn't speak Arabic. Jen valiantly kept her eye roll to herself.

"No doubt it is due to the brave efforts of soldiers like you," she told the guard. Her voice was sweet, but the words tasted like tar in her mouth. The Syrian Army were a bunch of jackbooted thugs, in her opinion. If they only knew some of the things she'd written under her pen names about the atrocities committed by this man's comrades, not only would they not let her into the country, they'd probably beat her to death.

She smiled again and bowed as she backed away toward the passenger side of the SUV. If what the guard had said was true, they might have a good shot at making it to Damascus safely. She tried to remember, were there three or four checkpoints between here and the capital?

A twinge in her side brought her attention to the still-healing gashes over her ribs. What had been an annoying, itching dull ache was suddenly ratcheting up the pain scale. She put her hand to her side and felt wetness. Looking down, she realized her shirt and the waistband of her khakis were soaked with blood.

* * *

Theron heard Jen's boots stumble on the gravel and looked back in time to see her clutch her side, bright crimson blooming in the spot where she'd been scratched by the zombie. Fear clutched his chest for a moment at the panicked look in her eyes.

"Jen?" He was at her side in an instant, and good thing, too, as her knees chose that moment to give out.

As gently as he could, he caught her and lowered her to the ground. Ignoring the looks from the border guards, he wrenched her shirt up to examine the wounds.

Gashes that had been scabbed over and well on their way to healing were open, the skin peeled back, and blood was pouring in a steady stream. At their worst, those gashes should have been oozing wounds. This wasn't normal. This wasn't right.

"Theron? What's happening? I don't feel right." Her voice was weak and a little shaky. Her body trembled beneath his hands as he took the pulse in her wrist.

He concentrated, opening his mage senses as he examined the wound. A red, sparkling haze seemed to hover over her skin, flowing in and out of the gashes over her ribs. Damn it! Blood magick.

"It's going to be okay." His voice was surprisingly steady, but his heart was pounding, and cold sweat had broken out over his skin.

He hooked his arms under her knees and behind her shoulders, carrying her slight body toward the SUV. She was so light and delicate. Fragile.

Thoughts raced as he ran for the vehicle. She'd bled in the fight with the zombies. They'd gotten some of her flesh with those gashes. It didn't take a genius to see they had used that material in a blood spell. How could he have overlooked that? Why hadn't he warded them both?

Blood magick was incredibly dark magick, only one step up from human sacrifice. It was one of the reasons mages were so careful to keep their blood from falling into anyone else's hands. Blood could be used to track you, but it could also be used to strike at you.

After they'd eliminated the sorceress in Ramadi, the cultists who were after them were probably wary of getting too close. They were too gutless to face Theron directly, so they were striking at them with blood magick like cowards.

This was bad.

Reaching the SUV, he fumbled and managed to get the back gate open without dropping Jen. She was still conscious, but extremely pale and very listless.

"Hang in there," he told her as he shoved supplies out of the way and laid her flat in the cargo area. He climbed in after her and grabbed for the first aid kit. Hands slippery with her blood, he scrambled for the shears and quickly cut her shirt away.

As he did, something stung his left eye and he closed it. Wetness trickled down his cheek. Reaching up, his fingers came away with fresh blood. A wave of dizziness washed over him. He'd been hurt in that fight, too. They had his blood. And now the wound over his eye that had healed up was gushing just like Jen's.

This was one hell of a nasty spell and he was going to need one hell of a ward to block it. Wards were easily his weakest area of magick and one he rarely practiced. He was more of a kill-it-with-fire kind of guy. Wards were for mages that couldn't handle a standup fight.

Still, he'd been drilled on protection wards like everyone at the Academy. Sifting through his memories, he came up with one that might work. He yanked Jen's messenger bag over and riffled through the contents. Luckily, she had a permanent marker in there, thank the gods.

Pulling the cap off with his teeth because of slippery hands, he began to draw on the left side of Jen's chest, just over her heart. The black ink was stark against her skin, pale from blood loss. The intricate and looping knots of the ward flowed from his mind, drawn out by some combination of adrenaline and fear.

Fat drops of his own blood dripped on her shoulder and arm and he tried to ignore it. In less than two minutes, he had the ward nearly complete. As he closed the last loop together, connecting the ward as one continuous line, he poured his own energy into the ward, powering it up. The magick snapped into place over her with a green flash of light.

A deep sigh escaped him as he saw the red glow fade around her wound and the bleeding slowed to a trickle. He worked quickly with the first aid kit, hauling hemostatic bandages and gauze pads out. He had her wounds taped up and bound with an elastic bandage in what had to be record time, fear for her making his movements quick and sure.

"You're bleeding," she murmured, her eyes half closed, but her breathing even.

He stripped off his own shirt and made quick work of drawing the same ward on his chest. His bleeding stopped, and the wound started to close on its own.

"What happened?" Jen asked, confusion knotting her brow.

"I'm so sorry, Jen." Guilt tore through him, a physical pain in his chest. "I screwed up. They got your blood during the fight in Ramadi and used magick to attack you. And me. It didn't occur to me that they would go for blood magick."

"What's with the fancy temporary tattoos?"

"Protective wards. I should have thought to put them on us a long time ago."

She reached out and touched his hand.

"It's okay. We're safe now, right?" she whispered.

A sharp knocking sound at the back window brought his attention around. It was one of the border guards.

He used his faster-than-sapien speed to get his shirt back on and Jen covered with a mylar blanket from the first aid kit, to hide the blood more than anything.

"Is everything all right?" the guard asked as Theron opened the back gate.

"Fainting spell," Theron said in halting Arabic. "She's a little dehydrated and hasn't been eating as much as she should."

"I thought I saw blood," the guard said.

"It's mine," Theron said quickly. "She scratched me when she passed out."

He indicated the closing gash above his eye.

"Head wounds bleed a lot," the guard said, nodding.

"We're fine," Theron said. "We'll be on our way in just a minute and get out of your hair."

The guard nodded, clearly uninterested in getting involved.

* * *

It was nearly midnight when Theron pulled the SUV to a stop and killed the engine. While they hadn't encountered any rebel or ISIS forces, each of the checkpoints (it turned out to be four) had been a lengthy ordeal nearly identical to the border checkpoint. Two thousand questions about who they were, where they were going, what they were doing and what had happened to her equipment.

And then they'd hit the traffic.

Before they'd even reached the city, traffic had slowed their progress to a crawl. Once inside the city, it had been even worse. What roads remained undamaged were gridlocked by other vehicles.

The blood loss had left Jen drained and she'd slept most of the way. Theron had fought the urge to constantly check her pulse.

Now, Jen looked around groggily, clearly confused about where they were. Her color was coming back fast now that she wasn't being attacked by blood magick.

"Where are we?"

"We're staying in a hotel tonight," he told her. "We'll get access to the Corps outpost here in Damascus in the morning."

The portal to the Citadel was in a heavily fortified building near the heart of the city. The portal itself was a rarity in the magickal world. It was one of a dozen static access points scattered around the globe. Because mages couldn't open portals, unlike the elven and fey races, they depended on these static portals to be able to operate effectively. Each of the portals remained open at all times, providing instant access to the Citadel. For that reason, they had to be carefully guarded.

Because of the long-running conflict in Syria, the Damascus team was shorthanded, so the portal was behind about seventeen layers of physical, electronic, and magickal security and located deep underground.

He'd notified Desic of his plans, and his trusty handler would let the Damascus team know they'd be there in the morning. They were almost home free.

"I'll grab the bags," he told Jen. "Cover your hair and face as much as you can."

She didn't question him, thank the gods, but just wound her scarf around her head and put on a huge pair of sunglasses.

As she looked up at him behind the shades, he said, "Good enough, let's go."

Moving through the parking garage, Theron was alert to movement, signs of danger, unusual scents, anything that might signal someone was coming for them.

They made it to a set of glass double doors without incident.

As they entered the lobby of the hotel, Jen froze in her tracks, and even with most of her face covered, he could read the shock running through her.

"You're kidding!" she hissed at him. "We are not staying at the fucking Four Seasons."

"Yes, we are." His voice was calm, his smile in place and he didn't look at her, his eyes roaming the sumptuous lobby. "They have a high security wing."

He didn't want to tell her that after all he'd put her through, he wanted her to have one night of safety and luxury. It might very well be the last night they had together. He was going to make sure she took a long, hot bath, pigged out on room service and slept like the dead while he watched over her.

Theron gently took her arm and led her to the desk while she looked around the lobby. He was pretty sure she didn't realize her mouth was hanging open a little. It had probably been a while since she'd seen anything like this.

The floor was inlaid marble in a rich cream color. Giant marble pillars in a soft tan rose to the ceiling and the curving grand staircase was done in marble and glass.

As they approached the desk, a clerk spoke in English, "Checking in, sir?"

"Yes. The reservation is under Steve Rogers."

Jen snorted as she tried unsuccessfully to stifle a laugh. He'd hoped she might catch the Captain America reference. He might as well embrace the inside joke that had sprung up between them, especially if he could use it to make her laugh.

Everything had already been taken care of, thanks to Desic, and the door to their suite was shutting behind them in a matter of minutes.

On the way up, he'd observed enough of the touted security measures to make him feel slightly more at ease. Their room was well positioned, not directly next to the emergency stairwell, but close enough that they could make a quick escape to the parking garage if they needed to.

He moved through the room, scanning for anything out of

the ordinary, and gave Jen the all clear. She was still standing by the door to the hall, her bag on her shoulder, her big sunglasses still hiding her eyes.

Theron moved to her side, careful to move slow so as not to spook her.

"You okay, princess?"

She nodded silently, looking around the two bedroom suite. He had to admit, the place was pretty swank. Everything was done in tones of cream, tan, and gold. The carpet was so plush his combat boots left impressions of the treads behind in the pile. There was even a fireplace against one wall, done in white marble veined with gold.

If anything screamed decadence, it was a fireplace in the desert.

The bathroom was all white marble, with gold plated fixtures. When Jen turned on the lights, it was almost blinding.

"Which bedroom do you want?" he asked.

The bedrooms were on opposite ends of the suite, with doors facing each other across the vast sitting room. Without saying a word, Jen wandered over to the one on the right, tossing her bag on the white duvet that covered the bed.

A frown drew his brows down. She was being far too quiet. Her shoulders were slumped just a little and a deep exhaustion seemed to drag at her arms. He didn't like it.

Striding into the bathroom, he turned on the taps in the lavish marble tub, with a heavy emphasis on the hot water. There were bottles of various potions along the rim of the tub, but the labels were in Arabic.

Opening one, he sniffed. It smelled like flowers and had the consistency of liquid soap. He upended it beneath the rushing tap and was satisfied when bubbles began to froth on the surface of the water.

Leaving the water on, he turned on his heel and marched back to where Jen was sitting on the bed. Those glasses were still in place, making her face hard to read. Her arms were crossed and her spine was curled slightly, like a weight was pressing down on her shoulders. She looked so tired, like she hadn't slept in a month.

The lines around her mouth looked deeper than they had when he'd first pulled her out of that hotel in Baghdad.

Not knowing what to do, he stood in front of her and said, "Your bath is running."

She didn't even nod. He'd put her through hell the last few days, he couldn't really blame her if she didn't want to talk to him.

Moving very slowly, he knelt and reached up to gingerly pull her shades off. She didn't meet his eyes at first, but was just staring straight ahead.

Theron snapped his fingers in front of her nose and she focused on him, but those normally laser-like dark eyes looked dull.

"What's up?" he said softly. "How are you feeling?"

She took a deep breath and looked away, turning her shoulders away, folding her arms more tightly across her stomach. One hand rested against her injured ribs.

"It's over," she said, her voice nearly a whisper.

Her hand was cold as he took it in his own. She didn't seem to notice that he was touching her.

"What's over?"

"This. Everything. My life. My old life, I mean. I don't know. I just don't know." She didn't look at him as she spoke, her gaze locked on the wall, seeing something he couldn't. "I'm not making any sense."

Theron had seen this before. More than a few times after a difficult mission, operatives went a little wonky. During the mission they were rock steady. It was only when they got someplace safe that they got the shakes. It was like they could only really process what had happened when they were in total safety. And, in his experience, it could hit the person like a ton of bricks.

Shit, that's what was happening to Jen. For the first time in days, she could stop long enough to process everything and she was vapor locked.

"Come on," he said, rising and tugging on her hand. "A bath will make you feel better."

Her eyes locked on his face and she finally looked at him.

"What's it like?" she asked.

"What's what like?"

"This place you're taking me. The Citadel."

"It's about what you'd expect from an underground military installation. It's pretty sterile. But it's not as crowded or as claustrophobic as you'd think. We had a lot of help from the Svarturans and the gnomes to build the place. They're both subterranean civilizations, for the most part, and they know what they're doing."

She nodded like she understood, but he knew she didn't. Her gaze was locked on the middle distance again.

Gently, he took her by the elbow and brought her to her feet. Her gaze drifted to his face again. Gods, she was beautiful.

He looped his arm around the small of her back, pressing her into his side, supporting just a little of her weight and took her into the bath. Hitting the tap, he shut the water off.

She seemed to like it when he told her stuff, so he kept talking.

"Have I told you about the Svarturans? I don't think I have. You might know them as dark elves, but they hate that term, so don't ever use it to their face. The Svarturans and the elves don't exactly get along. I mean, they can work together when they have to, but they're not happy about it."

She sat down on the edge of the tub and he started unlacing one of her boots while she watched him.

"You'll probably meet some Svarturans at the Citadel. They have really dark skin, like printer ink, white or silver hair and pointy ears. And they have kind of pronounced canines, so try not to stare when you see one for the first time."

He slid her boot and sock off and went to work on the other boot.

"They're a matriarchal society, so it makes politics kind of interesting. A friend of mine is actually the exiled prince. His name is Dumeril. You might get to meet him. Watch out, though. He's kind of a flirt, but he doesn't mean anything by it. He actually only dates guys."

He set her other boot aside and tucked her socks in the top of one.

"I'm kind of rambling," he said, running out of verbal steam. "But you're kind of freaking me out here."

Her voice was so quiet, he almost didn't hear her when she said, "Please don't stop."

"I want to give you some privacy," he told her, rising to his feet.

Her laugh was half-hearted and weak, her tone derisive.

"You fucked me last night, I think we're past modesty at this point."

He wanted to correct her. That hadn't been fucking. Not for him. Fucking had been the only thing he'd done up to that point.

Last night had been something else. It had been uncontrollable, unbelievable, a connection that rocked him to his core and spun his world on its axis. He wasn't sure what he'd call it, but fucking would be the last word he'd use.

This wasn't the time to argue about it. There would probably never be a time to argue about it.

Shaking himself, he moved over to the old fashioned vanity and pulled out the padded bench, facing it away from the tub.

"How are the ribs?"

"Scabbed over," she said. "Your ward must be doing its thing. Do I need to worry about washing it off?"

There was a rustle of cloth and the metallic hiss of a zipper. One by one, her clothes hit the floor.

"It'll hold for now. I can redo it when you get out. Might add a couple more for good measure."

He heard the soft splashing as she slid into the water and when he turned to look, she had settled in amongst the bubbles. They were so thick and so many that they came up to her ears.

He almost laughed at the sight, but he stifled it and settled for flashing her a grin. It was a good bet Jen hadn't thought about a bubble bath in years, much less actually sat in one. She pushed bubbles out of her way like she was shooing flies, mounding the foam at the opposite end of the tub and looking slightly annoyed with the stuff, like it didn't have the right to be so exuberant.

Theron watched as she let her head fall back in the water. As she rose, her back arched, and water and bubbles sluiced down her midnight hair. It looked extremely dark blue when it was wet. He wondered if she knew that. He took a mental snapshot of her, hoping he could remember that exact color later.

With a start, he realized that he was supposed to keep talking, but he'd gone silent as he watched her.

"Have I told you about my sister, Alayna?" he blurted.

Jen's gaze drifted slowly over to him, like it took her a lot of effort, and she gave a barely perceptible shake of her head.

"You'd like her, I think. She's bossy, like you, but a lot louder. Has a dark sense of humor, like you. She has this way with people. I don't really understand it. She's disarming, especially with the people that are determined not to like her. She's not very diplomatic, but somehow, everyone that meets her falls in love, in their own way."

Jen just stared at him, so he kept talking.

"She has these teammates, well, they're her subordinates, but they're also her friends. They're so loyal to her, they'd walk through hell and back if she asked them to. And I'm so jealous of that…" He trailed off.

He'd had that once with Jas and Bren. Except, they'd burned to death and he hadn't. No one was ever going to trust him again like that, and rightly so. He'd failed his two best friends in the world.

When he looked up, Jen met his eyes and nodded.

"She's the one I told you about who's probably never going to speak to me again. She's got a," he paused for a second looking for the right word, "man now. He loves her. So, she doesn't need her big brother to look out for her anymore. Not that I was ever very good at it in the first place."

The truth was, he was intensely jealous of Alayna. She had friends who loved her. She had Alex. Those two were beautiful together. In the short time he had seen them together, an intense love had been written in every gesture, every glance between them. When he'd seen Alex put his arms around his sister, it had made Theron hungry for something he'd thought he'd never want.

"She has a pet dragon," he continued.

Jen cocked an eyebrow.

"Those are real?"

Theron let a small cocky smile pull up one corner of his mouth. He knew that would get her attention. Jen was an intensely curious person.

"His name is Z. He's Alayna's familiar. He's got these impossibly black scales and big leathery wings."

"How big is he?"

"About the size of one of those short school buses, not counting the wing span."

"How many dragons are there? You'd think someone would have spotted one and put it on YouTube if they are real."

"We're pretty sure Z is the last one. The rest of them left this dimension a long time ago. Z was a runt and he got left behind."

Jen nodded and trailed her hands absently through the bubbles, creating mounds, towers and spires in the foam.

"Do you have a familiar?" she asked, quietly.

He was just so glad she was talking again, he'd answer any question she asked.

"I was never that lucky. Familiars have a really tight bond with their mages. That kind of bond doesn't happen for everyone. And familiars usually match up with a mage's element. Air mages usually end up with birds. Water mages are partial to sea life or animals that spend some time in the water. Earth mages get dogs and cats, sometimes the odd badger or chipmunk. Fire mages are usually out of luck. Phoenixes are very rare, and not too many animals like fire. Although, reptiles are somewhat partial to fire mages because we run hot. Some of the other fire slingers I know have snakes and bearded dragons and such.

They like to curl up on them, like they're giant heating rocks or something."

A slight smile touched Jen's lips when he said that.

"There it is," he said softly. "I was starting to wonder if I'd ever see that again."

* * *

Jen was disgusted and embarrassed with herself. She had only shut down like this a handful of times in her life. The last time it had happened was when she'd lost the pregnancy.

It was like her hard drive had crashed, she was completely locked up and unable to perform anything beyond breathing and maybe blinking once in a while. These episodes left her unable to make even the simplest decisions. But when she snapped out of them hours—maybe even a day later—she tended to act rashly. It was like all the decisions she should have been making had collected behind a dam. When the dam broke, all those unmade decisions coalesced into a huge wave that went crashing through her life.

The last time this had happened, she'd been booking a flight to Baghdad from her hospital bed before she'd realized what she was doing. She shuddered to think what kind of terrible decision she was going to make this time around.

But, honestly, how much more fucked up could her life get?

She realized with the sudden clarity of struck crystal that she didn't really have a life anymore, fucked up or otherwise.

She had no living family. Her so-called friends hadn't spoken to her in years. Some of her colleagues didn't know her real name, just one of her pen names. The few possessions she'd had were gone and she'd traded the tools of her trade to bandits to buy her safety and the safety of the strange man who sat across from her. The work she'd almost died for was over. She'd never work as a reporter again as long as she was being hunted for her power.

There was a strange kind of freedom in owning nothing, in having no ties, in being no one.

She had no idea what the future held for her. It was like standing in a doorway, looking into a pitch black room and trying to decide if she wanted to live in it.

It was terrifying and exhilarating and lonely all at once.

And then there was this man, this impossible, gorgeous, funny man who controlled fire with his mind and made her laugh until her sides hurt and killed monsters to keep her safe. Maybe this new place she was headed wouldn't be lonely with him. She'd shown him some of the darkest parts of herself and he'd seemed to accept that, but after she'd shared her body with him, shared her feelings, he'd acted like she'd done something wrong. No, not wrong. Disgusting.

She was secretly dying to ask him what had got his panties in a bunch, but she wasn't about to open her mouth and give away the fact that she was thinking about it. In fact, she wasn't thinking about it. She closed the mental image of the way he'd looked last night, first coming inside her, then later as he'd tossed her those wet wipes and sat himself on the other side of the fire, in a little box and wrapped it all in mental chains.

She didn't know why he was being so nice to her now. He was chatting, trying to fill the silence, pull a smile out of her. The gesture was appreciated, but she didn't understand it.

It was hard to admit it, even to herself, but Theron's rejection the night before had hurt. It had taken a lot of courage to open up, to lay out all those dark things on the table and let him look at them, but she had. He was literally the only person on earth she'd told any of that stuff. And then she'd let him into her body.

None of the guys she'd slept with in the past five years had known anything about her, really. They knew what she did, they knew what she wrote, but they didn't know her. That handful of men had fucked her because she was hot and mildly entertaining company, if you enjoyed sarcasm and a razor wit.

Theron had known all her dark stuff, and he'd held her like she was...like she was precious. There had been passion in the way he'd kissed her, the way he'd touched her.

So why had he pulled away suddenly?

Getting answers to questions was her job. And she was very good at it. She had a question to focus on now, and she was going to find the answer. She might not like it when she found it, but she'd worry about that later.

She rose from the water, pausing to let the bubbles slide down breasts and stomach and thighs. Theron's eyes went wide for a split second before he turned away. Now he was a little off guard. Good. All a part of her plan.

She laughed. "Theron, you came inside me last night. I think it's okay if you see me naked."

A blush crept up the back of his neck. He cleared his throat, but he didn't answer her.

Stepping from the tub, she snagged one of the luxuriously plush white towels from the rack beside her. Toweling off quickly, she squeezed the water out of her hair and wrapped it up in the terry cloth on top of her head. Redoing the bandages on her ribs didn't take long. The wounds seemed to be healing faster than normal. She pulled on one of the oversized plush white robes and opened the bathroom door.

A cloud of steam followed her out and Theron trailed in her wake, looking like he was trying to figure out what was going on.

When conducting an interview with a difficult or hostile source, it was always best to start the conversation by putting them a little off balance. Mission accomplished.

The next step was to make the interview subject more comfortable. It engendered a certain amount of subconscious gratitude toward the interviewer.

Jen padded in her bare feet across the soft rug to the bar built into one wall. Opening the cabinet, she found what she was after. A minute later, she wordlessly handed Theron a crystal tumbler with a generous measure of Blue Label whisky.

He met her eyes as his fingers brushed hers. The dark look in those indigo eyes of his made her stomach do a little flip, and she had to remind herself that with Theron, she was literally playing with fire.

She took up her own tumbler of whisky, flashing him a glance over the rim as she sipped. The whisky burned her throat and warmed her from the inside. Something that tasted like courage curled on her tongue.

Theron moved to the window that overlooked a city that sparkled with lights in odd patches because parts of the city still struggled to maintain power. For a moment, she was struck by the dichotomy of her situation. Dozens of stories above a city at war, she was surrounded by luxury and guarded by the fiercest of protectors, while down below, some people didn't have electricity. She shook off the dark thought and focused on her objective.

She put her hand to the glass of the window. "It's almost beautiful from up here, isn't it?"

He nodded without saying anything and cast a sidelong look at her, taking another sip from his glass. He was still a little on guard, but the whisky would probably take care of that soon.

She frowned and looked back at the window. Something was off about it. At her narrow-eyed expression, Theron spoke up.

"It's not a window. It's a high-definition LCD screen with a feed from a camera outside the building," he said, moving closer to her side. "The high security wing doesn't have any windows. Too risky."

She looked up and realized his eyes had been on her, not the window. He was too close, too big. He was taking up all the air, damn him.

Stepping away from the window, she moved to the small sitting area. There was a little couch and two wingback chairs done in dark wood and white silk brocade. She had to fight the urge to fling herself into one of the chairs. Instead, she sat slowly, displaying an ease and nonchalance she didn't feel.

Theron moved to the chair across from her, but he didn't sit. He leaned his forearms on the padded top and cradled the tumbler in his large hands. The casual pose made the muscles in his shoulders and chest bunch beneath his t-shirt. Did he have any idea how delicious he looked?

Shaking off that thought, she launched her initial volley. "Tell me about what's going to happen tomorrow."

Theron was silent a long moment, not looking at her. Finally, he said, "I've already sent word that we'll head to Damascus HQ in the morning. I'll brief the mages on that team about the death cult and what I've found out about what happened to the dead mages in the region. After that, we'll access the portal chamber. There's a lot of security to get through."

He didn't look at her as he spoke, his eyes on the glass in his hands.

"The portal can be a little spooky if you've never seen one. It's bright. Really bright. Lots of colors. But it looks like a tear in reality and that freaks some people out."

"I'm a little nervous about that whole thing. You're telling me, we just walk through a tear in space and we're suddenly on another continent?"

She wasn't actually nervous at all, but she wanted him to think she was. It was more likely to keep him talking.

"Nothing to be nervous about, really. It's the safest way to travel, believe me," he said. "It can be a little disorienting, at least the first few times, but it only lasts a few seconds. People almost never throw up."

She shot him a look and he gave her a sly smile behind the rim of his glass.

"Are you ever serious?" she asked him.

"Sometimes." He wasn't smiling when he said that and his eyes were locked on her face.

Jen took a deep draw on her whisky and as the warmth spread through her, something that felt like calm wrapped itself around her.

"What happens when we get to this Citadel of yours?"

His eyes darkened and again he wouldn't look at her.

"I'm not sure," he said. "And that's what I'm afraid of."

"What do you mean?" she said, genuine anxiety trying to crawl its way into her chest.

He sighed and moved around the chair to sit down. He braced his forearms on his knees and leaned forward. The muscles in his shoulders weren't just bunched from his position, they were tense. He was tense.

Finally, he spoke. "I've sent instructions to my handler that we are not to be separated when we reach the Citadel, but I'm just a ranger. There are a lot of people there that outrank me. You and I might have no say in whether we stay together."

"I thought you'd be glad to be rid of me," she said, laughing a little.

He was silent and she looked back at him.

"It's not like that," he said.

"What is it like, exactly?"

He gave her a hard look that gave nothing away and took a long drink from his glass.

His voice was rough. Jen didn't know if it was from the whisky or something else. "I dragged you into this mess. I've put you in so much danger. What happened today, the blood magick—they weren't trying to kill you. They were trying to slow us down long enough to catch us. I'm going to stick with you until I know you're safe and in as good a place as you can be and then I'm going to put some distance between us. For your safety."

"So this is about your sense of obligation," she said, her voice a little hollow. "It's about your honor."

"It's not just that," he said, his gaze tangling with hers for a moment before he looked away again.

"I'm your burden," she said, realization clear in her voice.

"No," he said emphatically, his voice hard. "You are not that. Never that."

"Then why are you doing this?"

He blew out a frustrated breath and rose to his feet, his steps agitated.

"We need you," he said, running a frustrated hand through his hair. "You don't know how much a seer could help us."

"We need?"

The heat in his eyes as he met her gaze was like the blazing blue of a welder's torch and his jaw was set hard, but he said nothing. Her heart almost stopped at that look. No one had ever looked at her like that.

But he looked away and that heat disappeared like it had never been.

A growl of frustration was crawling up her throat, and she drowned it with a mouthful of whisky. The heat of the alcohol was making her bold, and she miscalculated.

"Why did you push me away last night?"

Theron's head whipped around and he looked momentarily confused at the sudden shift in conversation. Jen's cheeks flared with heat. Stupid. She had jumped to the most important question too soon. Rookie mistake. Her anger was spilling out.

"What?" he asked.

Too late now, she supposed. Might as well forge ahead. She had nothing to lose. Her hands shook a little and she tried to still them against the chair cushion.

She shot up from the chair, agitated and trying to hide her face as she figured out how to move forward after that blunder.

Her back to him, she snapped, "Last night? You know, when you fucked me and pushed me away like I was a well-used whore?"

* * *

Shock exploded through Theron. What the hell?

"It was not like that," he said through clenched teeth. He found himself stomping toward her turned back and stopped.

He'd been horrified by his lack of control. He'd put them both in danger by losing focus. He'd proven today why that was so dangerous. The blood magick could have landed them both in enemy hands.

In addition, he'd violated a key rule that every mage lived by. Banging sapiens was allowed. Falling in love with them was not. Under any circumstances.

He'd been trying to put the brakes on the feelings she was developing. There was no chance the brass was going to condone a relationship. He'd be out of her life in a matter of days, and that was best case scenario.

Are you trying to protect her? Or yourself?

He'd thought she'd been angry about leaving her unprotected and vulnerable to the blood magick, but she was pissed about him pulling away last night. It was the last thing he wanted to do, but it needed to happen.

He'd put her through so much. He'd proven today that he couldn't protect her. There was something forming between them. She was feeling it, too. When they got to the Citadel, there was every chance they would be ripped apart and he wasn't prepared to cause her more pain.

He needed to tell her the score. She deserved to know why he was trying to put distance between them, to squash his feelings. And hers.

But deep down, he knew the reason he hadn't told her sooner. Anger he could handle. But if he told her what he'd kept from her, she might hate him. And that was something he didn't think he could bear.

She turned, anger flaring in her dark eyes, and took several quick steps toward him. They were just a few feet apart now. He could almost reach out and touch her. That was dangerous, but he couldn't seem to make himself move away.

"Why don't you explain it to me, then?" she shouted. "And maybe you should use small words so I can understand, huh?"

Anger flared within him, like a bottle of gasoline had been thrown on his inner fire. He had never implied that she was dumb, he never would do that. He wasn't sure when he moved, but he found himself within inches of her, staring down into her sparking dark eyes.

The words left his mouth before he could choke them back.

"Last night was the best thing that ever happened to me. You have no idea how hard it was to leave you there, all hot, wet, and naked."

"So why did you?"

The words were just falling out of him now.

"I put us in danger. I lost focus. You saw today what that looks like. You got hurt and I could have stopped it."

"You did stop it, Theron. We're safe. You couldn't have known what was going to happen. Unless seeing the future is one of the powers you didn't mention?"

"It's not just that. I lost control last night. You don't understand how dangerous that is for someone like me. The fire is always with me Jen. If I lose control completely, I could hurt you," he paused for a breath. "It's happened before. I make mistakes and people die."

She was silent, but she didn't step back and her eyes didn't leave his face.

"It's forbidden, Jen," he whispered. "I didn't tell you, and for that I'm sorry, but mages are forbidden from being with sapiens."

Her face fell and there was a sad and questioning look in her eyes. "What do you mean?"

Her hand reached out and touched his chest. He was pretty sure she didn't even know she was doing it.

He swallowed hard.

"Sex is allowed. But it can only happen once. Relationships aren't allowed because sapiens can never know who or what we really are. They outnumber mages. If we were ever discovered the sapiens would kill us all out of fear."

She nodded solemnly. She'd lived in a warzone for five years. She knew what sapiens did to each other for no other reason than they disagreed about the minor points of the same religion. What would they do to subspecies like mages and shifters and vampires that had been hiding among them, not to mention dimensional outsiders like the fey and the elves.

"I'm not a normal sapien. Does the rule still apply?"

"I don't know. I'm just a soldier, Jen. We have no control after tomorrow. We'll probably be separated. And even if the brass gives us a pass, my job is dangerous. You've seen that. I've practically got an expiration date stamped on my ass."

He looked down and realized his hand was on her shoulder. When did that happen?

She met his eyes again and for just a second he got lost in those dark depths.

"You said last night was the best thing that happened to you," she said.

"It was," he said softly. Without thinking, he closed the distance between them, pressing into her. "Followed closely by the night before when I held you in my arms while you slept."

The past two nights had shown him what connection was. He imagined it was like getting a couple of hits of the most amazing drug. It was instantly addictive. And it was disastrous. If they continued on this path, they were heading toward a place neither one of them would be able to walk away from without serious scars, the kind of scars that changed, the kind of scars that might kill you eventually.

She reached up and touched his cheek and he closed his eyes at the feel of her.

"Last night, I was feeling things. And I think you were, too. I panicked," he said, his voice rough. "You've lost so much. I didn't want to be one more thing you lost."

Her voice was soft and right beside his ear when she said, " We may not get tomorrow, but we can have tonight. No one ever has to know."

At her words, need exploded within him. He turned his head and captured her mouth, pulling her hard against his body. Her mouth was hungry against his, her tongue brushing his bottom lip and tearing a groan from his throat.

He could let himself have this. He could let himself have her. Just for tonight. Tomorrow, they would figure out how to go on. It might kill him to give this up, but he'd worry about that tomorrow.

For now, he lost himself in Jen's kiss, the feel of her breasts through the robe, pressing into his chest, her intoxicating dark scent as it wrapped around him.

If they only had this one night together, he was going to make it count. At least the digs were nicer than the ones they'd had last night. This was probably going to be their last night together, and he was going to make enough memories to last him for the rest of his likely short life. He was going to drink in every detail and savor every drop.

And he knew just how he wanted to start.

Chapter 13

Jen felt Theron's powerful arms tighten around her, and suddenly her feet were off the floor. She wrapped her legs around his waist without breaking the kiss. The feel of his hard mouth against hers made her head spin.

The heat of him seeped into her, melted away any doubts she had. If they had this one night together, she was going to soak up as much of this heat as she could to keep her warm on the cold nights to come.

She was dimly aware that they were moving toward one of the bedrooms, but she didn't care. Wherever this man wanted to take her, she'd go, willingly, enthusiastically even.

Suddenly, she was falling, and when her back hit the mattress, she bounced, and an uncharacteristic squeal left her throat. She laughed at herself as she flipped her hair out of her eyes. Theron stood at the foot of the bed watching her, his indigo eyes sharp and predatory. As he reached for the hem of her robe, she flashed him a small smile.

He froze, his eyes on hers.

"Oh gods, do that again," he whispered.

"What?"

"That smile. It kills me. I love that smile," he said, his big hand brushing the skin of her thigh, just above her knee. Little sparks of electricity danced up her nerves where he touched her.

"It didn't make an appearance very often before you showed up," she said, pushing up on her arms to put her mouth just a few scant inches from his.

It was his turn to smile, but there was no mirth in it. It was a knowing, sly smile full of dark promises.

Slowly, deliberately, he put those smiling lips to her throat. At the feel of that hot mouth on her skin, she moaned and let herself sink back on the mattress. She wanted to feel him on her again. Last night hadn't been enough.

She pulled at his shoulders, but didn't budge him an inch. In fact, he was moving in the opposite direction, down her body.

His big hands were hot on the skin of her breasts as he slipped them inside her robe. His thumbs caressed the sensitive skin just below her nipples. That, combined with the cool air slipping in through her open robe had her nipples tightening painfully. Her back arched and he caught the sensitive flesh between his teeth. She groaned at the wet suction of his mouth.

Her eyes fluttered closed and she ran her fingers through his hair, holding him against her. His groan of pleasure made her chest vibrate and she smiled again. If she kept this up, her face was going to hurt from smiling.

As his tongue flicked against her nipple, it sent little shocks right to her pussy, like the two were connected. It was unlike anything she'd ever experienced. Of course most of her lovers had spent all of five seconds on her breasts. There wasn't much to the things, so they tended to be an afterthought for most guys, but Theron seemed content to spend all night with them.

But heat and tension were starting to build further south, and she wanted to feel him penetrate her.

She pulled on his shoulders, but again, he ignored her. Instead, he released her nipple and gave her a sizzling look from beneath his copper lashes. There was no smile this time.

His gaze didn't leave hers as he undid the tie of the robe, which had loosened to the point of almost coming undone. He slowly parted the halves of the robe and left her completely bare. His eyes roamed over her exposed body and she felt her cheeks heat.

He hadn't gotten a look at her last night, what if he didn't like what he saw now? Insecurity like this was incredibly rare for her. In fact, she couldn't remember the last time it happened.

Theron kissed her again, right below her sternum and started moving down her body slowly. She reveled in the feel of his lips on her, his tongue stroking her skin. When he scraped his teeth over the sensitive skin of her flank, she cried out and arched off the bed.

As he kissed her hip, she realized where he was headed with this.

"Wait, no, I haven't…" the look he gave her was so intense the breath caught in her throat. Without breaking eye contact, he scraped his teeth lightly over her skin again, right at the top of her thigh.

Embarrassed, she said quietly, "I haven't had a chance to trim in a while."

Okay, it had been like two weeks. She hadn't been expecting to take anyone to bed, and Baghdad wasn't exactly covered in places offering bikini waxes. Still, when someone was going to be visiting, she liked her house to be neat.

His look was hard when he said, "You think I care about that?"

His fingers brushed over the short dark curls at the apex of her thighs. Those fingers stroked lower, just short of her clit, which was crying out for his attention.

"This is the most beautiful thing I've ever seen," he said, his voice rough and his hot breath feathering over her inner thighs.

She looked down her body and saw truth in his eyes. His gaze was reverent. As he met her eyes again, he moved slowly, giving her every opportunity to stop him. She didn't.

As he pressed his mouth against her, she moaned and arched, opening herself to him. All thoughts of embarrassment fled and there was only sensation, wet friction, heat, suction.

When his tongue found her clit, she nearly cried out. When he sucked the impossibly sensitive skin into his mouth, she did.

It wasn't long before the tension coiled within her snapped and sent her spiraling into an incredibly intense orgasm. She was vaguely aware of cries exploding from her throat, some of which might have been his name, and she just prayed that the high security wing was well soundproofed.

His tongue continued to move against her, inside her as she came down, little aftershocks making her jerk in his grip. She looked down at him as he sat back and wiped his mouth and she almost came again from the hot look in his eyes. Damn, the man could speak volumes with a look.

As her senses began to return, she realized that he was still fully clothed. Her first instinct was to pull the robe around herself, but instead, she slipped her arms from the garment and left it on the mattress. He rose to his feet and her hands found the hem of his shirt, pulling the tan cotton over his head.

He didn't resist her.

She kissed her way down his bare chest, running her fingertips over the ridges of his hard muscles, first his pecks, then his abs, then the ridges that dipped down into his waistband. When she reached this point, she dropped to her knees and started to undo the button of his pants.

At his groan, she looked up.

"Sweet, gods," he whispered, his breath starting to come faster.

His reverent words brought another smile to her lips. She fumbled a bit with his fly in her excitement to free his erection. She could feel the shaft through the black fabric of his fatigue pants, the ridge of the head evident.

As she freed him, she gripped the shaft and ran her fingertips over his tight balls. A satisfied smile spread across her face at his groan. His eyes closed and his head fell back as she moved her hand up and down, slowly stroking him.

Desperate to taste him, she ran her tongue over the velvet flesh and circled the tip before she slid him into her mouth.

Her name was a low growl in his throat and she would have smiled if her mouth hadn't been stretched around his cock. He tasted of salt and spice and his skin was feverishly hot against her tongue.

She took as much of him into her mouth as she could, but it wasn't anywhere close to all of him. The rest of him, she stroked with her hand, working his flesh. She gently squeezed his balls, and his cock jerked in her mouth.

When she looked up and met his gaze he cursed softly.

She sucked hard and then popped the head of his cock free from her lips, bouncing it against her tongue. When she sucked him into her mouth again, he spoke urgently, "Stop. Wait, I'm going to come."

She wanted him to. She wanted to taste him. He tried to push at her shoulder, but she gave him a look that said he had better lay off. HIs eyes closed, and his head fell back again.

He was breathing like he'd sprinted a mile and it wasn't long before he shouted, his cock kicking in her mouth. The hot taste of him filled her mouth and she drank it down, loving it. When she'd sucked every drop from him, and his shudders had let up, she released him and smiled.

With an impossible speed, he kicked off his boots, pushed his pants down his legs and he pulled her down onto the bed. She sprawled across his massive chest. His big hands maneuvered her hips until she straddled him. Bracing her hands against his shoulders, she pushed back, arching, one hand playing with her nipple as she watched him. The fingertips of her other hand lightly brushed her swollen mouth.

"Gods, you're fucking killing me," he said. "I'm already hard again."

He wasn't kidding. She could feel the rigid length of him against her thigh.

"Jen." Her name was a growl, a plea, a prayer.

* * *

T heron's head was spinning as Jen straddled him. She was completely naked, and all he could do was stare at her. Her long, black hair fell over her shoulders to cover the tops of her breasts. Her skin was gold in the dim light from the sitting room that spilled into the bedroom.

He circled her waist with his hands and his fingertips nearly touched. She made him feel huge and powerful. And the sight of her was making him come undone. When she'd dropped to her knees in front of him and taken his cock in her mouth, he'd thought he might lose his mind. When she'd silently insisted he come in her mouth, he thought he might die.

But this, having her above him, arching her back, touching herself, this was it right here.

He hadn't wanted to come during the blow job, not at first.

He'd wanted to save that for when he was inside her, but now he was glad he had. Because this sight right here would have had him orgasming in a heartbeat. Now, he had a shot at lasting more than a minute.

When she rose up on her knees and positioned the head of him at her opening, his entire body went still and he stopped breathing. But as she sank down slowly, taking him inside her, he groaned so loud, he was pretty sure the chandelier in the sitting room was shaking.

She began to move, rotating her hips as she rose and fell, the elegant muscles in her long legs shifting and flexing beneath her soft skin. He ran his hands over her hips and up to her breasts, memorizing the curves of her.

Her face was pleasure made flesh. Her mouth was swollen, her lips parted, her dark lashes resting on her flushed cheeks. Her breath was coming fast and little breathy moans escaped with each downward stroke of her hips.

The sight of his cock disappearing inside her over and over again was pushing him too close to the edge too quickly. As he watched, her hand drifted to where their bodies were joined. Her fingertips touched her clit and began to circle. As she threw her head back and began to moan, he cursed and had to slam his eyes shut or he was going to come right now.

Without sight, the sensation of her inner muscles gripping his cock threatened to overwhelm him. She was delicious slick heat and friction. He started to draw protection wards in his head to distract himself. He'd always been shit at wards and it was a serious challenge to remember all the intricate symbols, swirls and knots.

Suddenly, her cries intensified, and her pussy tightened around him as she came. His eyes snapped open and the look of pleasure on her beautiful face pushed him right over the edge, the orgasm ripping through him, his release filling her.

He rose off the bed as he came, his arms wrapping around her, crushing her against his chest as she continued to ride him. He buried his face in her sweet smelling hair as she stilled and they both shuddered.

As he pulled back and met her eyes, that was when it hit him. He loved her. Shit. He loved her. A moment of panic fluttered in his chest. He swallowed hard and tried to fight the urge to run again.

This could not happen. This was not happening.

Instead of running, he pulled her against him so she couldn't see his face. He lay back on the bed, tucking her beside him and pulling the sheets and blankets over them. Jen was boneless and heading for sleep. Meanwhile, he was panicking.

He didn't get emotional during sex. Ever. What was wrong with him? More than likely, he was going to have to let this woman go in the morning. The Corps brass was going to take her from him, whisk her into some kind of training, send him onto the next mission.

He might never see her again.

Something inside him screamed at that thought and a distinct ache started in his chest. He closed his eyes and reveled for a moment in the feel of this woman in his arms.

He tried to calm himself, bank his inner fire. He took a long look around inside himself, examining his feelings, picking them apart. In that calm, he examined his heart, mentally poking at it. Something was different about it.

It wasn't his anymore. It was hers. Slowly, over the last few days, it had been taken over, cell by cell, until it belonged to her. He hadn't noticed until the process was complete, but it was and there was nothing he could do about it now.

He looked over in the darkness at the woman asleep in his arms. Jen was a prickly, fiercely independent creature. Would she even want it? And if she did, could they stay together?

It was worth a try, he decided. When they got to the Citadel tomorrow, he'd explain that he needed to stay with her, to help her transition. He was the only one she trusted, he'd explain. She'd never work with them if they separated the two of them.

If the brass wanted her to join them, he needed to be with her. And if their relationship was discovered, it might not be condemned. Jen was valuable. And she already knew about their world. Heck, she was willing to join it. Maybe it would work.

There would be some pushback, he knew. Mages were supposed hook up with other mages so they could make little mage babies and continue to feed the ranks of the Corps. Mages and sapiens were just different enough that they couldn't have offspring.

He didn't care about that. If the brass fought him, he'd offer whatever genetic material they needed to make little test tube mages. He'd even let female mages use his body if that was what it took.

With a start, he realized he'd do anything it took to keep this woman with him.

As he felt sleep starting to drag at him, he made up his mind. When they got to the Citadel tomorrow, he'd get her alone and explain where he was and what he wanted to happen. He hoped she was in the same place, or at least in the same neighborhood.

They were a good team. They worked. They could do this.

His last thought as he drifted off was that come tomorrow night, he hoped he was right back here, with Jen naked, sated and asleep in his arms.

* * *

Jen's first thought after waking the next morning was that the air conditioning in the hotel must have quit sometime in the night because it was sweltering in here. She'd kicked off all the sheets and blankets in her sleep and she was still warm.

Then, she turned her head and realized where all that heat was coming from. Theron was beside her. And he was putting out heat like a stoked furnace.

He was gloriously naked, and the light coming in from this sitting room caught in the fine gold hairs that dusted his thighs, forearms and chest. It glittered along his jaw as he smiled slowly, realizing that she was awake. His eyes opened slowly and in the shadows, his eyes looked almost violet. For just a moment, she allowed herself to stare at those eyes. They were dark blue one minute, purple the next, their true color somewhere between the two. She realized that she wanted more time with him, to study those eyes. The color seemed to shift slightly in different lights, in different moods. She wanted to get to know every shade.

The desire surprised her a little. Even with Trevor, she'd never wanted to know what color his eyes were when he was sad or when he laughed in sunlight. Was she becoming infatuated? She reached out and ran her fingers through Theron's hair watching the light play through the golds, coppers and platinums. It was like watching a candle flame dance in the low light.

His eyes closed and a rumble of pleasure sounded low in his throat, a small smile twisting his lips at the corner.

She'd had crushes before, and those had felt similar to this.

The fascination with the way that he moved, the little details of his appearance, the sound of his voice, it had all the hallmarks of a crush.

She'd never had sex with anyone she'd had a crush on before. Her crushes in high school and college had never looked her way and eventually the crush had been forgotten.

Trevor was the only man she'd ever loved, but she'd never had a crush on him. They'd been a part of the same circle of friends in college, and they'd just slid into an easy relationship. She'd loved him, but she was never fascinated with him, not to this point.

Trevor had been ambitious, charming and polished. He'd known what a shrimp fork was and what kind of wine to order with fish. Trevor was everything she'd thought she wanted back then. They just fit. It was easy.

But she'd never lusted for him.

She'd had men since Trevor. There had been a couple of journalists she'd met at the bar in the Palestine Hotel. They'd been passing through Baghdad on reporting trips back when the war had been wrapping up. They'd connected over drinks and shop talk and the shared experience of their work, but they'd been little more than one-night stands. She knew better than to get involved with another journalist.

There was the Mossad agent she saw periodically. When he was passing through Baghdad or she was passing through Jerusalem, they'd text and meet up, but that was about sex. She wasn't even sure she knew his real name.

Theron was different than anyone she'd been with before, and not just because he was a slightly different human subspecies with super powers.

She liked him. He was funny. Even fake zombies and bandits

couldn't dampen his sense of humor. He was gorgeous and, she had to admit to herself, she had a crush on him. And the sex was phenomenal.

For the first time since her world had come crashing down five years ago, she allowed herself to think, just for a moment, what it might be like to have someone in her life. Someone that she looked forward to seeing and talking with and laughing with and making love with.

The thought absolutely terrified her. After five years of living in war zones, she'd thought she'd left fear behind. This mad run from Baghdad to Damascus had shown her that she could be scared again. It had also shown her that she could laugh and get pissed off and feel something for a man again.

His words from the night before slammed back into her. He'd told her they couldn't be together. It was forbidden. His people would offer her protection and a purpose, but they wouldn't let her have him. They were probably going to have to say goodbye today.

Wouldn't it just figure that the first person she'd been able to open up to, to develop some feelings for, would be the one she couldn't have? That was the story of her life, putting her heart and soul and energy in the wrong places, with the wrong people. She'd given her heart to Trevor; he'd thrown it away without a backward glance. She'd given her energy to her newspaper back in LA, and they'd thrown her away without a thought. She'd pinned her future on a child that hadn't lived. And just as the stone shell around her heart was cracking, she was going to have to harden it again and say goodbye to Theron. Today.

Chapter 14

Theron scanned the hotel room one last time as they prepared to check out and head to the Mage Corps Damascus HQ. As he shoved items in his bag, he noticed a metallic glint among the sheets. Sifting through the material, he came up with a chain. It was Jen's phoenix necklace. Looking closer, he saw that the little clasp had broken, and it had come off during their session the night before.

Knowing what the necklace meant to her, he palmed it. Jen was waiting by the door, her bag over her shoulder. He stepped up next to her and slipped the necklace in her pocket, fully intending to tell her that he'd found it and that she should get it fixed.

As he opened the door and his mouth to tell her, Jen's body went ridged and her eyes wide.

The necklace forgotten, he asked, "What is it?"

"It's one of them," she said, nodding to an empty space in the hallway. A frown creased his face before it dawned on him. A spirit. She was seeing a spirit.

"What do you see?"

"She's young, maybe twenty-one. Long hair, short dress, high heels, lots of makeup. She's beautiful. She looks like a model."

Jen stared for a moment, frowning. She waved a hand at empty space, like she was trying to get someone's attention.

"Hello?"

After a moment's silence, Jen turned to him.

"She's spacy. Too far gone to see me. They get like that if they've been around awhile," she said. Jen started heading off down the hallway. "Nothing we can do here. We should go."

They hit the elevator and he punched the button for the garage level. He'd set up automatic checkout with the front desk last night so they wouldn't have to go through the lobby. They were so close to home free now; he didn't want to risk even the smallest exposure if he didn't have to.

The ride to HQ was a silent one. The perpetual traffic jam that seemed to clog the streets of Damascus 24/7 was in full swing. Jen just stared out the window, seemingly lost in thought. He wondered if she saw spirits walking the streets. Her encounter in the hotel hallway had unnerved him a little. He'd almost forgotten about her gift. For just one night, they'd been two people, not a mage and a seer.

He wondered if she saw spirits often. Were they everywhere? What was it like for her to walk among the living and the dead at once?

When he got her to the Citadel, it should be relatively spirit-free. Deaths happened very rarely there. Members of the Mage Corps weren't particularly long-lived, but they died in the field. The ones who made it to the healers wing of the Citadel usually survived.

And if he took her to his place? He'd had the house built, and no one had ever died anywhere near it, that he knew of. The place could be a refuge for her. It had always been one for him. And if she was there, for him it would be paradise.

After what seemed like an eternity, he pulled the SUV up to a loading bay that was nestled in amongst the buildings of old

Damascus. The heart of the old city had narrow streets that barely allowed their vehicle to pass, and the rolling door set back from the sidewalk had just enough clearance to get the monster inside.

He pushed a call button on the side of the building. When he heard the click and the slight hiss of static that said the mic was live, he said, "It's Blackwell."

There was a long beep, and then the door began rolling back. Theron pulled the SUV forward and hit a ramp that descended steeply into the darkness. The bottom of the ramp opened up in to an underground garage level. Fluorescent lights flickered to life overhead, and a metal door opened to the left. A petite brunette woman stepped through and waved them over.

Theron parked the hulking SUV and killed the engine. The mage looked vaguely familiar, but he couldn't pull a name from his memory.

"Welcome to Damascus HQ. I'm Bridget," she told him as he opened the driver's door and hopped out. Jen was climbing down from her side and looping the strap of her bag over her shoulder.

He reached out and shook the other mage's hand. She was solidly built, but the top of her head barely reached the middle of his chest. Curly brown hair fell to her shoulders, and green eyes met his. The energy around her marked her as an air mage, and her scent was that of a cold mountain wind, with the hint of something underneath it that he couldn't place.

Theron could swear he'd seen her somewhere before, but he couldn't place it. She looked like maybe she was about his age. Maybe they'd been at the Academy together?

"As my handler probably mentioned, we need to use your portal, Bridget."

"Of course," she said, turning for the door. "We'll get you back to the Citadel in no time."

* * *

Jen trailed behind Theron and Bridget as they entered a brightly-lit corridor lined with rooms. They were dozens of feet underground, but these rooms looked like living quarters. There was one full of guns and other weapons, an armory maybe? Some of the rooms were set up like offices.

Theron spoke to Bridget. "Is Jeremiah around? I haven't seen him since the Academy, I was hoping to say hello while I was in the neighborhood."

As the little brunette turned her head to look at Theron, something shimmered in the air near her shoulder. Jen blinked hard. Maybe she'd gotten less sleep than she thought? Or perhaps it was a trick of the light? Or some mage thing she didn't understand? These people were magic, after all.

She caught the shimmering again, this time next to the woman's ear and it made Jen uneasy for some reason.

"The Commander and the rest of the team are conducting reconnaissance in the north. We've had some reports of unusual activity around some of the smaller outlying villages."

"And they left you to hold down the fort?"

"Something like that," Bridget answered.

Jen pushed away her uneasiness. She was just tired and worn out from the last few days. They'd be in a safe place soon, and she could relax and get some sleep.

As they turned the corner, the hallway opened up into a huge space full of gym mats, punching bags and free weights, a training center of some kind.

"We'd better head back to the Citadel then. I'll see Jeremiah the next time I breeze through," Theron said.

"Of course, sir."

Jen spotted a figure in the far corner of the gym. It was a large man, with shaggy brown hair and broad shoulders. The hollows of his cheeks were deep, and dark circles ringed his eyes. His eyes seemed to burn.

The man tilted his head as she made eye contact, considering her. His eyes widened in surprise. Suddenly, in the blink of an eye, he was beside her, and she nearly screamed. Bridget had said she was the only one here. This man was a spirit.

Theron sensed her distress and turned, took her hand.

"You okay, princess?"

"Just a spirit. Startled me."

The spirit's mouth was moving, but there was no sound that she could hear. She tried to read his lips to make out the words. There might have been "Stop" and "Them" and something looked like "Killer," but he was talking too quickly. And the spirit wasn't entirely solid now, blinking in and out as he tried to speak to her.

"Your handler wasn't kidding when he said she was a seer," Bridget said, a note of awe in her voice.

"She's the real deal," Theron told her. "Jen, what does he look like?"

"Brown hair, yellow eyes, tall, big shoulders. He's trying to say something, but I can't hear him. He seems pretty agitated."

"That sounds kind of like Jeremiah," Theron said, his eyes narrowing on the space in front of Jen like he could see the spirit if he tried hard enough."

"He's still alive," Bridget said emphatically. "It could be Ven. We lost him during a raid on a nest of rogue ghouls a couple of months ago."

The spirit was pointing at Bridget and shaking his head. Anxiety rose within Jen. She wished she could understand the spirit, but if it had been a few weeks, and this spirit might be starting to space. Sometimes spirits were only images or disembodied voices or just cold spots after a while.

"I'm sorry," she told the spirit. "I can't understand you. I wish I could help."

Theron looked uneasy. "We need to go, Jen."

The spirit looked angry and frustrated. He pointed at Bridget and drew his index finger across his throat in the universal symbol for kill. Jen's blood froze. She was rarely frightened of spirits, but this one scared her. He was angry, and angry spirits were the only ones—in her experience—that could affect the physical world.

"Bridget, I'm not sure it's safe for you here."

"What do you mean?" the female mage asked.

"I mean, this spirit is angry," Jen said. "And he seems to be angry with you."

Bridget suddenly looked nervous.

"I think we need to get you on your way," she said, turning and heading for the door on the opposite side of the gym.

"What about him?" Jen said.

Theron took her hand again and said, "Once we get things settled, we'll come back. You can talk him into heading into the light then."

Jen nodded. Glancing over her shoulder she could see the spirit was following them. His yellow eyes were rimmed in red, like blood. His stare was unnerving. Jen wanted to ignore him, but she couldn't help but watch as he followed in their wake.

At the far end of the gym, Bridget opened a door that led to a stairwell. They descended, Bridget in the lead, Jen bringing up the rear. Ven, the spirit, leaned over the railing above, watching.

She'd lost count of the flights of stairs when they reached the bottom and another door. Bridget pulled a set of keys from her pocket and unlocked it. Before she reached to open it, she traced a pattern on the door. It wasn't any pattern that Jen recognized. As she watched, an image flared to life, glowing yellow over the door. It looked like a giant Celtic knot, with runes around the edge, that had been drawn in liquid sunlight. As quickly as it had appeared, it faded, seeming to sink into the paint covering the door.

"Protection ward," Theron said in her ear. "Bridget is disabling them so we can enter the room. Let her go first. There could be more of them."

Jen nodded and watched as Bridget opened the door to reveal darkness that was shot through with shifting colored light. There was a sense of vast space as they stepped through the door and Jen saw what must be the portal about fifty feet away.

It was like a dancing rainbow had taken up residence in the rock wall of an immense cavern. The portal itself was a rough oval maybe six feet wide and maybe twelve feet tall. The ceiling of the cavern disappeared into darkness above them.

"Sir, do you mind getting the torches?" Bridget asked.

* * *

Theron turned his concentration to the torches hanging in sconces around the room and called his inner fire, sending it outward until the torches caught, one by one, around the cavern. The rock walls around him rose maybe seventy or eighty feet above them, the ceiling forming a perfect dome.

Bridget moved forward and disabled two more wards set into the floor between the door and the portal. Theron eyed the shifting colors of the rift that would take them straight to the Citadel. No one alive was sure how old the portals were or exactly how they had been created. The prevailing theory was that ancient mages or elves or fey or some combination of those races had tapped into the naturally occurring energy at key points around the globe to create a network.

The ancient city of Damascus had sprung up around this place. Humans were drawn to places of power, just naturally gravitated there. All the thousands of people hundreds of feet above them had no idea that a portal to the remote Rocky Mountains existed right below their feet.

He snagged Jen's hand and stepped forward.

"It's going to feel a little weird at first," he told her. "When you step in the portal, you're going to feel like you're falling up, down, and sideways at the same time. It only lasts a few seconds. Just hang onto my hand, and we'll be there before you know it."

Jen nodded at him. She looked a little pale, a little nervous. That spirit upstairs had rattled her. He stroked her cheek with his thumb and looked into those dark eyes.

"Everything is going to be okay. I'll be with you every step of the way," he said. There was a lot more that he wanted to tell her, but that could wait until they got to the Citadel.

Bridget was standing by the portal waiting for them, the shifting rainbow lights catching in her hair and seeming to sparkle in the air around her. As he stepped forward, Bridget raised her hands, palms out in front of her.

Jen's hand was ripped from his grasp, and she flew backwards, slamming into the rock wall with a sickening thud.

What the fuck? Shock ripped through him as he turned back to see Bridget step toward him. Her eyes were locked on him. He called his fire in his left hand and went for the .45 on his hip with his right.

The air was suddenly ripped from his lungs in a rush, like he'd been kicked in the diaphragm. He choked, trying to pull in another breath, but his lungs wouldn't inflate. The fire in his left hand went out as he lost concentration, his brain screaming for oxygen. He raised the pistol in his right hand and pointed at the air mage.

Why was she doing this?

A hurricane gale slammed him from above and knocked him flat, grinding his cheek into the rock floor of the cavern. His gun hand was pinned to the floor, useless. Straining with all the strength he had, he couldn't raise the weapon an inch.

His lungs were really burning now, and he still couldn't draw a breath. The only sound he could hear was the howling wind that was pinning him and the sound of his own pulse hammering in his ears. He tried to twist his head around to see where Jen was, where Bridget was, but he couldn't move.

The downward pressure lessened slightly, and Theron could feel himself being pushed along the floor, the stone grinding into the skin of his face. He gritted his teeth as his vision began to go dark. As consciousness faded, he tried to call out to Jen, but there was no air.

Chapter 15

Theron regained consciousness slowly, swimming up out of the darkness into flickering torchlight and shifting rainbow colors. He could breathe again, so that was an improvement. Pain registered in his shoulders and wrists. Looking up, he saw that there were manacles around his wrists, which were connected to chains bolted to the rock wall.

Shit, that wasn't good.

Frantically, he looked around for Jen. He found her sitting against the rock wall about twenty feet from him. Bridget was several feet away, holding his gun on Jen. Anger flared within him, and he jerked against the chains. They chimed in a very distinct note, and Theron's heart sank.

Fairy steel. The chains were made of fairy steel. It was virtually indestructible. There was no way he would be able to melt it or break it.

At the sound, Bridget glanced his way, but kept the gun on Jen. The little air mage was smart. Given an opening, his Jen would jump her. He wouldn't be surprised if she still had her switch blade on her. But Bridget was an Academy-trained mage, and she was more than a match for Jen hand to hand, not to mention she had mage strength and could, apparently pull the air right out of your lungs.

"You traitorous bitch," Theron spat.

"Oh, good. You're awake," Bridget said. "I was starting to wonder."

The mage pulled a radio from her belt and spoke into it, "He's up."

Theron scanned the room for weapons. And took inventory of what he had on him. She'd taken his guns and his belt, but he could feel the knife he kept in a sheath in his boot. And his backup cell was in his other boot. Thank the gods. He might have a shot at getting out of this.

The door on the far side of the cavern opened, and a tall elf with dark hair stepped through. Ritual scars on his face and neck marked him as a member of the death cult. Damn it. They were inside the Corps, maybe inside the council itself. He had to warn someone.

Odds were good the entire Damascus team was dead. The Corps had no idea. And the bad guys had a direct path into the Citadel with this portal.

"Kahler, are we ready to open the portal?"

"It will take a few minutes."

"Then get started. We need to be on our way."

Theron's thoughts spun. If they were opening another portal, it meant they weren't going to the Citadel. And given the energy in this place, it would be easier to open a portal wherever they wanted to go, even the Fey Realms.

The elf—Kahler she'd called him—began the process of tearing open the fabric of reality. A blue portal, smaller than the fixed one across the room, began to appear, opening slowly.

"Why are you doing this?" Theron asked Bridget, trying to stall, trying to keep her talking.

"Isn't it obvious? Your girlfriend here is the key to bringing the walls down."

There was a manic light in Bridget's eyes that Theron hadn't seen before, and there was an edge to her voice that made something twist in his gut. She was insane.

"The walls?" He needed to keep her talking.

"Between this dimension and theirs."

Something stirred in his memory. Something from the report his sister had filed after she'd killed Dominic and destroyed the revenants he'd created. The vampire had been driven mad, but in his final moments, he'd been lucid. He'd told Alayna as he lay bleeding from the mortal wounds she'd inflicted that creatures from another dimension, he'd called them demons, had been speaking in his mind, directing his actions, driving him to try to destroy an entire city by unleashing hordes of the ravenous dead.

That kind of terror, pain, and sorrow would weaken the walls between dimensions, in theory, Alayna had said, allowing gods knew what to invade the Earthly Realms.

They currently sat under Damascus, a high energy point that was already prone to portals, and had been embroiled in a vicious and deadly war for years. If anyone were to stage a dimensional invasion, this was the place to do it. They could decimate this realm's defenders with little effort.

"Eurus. The one who put out the bounty. The one giving orders to the death cult. That was you, Bridget," Theron said, realization dawning.

The question that occurred to him next was even scarier. Why was he still alive? Bridget didn't need him, just Jen.

Jen's voice penetrated his thoughts. "There's something on her, Theron! I can't quite see it, but there's something—"

Theron's heart stopped as Bridget pulled the trigger, and a

gunshot echoed through the cavern, as loud as a cannon blast.

* * *

Jen screamed. Fiery needle points of pain lit up her right cheek. The bullet had struck the rock wall maybe twelve inches from her head, and the tiny shards of rock were in her skin now.

"The next one goes in your kneecap," Bridget told her.

Jen was sure of it now; there was something hovering around Bridget. She'd catch random shimmers in the air, a hint of something that was there, yet not there. In addition, Bridget periodically tilted her head or nodded as if she was hearing something speak that no one else could see.

The spirit she'd seen earlier was standing by Jen's side, glaring at Bridget, looking back and forth between her and the mage, tight-lipped, watching with his burning red eyes.

Jen wanted to cry. They'd been so close. Then Bridget had slammed her into the wall and suffocated Theron until he'd passed out. She'd been too dazed to do anything but watch as she'd chained him to the wall, wrenching his arms painfully over his head.

Where were they going to take her? What were they going to do to her? What were they going to do to Theron?

Jen thought about rushing Bridget, forcing the mage to shoot her dead. Dying here was better than whatever they had planned for her. But what about Theron? Could she sacrifice him, too?

"It's ready," the dark haired man with the pointed ears said, standing to the side of the new glowing blue opening in the rock wall.

"On your feet," Bridget said.

"No," Jen said.

"Move your ass or I will shoot him," Bridget said, pointing the pistol at Theron. So that was why she'd left him alive. He was leverage over her. And it was going to work.

Fear choked her and she heard herself begging, "No, please!"

Theron's voice reached her. "Don't do this, Bridget. It's not too late!"

"It's been too late for a very long time, Blackwell," Bridget said, venom in her voice, her words coming too fast. "The Mage Corps isn't worth saving. The Council and the sapiens aren't worth saving. The demons are coming, and there is nothing anyone can do to stop them. You can work with them and live or stand against them and fall. I plan to live."

"You're working with demons, Bridget. Do you really think they'll keep their word?"

When she remained silent, he continued. "Please Bridget, I'm begging. Don't take her. You can have me, but don't take her."

Bridget tilted her head and seemed to be listening to something. A sick smile spread across her lips.

"You care about her."

Theron hesitated for a moment, his eyes going to Jen's for a heart-stopping moment. His gaze snapped back to Bridget's.

"Yes," was all he said.

Bridget fell silent again, nodding as if agreeing with someone. Finally, her eyes slid back to him and that sick smile got a little wider.

"They have a deal for you."

Bridget moved away from Jen, far out of range. Jen could try to tackle the crazy bitch, but she'd have plenty of time to bring that gun to bear before she could get to her. Taking a bullet wouldn't save Theron.

"We're going to Hell and there's only one way you can follow her," Bridget said. "Willingly take your life and follow her to the other side."

"What?" Theron's voice held a dangerous edge. His gaze flashing between hers and Bridget's.

Bridget moved up next to Theron, the gun pointed at his throat.

"Hell is just another dimension folded in on top of this one. I've been there. It's an incredible place," she said. "Jen will live in her human body, serve the demons with her power. Your spirit can go with her, stay by her side. It would be perfect, don't you see? Don't you see the gift they're offering you both?"

Bile rose in Jen's throat.

Hell? They were going to drag her to Hell? And they wanted Theron to die and go with her?

"Don't do it, Theron!"

"Shut up!" Bridget screamed.

His gaze locked on Jen's for a second, considering something.

His voice was strong when he said, "Not a chance. I don't make deals with demons. And you shouldn't either, Bridget."

From over by the glittering blue dimensional doorway, the dark-haired man spoke up. "This portal is becoming unstable. We need to go."

Jen spoke up.

"I'll go with you. Just let him live."

"Jen, no!" Theron shouted.

Jen rose to her feet and headed toward the portal. "I'll do whatever you want, just please let him go."

Bridget moved toward her without taking the gun off Theron. The mage grabbed Jen's arm and dragged her the last several feet to the portal. Jen could feel something, some force, dragging on her, pulling toward the portal. Anxiety rose within her, like ravens flapping giant wings in her roiling stomach.

She kept her eyes on Theron, willing him to understand why she was doing this. A roar filled her ears and the dragging sensation became stronger. Another step and she knew in her bones the portal would take her.

"I'll find you, Jen!" Theron shouted at her.

She felt herself starting to fall. Time slowed.

She saw Bridget raise the pistol and point it at Theron, but the mage seemed a mile away and at the same time inches from her. Jen heard Theron's voice.

"Jen, I lo—"

The gun barked. Twice. Jen could swear she saw the bullets flying as time continued to slow. The last thing she saw was blood spraying as they both hit Theron in the center of the chest. Darkness closed around her then, and she was falling.

* * *

Theron's heart pounded impossibly loud in his ears. His breath sawed in and out of his chest. The bullets had left trails of fire as they tore into his chest, but now ice was starting to seep in behind them.

He was alone. He'd watched Bridget shove Jen back through the portal just as she'd shot him. Kahler followed them a few seconds later.

He'd told Jen he would find her. He'd tried to tell her he loved her.

He swallowed hard and looked down, watching red bloom across his shirt. He hadn't worn his vest. He'd thought they were safe. And he hadn't worn his vest.

His breath was coming faster now, in little gasps. He closed his eyes and tried to slow his breathing, tried to remain calm. He could feel the bullets, feel the pathways they had cut through his body. They'd missed his heart, and somehow missed both lungs, but he was losing blood fast.

His hands were still chained above his head, so there was no way he could apply pressure to his wounds.

He still had his knife, but that was no good against fairy steel. Cutting off his own hands wouldn't help the blood loss situation.

The cell phone! It was in his boot. There was a chance he could call for help.

He tried to raise his boot to where his hands were chained above his head, but he wasn't that flexible. Settling his weight in the manacles, he lifted both feet off the floor and let himself hang. The fairy steel manacles bit into his wrists, but the pain helped him focus.

His heart began to pound, and his vision started to go dark around the edges as he slowly bent at the waist, raising both legs until his body hung like a teardrop, his boots near his wrists.

Consciousness started to slip, and his boots hit the concrete. If he'd known he was going to be in this situation, he'd have stretched this morning. He laughed a little to himself. That was a bad sign. He was starting to lose touch.

What he needed was a way to stop the bleeding. He didn't have healing powers. Only water mages or a whisperer, like his sister, could do that.

Fire could cauterize a wound, but his own fire would never burn him. It was a fundamental survival mechanism, and he knew of no way to bypass it. It was the same mechanism that kept his stomach acid from eating through his own guts or the one that kept his immune system from attacking his own cells.

He eyed the torches. While he'd lit them with his inner fire, they were burning on their own now. His inner fire wasn't the only fire he could control. He called to the flames in the torch nearest him, caressing them with his mind, learning their shape, their intensity.

Fire had never burned him. Even when he was unconscious and his best friends were burning beside him,

But he'd never commanded it to burn him. It had never occurred to him to try. Fire was his element. It lived within him, would it obey him this time? The ice was spreading out from his chest, he didn't have much time. Summoning all his concentration, he felt his consciousness slipping around the edges. If this failed, and he passed out, he'd bleed out before anyone found him.

Counting to three in his head, he called the fire to him. It leapt across seven feet or so, and a tongue of flame touched his shirt. He willed it to catch. The cotton of his shirt caught a few inches above the hem, little flames beginning to lick their way up his chest.

He poured every ounce of his concentration and magick into willing the flames to burn him. Searing heat and pain bloomed against his skin. It was an entirely new sensation, and he welcomed it.

Fear, anger, pain, despair, they all became fuel for that fire. Theron poured it all into the flames until it became a living thing made of his will.

He directed the fire that was consuming his shirt, concentrated it, shaped it like a scalpel. And sent it tunneling inside his body along the pathways the bullets had cut.

He heard himself screaming as the pain devoured his consciousness.

Chapter 16

Consciousness came roaring back to Jen and every muscle in her body tensed and jerked, her brain still thinking it was falling through space...and time? And dimensions?

Where the hell was she?

Well, she might have answered her own question with that one.

Jen rolled onto her side and felt a surface that was as smooth and hard as glass beneath her, but it rose and undulated in odd patterns. Obsidian. She was lying on a field of volcanic rock. Above her, the ceiling of a massive cavern that echoed the one in Damascus rose above her. In an eerie parody, the cavern was lined with guttering flames. However, these were not torches. The flames shown an electric blue and looked more like gas sconces.

The air smelled strongly of sulfur and hot metal. It reminded her of the volcanoes she'd visited in Hawaii. Bridget, the bitch who had dragged her here, was standing a few dozen feet away, gesturing like she was speaking to someone. The shadows hung heavy in the cavern, the odd sulfur flames not casting much light.

"You are needed back in the Earthly Realms, Bridget," a female voice said. "But you cannot return to Damascus. You did well to bring us the seer, but those rats who command the corps of mages will discover what you have done. Kahler will insure that you are transported to a safe location. You must return and prepare the way for us."

Bridget had her back to Jen, and she couldn't see the mage's reaction. If Jen had anything to say about it, that traitorous backstabber would be dead on the ground before she went anywhere.

Jen stayed her homicidal impulses and stayed where she was, feigning unconsciousness. She'd seen what Bridget had done to Theron, first suffocating him and then slamming him with hurricane-force winds. Jen was no match for that kind of power, but she was a patient woman.

"I understand," Bridget said. "Just tell me where I'm needed."

Eventually the bitch would turn her back at the right moment, and Jen would avenge Theron. At the thought of him, her chest clenched painfully. Oh, god. She'd watched the bullets hit him, watched the blood spray. He hadn't been wearing his tactical vest. The slugs had torn right through the thin cotton of his shirt and into his flesh. Both had hit his chest, one high, one low.

He was probably dead by now. Jen had no idea how long she'd been out. He'd been chained in that cavern. There hadn't been anyone else in the building, Bridget had said. If Jen had to guess, those other teammates were either dead, incapacitated, or in on the plan.

Jen balled up the pain and shoved it to a corner of her chest. She'd deal with it later, if she lived long enough.

"You've done good work here, Bridget," the female voice said. "Stay safe. We need you."

Bridget moved to the far side of the cavern and disappeared.

As far as Jen could see, she was alone, but she'd only heard Bridget's footsteps leaving. Probably a good idea to stay unconscious awhile longer, then.

"I know you're awake, seer," the voice echoed through the cavern, sounded bored and slightly annoyed.

Well, shit.

Jen opened her eyes and sat up slowly, her body aching like she'd been beaten. Casting her eyes around the flickering blue and purple shadows, she couldn't see who had spoken. A frisson of terror chased its way through her chest, but she pushed it into the same corner she was keeping her pain, grief and anger over Theron. That corner was getting a little full.

"Who are you?" Jen asked. "Show yourself."

A form moved slowly out of the shadows. She looked human. In the electric blue light of the sulfur flames, her hair looked light blue, so it was maybe blonde in normal light. Her face was like something out of a fashion magazine for teenagers, with big eyes, a cute little nose that turned up at the end and full, glossy lips. She looked to be no more than twenty years old.

She wore a simple dress that was probably white in normal light.

"I'm Lillith," the woman said, a brilliant and seemingly genuine smile lighting up her beautiful face. "You must be Jen."

* * *

Theron came awake and heard someone moaning, the sound heavy with pain. He wished whoever it was would shut the hell up so he could get some sleep.

With painful realization, he recognized his own raw voice.

His wrists were numb, but the joints in his elbows and shoulders burned. Those sensations were like tiny, flickering candle flames next to the inferno of his chest.

His shirt was gone and his skin was painfully blistered and burned. Two twin paths of liquid heat blazed through his chest. It all came back to him. He'd cauterized his gunshot wounds and passed out. The fire must have continued to burn until it consumed his shirt.

It had burned him. He'd asked it to. Damn, that really hurt. He'd never been burned before. As a fire mage, he wasn't even sure it was possible. Apparently, it was if he passed out while his shirt was on fire.

He took deep breaths to try to gather his thoughts around the pain. On the bright side, at least he wasn't bleeding anymore. And his pants hadn't caught fire. That was definitely a plus.

HIs next step would be to get out of here before someone hostile showed up or infection or shock set in and killed him.

He eyed the shackles over his head and the chain that was anchored with a metal bolt into the rock wall. No way he could burn through it. He didn't have that much juice yet.

Theron needed help. Badly.

He remembered the cell phone in his boot and tried to lift his feet and legs toward his hands. He'd nearly passed out from blood loss doing this before and had failed miserably. Now, he had a better shot, although his blood pressure was still dangerously low, and he saw black spots in his vision as he contorted his body in half.

Regretting that he had never taken a yoga class in his life, he cursed and groaned and ground his teeth until he was able to, miraculously, work the cell free from his boot.

It was an older style phone with buttons instead of a touch

screen. He hated touch screens, and he was very thankful for that now, as he could barely make out the screen while punching the numbers.

He hit the first series that came to his head. He waited until he heard the ringing stop. He wasn't sure if anyone was on the other end or if he'd gotten voicemail.

"Alayna!" he shouted, hoping the speaker could pick up his voice. "I need help!"

* * *

Theron floated in a haze of pain, physical and emotional. He wasn't sure how much time had passed since he'd called Alayna. He wasn't even entirely sure she would come after the way they'd parted last, but she was the only one he could turn to.

He thought of Desic, his handler. If he called him, the Corps would come roaring through that portal. Water mages would heal his wounds in a matter of minutes. They could secure the location. He could warn them about Bridget and her plans.

But there was no way they'd let him go after Jen. They'd put him in chains first. Theron knew the kind of math the Corps brass would do and he knew they'd choose to leave Jen trapped in a Hell dimension before they risked anyone going in after her.

The course he'd chosen was risky, and not just for him, but he found he was willing to risk a lot to get Jen back. He would put measures in place so that if he failed or died, the Corps could still be warned.

But first, he needed help.

As if on cue, he heard a male voice say, "You look like shit, Blackwell."

Theron's eyes snapped open and he stared into the violet eyes of Dumeril D'Nailo, his sister's second-in-command.

Dumeril was a Svarturan. His skin was inky dark and his teeth shone impossibly white as he flashed Theron a smile, his long canines giving him a slightly wolfish appearance. His long silver hair fell to the middle of his back, but was done in intricate war braids at his temples.

His sister's team medic was dressed head to toe in black fairy leather that was almost as dark as his skin. A pack was slung over his shoulder, his kukris were strapped to his back and he had twin .45s on his hips.

"Not that I'm not glad to see you," Theron said, his words coming slowly, exhaustion evident in every word, "but where is my sister?"

Dumeril ignored him and stood on his tiptoes and craned his neck to see the manacles that held Theron's wrists. Nodding to himself, he turned to rummage in the pack and came up with a set of tools. In less than a minute, Theron heard a snick, and he fell to his knees as the only thing holding him up was released.

"Alayna couldn't make it," Dumeril said, putting his lock picks away and pulling a med kit free from the pack.

Worry creased chased through Theron's gut. "She okay?"

"She's fine. It's been three months since her way-too-near-death experience."

"Then she's still mad at me."

"She is not," Dumeril said, pulling antiseptic and bandages out. The gel spray that Dumeril hit him with burned as it touched his raw skin and Theron saw black spots around the edge of his vision. "She understands you were just following orders. We all were."

"Then why isn't she here?"

Dumeril eyed him hard before he finally said, "She's pregnant."

"What?"

"I told her I didn't want her to risk the portal jump. She's only about six weeks along. In these early days I don't like her walking up the stairs, much less riding rifts in space-time."

Theron was still stunned at the revelation that his sister was carrying a child. Until a few months ago, that was not an option on the table. She was a whisperer who was destined to die young. Male mages wouldn't touch her, which had been just fine with her big brother, and she hadn't wanted to risk leaving a child motherless. Her job was still extremely dangerous, and Theron thought she hadn't changed her mind about the no kids thing.

"Wait a second, who's the father?"

"Alex."

"He's a sapien, Dumeril. He's a nice guy, but he can't overcome basic biology. Sapiens and mages can't have babies. So she must be banging a mage on the side."

"Trust me when I say that she's not with anyone else," Dumeril said emphatically. "She only has eyes for that man. Unless you believe in immaculate conception, Alex is the father."

"It's impossible."

"I ran the tests myself."

"No way," Theron said. "There's just no way. How could this happen?"

"When confronted with the seemingly impossible, I generally find that the simplest explanation is true. The simplest explanation in this case is someone be lyin'."

"I'm exhausted here and not in real great shape," Theron said. "Who's lying?"

"The Council," Dumeril said. "I think they've lied to the mages for years about the impossibility of offspring between sapiens and mages. The Corps wanted to insure a steady supply of little mages to feed the ranks. They want purebred, but they'll take mutts if they can get them. I bet they've been taking half-mage babies born to sapien mothers for centuries, wiping the mother's memories. And the half-breeds born to mage mothers, well, the moms probably convince themselves a mage is the father, or they're ordered to stay quiet.

"Until Alayna and Alex went and fell in love and broke all the rules," Theron said.

"Alayna has always been really good at that."

HIs sister was going to be a mother. He was going to be an uncle. Shit.

Shit. The blood drained from his face as one thought hit him like a runaway freight train: he and Jen hadn't used protection. The woman he loved could be pregnant. With his child. In Hell.

Terror and guilt gripped him, sending panic skittering over his nerves. He had to take several deep breaths to calm his thoughts, which were spinning faster than the speed of light.

Theron vaguely felt Dumeril's fingers on the pulse in his throat. He could hear the Svarturan's voice echoing in the distance but couldn't make out the words.

"Don't you shock out on me, Blackwell," he heard Dumeril shout. "Your sister will kill me."

The bare skin of his back touched the rough rock floor of the cavern, and he felt Dumeril's hands on his chest. The sensation of ice water pouring over his blistered skin was a relief and cleared his thoughts slightly.

Looking down, he saw the ravaged skin changing as Dumeril passed his healing hands over it, the blisters receding, the color fading from angry red to the tan it had been before. He felt like he could breathe again as his gunshot wounds healed.

Theron wasn't sure how long he lay there with Dumeril running his hands over him, healing his wounds. He only knew that Dumeril couldn't heal his most serious wound: Jen's loss. He had to get to her. Now. They'd wasted too much time already.

"I need to tell you something, Dumeril."

The big Svarturan sat back and looked at him, Theron's serious wounds having been taken care of.

Theron told him everything that had happened, as quickly as he could, about finding a seer, taking her into protective custody, running from the death cult, making it to Damascus, Bridget's ambush.

"They've got her, D. I have to get her back."

Dumeril pointed at him accusingly. "Don't give me that look. I know that look. That's the look of a Blackwell in love. And every time I see that look, some epically bad shit's about to go down."

Theron sat up, moving his shoulders experimentally.

"They opened the portal right over there," Theron said, indicating the far wall where Kahler opened the way into Hell. "Think you could rip it back open?"

"It's not a question of if I could," Dumeril said. "It's a question of if I should. You're talking about strolling into a Hell dimension. You have no idea what the situation is on the ground. You don't even know if there is a ground. Or air."

Dumeril eyed the now empty space where the portal had been.

"I can open it, but it might not spit you out exactly where they went through. Portal jumping is an inexact science on the best of days, and this is far from that. You could end up miles from where their group came through, although that might not be a bad thing. Less likely to land right in the middle of a group of hostiles."

"I'm going," Theron said, adamant. "Figure out a way to get me there."

"Gods save me from Blackwells and their good intentions," Dumeril muttered.

Chapter 17

Jen eyed the hand that was offered. The fingernails were done in a French manicure. The hand was pale and slender and very human looking.

"Who are you?" Jen asked.

"I think the question you really want to ask is, 'What are you?'"

"You're not wrong," Jen said cautiously.

The thing that looked like a woman was silent for a moment before she answered. "I'm a demon," she said, continuing quickly. "But it's not, like, as bad as it sounds, okay?"

"I'm sitting in Hell talking to a demon. How is that not as bad as it sounds?" Jen said, astounded that she was having this conversation. Before she'd fallen for a fire mage, met a genie and fought beside an Egyptian goddess, she'd have blamed all this on a concussion, but now, she knew better.

"I feel like we've gotten off on the wrong foot, and that's totally Bridget's fault," Lilith said, wiggling her fingers in invitation for Jen to take her hand so she could help her up off the floor. "C'mon. Let's get a drink and talk about this."

Jen stood on her own, and Lilith looked slightly miffed that she had refused her help. She wasn't sure she should take anything that was offered here. Her memory conjured pieces of some ancient myth. Persephone had eaten three pomegranate seeds in the underworld, and she had to stay there three months out of the year. Might be mythology, might have the ring of truth in it. She had no desire to spend winter vacation in Hell.

Lilith turned and Jen had little choice but to follow, unless she wanted to stay in this cavern. There was a long hallway, carved from the same black, volcanic rock of the cavern, lit with the blue gas sconces. Eventually, they emerged into the open and Jen's mouth fell open.

They stood on the bottom level of a huge atrium that towered hundreds of stories above them. The entire thing was made of mirror polished obsidian. The same blue lights flickered on the wall.

The spire was maybe a hundred feet around. Balconies wrapped the atrium at every level, extending out over the floor on which Jen stood. Everything was slightly irregular, like the place had been grown from volcanic rock instead of built. The spire twisted slightly as it climbed, and it made Jen a little dizzy to look up at it.

Around the space, dark, vaguely humanoid shapes moved. They looked like shadows that had become three dimensional. As one moved past Jen, she recoiled and Lilith caught her with a hand on her arm.

The demon's skin was pleasantly warm, and she smelled like Armani perfume.

"It's okay. They're just shades. They won't hurt you," Lilith said in her ear.

Jen moved carefully away from the demon so as not to appear as terrified as she was.

"Shades?"

"The spirits of the long dead," Lilith explained. "When they're fresh, they still look like they did in life, but as time goes on, they lose their identity. When they're all used up, they look like this. They're a bit mindless, so we use them for servants until they dissipate completely."

The casual way the demon spoke of what had once been human spirits sounded exactly the way her girlfriends used to sound when they talked about hitting the shoe sales. Lilith sounded the way she used to sound, before her life imploded, dressed like she used to dress, even smelled like she used to smell. Bile threatened to climb her throat and she swallowed hard.

"Let's go. I've got some people I want you to meet," Lilith said, excitement bubbling in her voice.

Jen followed Lilith up stairs and ramps, down twisting corridors. She lost track of their route within the first five minutes. This place was a rabbit warren designed by a madman. She might never find her way out of here and back to the cavern. That was obviously the point.

They passed by a window cut in the obsidian and Jen ground to a halt and stared.

A city of obsidian stretched out before her. There were squat little constructions that looked like giant bubbles of lava had frozen and cooled, with blue gas lights flickering inside. Huge spires rose hundreds of feet in other areas, but were nowhere near as tall as the one she stood in.

Thousands of windows flickered with blue gas lights in spires that reached like skeletal fingers toward a black sky devoid of stars.

The air was warm and very dry, but it wasn't as hot as Jen had thought Hell would be.

"Ahem," Lilith cleared her throat and Jen followed. After what seemed like hours, they arrived at a set of huge, ornately carved doors that opened seemingly on their own as Lilith approached.

The room was vast, with a raised platform at the far end. A massive opening was cut into the obsidian and a balcony extended out to look over the city. The view was dizzying.

Two women, who were dressed similarly to Lilith, in skin tight dresses that hit them mid-thigh and sky-high stilettos, tottered over and started chattering in high-pitched breathy voices. One had curly brown hair, and the other had long blonde hair that was straight as a pin.

They looked for all the world like a trio of gal pals out for a night in the clubs back in LA. They were dressed exactly the way she and her friends used to dress.

The brunette extended her hand in that slightly tilted way that wasn't really a handshake. Jen politely grasped her fingers and let go.

"I'm Jezebeth, but everyone calls me Jezi."

"Nice to meet you." Jen's voice went up on the last word so it sounded more like a question.

"I'm Astaroth," the blonde jumped in. Jen repeated the process with the finger grasp. Her girlfriends back in LA had all done that too, like they'd been afraid a real handshake wasn't feminine enough. She'd never thought twice about it back then, but it annoyed the shit out of her now. "But I go by Asti."

"We're so excited you're here," Jezebeth said.

"You're going to love it! Lili's the best. We got you, girl," Astaroth continued, their voices mixing into a high-pitched chatter that was, if not pleasant, at least familiar.

"Oh my gosh," Lilith exclaimed. "Look at us chatting away, you must be exhausted. Asti, can you get something for Jen to eat. And Jezi, can you get a bath ready in Jen's room?"

"Of course, Lili," Astaroth said. "We'll be right back."

The two women—demons! It was important to think of

them as demons—clicked over to the door in their stilettos and disappeared.

"Love those bitches," Lilith said. "But they can be as dense as a dying star sometimes."

"It's fine," Jen muttered.

"I know this must be incredibly overwhelming for you," Lilith said, her voice gentle. "This is not the way I wanted to introduce myself, but because of Bridget's fuck up, we had to move the timetable up a little."

Jen stayed silent, watching the demon as she paced about, one finger twirling in her platinum hair.

"The truth is, we need your help. You're our only hope, Jen."

* * *

"Have I mentioned that this is absolutely crazy, ridiculously stupid, and an epically bad idea? "Your concerns are noted, Dumeril," Theron said as he adjusted his pack. It was loaded down with supplies from upstairs, protein bars, water, medical supplies, ammunition. He had no idea what he was walking into, but he was loaded for demon bear.

"Remember, the laws of physics don't necessarily apply in the same way in Hell," Dumeril said.

The Svarturan had been talking at him for several hours, first while he healed Theron's burns and the damage from the gunshots, and later, while they prepped. Dumeril had clearly been hitting the books, researching everything he could get his hands on since his first encounter with evidence of demonic influence three months before, back in Austin.

There was surprisingly little information about Hell, and all of it was conflicting. It was almost like no one came back from there. Theron kept going back to what Djinn Bin Jaan had said back at Dreamland. Thought has form.

The demons, they knew more about them. As near as anyone knew, they were beings of pure energy. They fed off human emotions, namely the negative ones like anger, fear and sorrow. They fed from the spirits of the dead, but there was nothing to say they wouldn't do the same to the living. "Just be ready to open the portal once every twelve hours," Theron said.

"I still think I should come with you. What shot do you think you have alone in an alien dimension?"

"I can't risk it. If you're hurt or killed, how do we get back? You're the only one who can open the portal." Theron's jaw clenched so hard it hurt.

Centering himself, he turned to where he'd last seen Jen falling through a portal into Hell. His chest hurt, and his gut churned at the thought of her trapped over there. Gods only knew what was happening to her.

"No time like the present, D." He nodded at the empty space, and Dumeril stepped forward, his hands moving as he searched for the seam where the previous portal had been torn open. That was the thing about portals, they might look closed, but one could never completely seal the tear in space once it was created.

Slowly, a blue pinprick of light formed in the wall. It grew gradually until it was as tall as he was and twice as wide.

This was it. Steeling himself, he stepped forward.

A voice he hadn't heard in years made him freeze mid-stride. "Wait! I'm coming with you."

* * *

Jen had to admit, for a place that claimed to be Hell, the steamy bath certainly felt like Heaven. Too bad it couldn't penetrate the cold spot in her chest that had appeared the moment she watched Theron get shot and hadn't dissipated since.

Was he dead? At least one of those bullets had hit him, she'd watched the blood splatter. Was he dying, even now? Was he in pain?

Would he come for her?

The chattering of three animated demons intruded on her dark thoughts, and she lifted her head, even though the effort took much more energy than it should have.

Lilith, Jezebeth, and Astaroth reclined on separate white couches that were trimmed in what looked like gold filigree. The couches hadn't been there when they'd entered the room, but had appeared out of thin air as the women—demons!—sat down.

"Thought is form," Jezebeth had said by way of explanation at Jen's startled expression. "The energy of your thoughts takes solid form. Emotion makes it particularly solid. You can try it later, but you should relax for now."

Fat fucking chance.

Her bathtub was actually a pool cut into the black glass of the floor. The water was almost hot enough to scald, but it was actually helping her tired, aching muscles. Perfumed bubbles reached to her chin. Beside her on the floor was a plate of bread, cheese, and fruit. Jen had picked at it. The stuff was delicious, but she wasn't particularly hungry.

She listened to the demons chatter amongst themselves. They talked about people she didn't know, but the sounds they made were so familiar.

"Oh my god, I cannot believe she did that. What a bitch!"

"The absolute nerve of him. I hate him!"

During a lull in the conversation, Jen finally jumped in.

"Um, is anyone going to tell me what I'm doing here, exactly?"

She hated how hesitant she sounded, but being around these women had her sliding back into old habits and patterns. Everything became a question, her voice was higher, she felt small. Who was she all of a sudden? The answer was, her old self, from before the implosion.

With a dazzling smile, Lilith turned her full attention on Jen.

"You, seer, are the answer to our prayers."

"How exactly?"

"Okay, it's like this. There's two teams here in Hell. I lead one," Lilith said. "And Falak and his stupid frat boys lead the other."

"Falak?"

"I think your culture calls him Satan or something. Falak is a lot older than that. He is the serpent that seeks to devour creation. And he's a total douchebag who's trying to organize an invasion of your dimension."

"Okay?" Jen said, her voice rising on the end of the word. "And you're Lilith, like the Lilith from the Adam and Eve story?"

"First of all, that story is fucking slanderous," Lilith said, her voice snapping with anger and a well-manicured index finger rising to emphasize the point. "Second, I'm millennia older than that story. I was around when your ancestors were just crawling out of the ocean."

"Gotcha. I sense that topic is off limits," Jen said.

Lilith gathered herself, pasted her smile back in place, and continued. "That bastard Falak is going to rip the walls down between our dimensions and tear your world apart. I happen to like things the way they are, so we're trying to stop him."

"How exactly can I help you?" Jen asked.

"You see spirits," Astaroth chimed in.

Jen gave her a yeah-and? look. "We need spirits to live," Jezebeth supplied.

Jen must have looked confused because Lilith jumped in.

"We live on human emotions, negative ones."

Jen recoiled. "You eat them?"

The demon held up her hands defensively. "It's not like that. We just sort of hang around them while they're all sad and in pain and kind of drink it in. They're in Hell; it's not like they were happy people to begin with."

Jen sat still, staring at the water that covered her hands.

"So, it's like the stories? Only bad people end up here?"

"Kinda," Lilith said. "Only people who think they're supposed to end up here end up here. People know deep down if they're bad or not, and their spirits are drawn here after death. Others make deals with one of our kind, and we take possession when they die."

The words chilled Jen to her core. All the spirits she'd seen throughout her lifetime, had they ended up here? What about the people she'd lost? Her mom? Her daughter, who'd never really lived in the first place?

Theron? Was he here?

Ripples spread out on the surface of the water as her tears fell.

"Oh, honey, don't cry," Jezebeth said in a soft voice beside her. A gentle hand smoothed her hair. "Lili told me you lost your man."

"Bridget killed him," Jen whispered.

"That was a mistake and Bridget will be punished for that, but she had her reasons," Jezebeth continued. "The Mage Corps is corrupt and misguided. The mages are little better than brainwashed slaves. Some of them mean well, but they can't stop Falak's invasion."

Lilith chimed in, "I'm sure your mage is not here, and he wouldn't want you to cry. He'd want you to go on. He was a hero, and he'd want you to do everything you could to save your dimension. We need you to go back to your dimension, Jen. We need you to find the spirits that belong here in Hell with us. If we're going to stop this invasion we need to be strong. We need the fuel those spirits can provide."

"We can't do it without you," Astaroth said, joining the other two beside the pool. "We have no form in your dimension. We can't find the spirits. Only you can do that. Only you can save your world."

* * *

"Xander," Theron said, turning to face his older brother. "What are you doing here?"

Dressed in a black hooded cloak, Xander strode into the cavern radiating dark menace. He pushed the hood back, revealing his jet black hair, which was cut short. His indigo eyes, an exact match for Theron's own, snapped with a frightening intellect and determination.

"Alayna called me in a panic and told me to get here as soon as I could. What's going on?"

Theron filled him in as quickly as he could while Dumeril injected his opinion about the risks of this mission.

"When do we leave?" Xander asked.

"I'm leaving now," Theron stated as calmly as he could. "You're staying here."

"Bullshit! I'm not letting my only brother walk into Hell alone."

Theron sighed in exasperation. Not for the first time in his life, he thought about how much easier it would be if he was an only child.

"Won't the Council miss their personal death dealer?" Theron snapped. Xander was a Wraith, an elite group of mages who served as the Council's assassins and spies. Xander could kill with a touch, and he was very good at his job.

"The Council can suck my dick. Let's go save your girl."

Theron growled, but realized he would never be able to persuade Xander not to follow.

"Fine. Get your shit together."

A few minutes later the two brothers stepped through the portal together. It felt just like any portal jump, that impossible sensation of falling up, down and sideways at the same time.

When the sensations stopped, Theron found that he and Xander were standing on open ground that looked like obsidian, covered by a thin layer of sooty soil. The sky was a shifting grey and black, with something that might have been a sun or a moon trying to peek through the heavy clouds above them.

Cracks in the rock around them glowed with an electric blue fire. It was hot, and the air smelled of sulfur. But there was oxygen. He could breathe.

"Huh, so this is Hell?" Xander's voice reached him. "Somehow I thought it would be...more hellish."

Theron ignored him and looked around. The landscape was mostly flat, with the occasional boulder, ridge, or rise cropping up here and there. It looked like a lava field. In the middle distance, a sharp line of mountains rose like sawteeth. Blue fire shone at several of the peaks, and glowing blue lines trickled down the sides.

"Sulfur must be a predominant mineral here," Xander said at his side. "It glows blue like that when it burns."

"Thank you, Mr. Spock. The real question is how do we find Jen?"

"My suggestion? We head for those mountains and get the lay of the land. Dumeril wasn't kidding when he said we might end up miles from where Jen got dragged through. It doesn't look like there's anything sentient for miles."

It was as good a plan as any, Theron supposed. Without a word, they began to walk in the direction of the mountains, black clouds of dust rising around them with each step.

* * *

Jen sat alone in the room the demons had shown her to so that she could rest and consider their offer. The floors, walls and ceiling were the same mirror finish obsidian that everything else was made out of. A huge four poster bed stood in a corner, covered in gleaming white bedding that looked soft and inviting.

She should lay down and sleep, she knew, but her thoughts were swirling. So, she sat in a white chair by the window, looking out at the dark city below and the flickering blue lights.

Her thoughts kept returning to Theron. Was there something she could have done to save him? Her heart squeezed at the thought, constricting painfully in her chest. Tears welled in her eyes. How long had it been since she'd cried? Before a few days ago, she hadn't thought there were any tears left inside her, but Theron had woken something up in her. He'd made her laugh. He'd opened her up to feeling things again, joy and pain. And he'd made her love him.

Damn it. Why hadn't she told him? Now she'd never get the chance.

Her life was full of missed chances and things that had gone wrong. Everything went wrong. Why had she thought this would be any different?

Suddenly, the hairs on the back of her neck stood up, and her skin tingled. She wasn't alone. Could one of the demons be coming back?

Looking around, fear twisted in her stomach as she caught sight of a figure in the dark corner of the room. Was it one of those creepy shade things? It moved forward, into the light and Jen gasped.

It was the spirit she had seen in Damascus, just before Bridget had betrayed them, the one that had been silently screaming at her.

"I won't hurt you," the spirit said. His voice was clear now, if a little rough. He put a hand out toward her like she was a nervous animal that might bolt at any second. It was a fair assessment.

"I saw you, before," was all she could manage.

The spirit's eyes were bright red, full of burst blood vessels and there were claw marks on his neck that looked like they'd been made by fingernails.

"I was there in Damascus. I tried to warn you."

"I couldn't hear you," Jen said. "That happens sometimes with spirits. I wish I'd known."

"Me too," he said, his voice sad. "I'm Jeremiah. I was the commander of the Damascus team. Before." Jeremiah had probably been a handsome man before his death, if his spirit was any indication. He was tall, well-muscled, with dark hair and eyes. His spirit wore clothing much like Theron had, fatigue pants, tight T-shirt.

"What happened to you?" Jen asked.

"Bridget," the spirit said, his voice shaking with anger and his lips pulling back from his teeth in a snarl. "That fucking traitor. She suffocated me. Used her powers to pull the air right out of my lungs. Attacked us in our sleep. She killed the whole team."

That explained the red of his eyes. Petechial hemorrhaging. It happened when people suffocated or were asphyxiated. She'd seen it before. He must have clawed at his throat as he was dying, leaving those furrows in his neck.

"She came to us from Baghdad a while back. Last surviving member of that team. Now, I realize she probably set them up and got them killed."

That fit with what Rafi had told her about his death.

Jeremiah moved closer and Jen didn't shrink away.

"I saw what happened to Theron. I followed you and Bridget through the portal and hid myself."

"Why would you throw yourself into Hell?" she asked, incredulous.

"I knew Theron Blackwell, and he was a good mage, one of the best. He wasn't in a position to help you and I was. You're a seer, maybe one of the last. And you're the secret weapon the demons need to take this war to the next level."

"Lilith said they're trying to stop the invasion."

"I heard all of that," he said, waving a dismissive hand. "I don't buy that for a minute, and you shouldn't either."

He stepped forward and put a hand to her shoulder, not yet having lost the gestures he'd used in life.

Jen almost fell out of her chair when his hand didn't pass through her shoulder. He was solid!

Leaping to her feet, she backed away quickly.

"How did you do that?"

"You heard them. Thought has form here. Spirits have form. Demons have form. Give it a try, think of something."

She decided on something harmless and turned all her concentration on one image. Holding her palm out, a red rubber ball appeared in her hand. She almost dropped it. The thing was solid. It even smelled like rubber. She threw it at the floor, and it bounced, hit the wall, and traveled through the air until Jeremiah snagged it.

Whoa.

The moment she stopped thinking about the ball, it popped out of existence.

* * *

Theron wasn't sure how long it had been. He never wore a watch, because they tended to melt when he started throwing his fire around. He'd left his phone on the other side of the portal, knowing the thing would be worse than useless here. It had maybe been twelve hours, he guessed.

He and Xander had reached the base of the mountains.

"Should probably make camp and start the climb after a few hours of sleep," Xander said.

"I don't want to stop."

"Look, dude. There's no sunlight here, not really. You're gonna drain pretty fast if you don't preserve your strength. You don't want to be spent by the time we get to the fight, do you?"

Xander had a point, damn it. His older brother was ever the pragmatist. Theron had always been the impulsive one.

"What if they're hurting her?" Theron said softly.

"She's the freakin' golden goose, by all accounts. They're probably treating her like a queen."

"Or torturing her until she breaks."

"You can't think that way, man," Xander said, his hand gripping Theron's shoulder reassuringly.

What the hell did Xander know? He'd never loved anything or anyone in his life. He was an assassin, for the gods' sakes. His emotional armor was a mile thick and Theron wasn't sure he actually cared about anything in this universe, even his own life.

Theron gazed up at the glittering black mountains. It was going to be a heck of a climb. His heart demanded that he keep going until he had Jen safe in his arms again. His aching body was quick to remind him that he'd been shot and severely burned just a few hours ago and had then undertaken a grueling march.

"Fine. We eat and then rest for four hours," Theron said, slipping his pack from his aching shoulders.

Just as they were settling down and ripping into their protein bars, a rumbling growl split the air. Every hair on Theron's body stood on end at the sound of that growl. He froze, then slowly turned.

He and Xander had made camp in a circle of huge boulders that provided some protection from the hot wind that blew down from the volcanoes around them.

From behind one of the boulders, a form moved on four legs, creeping toward them. The first thing Theron saw was the eyes, burning red like hot coals. They were set in a canine face Below the eyes, fangs gleamed black, like the obsidian landscape around them.

Theron rose to his feet, extending a defensive hand toward

the creature as he backed up. Glancing behind him, he saw that Xander was also on his feet, his daggers in his hands.

Theron's free hand went to the .50 cal he had strapped to his hip. He was ready to call a fireball if he needed to, but this creature looked like it was made of fire, so he wasn't sure how effective his powers would be.

The creature was covered with glowing red lines, running like cracks over its skin. It reminded Theron of a lava flow he'd seen in Hawaii. It had stopped growling and had instead raised its head, looking for all the world like it was sniffing the air. The two mages stayed perfectly still, barely breathing.

After a few moments, the creature approached slowly, it's head down, its glowing gaze locked on Theron.

"Xander," Theron whispered. "What the hell is this thing? What do I do?"

"Fuck if I know," Xander snapped. "But if I had to guess, I'd say that's a Hellhound. And it looks like it wants to make friends."

"Or eat me," Theron said.

The creature continued to creep forward. It was huge. Its head came up to Theron's waist; its body was compact and rippling with muscle, with no tail and a build like a mastiff or similar hound.

The creature's head was within inches of Theron's outstretched hand, but he stayed frozen. The hound slowly placed the dome of its head against his palm. The thing's skin was rough like pumice and almost scalding hot, but Theron used his powers to absorb the heat in a way that didn't hurt him.

"Good doggie," Theron said softly. Glancing at Xander, he said, "I think he's friendly."

Suddenly, images, sounds, and thoughts that were not his own bombarded his brain. He winced and almost screamed. Fire.

Stone. Running on all fours, chasing prey. A pack. Rejection. Hunger. Loneliness.

The images stopped, and there was just the darkness of his closed eyes. And a rumbling voice that sounded like a concrete mixer.

"What are you?" the voice asked. The thing had spoken in his head.

"I'm a mage," Theron replied with his voice, but the thing seemed to understand him.

"Why do you smell like fire?"

"I have fire inside me."

"So do I," the hound said.

"Can I ask what you are?" Theron said.

"Can't find the right word in your mind. You want to call me hellhound. This is appropriate."

"How do you speak my language?"

"I see the words in your mind."

"Freaky."

"Hardly. This is how all Hellhounds communicate. But you are not a Hellhound. Is this not how you communicate with your kind?"

"No, it's not," Theron said.

Xander's voice intruded on the conversation, and Theron's eyes snapped open.

"I hate to interrupt what's happening here, but can you clue me in on whether I need to stab this thing to death or not?"

"No!" Theron shouted at the same time the Hellhound growled.

"Everybody, chill," Theron told them. "What's your name, Hellhound?"

"What is name?"

"The thing you're called by others. My name is Theron."

"I am not called anything," the hound replied.

"What is it that you want?" Theron asked, a little nervous about the answer.

"You smell like food. You are in pain and it's delicious. Fills up my belly. I like your fire. Feels like pack. But you are not pack."

The animal tilted its head, as if it was confused, looking for all the world like a typical dog trying to figure out what its master was saying.

"Excuse me a minute," Theron said, removing his hand and stepping away.

Xander's eyes were wide, his posture tense and his daggers held at the ready.

"What the fuck, man?"

"I think he's friendly," Theron said.

"What?"

"He seems to like me."

"I do like you," the voice spoke inside his mind. Theron's head jerked around like he'd been slapped.

"That thing is talking in your head, isn't it? Just let me kill it."

"No!" Theron and the hound shouted at the same time.

They were all quiet for a moment, looking at each other. Finally, Xander looked back and forth between them, his gaze bouncing in rapid succession.

"Holy shit," he said. "I think that thing just became your familiar."

"What? No way. It doesn't happen that fast."

"It did for Alayna and Z. It did for me and Katya."

Theron had never had a familiar, so he wouldn't know. It wasn't unusual for fire mages to go their whole lives without one. Not many animals liked hanging around fire slingers. And wouldn't it figure that he ended up with something as unusual as a Hellhound for a familiar. His sister had a dragon for a familiar. Xander had a rusalka, an undead, vengeful water spirit who was most likely hanging out in the waterskin that hung at Xander's belt.

It seemed the Blackwells couldn't do anything normal.

* * *

"I'm going to have to call you something," Theron told the Hellhound. The three of them were hiking the steep slopes of the mountain range now, Theron in the lead, the Hellhound by his side and Xander bringing up the rear.

He and Xander had been able to get some sleep, although Xander had insisted they do it in shifts. The Hellhound had offered to keep watch since he, apparently didn't require sleep, but Xander wasn't ready to trust the creature yet.

Theron could sense the creature's thoughts, and while he was relatively new to the practice, he was pretty sure he'd know if the hound was going to double cross them. He and the hound continued to test their new bond.

The hound had explained that like all life in this realm, he fed on the energy of emotion, namely negative ones. Pain, fear, anger, and sorrow were his favorites, he'd explained as they'd settled in to rest hours ago.

"You are feeling all of these," the hound had said. "And guilt. So much guilt. This is particularly delicious. I have not been this satiated since my pack rejected me."

The hound had explained that he was the runt of the pack, which made Theron nervous to see what a full-size Hellhound looked like, since this one was big enough to put his paws on Theron's shoulders if he stood on his hind legs.

The hound's pack was starving. Food was scarce because the demons had rounded up nearly every spirit in the realm and were keeping them corralled somewhere. The Hellhounds hunted spirits, fed off their fear and pain. As the runt, this hound had been rejected to prolong the pack's survival.

The hound was a font of knowledge about this realm. In exchange for his guidance and protection, the hound only wanted to hang around and feed off all the painful things he'd been feeling since Jen was taken. If someone could benefit from the guilt that was clawing at his guts, then that was just great.

"I call break," Xander said breathlessly behind him.

"What? We need to keep going," Theron snapped at him.

"We need to eat something and rest for a few minutes," Xander said. "You're not getting your solar recharge, and there sure as fuck isn't any water in this dimension, so I'm out of luck too."

While fire mages needed sunlight to recharge, water mages needed flowing water to recharge their magickal batteries. There wasn't a drop of moisture in this realm, and the water in their packs wouldn't cut it. It had to be a lake or a river or the ocean to do any good.

Theron knew Xander's familiar, Katya, would be able to provide him some energy, but Xander didn't want to risk bringing her out of her waterskin in this realm. Katya was technically a spirit and everything in this realm seemed to eat spirits. He wouldn't risk her.

If Katya were destroyed, the psychic wound would incapacitate Xander, possibly kill him. That was the danger of bonding with a sentient, intelligent creature.

Xander parked it on a boulder and tore a protein bar open.

With little choice but to follow suit, Theron settled down, his back to a rock wall. They chewed in silence for awhile before Xander's voice broke into his thoughts.

"You might not have heard, but apparently the prophecy is back in play."

Theron laughed softly. "The one that says the Blackwell siblings are supposed to save the world? That prophecy? I thought they decided that wasn't about us because Alayna is a whisperer."

"The very same. When Alayna pulled her return from the dead act a few months ago, the Corps and the Council started blathering about it again."

The words of a prophecy hundreds of years old floated up through Theron's memory.

Four and four and four They will stand against the darkness They will bar the door against the ravenous ones A child of the golden air A child of the burning sun A child of the troubled water And a child of the wild earth Born of the same womb Will unite the people of the sun and moon In victory, there will be peace

Supposedly, it rhymed in the original Elvish language.

"I don't particularly want to be a chosen one, do you?"

"Definitely not," Xander said. "But we may not have much of a choice."

"We don't even know if Kayla is still alive. There may not be four Blackwell kids anymore."

Their oldest sister had disappeared when Theron was 14. It had been the eve of Kayla's graduation from the Academy. She'd left without saying a word to anyone. A short note had expressed her love for her family and asked that she not be followed or contacted. Kayla had always chafed under the rules of the Corps. After their father died, she'd been rebellious and difficult to control. When Alayna had been identified as a whisperer, a powerful mage who was destined to die performing a fatal spell, that had shattered Kayla. And her disappearance had shattered their family.

"She's alive," Xander said. "I think she's doing some kind of job for the Council and they know where she is. Otherwise, she would have been labeled a rogue and hunted down by the Wraiths. Her kill sheet would be in the files."

"It's been almost 15 years. If she was alive, you'd think we would have heard something."

They both fell silent. They could worry about their wayward sister if they lived through this. Beside him, the hound shook himself like a dog, sending embers off his skin that danced in the air like the sparks of a campfire. It was actually kind of pretty.

"Sparky," Theron said aloud, smiling a little to himself. The hound spun three times and curled up on the ground. "I'll call you Sparky."

The hound raised his head and looked at Theron for a moment.

"This designation is acceptable," he said before settling back down again.

Theron chewed his protein bar, not even tasting the thing, his right boot bouncing anxiously in the black dust. HIs thoughts were with Jen. Where was she? Was she hurt? Was she even still alive?

Fear for her made his stomach churn. Guilt made his chest burn. What if he'd been faster? What if he'd been stronger? What if he'd been smarter and had seen the double cross with Bridget coming sooner? Could he have saved Jen?

You couldn't save her then, and you can't save her now.

It was like a voice whispering in his ear. He looked to Xander and Sparky, but they hadn't reacted like they'd heard anything.

You're going to fail, just like you've failed at everything else.

There it was again. Theron looked around frantically, his eyes darting between boulders and outcroppings, searching for the threat.

You couldn't save your father. You couldn't save your best friends. You couldn't save your sister. You won't be able to save the woman you love, and you're going to get yourself and your brother killed trying.

"Shut up," Theron said, his voice low and hard.

Xander shot him a narrow-eyed questioning look, but Theron waved a hand to dismiss his concern.

You can't stop what's coming. Let me show you the destruction you won't live to see.

Suddenly, images assailed Theron's mind. He felt himself sinking to his knees in the dust, clutching his head in both hands as pain ripped through him. When he opened his eyes, a city burned around him, smoke filling his nose and mouth, choking him.

He knelt on a street, tall buildings rising around him. The structures were cracked open, half destroyed, bombed out. Human bodies littered the ground and blood decorated the walls at street level. It looked like there had been a battle here.

Rising to his feet, he stumbled along. How had he ended up here? What was going on?

A flash of silver among the bodies caught his eye and something within him compelled his feet to move in that direction.

It was hair. Platinum blonde hair. Some of it had been stained red with blood. The woman wore shimmering black armor made of dragon scales. Her indigo eyes were open and starting to go cloudy in death.

Her belly was slightly swollen under her armor.

An agonized moan slipped from his lips as he sank to his knees beside the body.

"Alayna," he cried.

Reaching out, he found she was solid. This was real.

She hadn't died easy. Her body was covered in blood, she'd lost an arm below the elbow and half her face was gone. But it was her.

Beside her lay Alex, the love of her life. He'd been shot through the neck, his blood a dark pool around him. Looking around, Theron could see others. Dumeril lay on his back with his entrails spilling on the pavement. Lu, the shapeshifter, was mostly naked, lying on her side a few feet away having shifted back to her human form in death. A small body, the size of a child's, lay face down covered by her cloak, her daggers laying near her outstretched hands. That was Ellie, the gnome.

This is coming, and there is nothing you can do to stop it because you're not strong enough.

Theron shook his head and put his arms around what was left of his sister. She was heavy in death, he noted, as he pulled her head into his lap and stroked her hair.

You might as well take that pistol on your hip and put a bullet through your head. You're worthless and they'd all be better off without you.

Theron eyed the .50 cal on his hip. He'd never thought about suicide before. It had always seemed like such a waste, but maybe the voice had a point. Maybe he could save everyone a lot of pain if he just ended it now.

His right hand caressed the weapon. This would be easier than the crushing failure he was going to face. He wasn't strong enough.

Suddenly, a hot wind blew across the back of his neck, and he raised his head, the crushing fear of failure dissipating for a moment. A sensation like wet, rough rock scraped along the side of his face and he recoiled. There was nothing there! What was going on?

Staring back down at his sister's body, the image blinked, twisted, faded. For a second, he saw nothing but rock and dust before him. Blinking and shaking his head, he tried to focus. The wet stone sensation hit his face again, dragging up his cheek. Ugh, what was that?

The burning city around him began to fade in and out again. Another voice was in his head now.

WAKE UP, MAGE!

In the blink of an eye, the burning city was gone and he sat on his knees in the dust, Sparky beside him licking his face with a tongue that was like a hot, wet pumice stone.

Recoiling, Theron backed up against the stone wall and ran a shaking hand over his face.

"What the fuck just happened?" His voice shook as badly as his hands.

"Agramon, the demon of fear," Sparky said. "These are the Mountains of Terror, his domain."

"Why didn't you tell me we were going through the territory of the fear demon?"

"You seem a brave creature," Sparky said. The hound shook himself slightly and it looked for all the world like a shrug. "And this is by far the easiest route. Fear can be overcome. There are other demons out there who are not so easily defeated."

Theron's head snapped up. Where was Xander?

A few minutes of searching and he located his brother curled in a ball on his side staring into the far distance, trembling like a leaf in the wind.

Theron didn't know what Xander was seeing, but he knew he had to snap him out of it. Taking a page from Sparky's book and using physical stimuli to dissipate the illusion, Theron drew his hand back and slapped his big brother across the face hard enough to leave a red handprint on his cheek.

With a cry, Xander brought his hand to his face, his eyes darting about in confusion before landing on Theron.

"What the hell just happened?"

"Hell. Hell just literally happened. We both got mind fucked by some fear demon."

"For real?"

Theron nodded.

"What did you see?" Xander asked.

"What's going to happen if we don't stop this invasion. Trust me, it wasn't pretty," he replied. "What did you see?"

Xander was silent for moment, looking everywhere and nowhere at once.

"I don't want to talk about it," he said finally.

"Fuckin' fine. Let's just get moving."

Catching up to Sparky and shouldering his pack again, Theron thanked the hound for snapping him out of the vision, or whatever that was.

"I said I would protect you."

"But you must have been getting a negative emotion feast during that little episode," Theron said, wondering why the hound hadn't taken the opportunity to gorge himself.

"I was already full," Sparky replied.

Better to drop the conversation, Theron decided, as he fell into step beside the creature.

"You think that demon will take another run at us?"

"Oh, definitely," Sparky said, his tone matter-of-fact.

* * *

After what seemed like days, but was probably closer to a few hours, their little band had reached the summit of the peak, and Theron reluctantly called a halt for the "night." It had been a hard climb, especially given that they had no climbing equipment, but they'd been able to do it.

The three of them had stumbled on an outcropping that created a nice little shelter and put solid rock around them on three sides. Sparky sat at attention near the opening to their little cave and stared out at the rocks lit by the blue fire of the volcanic craters around them.

"Still not entirely sure about that hound, but you two seem to have taken to each other," Xander said, tearing into a protein bar.

Being an assassin, he was always looking for the knife in the dark, the sudden but inevitable betrayal. He could count on one hand the number of people Xander trusted in this world, but luckily Theron was on that list. As distrustful as he was, Xander would likely keep his daggers in their sheaths. For now.

"What's our next move?" Xander asked.

"Rest, refuel, and find the tallest vantage point we can to get the lay of the land. With any luck, we'll find some indication of where Jen is."

"You're telling me you didn't tag this chick?"

"Protection wards only, no tracking wards. I've got this," he said, pulling the tracking crystal from a pocket. "It's keyed into her DNA. But it's been dark since we got here."

He'd checked the thing as soon as they'd landed on this side of the portal. The crystal being dark could mean a few things. They might be too far away. The demons holding her could be jamming the magick. Maybe his magick didn't work right here. Or she was dead.

He refused to think about the last one.

"This girl must be pretty special," Xander said.

Theron didn't answer, not sure what to say, unable to put into words how special she was.

"Because you look like shit, man."

"Is that why you're here, Xander? Because I'm falling apart?"

Xander was silent for a while as he chewed through his protein bar. When he finally spoke, his voice was quiet.

"Look little brother, you're the only ray of sunshine in this dark, fucked-up family of ours. It's pretty obvious how you feel about this woman. I'm afraid we're going to lose you if we don't get her back."

"How do you know so much? We barely speak." Theron said, trying to keep the note of accusation out of his voice.

"I've known you from your first moments of life. I also know that you only managed to survive Jas and Bren's deaths by the skin of your teeth." He paused for a long moment. "I'm not here because you're falling apart. I'm here because I've done a lot of really terrible things. There's a lot of blood on my hands. There's been so many times when our family needed me, and I wasn't there." He paused and took a deep breath. "I can't redeem myself, but maybe I can keep you from ending up like me."

Theron sat in shocked silence for a long minute, not knowing what to say.

Xander saved him from answering. He put his back to a rock wall, tipped his head forward to rest on his knees and shut his eyes.

"You can take first watch," Xander said.

* * *

Theron was absolutely exhausted. He still had hours left on his watch. But his eyes were so heavy, and Sparky could keep watch. The Hellhound would wake them if anything happened. Yeah.

He closed his eyes, just for a moment, just to rest them, but he found himself drifting in a grey, dreamless fog. The sound of footsteps jerked him from sleep and into wakefulness in a split second.

The sound of boot treads on the rough black dust that covered the obsidian rock was unmistakable. Two sets of footsteps. Theron waited, his hand on his .50 cal. He didn't see Sparky around. Where had the hound gone? He couldn't see Xander either. How long had he been out?

He couldn't spare another thought for them as two figures emerged from the darkness, walking side by side. Theron couldn't see their faces, but after a moment, his heart skipped a beat. He knew the walk, the movement of each man like he knew his own.

His breath came hard and fast as they emerged from the shadows and he saw their faces. Their horribly burned faces.

Jas. Bren. His best friends. Who had died because of him.

Chapter 18

Bile rose in Theron's throat at the sight of what had once been his friends, burning. Unlike the fire that had left him untouched as it consumed his friends.

"Guys?" Theron's voice shook as he rose to his feet. His legs were a little unsteady as he looked at the two of them. "Is this real?"

"As real as you are, T," Bren responded. HIs red hair was gone, burned away.

"Why are you here? You don't belong here," Theron said.

"Are you so sure about that? We killed a lot of people. Some of them didn't deserve what happened to them," Jas said. The skin of his handsome face was mostly gone, leaving charred muscle and bone behind. For some reason, his eyes were as sharp and clear as they'd ever been in life.

"We didn't deserve what happened to us," Bren said, moving closer.

"We trusted you, T," Jas said, taking another step. Theron was backed up to the rock wall now and they were still coming.

"We thought you were our friend, our brother," Bren said. Another step and they'd be within arm's reach.

"But we were wrong, and we paid the price," Jas said, reaching toward him.

Theron bit back a scream as their skeletal hands landed on

each of his shoulders, gripping with inhuman strength.

"And now it's time to make it right," the voices of his dead friends said in unison as darkness pulled him down.

The next thing he knew, he was back in that warehouse a year ago. Looking around him, he saw Jas and Bren moving on either side of him, suddenly whole and healthy.

They moved silently, weapons at the ready as they moved through the warehouse where they'd tracked the rogue mage. The bastard had already left a trail of bodies in his wake, it was time to take him down.

He and Jas and Bren moved like the well-oiled machine they were, checking and clearing rooms with practiced speed. As they reached the open warehouse floor, they knew their target had to be here. Popping out from cover, they took aim and began firing.

The rogue was an air mage and used wind currents to send their bullets off course. They pressed forward.

That's when Theron heard the twang of a tripwire snapping and Bren curse in the same instant. He sensed the grenade igniting beside them, just inches from where Bren stood. In a split second, Theron put every ounce of strength into directing the fire of that blast away from them.

He cheered inwardly as the fire sprayed away from them. In the space between heartbeats he realized he'd sent the fire directly into an old propane tank. He couldn't react quickly enough. The tank exploded.

He remembered losing consciousness at this point. When this had happened a year ago, he'd regained consciousness in the field outside, having been thrown clear of the building by the blast.

Jas and Bren hadn't been so lucky. He'd found their burned

bodies inside. His friends had burned to death while he'd lain outside, safe and sound.

But this was not then. This was now. They'd said make it right. And he would.

He'd realized what was happening too late to stop the tripwire, but he directed the blast at where the rogue hid behind some metal crates, instead of into the propane tank. He turned, grabbing Jas and Bren by their tac vests and dragged them toward the window.

When this had happened before, he'd been blown through that window. Now, he was going to jump through it, with his friends alive by his side. This time, he would save them.

The window was in front of them, his boots pounding heavily across the wooden floorboards. One jump and they would be through.

An unseen force slammed into his knees, sending his world spinning. Impact. Disorientation. Pain. He was suddenly on his back, looking up, when he felt the crack of an invisible palm across his face.

What the hell?

Crack. Again, stinging pain bloomed along one side of his face and out of the shadows, Xander's face swam into view.

"Where are they?" Theron said, his voice desperate as he tried to sit up. His hands were empty. His friends were gone. There was no window, only black dust and stone and the electric blue-purple glow of the sulfurous magma veins.

"Where are who?"

"Jas and Bren! I had them. We were almost clear—"

"You almost ran off a fucking cliff is what you did!" Xander told him, grabbing his chin and turning his head toward the drop off a mere six feet away.

The chasm yawned below them, impossibly deep, the mouth of an abyss that would have swallowed him. He went utterly still for a moment before tremors began to move quickly through his body. Something between a groan and a scream tore from his throat as he slammed his eyes shut.

"I had them," he said, his voice a tortured thing.

Xander put his arms around him and pressed Theron's face into his chest. There was some screaming and some cursing, and if Xander's shirt was a little wet when Theron finally let go, neither was about to say anything about it.

* * *

Theron reached the peak with little difficulty, Sparky hot on his heals and Xander following slowly behind. After the latest encounter with the fear demon, they'd decided to continue, despite having gotten barely any sleep. It wasn't like he was going to be falling asleep any time soon. Maybe not ever again if he could help it.

He'd had Jas and Bren with him and it had felt so damned real. He had been convinced he'd somehow gotten a second chance to save them. Instead, it had been an illusion designed so that he'd throw himself off a cliff.

Had that been what they'd meant when they said he had to make it right? He couldn't save them...but he had to join them? Had those been the spirits of his friends or just a demon's illusion? They'd known everything that had happened.

"Demons can read minds," Sparky spoke in his head.

"Huh?"

"You didn't see your friends. I would have seen them if they were there. The demon was manipulating you."

"Think so?"

"Know so," the hound said. "Agramon is crafty. He likes to play with his food. He's trying to break you and he's getting better at it. You couldn't hear me when I tried to wake you."

Theron nodded, but didn't say anything.

"The demon was in your brother's head, too," Sparky said.

"Yeah?" Theron looked back at Xander. There was a dark, haunted look around his brother's eyes. He'd attributed it to witnessing Theron almost throw himself off a cliff, but maybe Agramon had forced Xander to see something just as horrible as he'd seen.

Xander's familiar, Katya, hovered a couple steps behind him. The spirit creature still made Theron uneasy, even after all these years.

She'd been a beautiful maiden once, living in turn-of-the-century Russia. She'd been raped and murdered, drowned in a river. Her thirst for vengeance had transformed her spirit into a rusalka, the terrifying river ghost of Russian legend. She could take flesh if she chose, either as the beautiful maiden she'd been or as a truly grotesque undead creature with wet black hair and skeletal limbs covered by soggy, white flesh. The empty black eye sockets were what really gave him the willies when he saw her like that.

Her spirit would have been released if she had ever found her murderer and drowned him in the same river. But she hadn't, and the dude had most certainly died of old age by now. Xander had run across her on one of his missions just out of the Academy, and they'd bonded. Now, she was Xander's familiar and took pleasure in draining the life from other murderers at his command.

Xander had been concerned for the spirit's safety in this realm, convinced that she might become a snack for a demon or a hellhound, despite how powerful she was. She drifted in her semi-transparent form, her ghostly eyes on Xander.

Theron slowed his steps and let Xander move up beside him.

"Was it Katya that brought you out of the demon's vision?" Theron asked as nonchalantly as he could.

Xander opened his mouth to speak and froze. His eyes slid to Theron's and he closed his mouth.

"She's hovering," Theron continued.

"I don't want to talk about it," Xander snapped.

"We need to compare notes if we're going to understand what we're up against."

An exasperated sigh left Xander. "Fine. Yes. Katya was able to snap me out of it. That's when I saw you running for the cliff. Had to do a flying tackle at your knees. You're lucky I didn't dislocate something."

Ignoring Xander's attempt to steer the conversation, Theron asked, "What did the demon make you see?"

Silence stretched between them.

"You're not going to let it go, are you? We're in the middle of Hell, but you're going to charm and smile until I spill my emotionally damaged guts, aren't you?" Xander said flatly.

Theron just sent him a close-lipped smile that said there was no escape.

"My worst fear. That seems to be this bastard's MO."

Theron waited, letting the silence stretch between them. Jen had used this trick on him. A stab of pain spread out from his chest at the thought of her, and he rubbed absently at the spot.

He almost didn't hear Xander when he said softly, "I saw my targets. All of them."

Xander was a Wraith, a rogue mage hunter and a personal

assassin of the Council. His power over water allowed him to kill his targets with a touch, causing raging fevers, strokes, aneurisms and heart attacks.

"The Council doesn't send a Wraith unless the person needs killing, Xander."

"My greatest fear is that some of them may not have deserved it."

"Talk to me. Tell me what you saw."

"I saw Grayson Kingfisher, the first mage I ever killed. He was nineteen. So was I."

"Grayson Kingfisher cut the throats of two sapien women in a ritual sacrifice in an attempt to work some seriously deadly blood magick. If anyone deserved to end up six feet under, it was that piece of shit."

"I was just told he did those things," Xander whispered. "What if I was lied to?"

They were soldiers. Questioning orders was a dangerous pastime. For Xander, it was more dangerous than most.

Xander continued, saving him from answering.

"I saw Fiona Woods. First woman I ever killed."

"She was in my year," Theron said. "She ran. Desertion is death. We all know that."

"She told me in the vision that her only crime was wanting to live to see twenty-five. Was she wrong?"

Theron ran a frustrated hand through his hair, wincing at the gritty soot that was collected there.

"The Council would have ignored her if she hadn't fallen in with a group trying to overthrow the Council."

"Maybe so. Maybe not," Xander said. "During the vision, I was convinced their spirits had ended up here in Hell and had found me. And because thought has form, they were tearing me apart. They turned into corpses and were sticking their rotting hands down my throat."

***

Jen paced to one end of the polished onyx floor and back again. The room the demons had stashed her in was expansive, filled with comfortable furniture all in stark white. Jen's thoughts spun around in her head like a roaring tornado. She could only hold on to one thought for a few seconds before it was torn away. Guilt, fear, anger, sorrow. Theron was dead. She'd never see him again. Spin, spin. How was she going to get out of here? Was there some escape route she was missing? Spin, spin. She shouldn't trust the demons. But could she use them to get back to her own dimension?

The sound of the door opening behind her froze her whirling thoughts.

"Hey, sweetie," Lilith's voice came from behind her. "You're going to wear a hole in the floor if you're not careful."

Jen turned slowly and looked at the demon. She was dressed in a short white dress that hugged her model-thin body. Her pin straight blonde hair fell to her waist and she looked like she belonged on a catwalk in Milan, right down to her sky-high white heels.

Jen didn't say anything. A tiny part of her wanted to unload the stuff swirling in her head to Lilith. She needed a friend, and this creature was certainly acting like she wanted to be her friend. Lilith had done nothing to harm her since she'd been here. In fact, she'd taken care of Jen, going out of her way to make her comfortable.

"Let's take a walk," Lilith said. "I've got a little surprise that I think might cheer you up."

Jen followed, unsure how a demon could possibly cheer her up. Down twisting black corridors, she followed Lilith until they came to a set of large doors. When Lilith opened them with a sweep of her hand, a dark, cavernous space was revealed. Jen stepped back, fear twisting her stomach.

"Trust me," Lilith whispered. "Just step inside. You're going to love it."

Not wanting to anger the demon and feeling a strange, compelling curiosity, she stepped past the door into the darkness. As she did, the cavernous space suddenly shifted, and Jen felt a disorienting moment of vertigo.

Blinking hard, her eyes focused and revealed…a house. She was standing in a house. Hardwood floors, a homey looking kitchen, a living room done in blues and greys. Sheer white curtains stirred in a breeze through open windows. Beyond them, Jen could see—was that the ocean?

"It's your dream house!" Lilith squealed, throwing her arms wide.

She wasn't lying. It was Jen's dream house, down to the last detail, including a picture-perfect beach outside.

"How did you—" Jen began, walking numbly to one of the windows. "Did you read my mind?"

"Just a little," Lilith said, looking a little sheepish. "I wanted it to be perfect."

"Why? Why are you doing all of this?"

Lilith was silent a moment before she turned to Jen, stroking her shoulder affectionately.

"You're very special, Jen. You don't understand how long we've been looking for someone like you. And you're here just in time to help us stop Falak and his minions. With your help, we can save your world and mine. Honestly, I'd give you anything you wanted. You're that important to me."

Jen was taken aback by Lilith's words. She hadn't been important to anyone in a very long time. The only person who had really ever cared about her was her mother, and she'd been gone for what seemed a lifetime.

You were important to Theron, a little voice chimed in, sending a spear of pain through her chest, but she squashed it. No use thinking about that now. He was dead.

And now there was Lilith. It was so tempting to take what she was offering. The dream house, a purpose in stopping the invasion, a friendship, something she had been without for so long.

"How are you doing this?" Jen asked, waving a hand at the white painted walls.

"Thought has form in this dimension," Lilith reminded her. "I instructed some of the minions of the lower demon classes to create this place for you."

"It's an illusion?"

"As long as they're thinking about it, it's as real as you are," Lilith replied.

Jen ran her hand over the white granite countertop to her right. It was solid and cold to the touch.

"There's one more thing," Lilith said, a smile spreading across her perfectly glossed lips. "I have someone I want you to meet."

Chapter 19

"I said I don't want to talk about it anymore," Xander repeated for the third time. Theron had kept pressing Xander for more details about his visions from the demon of fear, trying to pick apart how Xander had been able to snap out of it and Theron hadn't.

His older brother had always been a closed book to him, for as long as Theron could remember. Xander was only two years older, but the gap between them had always felt like decades because Xander seemed so much older at heart.

Theron could never remember the water mage playing and laughing as they grew up. He'd always been on the sidelines, watching in silence. Xander's sense of humor was best described as gallows. He didn't speak unless he had something to say, preferring silence over chatter. And pessimist didn't even begin to cover Xander. The guy saw the worst in every situation and was constantly calculating the worst-case scenario. He didn't let it stop him from completing his missions, but he didn't seem to take joy in anything either.

"What do you want to talk about then? I'm going bugfuck in this silence," Theron responded.

"I don't know. What do normal brothers talk about?"

"They talk about normal stuff, like their lives and sports and jobs and current events," Theron said, exasperation filtering into his voice.

Xander stopped walking, the black dust settling around him.

"You want to talk about my life? I live alone and barely speak to other human beings. Most of my conversations are with the undead, vengeful spirit who lives in a canteen on my belt."

He paused and Theron opened his mouth to respond, but Xander launched into the rest of his tirade, saying more words at once than Theron had heard from him in years.

"Neither of us follows sportsball of any kind, so that's out. You want to talk about my job? You want to hear about all the people I've assassinated recently? I'm sure that will make for riveting conversation," Xander said, his voice dripping with disdain. "And fuck current events."

With that, Xander readjusted his pack, turned away and started trudging through the dust again, leaving Theron with a frown creasing his brow and his mouth hanging open slightly. What could he say to that?

Theron turned and followed, deciding that he preferred silence after all.

It seemed like hours later, but may have only been a few minutes when Xander ground to a halt in front of him, almost causing Theron to collide with his back.

His brother's body was rigid, on high alert, his breath coming a little fast. Theron peered around him.

The path they were on wound through rocky outcroppings on either side, their shapes jutting sharply and glossy black. They were in the foothills now, almost free of what Sparky had called the Mountains of Fear.

Maybe twenty yards ahead of them, a flash of something light could be seen against the dark rock. The shape was vaguely human. Theron moved cautiously around Xander, motioning silently for the water mage to cover him while he took point. Nodding, Xander took up position behind him and to the right, the air around them both crackling with energy as they readied to call on their powers.

Theron moved quietly in a half crouch toward the figure. As he approached, he saw that it was an emaciated human in ragged khakis and a T-shirt. Long, dark hair was a wild, matted tangle around the thing's head.

Theron almost didn't hear the sound over the rushing of blood in his ears: soft feminine sobbing. Time felt like it was moving too slowly. His stomach fell to his knees as the figure turned to face him.

Jen's dark eyes met his, and he almost screamed. She was emaciated, the bones in her face far too prominent. Her collar bones and ribs were visible through the torn neckline of her tattered shirt.

Theron nearly launched himself into a breakneck run to get to her, but the thing she held in her arms kept him rooted to the spot, unable to make a single muscle obey him. It was a baby. Or, it had been once.

The tiny dark-haired child had been dead a couple of days at least, the skin gone grey and purple.

Was this real? Another trick of the fear demon, it's last ditch attempt?

Theron saw his own horror reflected in Xander's face and knew that his brother was seeing this too. In every other vision the fear demon had shown him, Xander had been hidden from him. The demon showed each person their worst fears. If Xander was seeing this too, it must be real.

As he stepped forward, his legs moving like a drunk's, his mind spun. How could this have happened to Jen? She'd gone through the portal two, maybe three days ago. How could she have become so malnourished and had a baby in that time?

Time passes more quickly here. While you healed and collected supplies, she's been trapped here for months. Carrying your child.

The voice echoing in his head sounded like his own, but rough and dripping with anger. He shook himself trying to dislodge the words, but the idea had taken root. Jen had suffered because of his delay. She'd lost another child, their child, because of him.

Jen's voice, cracked and dry, sounding of rattling corn husks, snapped his attention back to her.

"I couldn't save her, Theron. I'm sorry. I tried so hard. She was born blue and I couldn't make her start breathing. I tried everything—" her words became a stream punctuated by sobs. After a moment it was just gibberish.

Theron was at her side now, and he knelt beside Jen. She was a broken thing. Starved, covered in cuts, lesions, and bruises. What was left of her clothes was stained with blood and other things he didn't want to think about.

Her lips were cracked and bleeding and as she babbled the blood smeared over her teeth.

"Xander, bring the med kit and some water!" he barked over his shoulder. When he didn't hear movement, Theron looked behind him. His brother and Sparky were gone.

Turning back to Jen, his thoughts jumbled for a moment. He'd been worried about something a second ago, something about his brother—

"You said it was safe, Theron. You said we were safe. Said it was safe, said it was safe, said it was safe…"

Whether she was talking about the unprotected sex or the fact that he'd dragged them into Bridget's ambush, it didn't matter.

Jen was right either way. He'd said they were safe and here they sat. She'd spent months in Hell, given birth in these conditions and was holding another dead child because of him.

He'd had a daughter. The thought clawed at the inside of his chest. He couldn't protect her, hadn't even known she existed.

"Xander, bring the med kit!" Where was his idiot brother? Couldn't he see she needed help? Something niggled inside his mind. It itched like a mosquito bite. He started to turn, to look for Xander but Jen's hand on his face stopped him.

He met her eyes.

"Gods, Jen. I'm so sorry. So fucking sorry. I didn't know," he said, feeling hot tears spill from his eyes. "Jen, we have to go. We have to get you out of here."

She laughed a little, a rasping sound in her throat, that still managed to capture the dark humor he loved about her.

"We both know I can't walk out of here," she said, gesturing to her emaciated form.

"I can barely sit up," she ground out. "I'm not leaving this rock."

"Don't say that," he demanded, reaching up to smooth her hair back from her face. Her gaze slid from his face and landed on the .50 cal at his waist, a tiny smile twisting her bloody lips.

"You can do something for me, though," she said, her voice sad. "You can end this for me. Quick. Easy."

Theron recoiled.

"Not a chance. Xander's got some healing skills. He can help, if I can just find him. We're getting out of this together or not at all."

"That second part is looking pretty likely," she said softly. Her hand caressed his face again. The other held their dead child. She leaned forward, until her lips were just inches from his.

In a voice that was almost too soft to hear, she said, "All you have to do is pull that trigger twice and we can be with her, with our baby, forever."

Time seemed to stretch, elongating until a single second felt like hours. Jen's words were like dark snakes invading his mind, twisting and writhing, sinking their fangs into every part of him. For that eternal moment, he believed her. He should do it. Darkness swallowed his mind, snuffing out everything as he felt the .50 cal clear the holster and come to rest in his palm.

***

In the blink of an eye, Xander found himself standing alone on the path. He'd seen Theron run toward the skeletal woman only to disappear as soon as he'd reached her. Looking around, he saw that Sparky wasn't around either.

This shit was getting so old.

"That all you got, you demon motherfucker? Show yourself and let's dance."

Dropping his pack to the ground, he drew his daggers from the cross-draw sheaths on his hips and stood ready, letting the edges of his cloak fall over his arms to hide his movements.

"I'm right here," a voice whispered in his mind.

Xander was only able to keep himself from flinching by clamping down on every muscle in his body with an iron will.

"You are not a man who is controlled by his fear, I see that now," the voice said. "You have no idea how rare that is."

Xander laughed. "Flattery gets you nowhere."

"Most people crack when I throw their worst fear at them. I showed you the faces of the innocents you murdered, and you saw through it. Your mind and will are strong. It's all about completing the mission for you, isn't it? You'll push past fear and pain and what's left of your conscience, all for the mission."

Xander stayed silent, instead concentrating on his breathing, feeling the daggers in his hands, staying alert for the attack he knew was coming, waiting for some monster to leap from the darkness.

"What would you do to complete this mission, Xander? What would you do to get your brother and his woman out of this dimension, alive and healthy?"

That got his attention.

The demon had read him like a book. He would do anything to complete a mission. And today, his mission was to protect his brother.

"Now that you're listening, let's get down to business. I need a way out of this dimension. One of the only ways to do that is ride out in the body of a living human. As you might have guessed, not too many of the living come wandering through here."

Xander stayed silent waiting for the other shoe to drop.

"I'll show you exactly where this woman is being held and give you the power you'll need to fight your way out of here. In exchange, you let me hitch a ride to the other side."

"And unleash the demon of fear on Earth? Not gonna happen. We'll find our own way out of here."

"You're going up against Lilith, the queen demon herself. Your brother nearly cracked under my assaults. Do you really think he can withstand her?"

The tiniest niggling doubt passed through Xander's thoughts. Could Theron survive that? What about Jen? What hope did they have of finding her on their own? And getting back out again?

"You might be able to do this on your own. But this is his life we're talking about. Why risk it? Why not get a guarantee?"

The demon was right. If Xander said yes, they'd have their best chance to make it out of here. Theron had to survive. He was the good one. He was the one who held everything together. If he died, not only would Xander be lost, it would kill Alayna and their mother.

And without Jen, Theron would be a broken man. She had to make it out, too.

Xander considered his own dark soul. It wasn't worth saving, couldn't be saved. Throwing a demon on top of that wouldn't change a thing.

"On one condition," Xander said quietly. "When we reach Earth, you don't leave my body. I'm not letting you loose."

The demon was silent a long time and Xander thought the creature may have gone when it finally spoke again.

"You see, mage, I have no grand designs on invasion and conquest like Lilith and Falak. I just want free of this place. I will gladly live quietly within you until your death, feeding on the fear of the people you kill. I have no doubt that I will never go hungry, and you'll never even know I'm there. I could even give you a small portion of my power to control fear in others. Think of what you could do with that."

This was about saving his brother. Xander took a deep breath.

"It's a deal."

✳ ✳ ✳

"I have someone I want you to meet." Lilith's words echoed in Jen's ears as she turned to see a figure standing in the living room of the dream house the demon had created from her thoughts.

He looked just as he had in the moments before Bridget put three bullets through his chest. Those bottomless indigo eyes were just the same, the perfect combination of blue and violet. The hair was just the same, that mix of blonde and red, the color shifting as he moved, looking for all the world like the flames he controlled. He was just as tall, just as broad and just as overwhelming as he had been.

The copy was perfect.

And it made her want to scream and vomit at the same time.

Turning away from the facsimile of Theron, she came face to face with Lilith's excited grin. The grin quickly turned to a frown when she saw Jen's face.

"What's wrong, sweetie?"

"It's not him! He's not here!" Jen didn't mean to scream in the demon's face, but that's exactly what she found herself doing.

Lilith put out a calming hand and tried to quiet her.

"Of course not, sweetie. I made him. Just for you. From your memories. It's my gift to you."

"Send it away!" Jen could feel hot tears streaking down her face.

A frown creased the demon's face, and Lilith's eyes narrowed angrily for a moment. But like a cloud passing in front of the sun, it was there and gone in a moment, the bright light of a smile returning to her impossibly beautiful face.

"I'm so sorry," Lilith said, waving her hand and causing the not-Theron to disappear in an instant. "I should have realized it was too soon for you. Ugh, I'm so fucking stupid sometimes. I don't get to hang out with living humans very often. Can you forgive me, sweetie?"

Jen tried to breathe through the pain that had taken up

residence at the sight of Theron here in this dimension. The only thing that was keeping her from being a blubbering pile on the floor was the sure and certain knowledge that while he was dead, he was not here.

He'd been a hero. Her hero. And if there was any justice in the universe, he was in a much better place than this one.

"I just need a minute, Lilith. Can you just give me a little time alone?"

"Absolutely," the demon said, backing up toward the door of the little beach house. "If you need me, just call my name."

And then she was gone and Jen was alone.

Sinking to her knees, she tried to stop the flow of tears, to find her center, to be the strong person she knew she was and that Theron would want her to be. But the tears just kept flowing.

* * *

Theron looked down at the pistol in his hand. It whispered a dark promise of relief. He looked up into Jen's exhausted eyes.

"This is what you want?" he asked softly.

"I want the pain to stop," she said, her voice crackling. "Don't you?"

The thought that he had done this to her, put her here, clawed at him. The thought of their dead child tore his heart out. But the thought of losing her, going on without her, that was killing him.

He raised the gun slowly. And stopped. And frowned.

This wasn't right. Something about this wasn't right. A little bell was chiming in his skull, trying to tell him that something wasn't right.

It was the eyes. Jen's eyes, his Jen's eyes, had never held defeat.

That woman had faced pain and adversity, had walked into the teeth of a war zone and out the other side. If he hadn't convinced her to work with him, to trust him, he had no doubt she would have eventually found a way to defeat him.

His Jen wouldn't give up, not as long as there was a breath left in her body, and maybe not even then. That meant this wasn't his Jen.

He leapt to his feet springing back from the creature. In a split second he called his fire to his left hand, directing a blast squarely at the thing that dared to wear the face of the woman he loved.

The ferocity of the flame startled him for a moment, but he recovered. It was electric blue, like the hellfire around them, and it erupted from him in a roar that knocked the creature back.

It screamed with an inhuman voice, morphing into a shadowy form twice as tall as he was. The flames covered the thing as it writhed in pain.

Theron hit it again, pressing his advantage and pouring everything he had into the torrent of flame that came roaring from him. His anger, pain, fear and sorrow he kept back, shoving them away for fear it would feed the demon. Instead, he fed the flames with a sense of righteous justice.

The thing screamed again, climbing up the octaves to ear splitting frequencies. Theron felt a warm body press against his leg and looked down to see Sparky at his side. He felt heat flowing up his leg as the hellhound fed some of his energy into Theron.

"The demon took flesh, and now it's trapped. Finish it!" Sparky said.

Dropping the pistol, Theron raised his right hand and released a second column of flames. He brought the two streams together at what he guessed was center mass on the vaguely human-shaped form.

The shadowy form began to dissolve from the middle out, the screams fading to a gurgling choking sound. Suddenly, Theron found himself thrown back by the force of a blast, his feet leaving the ground for a moment before his back slammed into the rock wall behind him.

Sparky hit the wall beside him and he just hoped the hellhound was okay.

Theron shook his head and looked around trying to get his eyes to focus. The creature was gone, and Xander was running toward him, the hood of his cloak blown back.

"What the fuck was that?" Xander shouted as he skidded to a stop, his eyes wide.

"I think that was a fear demon getting roasted," Theron said.

"Well, yeah," Xander said, waving a hand to dismiss the comment. "I'm talking about your fire, man. You're normally more flamethrower meets roman candle. That was more firestorm. I've never seen anything like that."

Xander's voice was a mix of amazed and worried.

Theron looked over at Sparky.

"You know anything about this?"

The hellhound shook itself as he rose, tilted his head and raised a shoulder in a gesture that looked disconcertingly like a shrug.

"When we connected, it appears you picked up the ability to control hellfire," Sparky told him. "And I might have given you a little extra energy."

Theron shook his head.

"Just glad you're on my side."

A few minutes later, the three of them were moving down the path at a good clip, nervous that something might have been attracted to the light and noise of the battle with Agramon. Theron wasn't sure the demon was dead. Wasn't even sure if demons died. It was probably a good bet they wouldn't hear from him for a while. Still, best to clear out.

Xander explained that he hadn't been able to see Theron. He'd thought he was alone until Theron had hit the demon with his fire, then he and Sparky had reappeared.

Theron told him everything the demon had said, it's last ditch attempt to get him to take his own life. And how it had almost worked.

Xander stared at him, something dark moving in his eyes.

"That's fucked up, man," was all he said.

Silence descended between them and they walked on.

Chapter 20

J en sat on the bed in the sunny bedroom of her beach house, her back resting on the headboard while hugging her knees to her chest.

What the fuck was she supposed to do now? Lilith was trying to tempt her with the things she wanted most in exchange for her help. She could see that. Ultimately, she had two options in front of her: fight and probably die in the process, or let the demon give her everything she wanted in exchange for using her gift to lure spirits of the dead into becoming food for demons.

Hell of a choice.

She smiled a little at her unintentional pun. Suddenly, Theron's smile popped into her head, and she felt a stab of pain.

Damn it. For a few short days, she'd had something so good and so real. She'd held love in her heart, had felt the edges of it, learned the shape of it. And now it was gone, but her heart still remembered the shape, would always remember.

As she sat, lost in her thoughts, a shadowy shade floated through the room, passing through the walls as if they weren't there. The walls weren't actually there, she supposed. Her head started hurting every time she thought about it.

Shades had been periodically drifting through the house since

Lilith had left her. That was going to take some getting used to. She wished they'd steer clear. Things gave her the creeps.

"Jen," a man's voice whispered beside her.

She jumped and turned to find Jeremiah, the spirit of the dead mage from Damascus, standing beside the bed.

"Fuck! Give a girl some warning next time," she shouted, her hand pressing to her chest to slow her hammering heart.

"Sorry to startle you. I'm still getting the hang of this taking solid form thing."

"What do you want?" she asked him.

"To keep you from making a terrible mistake."

"What mistake would that be?"

"Taking Lilith's deal. I've been talking to a few of the other spirits that are still lucid. Lilith has been feeding you a line. She's not trying to stop Falak's invasion of our world," Jeremiah said. "She's trying to beat him to it."

"What does that change?"

"You mean you'd still take the deal?"

Jen blew out a frustrated breath. "I'm not sure I have much of a choice, not if I want to survive."

For just a moment, Jen sank into all the feelings rushing through her. She was scared, more scared than she'd ever been in her life. She was at the mercy of powerful beings that she didn't understand, beings that wanted to use her.

Grief was like a heavy stone, pulling her under dark waters. It threatened to drown her. She'd lost everything and everyone she'd ever loved. Because she'd been betrayed at every turn. For a few brief hours in Theron's arms, she'd learned to hope again, hope for a future that had happiness and love in it. She'd been so stupid.

Anger raged within her, a black bonfire that threatened to

consume everything she was, everything she would ever be. For the barest moment of time, she thought about what it would be like to give in. Join the demons. Go full dark side. Let them give her everything she'd ever wanted. Take her revenge on the people and things that had hurt her.

And let the world burn.

Horrified, she pulled back from those thoughts. What was happening to her? Was she about to go supervillain?

Her fingers went to her throat, but her phoenix necklace was gone, lost amid the confusion. She'd even lost her talisman, but the thought of it still comforted her. She'd been reduced to ashes again, but she'd risen once. She could do it again.

"It's not a choice between saying yes or no to the deal," Jeremiah's voice interrupted. "There's a third option: run."

"Run where?" Jen asked, rolling her eyes. "There's no food or water out there. I'd be dead in a matter of days. And that's if they don't catch me first."

"Maybe death is better than being a tool of the demons trying to invade our world," Jeremiah said, his face twisted with anger.

"So I'd go from being their tool to their food. No thanks!"

"I'm just trying to tell you the score, what you do with that is your business. But don't think I'm going to stand by and let you have any peace if you help them."

Anger boiled within her.

"Get out!" she shouted at him.

As if a gale force wind had whipped through the room, Jeremiah was tossed backwards right through the wall and was gone.

* * *

They were fucked.

Theron stared out at the city that spread out below them. They'd made it out of the foothills of the Mountains of Terror. Obsidian spires of all sizes reached toward the starless black sky. Eerie blue-purple light from the burning sulfur seeped out of windows and openings of the spires and out of cracks in the ground.

Was Jen in that city somewhere? There was no way to tell exactly where or even if she was anywhere near here.

Theron started to voice his concerns when Xander started his descent from the ridge they were standing on.

"Where are you going?" Theron called. "We have no idea where she is."

Xander remained silent. Theron dropped his boots onto the steep incline and started skidding down after his brother, black dust rising up at their passage. Sparky loped along behind them, casting glances over his shoulder periodically.

As they reached the outskirts of the city, the first formations—Theron couldn't bring himself to call them buildings—just a couple hundred yards off, he grabbed Xander's shoulder and spun him to face him.

"Where are we going? We need a plan here, or we're going to get slaughtered."

Xander stared at him hard for a long moment before he turned and gestured at a huge spire that towered over the city.

"I think it's pretty obvious where she is," Xander said, jerking his arm from Theron's grasp and walking away. "And if she's not there, someone there will know where she is."

"What makes you so sure?"

"Don't ask questions you don't want the answer to," Xander growled, his hands clenching into hard fists.

That brought Theron up short. What the hell was going on with Xander? He knew better than to push his brother when he was like this; he'd just shut down completely. But this wasn't done. Not by a long shot. Theron made a note to circle back to this when they were safe.

If they were ever safe again.

The formations on the edge of the city were like giant lava bubbles that had cooled to smooth obsidian glass. Small openings were peppered across the surface, and the blue glow that seemed to be the only source of illumination in this world emanated from them.

As they moved past the bubble formations, shadows shifted within. Were these dwellings? Theron couldn't spare the attention to contemplate the architecture. His senses were on high alert, watching for threats from every direction. His pistols were holstered to keep his hands free. He wasn't sure how much good bullets would do against these things, but he knew for certain that his new hellfire enhanced powers could get the job done.

If the demons took solid form, he reminded himself. Even now, a thousand invisible demons might be watching them from above. He shoved the thought away. Start thinking like that and he'd paralyze himself.

The streets were eerily empty. Nothing moved but a hot wind that stirred around the cracks where liquid blue magma glowed.

The layout of the spires and bubbles made no sense. There wasn't anything that could be called streets. Order was a foreign concept to this place, it seemed.

Suddenly, Xander, who had taken point, threw up a fist to signal Theron and Sparky to stop. They all crouched in the shadow of a spire that towered five or six stories above them.

Several shadowy, humanoid shapes moved along past them, seemingly unaware of the presence of humans or a hellhound.

"Shades," Sparky's voice spoke in his head. "They are used up spirits. No memories, no emotions. Barely have form. They serve the demons as mindless drones."

"Are they a threat?" Theron asked.

"Only if one of the demons who controls them orders them to hurt you."

Nodding, Xander motioned them forward and they set out again, Xander on point, Theron shifting his focus forward and rear, and Sparky watching their sixes.

* * *

"Go stand in that corner," Jen said, pointing to the far corner of her illusory beach house.

The shade silently obeyed, then stood motionless with its spindly shadow arms by its sides.

In the hours since she'd banished Jeremiah, she'd been practicing her powers on the shades that wandered through her house. She'd captured and released several of them now, collecting as much data as she could. It seemed she could easily command them if she told them what she wanted and thought about it at the same time. Voice alone didn't cut it.

It was time for the next phase of the experiment. She was going to test whether thought alone could control the shades.

Jen focused, picturing the shade moving to the opposite corner and standing there. She sent her thoughts in the direction of the shade. And it moved.

Her focus faltered for a moment in her surprise, and the creature halted. Resuming control, Jen was able to send the shade around the room at a whim.

This was incredible. Had she always had this ability? And why had she never realized it before?

Thinking back over all the encounters she'd had with spirits over the years, she realized it was possible she'd just never known about this.

As a child, she hid in fear from the spirits, never interacting with them. As she grew older, she worked so hard to ignore them. She'd done such a good job that for a few years in her late teens and early twenties, she'd stopped seeing them all together.

She thought back to that victim from the bomb blast in Baghdad. She'd told the woman to let go, to go with god. And she had, dissolving, going off to some other plane of existence. Hopefully not this one, Jen thought bitterly.

So, she could command shades and even more lucid spirits, like Jeremiah. Had the demons known about this ability? Could other seers do this?

Lilith had said that on Earth, demons had no form and couldn't see spirits. Something about being on the wrong frequency. That's what they'd needed her for, to spot the spirits, to lure them to Hell where the demons could feed on their emotions, draining them until they were mindless shades.

Hours later, Jen found herself exhausted and sitting on the wicker sofa in her living room. Fifteen shades wandered about the house, completing tasks she had set out for them: stand here, walk there, put this object over there, bring this object here.

She could plant the command by thought and like little computer programs they would complete their tasks and stand silently waiting for the next instruction.

Her shades could work independently or as a unit, and so far, the only limit she had found on her powers was the number of shades in her vicinity. It was easier to command them if she could see them, but she found that if she let her mind get quiet, she could feel others around her that weren't in her line of sight. If they wandered close enough, she could pull them to her. That was how she'd ended up with the fifteen now moving around her house.

This could change everything, Jen decided. And as far as she knew, the demons didn't know she could do this.

As if she had summoned her, Jen felt a tightness in her chest that she had come to associate with Lilith. The demon was close.

Jen silently ordered the shades to disperse and as the last one melted through the wall of her house, she heard Lilith's voice.

"I came to check on you, sweetie," the demon said, breezing in through the open front door of Jen's home. Hair that looked like it had been styled by Hollywood's finest was piled on Lilith's head. Sky high white heels clicked on the raw pine floor boards. A white peplum top and tulip skirt hugged her supermodel body.

"I know you're still mad at me about my little snafu earlier," the demon said, a little pout on her lower lip as she sat down on the loveseat opposite Jen.

Jen stayed silent, watching.

"I realize, now, that his death is too fresh for you. I get that."

Jen closed her eyes for a moment and nodded. Let Lilith think she was still broken up about it and unable to speak.

"I just want us to be friends. And I want us to defeat Falak together. Don't you want that, Jen?"

Jen nodded again. As soon as they opened a portal back to Earth so that she could start the work of luring spirits to Hell,

Jen was going to play her ghost whisperer trump card. Demons couldn't take physical form on Earth. She could break free.

After that, who knew? Maybe she could hook up with the mages, find this Council that Theron had worked for. He'd mentioned siblings, two sisters and a brother. Maybe they could help her.

Jen kept these thoughts hidden under layers of beach scenes. The demons, she had discovered, could pluck memories out of her head easily, but deeper thoughts, particularly of the future didn't seem to register. Not that they'd let on, anyway.

"I want that, too," Jen said quietly, trying to convey the picture of passivity.

Let the demon think she'd been bought off by the illusion of this beach house. As soon as her boots hit the Earth, she was gone. The demon had failed to do enough to tether her here.

"I was hoping you would say that," Lilith said, a dazzling smile spreading over her perfect red lips. "Because I have something that I know you're going to love."

Lilith turned to the door and waved a hand in a beckoning gesture. Jen's stomach fell through the floor.

A little girl of about five stepped through the door. Long, jet black hair fell to her waist. She wore a white dress with a blue sash and a matching blue bow in her hair. And her eyes. Jen knew those eyes. They were the same eyes she saw in the mirror every morning.

The child spoke, her voice as clear as ringing bells.

"Mommy?"

* * *

"This is it," Xander said, indicating the huge set of ornately carved black doors.

"You sure?" Theron said, his eyes on the stairs behind them, watching for threats.

He and Sparky had followed Xander through the demon city to this, the spire that towered over everything. They'd wound through a maze of stairs and ramps, climbing ever higher. Theron wasn't sure how his brother knew where they were going, and it was kind of freaking him out.

"You keep asking me that," Xander said, exasperation coloring his words. "And I keep telling you that I'm sure."

He met Xander's eyes, then flicked his gaze at the stairs behind them. Xander got the message and took up a guard position. Sparky kept his glowing eyes on the stairs above them.

Theron put his hand tentatively to the black glass of the doors. They were cool to the touch. No wards or traps that he could feel. He gave one of the doors an experimental push and was surprised when it swung open easily.

Stepping through the door was like stepping into another realm. He stood on a stone path that led to a little white cottage surrounded by a white fence. Stepping through the gate, he was greeted with a riotous English garden, lavender and roses and sunflowers competing for space. Beyond the cottage, a white sand beach and rolling waves stretched to the horizon. The sky was a perfect blue dotted with little white clouds. Though no sun was visible, the air was warm.

Was this some kind of demonic holodeck?

The doors and windows of the cottage were open, white sheer curtains dancing in the breeze. A figure moved inside.

Cautiously climbing the three steps to the door, Theron realized he had never felt this nervous. He had no idea what he was going to find here.

Whatever he had been expecting, it wasn't this.

Stepping through the door, he found himself in a beach house right out of Martha Stewart's wet dream. Raw pine floors, white wicker furniture with navy blue cushions and flowers from the garden in crystal vases.

Jen was in the kitchen chopping vegetables, occasionally throwing handfuls of celery and carrots into a pot on the stove. Her long hair was loose around her shoulders, not pulled back in the braid she usually wore. She still wore the same t-shirt and khakis he'd last seen her in. She looked whole and healthy.

At the sound of his footsteps she looked up. And froze, wide eyed. Anger flashed over her face and she gripped the knife in her hand. Her eyes were hard as she looked at him.

Not exactly the welcome he'd been expecting.

"Get out!" she screamed.

"Wha—" Theron started, but before he could so much as get a word out, Jen started in again.

"Tell Lilith that her sick little games are getting old. I'm tired of her sending these copies. You're nowhere close to the real thing."

Her eyes glinted like black steel as she stared at him, concentration creasing her brow.

"Why aren't you moving?" she asked in confusion.

"Because I love you and I'm not leaving here without you," he said, taking a step toward her.

The knife in her hand rose between them, a threat and a promise.

"Oh, that's rich, throwing out the L-word. Nice try."

He searched her face, hoping to find some clue to what she was talking about.

"What did they do to you, Jen?"

Her eyes scanned him carefully, no doubt taking in his stained and dusty clothes.

"This new tactic is clever, making it seem like you're mounting a rescue mission, but you're just another copy."

Keeping his eyes on the knife, he reached out and put his hand on her arm, "I'm real, Jen."

"Stop it!" she shouted, shrugging his hand off. "You're dead!"

"The bullets didn't kill me, Jen. I got help. A friend healed me. My brother's here with me. We came to rescue you. You have to believe me. And we need to get out of this place before the demons know we're here."

Her dark eyes were wide, shining with unshed tears, and her lips were a thin, angry line.

Reaching out slowly, he took the knife from her hand, setting it out of her reach on the granite counter. He pulled her stiff, shaking body into his arms.

It was her. He knew it on some fundamental, atomic level. This was his Jen. Ever the fighter.

His body reacted to her, despite the pain and fatigue, coming to life at the feel of her pressed against him.

"How do I know it's you?" she asked softly.

He wracked his brain.

"You told me what happened in LA. Your mother's death, Trevor splitting on you like a coward, Madison's stillbirth. You said you'd never told anyone else about that."

"Nice try," Jen said sadly, stepping away and taking up the knife again. "I know Lilith can see my memories. That's how she knew what my dream house looked like."

She gestured at the cottage around them.

Shit. Could he cut himself to show her that he could bleed? No, the copy of Jen that Agramon had shown him could bleed.

Wait. His brain flashed on a memory. The phoenix necklace.

If she hadn't found it yet, that was something she didn't even know about. And something only the real Theron would know.

"Back in the hotel in Damascus, you lost your phoenix necklace in the sheets. Right before we left, I slipped it in your pocket. Your left pocket. Check it."

Surprise and confusion crossed her face. Slowly, her hand went to her left pocket. He knew the moment when her fingers found the little gold necklace. Her eyes closed, her features crumpled, and the knife clattered to the floor.

He wasn't sure which of them moved, but she was in his arms in an instant, his mouth on hers. Her hands speared up through his hair and he groaned. Without breaking their kiss, he lifted her hips until she sat on the counter, her legs wrapped around him.

Her tongue was in his mouth, and he reveled in the feel of her against him. He'd found her. Against all the odds, she was alive and they were together. And he was never letting her go again.

She pulled back, her hands on either side of his face, her eyes moving over him.

"You're here. You're real," she said, incredulous. "How are you not dead? I saw Bridget shoot you."

He pressed his forehead to her hers and squeezed his eyes shut for a moment.

"The bullets hit me. I was pretty sure I was going to bleed out chained to that wall."

He told her how he'd called the fire, cauterized his wounds enough to slow the bleeding. He told her about Dumeril and how he was waiting to open the portal for them back in Damascus, if they could just get back to where they'd come in.

Left out was the part about how a fear demon had flayed his

mind and almost talked him into blowing his brains out.

"Xander's waiting outside. What do you say we get out of here?"

He'd just taken Jen's hand when he heard a child's voice behind him say, "Mommy, who's that man?"

* * *

Jen watched as Theron turned slowly. His gaze remained locked on Madison as he leaned over and whispered to her, "Jen, who is that?"

How was she going to explain this one?

"That's Madison," Jen said softly. "Madison, this is Theron."

Theron turned slowly and looked at her, eyes wide and nervous.

"Madison?" he said carefully, swallowing hard before he continued. "As in, the daughter you lost?"

"She'd be about this age," Jen said, a note of sadness in her voice. "Lilith brought her to me."

Theron turned to face her where she sat on the counter. His hands rested on her shoulders and he brought his face into her line of vision.

"Jen, look at me. That is not your daughter."

Jen squeezed her eyes shut against his words.

"I know," she said softly. "But she could be."

He didn't understand. When Lilith had brought Madison to her, Jen had been horrified at first. But the child had run to her, leaping into her arms. Her little body had been solid and warm. Her hair smelled like Johnson's baby shampoo. And she'd softly whispered, "Mommy, I missed you."

On an intellectual level, Jen knew the creature was not her

daughter. But her heart said different.

She knew this was a temptation that Lilith offered in order to keep her in line and feeding the demons. It was effective.

On an emotional level, she wondered if she'd been given a second chance to be Madison's mother.

Theron stepped in close, his hands cradling her face. His indigo eyes were bright as he asked softly, "Is this what you want? This house? Children?"

She hadn't thought of it that way, but Lilith had tapped into desires she had never really acknowledged. After her world fell apart, she'd never let herself think of what she actually wanted. She could only see what was right in front of her, the next story, the next conflict, the next war-torn city. Because wanting something meant it could be taken away—or never happen at all, despite all her efforts and struggles.

But there was a part of her that did want the perfect little beach house. And it wanted children. Preferably ones with Theron's indigo eyes.

That part of her had always been there, but it had been buried so far down she'd forgotten it or thought it was dead. Until this man had shown up and made her want him. And now, she wanted a lot of things.

Looking into his eyes, she nodded.

He swallowed hard and pulled her into his arms, burying his face in the hair that tumbled around her shoulders.

"I'm sorry, Jen. I've made such a mess of things. From the very beginning, I should have asked you what you wanted. I should have worked with you to find a safe place for you instead of dragging you in the direction of what I thought was safety. I was so wrong and I hope you can forgive me someday."

He took a deep breath and let it out slowly.

"If this is what you want," he said, his voice rough, "I want to make this happen together."

Her heart hammering, she pulled back and looked at him. Everything was on display in those gorgeous eyes and he let her see it, didn't try to hide it. He loved her. He'd even said it. When he'd first come in, he'd said that he loved her and wasn't leaving without her, and she'd missed it in her shock. He'd tried to say it, just before Bridget had pushed her through that damn portal. He'd walked across Hell to find her, and didn't that say louder than anything else how he really felt?

Was she ready to accept that kind of love? A terrified part of her asked, would she ever be able to return that kind of love?

She thought about the devastation she'd felt when she thought Theron was dead. She'd been ready to join up with demons, go full dark side. Because he was gone, and what was the point anymore? She had been ready to watch the world burn without him.

"I love you," she said, the words coming faster than she'd meant them to. She'd almost spit them out in surprise at her own feelings.

Theron's eyes went wide for moment before a huge smile spread across his face. Even in the worst situations, even in the middle of Hell, surrounded by demons, with only a narrow chance of survival, Theron could pull out the most dazzling smiles.

Jen frowned as she remembered something he'd said.

"I thought you said you couldn't have children," she said. "Not with me, at least."

He looked almost sheepish as he said, "About that…It seems I may have been misled about my fertility with sapiens."

At her questioning look, he continued, "Dumeril, my friend

that showed up to heal me and open the portal here, he delivered some news: my sister is pregnant. Her lover is a sapien."

"Oh."

"Exactly. And after our unprotected escapades over the past few days, I was terrified I might have, well, I might have knocked you up."

Laughter exploded from her lips and she quickly stifled it with a hand over her mouth. At his concerned look, she said, "That's sweet, in a way. But Theron, I lived in a warzone for five years. You think I didn't take precautions? I have a ten-year IUD."

Theron blew out a relieved breath.

"Okay. Decision time. We need to get out of here fast if we want any hope of getting back to the portal. Xander and I got a little taste of what the demons can do, and I don't want to tangle with them again if we can avoid it," Theron said, sounding like he was planning battle strategy.

His voice got softer, dropping nearly to a whisper as he pulled her into his arms, his forehead resting against hers. "You can stay here with the thing that looks like Madison in the illusion that looks like your dream house and enslave yourself to demons that want to destroy our world. I won't stop you and I won't take choices away from you again. I'm not sure what I would do if I was offered everything that had been taken from me.

"Or you can come with me. We're staring down the barrel of an interdimensional war in which you'll be a prime target, so safety is far from a guarantee. I can't give you this house quite yet, but I have a little ranch outside San Antonio that is one of the prettiest places on Earth. I can't give you Madison back, but if you want children, I will make sure you have them, one way or another. The one thing I can give you is my heart, but you've had that on lock since you reset my shoulder in Ramadi."

He pulled back and gave her that smile again. Her hand floated up to caress his face and his eyes drifted shut.

"What I'm offering isn't perfect, or easy, but it's real," he whispered.

He wasn't offering her the moon and stars, and they might not live long enough to seal that deal, but it was very real.

"I can get you home," he said, his voice rough. "Even if you decide to have nothing to do with me. Whatever you want your life to look like back on Earth, I'll do everything I can to make it happen. Even if I'm not a part of it. You can tell the Corps and everyone else to go to Hell. I'll back you."

Her hand shook a little as she ran her thumb over his cheek.

"I pick you," she whispered as she stared into those indigo eyes. She leaned forward and pressed her lips to his. She'd meant it to be a quick, chaste kiss before they made the mad dash for safety, but his arms came around her like hot steel and his tongue teased her lower lip. She opened for him and reveled in the feel of him in her mouth. His hand found her breast and—

"I hate to interrupt the tender reunion, but we've got company," a harsh voice said from the doorway.

"Jen, this is my brother, Xander."

"Charmed," Jen said, catching sight of the dark-haired man with the same startling indigo eyes as Theron.

But that was where the similarities ended. Where Theron was a light in the darkness, this man was a part of it. He was as tall as Theron, but leaner through the frame. Xander was still an imposing figure, though. It was just that he was less Captain America and more Daredevil.

"I think I might have a way out of here, but we need to get moving," Xander told them.

Theron pulled away from Jen, his expression grim as he unholstered a pistol and checked the magazine. "How many are we dealing with?"

"Looks like two runway models. You know them, Jen?"

"Yeah. Couple of demon lieutenants. You two, in the back bedroom. I'll deal with them."

The brothers exchanged a look that communicated volumes in nanoseconds, but moved to the back bedroom and shut the door.

Jezebeth and Astaroth came breezing in the front door about thirty seconds later, their heels clacking on the wood floors. No knock, no tentative, "Hey Jen, it's just us." They rolled in like this place was theirs. And it was. These demons never had any intention of giving her anything. This place was her prison cell, and they were the guards.

Jen did her best to paste a smile on her face as she went back to cooking the food that had been brought in from the Earthly realms for her. She focused on chopping vegetables while resolutely not looking at the bedroom door.

She did glance at the thing that looked like Madison where it sat in the living area playing with a doll, wondering how well the creature would play the part. Would it alert the demons that her rescuers were hiding in the house.

"Lilith needs to see you upstairs, Jen. She sent us to get you," Jezebeth said, tossing her blonde hair over her shoulder and smiling a little too wide.

"Did she say what it was about?" Jen asked, not taking her eyes off the cutting board. She couldn't go with them, not now. In her head, she called to the shades nearby, feeling dozens begin to coalesce beyond the exterior wall of the not-house.

"No," said Astaroth. "But we have a lot of work to do if we're going to stop Falak from invading your world. That means we need to start collecting spirits to feed o—I mean power up with."

"Does that mean we're going to the Earthly Realms?" Jen asked, trying desperately to keep her tone casual.

"It will mean portal travel—" Astaroth started to say. Jezebeth stopped her with a hand on her shoulder. Her dark eyes narrowed sharply as she stared at Jen.

"The details aren't important," she said. "We don't want to keep Lilith waiting. Trust me."

Panic gripped Jen low in the gut.

"I just need another minute," she said, her words coming too fast, her nervousness plain.

Jezebeth moved impossibly fast around the counter and grabbed Jen's upper arm hard.

"We need to go now," she growled, her features twisting into a terrifying facsimile of human.

There was a soft thump from the bedroom as something shifted, and the demon's head snapped around with a lizard-like quickness. Jen's heart kicked into a gallop and tried to claw its way out of her chest. It was now or never.

In her mind, she called to her shades, watching as they oozed through the wall, obeying her with a frightening speed.

"Restrain the demons," she said, her voice a croak as it squeezed past a throat constricted with fear.

Shadows wrapped themselves around Jezebeth and Astaroth and the Madison-thing. The girl-copy wailed, and Jen's heart squeezed for a moment. It wasn't real. That thing was a demon wearing the face of a child to manipulate her. Nothing more.

"What are you doing, Jen?" Astaroth hissed.

"I'm not going anywhere, and neither are you," Jen said, proud of herself when her voice didn't shake. She kept the butcher knife she'd been using to chop veggies in her hand as she came around the counter.

"What we are going to do is talk about how we open a portal back to Earth." Jen loomed over the two demons. By now, her shades had pinned them to the wicker sofa.

"Release us!" Jezebeth screamed at the shades.

"They're under my control, now," Jen told them. "There may be no free will left in them, but there are still some echoes of feelings in there. And they don't like you."

The three demons screamed in frustration, but they were completely immobilized in the embrace of the shades.

"Tell me how to get out of this city and open the portal back to Earth, and I'll make sure they let you go when I'm gone," Jen said, trying to keep the words slow and even.

Jezebeth let out a derisive laugh. "We're going to break your mind, you stupid bitch. You'll be as compliant as these shades when we're done with you. I told Lilith we should have broken you instead of trying to befriend you, but she never listens to me."

A white hot anger bubbled through Jen's chest at those words. How could she have been so stupid to have considered even for one second that these creatures would ever treat her as anything more than a tool? It didn't matter that she'd thought she'd lost Theron. It didn't matter if she'd been two steps from full dark side.

The knife was at Jezebeth's throat before she could even think about it. The demon chuckled.

"You think that's going to hurt me?"

Jen didn't answer, the knife shaking in her hand from the incredible rage. The knife moved, slicing the white skin at the demon's throat.

A neat cut appeared, but no blood. The cut knit back together as Jen watched.

Jezebeth laughed again. "We're beings of energy. While everything takes form in this dimension, we control the form. That's our gift. We don't bleed."

Jen heard heavy booted footsteps behind her.

"They don't bleed, but they do burn," Theron's voice said behind her. Turning, she saw him, one hand wreathed in a bluish purple flame.

The demons' eyes all went wide.

"Hellfire," Astaroth whispered in a quaking voice. "How can he control hellfire?"

"Not important. What is important is that I destroyed Agramon with it, and I'll destroy you, too, if you don't answer Jen's questions," Theron said, a small smile tugging at his lips. Xander stood behind them, a twin set of daggers in his hands.

"You got an upgrade to your powers," Jen said quietly.

"So did you," Theron said, eyeing the shades.

Theron reached toward Astaroth and the demon flinched back as much as she could. He closed the distance so slowly, it was almost imperceptible. A strange thrill went through Jen. She wanted the demons to hurt, to scream. They'd hurt her, they wanted to hurt other humans. She wanted revenge.

"Do it," Jen whispered, not even realizing the words had slipped from her until Theron shot her a shocked look.

"Don't!" Astaroth whimpered. "I'll tell you!"

Theron backed off slightly.

"The elf. You need the elf, Kahler. He's the only one that can open the portal. You'll find him in the chambers off the lower level. Near the room where Bridget first brought you through."

"Astaroth! Lilith will kill you for this!" Jezebeth screeched.

Xander spoke up. "We need to get moving. I think she's telling the truth. Do you think the shades can hold them?"

"For a while, at least," Jen said.

With a thought, the shades completely enveloped the demons, cutting off their screams as they closed over their faces.

* * *

Their group moved quickly through the complex, flat out running down the winding obsidian stairs. Jen only paused for a moment when they encountered the hellhound out in the hall. Theron had explained as they moved that Sparky was his familiar now and the source of his newfound hellfire powers.

She told him about discovering her new powers and how they worked.

As they moved, she called shades to her, forming a billowing shadowy wave behind them. They encountered two minor demons on the descent. The shades enveloped them, pinning them motionless and silent to the ceiling.

Xander took point, and he seemed to know the way far better than she did. She shook off the questions she wanted to ask him. They had bigger things to worry about.

In a matter of minutes, they were back in the room where she'd first arrived in Hell. The bluish purple flames of torches were still burning. Just as Astaroth had described, they found the elf, Kahler.

Xander took the elf from behind, moving with an uncanny silence. His dagger was at Kahler's throat in the space of a heartbeat.

"One move and I'll end you," Xander said. "Open a portal back to Damascus and I'll let you skip off into the damned sunset."

The elf's voice was steady, almost bored, as he said. "You must be the Wraith. Bridget warned us you might come looking for vengeance for the fire-slinger."

Xander maneuvered the elf around and began pushing him out to the main chamber. The elf's eyes went wide as he caught sight of Theron.

"No vengeance needed," Theron said, hellfire leaping to life in his hand. "Not dead, yet."

"Open the portal," Xander growled in the elf's pointy ear.

"Why should I? Wraiths leave no one alive. I might as well take my chances that the demons will arrive soon. You'll likely kill me either way."

"There are worse things than death," Xander said through clenched teeth. The dark mage's eyes narrowed in concentration and he pressed his free hand to the elf's back. Kahler's eyes went wide for a moment and his face twisted in pain.

Suddenly, he dropped to his knees, a strangled scream escaping him, and Xander let him fall.

Leaning down, Xander said softly, "I just ruptured all the ligaments in your knees. Elves heal fast, but you're still looking at days of agony knitting those back together. Now, open the fucking portal before I start getting creative. I'm a water mage. You're about seventy-five percent water. I can make all kinds of things burst, rip, and boil."

Xander's expression was cold as a stone, except for the small twist of his mouth on one side. He'd done this kind of thing before. A long time ago, Jen would have recoiled at this kind of violence. Now, she felt relief. Kahler deserved all of this and more.

Panting, the elf levered himself around to a sitting position, pain contorting his slender features. His hands moved in a complicated pattern and a hole appeared in reality, spinning with a hundred bright colors.

The three of them looked at each other.

"How do we know it's Damascus on the other side and not the middle of the Atlantic or something?" Jen asked.

"We don't," Xander said, turning resolutely toward the portal that was increasing slowly to the size of a person. "I'll go through and check. If it's safe, I'll come right back through."

"Isn't there a safer way?" Theron said, stepping to his brother's side.

Xander laughed loudly and harshly. "Safe is a fucking relative term right now, man. I'm a water mage, if it's the middle of the Atlantic, I'll be fine."

"And if it's a volcano, or two hundred feet off the ground or two miles underground?"

"Then I'm screwed, and it's been nice knowing you."

"I can't let you do this."

"Yes, you can," Xander said with a sad smile. "You need to protect Jen. Get her back to the Council. They need her and she needs you."

With that, Xander stepped through and disappeared in the swirling rainbow.

Theron drew one of his pistols and pointed it at the elf.

"Any sudden moves, or you drop that portal, or he doesn't come through, you're done for," he told the elf.

The silence and tension stretched as they waited. What must have only been a few seconds felt like hours.

"How long will it take?" she asked.

"Hard to say. We'll give it a minute or two. Time doesn't seem to line up well between the dimensions. A few seconds there, might be a few minutes here."

Jen felt the pressure around her change just before her feet left the floor. A scream tried to escape her throat, but the air was being sucked right out of her lungs. Fear gripped her as she realized that she'd felt this before, back in Damascus.

As her back hit the stone wall, her body pinned by a gale force wind, she was able to take in a few details. Theron was similarly pinned across the room, his gun ripped from his hand. He was gasping for air, just like Jen was.

Bridget stood in a doorway that hadn't been there before. It was happening all over again. If she could have screamed in rage she would have.

"You two are so fucking bad at this." Bridget laughed.

Theron's eyes were wide as they locked on Jen. She could see that he tried to call his fire, but it was disappearing in the gale force of the wind. They were going to lose again. Despair ripped through her. Bridget wouldn't leave him alive this time.

The air mage's curly hair didn't even move in the wind as she stepped forward and retrieved the gun, aiming it at Theron's head.

"Point blank, this time, I think. I'm going to empty this clip in his head. There is going to be nothing left when I'm through."

As she raised the weapon, rage poured through Jen, hot and icy cold at the same time.

"Stop her," she gasped.

Her shades leapt to obey, surrounding Bridget in a swirling cloud of shadow. A shot went off, but the bullet ricocheted off the stone ceiling.

Slowly, the force of the wind pinning Jen to the wall let up.

Theron slid down the wall across the room.

"Restrain her," Jen whispered.

She pointed at the elf, who was trying to drag himself across the floor toward the newly opened doorway.

"If you go any further or let the portal drop, I'll have those shades tear you apart," she told Kahler. "Got it?"

The elf froze and nodded.

Jen walked slowly to where Bridget stood. Her body was obscured from the shoulders down by the shifting shades. Her face was red as she strained against their hold. Wind whipped around her, but it wasn't concentrated, merely pulling at Jen's clothes and hair.

"I should tear you apart piece by piece for what you did," Jen said, her voice shaking with her rage.

Theron moved up beside her, one pistol trained on Bridget's head, the other on the elf.

"What I did? Ask your precious fire-slinger about what he's done. About what the Council has done. The mages have been ground under the boot heels of lesser races for thousands of years. We're just pieces of meat for their endless war machine.

In a mocking tone she grated, "Keep the peace. Restore the balance. Risk your life. Watch the people you love die violent deaths. And give your children to the Academy on their seventh birthday.

"Yes, I made a deal with the enemy. I murdered my brothers and sisters in arms. It was still better than living in that system. Dying is still better than living in that system."

Jen stepped back, stunned. A murderous madness shone in Bridget's eyes. Bridget had betrayed her people, her comrades. She'd nearly killed Theron and had put Jen in the hands of demons. She'd plotted the invasion of their world, planning to hand innocent humans to a demon army. Nothing justified that, not even a brutal system.

Rage rumbled within her again. Without speaking, the shades tightened around Bridget, causing her to grimace in pain.

"If you're going to do it, fucking do it," Bridget said in halting gasps, unable to draw a complete breath.

But hadn't Jen been on the verge of joining the demons herself? She'd been on the edge of a supervillain origin story just a few hours ago.

Theron caught Jen's gaze with his. "You don't have to do this. If you want to kill her, I won't stop you, but it will mean human blood on your hands. Trust me, it haunts you. No matter what. We can take her back through and hand her over to the Council for justice."

Theron was right. Did she want to live with Bridget's death on her hands for the rest of her life? "She might have information," Jen said. "We should take her back."

She looked into the traitorous mage's eyes, the rainbow colors of the portal swirling behind her. Suddenly, Bridget's head tilted backward and a wound opened in her throat, blood pouring in a gurgling stream down her chest.

As her head fell forward, Xander appeared behind her, a dagger gleaming in his hand. Shock coursed through Jen for a moment. Theron stood in stunned silence.

"She was a rogue mage. The kill was mine," he said softly, wiping the blood on his cloak and stowing his dagger somewhere hidden. "Portal's good. Dumeril's on the other side."

With a thought, the shades released Bridget's body and it slumped to the floor. Xander stood over the mage as she died, staring at her face as the light left her eyes, like he was drinking it in. A chill raced across Jen's skin despite the heat of the room.

Slowly, Bridget's eyes closed, and she stopped breathing. Something inside Jen broke open at the sight. It was relief, it was pain, it was even a little sadness. What kind of pain could drive someone to the lengths Bridget had gone to? She looked away from Bridget's body and Theron caught her gaze. He stepped toward the portal and held out his hand.

It occurred to her then, in a moment that seemed to stretch forever, that true pain put you on one of two paths. You could choose love or you could choose hate. For so many years, she'd walked the fine gray line between the two, choosing neither, only existing.

Now, she chose.

Jen took Theron's hand, took a deep breath and stepped through the portal to the other side.

Epilogue

"Want to watch another episode?" Jen asked. Theron could tell from the excited tone of her voice that she desperately wanted to keep watching. They were bingeing the latest season of a superhero drama on a streaming service. It was a good show, but Theron was barely paying attention to it. He'd spent the last few hours mostly watching Jen as they snuggled on a couch in a set of spare quarters in the Citadel.

When he wasn't watching her, he was plying her with food and doing his best to empty out the kitchens' stock of comfort food.

They'd been in the Citadel for a couple of days now. He'd firmly told the brass to leave them be after the initial debrief. They'd gotten healed up in the hospital wing. His mother, the Citadel's chief healer wasn't there, having been sent on a mission for the Council.

Dumeril had headed back to Austin with a back pounding hug and backward wave, promising to pass on Theron's well-wishes to Alayna and Alex. He'd have to stop in to see them, apologize for the way he'd left things, and introduce them to Jen. Rather than dreading it, he was excited that he had the chance to do that. Maybe there was a chance to salvage that relationship. Alayna had survived the Reckoning. She was involved with a sapien and the Council had backed off, given them their blessing. They were expecting a baby. Maybe there was some kind of hope for their broken, shattered family after all.

Xander had disappeared without a goodbye, but that wasn't entirely unexpected. He'd said hardly a word as they'd come through the portal in Damascus and headed right for the Citadel. They'd handed an unconscious Kahler off to Mage Corps guardians.

Xander had never been a big talker, but the silence had unnerved Theron a little. Theron had been so focused on Jen that he didn't notice when Xander had slipped away. A random guardian had informed him that Xander had left the Citadel to head back to New Orleans, his home base.

Theron vowed to himself that he would catch up with Xander soon. He wouldn't let it go so long again. He owed his brother everything.

As they'd prepared to leave Damascus behind and head to the Citadel, Jen had discovered that Jeremiah's spirit had followed them out of Hell. She'd managed to help the fallen mage commander move on.

After all that, he and Jen had settled into these quarters and hadn't left. Their days had been filled with love making, eating, sleeping and binge watching. It had easily been the best two days of his life.

As the gloomy opening sequence of the show transitioned into the opening scene of the episode, he hit pause.

Jen looked at him curiously.

"Can we talk about something?" he asked.

She nodded, not saying anything, but looking a little worried.

"We have a meeting with some of the Corps brass in the morning. Have you decided what your plans are? In my experience, it's better to go into these meetings knowing exactly what you want to ask for."

Jen was silent for a long time. The question of what came next hung between them and his heart pounded.

"I'm going to ask for some time off," she said, finally. "A few weeks maybe? To get my head right. It's been a long time since I've had to work with anyone or really be around anyone. During our debrief, General Silverthorn mentioned something about training. I think I'd like that. I'd like to learn how to fight, protect myself, use my new powers."

They had been very vague with the brass about those powers. They knew from his reports that she could see and communicate with the dead. They didn't know that she could control them. They hadn't mentioned that her shade army had come back through the portal with them. The shades weren't visible, but Jen said she could feel them around her. They weren't sure what effects the shades could have in this dimension, but Jen was hoping to find out.

They hadn't told the brass about Sparky either. Theron could see the hellhound, but he only became visible to other people if Theron asked him to. It required the hellhound to draw on Theron's power, just a little to phase into their reality. Through his connection to Sparky, Theron could still call on hellfire, an ability that would definitely come in handy if the demons did manage to slip through into their world.

They could decide later exactly what they wanted to reveal to the Corps leadership. They'd seen one turncoat in the ranks already. Who knew how many more there were?

"My journalism career is shot, unfortunately, but I still have a lot of skills. Investigation, research, sourcing information, interviewing. I can use my seer abilities. And best of all, no one in the shadow world knows me. We're going to need information and solid intel if we're going to stop this invasion. I think you and I could team up. I mean, most people sign up to be journalists to save the world. There's a good chance I'll get to do that for real."

A big smile spread over his face. "Have I mentioned how brilliant I think you are?"

"Only a few times," she said kissing him just below his ear. "But you can tell me that any time you want."

"This time off you mentioned. Where do you want to spend it?"

The smile she turned on him was dazzling. "I want to spend it where ever you are." She threw a leg over his lap and straddled him, kissing him hard. Heat bloomed within him.

As she broke the kiss, her midnight gaze kept him locked in place. "I love you, Theron. It took me a while to admit that to myself. I'm sorry I didn't say it sooner. I knew it that night in Damascus and I should have told you. I was just scared."

Her hands cupped either side of his face.

"I told you before, the road ahead is going to be hard. There is no guarantee we both make it out the other side of this."

"We've already been through Hell. Literally. Everything after that is Disneyland," she told him.

He pulled her into his arms then, burying his face in her loose black hair. It smelled like soap and sunshine.

"You asked me where I wanted to spend this time off," she said against his throat. "I heard about this little place outside San Antonio that is supposed be one of the prettiest spots on Earth. Maybe we could go there?"

His arms tightened around her again as his heart leapt within his chest.

"Yes, ma'am."

Acknowledgements

A lot of people made this book possible. Most of the credit has to go to my husband, who did more than his fair share of housework and childcare so that I could put these words down on paper.

Thank you to my mother, who put in many hours of babysitting and never let me doubt that my words matter. You are a gift.

Big thanks to my editors at Chimera Editing. Jami Nord and Emmie Mears took a rough manuscript and polished it until it gleamed.

To all the members of the Austin RWA chapter, thank you for your support, advice and wisdom.

Thank you to my amazing cover designer, Amala Benny. Check out her dazzling covers at mayflowerstudios.com.

And thank you to my readers. I'm so excited to be on this adventure with you. Hang on tight, we've got a long way to go!

About the Author

Rose has been obsessed with ghost stories and the paranormal for as long as she can remember. In the first grade, she made up a ghost story and convinced her entire class that their school hallway was haunted. Kids cried. Parents were called. And a writer was born.

A Texas native, she loves horseback riding, knitting, practicing martial arts and archery. She lives with her husband and offspring in Central Texas.

You can connect with me on:
- https://roseobrienauthor.com
- https://twitter.com/roseowrites
- https://facebook.com/roseowrites

Subscribe to my newsletter:
- https://roseobrienauthor.com/contact-us

Also by Rose O'Brien

Air of Darkness
Elemental Mages Book 1

A powerful mage destined for an early grave. An FBI agent out for revenge. They are both on the trail of a supernatural killer. Can they work together and ignore the sparks that fly between them? When love wars with duty, which one wins?